THE DREAM *of* SCIPIO

ALSO BY IAIN PEARS

An Instance of the Fingerpost

THE DREAM *of* SCIPIO

IAIN PEARS

RIVERHEAD BOOKS

a member of Penguin Putnam Inc.

NEW YORK

2002

This is a work of fiction. Names, characters, places, and incidents either are the product of the author's imagination or are used fictitiously, and any resemblance to actual persons, living or dead, business establishments, events, or locales is entirely coincidental.

Riverhead Books
a member of
Penguin Putnam Inc.
375 Hudson Street
New York, NY 10014

Library of Congress Cataloging-in-Publication Data

Pears, Iain.
The dream of Scipio / Iain Pears.
p.   cm.
ISBN 1-57322-202-X
I. Title
PR6066.E167 D74   2002   2001058916
823'.914—dc21

Printed in the United States of America
1   3   5   7   9   10   8   6   4   2

This book is printed on acid-free paper. ∞

Book design by Judith Stagnitto Abbate
Map by Jeffrey L. Ward

TO MY FATHER

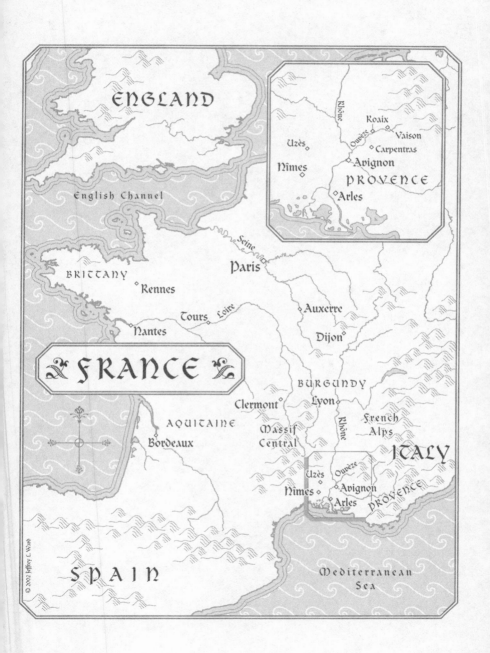

PART ONE

JULIEN BARNEUVE died at 3:28 on the afternoon of August 18, 1943. It had taken him twenty-three minutes exactly to die, the time between the fire starting and his last breath being sucked into his scorched lungs. He had not known his life was going to end that day, although he suspected it might happen.

It was a brutal fire, which took hold swiftly and spread rapidly. From the moment it started Julien knew it would never be brought under control, that he would be consumed along with everything around. He didn't struggle, didn't try to escape; it could not be done.

The fire ravaged the house—his mother's old house, where he had always felt most at ease, and where he always thought he had done his best work. He couldn't blame those nearby; any sort of rescue would have been foolhardy. Besides, he wanted no assistance and was content with the privacy they had granted him. Eight minutes between the fire starting and his collapsing into unconsciousness from the smoke. Another three minutes before the fire reached him and began to make his clothes smoke and skin bubble. Twenty-three minutes in all until his heart gave out, his breath stopped. Another hour until the fire finally burned itself out and the last charred rafters crashed to the floor over his body. But to Barneuve, as his thoughts broke into pieces and he stopped trying to hold them together, it seemed to have taken very much longer than that.

IN SOME WAYS, his fate was sealed the moment Olivier de Noyen first cast eyes on the woman he was to immortalize in his poems by the church of Saint Agricole a few hundred meters from the Pope's new palace in Avignon. Olivier was twenty-six, having been fated to live and die in what was possibly the darkest century in European history, an age men called cursed, and which drove many all but insane with despair at God's vengeance for their sins. Olivier, it was said, was one such.

Isabelle de Fréjus had just turned sixteen and had been a wife for seven months, but was not yet pregnant, a fact that was already causing old women to gossip knowingly, and to make her husband angry. For her own part she was not displeased, as she was in no great rush to embark on the great gamble that left so many women dead or permanently afflicted. She had seen in her mother the terrible damage caused by her own birth, so swiftly followed by another and another, and was afraid. She did her duty by her husband, and prayed every night (after she had taken such precautionary measures as she knew) that her husband's assaults would prove fruitless for a while longer. Every second day she went to church to beg forgiveness for her unruly, rebellious wishes, and at the same time to place herself at the disposition of the Virgin in the hope that Her mercy and forbearance would endure a while longer.

The effort involved in this celestial balancing act required such concentration that she left the church in a haze of thought, her brow furrowed and showing off a little wrinkle just above her nose. Her veil was ever so slightly disarranged, as she had pushed it back a little when she knelt down to pray. Her maid, Marie, would ordinarily have reminded her of this small lapse, but knew her mistress well, and knew too what was going through her mind. It had been Marie, in fact, who had taught her those little tricks that were helping to make Isabelle's husband so increasingly concerned.

A small wrinkle and a veil askew were perhaps enough to inspire a painter, but not in themselves sufficient to have such a devastating effect on a man's soul, so some other explanation must be sought. For Olivier, standing nearby, felt as though some immensely powerful beast had torn at his breast, sucking the very life from him. He gasped in shock, but fortunately no one heard him. So intense was the sentiment, that he had to sit down on the steps and remain there, staring long after the receding form had disappeared from view. And when he stood up, his legs shaking, his brow damp with sweat even though it was still morning and not yet hot, he knew that his life had changed forever. He did no work for days.

Thus began a tale of the doomed love between a poet and a young girl that was to lead to such a calamitous and cruel ending.

PERHAPS IT was her youthful beauty? Julien Barneuve thought so, at least when he first read the account of this fateful encounter, elaborated through the years and finally set down with all the romance that hindsight can offer around 1480, nearly a century and a half later. The pedigree of the anecdote was always suspect, seeming too close to Petrarch's encounter with his Laura to be comfortable. But it had tradition behind it, as well as one of Olivier's finest verses, the ten-line poem that begins (in the wholly inadequate 1865 translation of Frédéric Mistral), "My eyes have stabbed my soul . . ." And the essence was surely true, for Olivier's dreadful fate a few years later when he fell into the hands of Isabelle's husband could not be contradicted. If he had not loved her, why would he have killed her and been attacked himself in such a way?

For Olivier was tainted with madness, it seemed; the story recounted how the girl had wished to go with her husband to flee the plague and the poet begged her to stay in Avignon, that they might die in each other's arms. And when she refused, he killed her, unable to let her go. The deed revealed his secret, and he was set upon by the Comte de Fréjus's hirelings in revenge, beaten, and his tongue and hands cut off. Olivier was, quite literally, silenced, his voice forever quieted. He could no longer talk, write, or even make signs so that others could understand him well. More still, the outraged and humiliated husband had destroyed all but a few of his poems. No one could now tell whether his poetry, for which he was beginning to become known, was indeed the first flowering of a literary Renaissance, the model beside which Petrarch ranked a lowly second, or merely appeared so to those few who had read his work during his life. Only a dozen or so remained, not enough to captivate a man like Barneuve until he came across some documents in the Vatican library on a cold day in February 1926 while going through the papers of Cardinal Annibaldus di Ceccani, a collector of manuscripts and the poet's first—and only— patron.

It was the first section of a twenty-page manuscript in Olivier's hand that kept Julien awake at night in excitement, when he finally made the connection and understood its importance. 'According to Manlius.' A brief sentence that meant nothing to most people, but all the world to him. In a moment of jest he said it was worth selling his soul for.

THE WRITINGS that Olivier passed down were begun by Manlius Hippomanes over a series of months at his villa a dozen leagues outside Vaison, some sixty kilometers to the northeast of Avignon. "Writings" is the wrong word, perhaps, for like many men in his position, Manlius rarely wrote himself, although he could do so quite easily if he chose. He dictated, rather, and his words were taken down by an amanuensis, his adopted son, whose life was made unreasonably difficult because of the speed at which his master spoke. Syagrius—an amiable young man of some twenty-three years who worked hard to make the best of his good fortune—had to scribble to keep up, then work long into the night to decipher his markings when preparing the fine copy. And no mistakes were tolerated; his master had a good memory and the highest opinion possible of his own prose, and could be punitive if so much as a word was changed. Besides, Syagrius desired nothing so much as to please, and attract a word or two of praise.

What he dictated, what so excited Barneuve, was a digest of philosophy, cut down and reduced to its essentials for dissemination among his circle and perhaps, should opinion be favorable, beyond that. Few now had any familiarity with such matters and must drink their wine watered to make it palatable. After it had been read, and if it was found suitable, he might pay a copyist for up to a hundred versions—perhaps fifty would now be more than sufficient—which he would send throughout Gaul, to his friends.

Manlius was a host that evening; as he worked, the sun set so gently, leaving a rosy hue in the sky, and the first hints of cooling air began to blow through the open courtyard that was used as a dining room in summer. A few of the party outside began composing verses to amuse themselves and show off their learning. It used to be a regular occurrence amongst them; for Manlius had always surrounded himself with the cultivated, the men of learning whom he understood and who understood him. He had done so all his life; it was his duty and often his pleasure, especially when he could patronize the worthy, or give entertainment to friends of equal rank.

Courtesy required that he play the part of the charming host at dinner as he had done countless times in his past, and he did his duty, even though he had little taste for it that evening. He conformed, as always, to the wisdom of Varro, that the number of guests should be more than the Graces and less than the Muses; he took trouble to ensure they were neither too eloquent, nor yet too silent; discreetly directed the conversation so that, although not trivial, it was not too ponderous, with readings to match. And he accomplished with ease that most delicate task of being free from meanness in his provision of food, without trying to impress his guests with its expense.

Despite his efforts, though, it was not a happy occasion, as it was becoming increasingly hard to assemble even a small group of like-minded spirits. Half the guests were clients, dependent on his favor and keen to eat the dishes of larks and partridges, carp and trout he had ordered, but too ill at ease in such illustrious surroundings to make easy conversation. His adopted son, Syagrius, watching carefully, fearful of making a mistake or saying the wrong thing, ate clumsily, blushing with embarrassment, and said nothing. There were two true friends, Lucontius and Felix, who tried to make things easier, but instead ended up dominating the conversation, interrupting when others tried to speak, being unnecessarily contemptuous of the clients and overly familiar with Manlius himself. And then there was Caius Valerius, a cousin of Felix's whom Manlius tolerated only because of his friend; he was a coarse man who wrapped himself in piety like a suffocating blanket, which only partly concealed his ill humor and vulgarity.

The three friends set the tone, swapping verse and epigram in the manner of the golden age, bathing themselves in the meters and resonances of the great authors they had revered since they had been schoolboys. It was Lucontius who introduced the lapse in taste—rare for him—that made the evening so much less than agreeable.

> *Yet now the breath of the Academy*
> *blow the winds of the church of Christ.*

Elegant, witty, refined. Felix smiled briefly and even Manlius barely managed to suppress a nod of approval.

But Caius Valerius turned dark with anger. "I consider there are some things at least which should be above jest."

"Was I jesting?" responded Lucontius in mock surprise, for he realized that Caius was slow-witted enough to be unable to distinguish between respect and mockery. "Surely I speak only the truth? Surely we see the Revelations of Our Lord solely through Greek eyes? Even Saint Paul was a Platonist."

"I do not know what you mean," Caius replied. "The truth is told to me in the Bible. I need no Greek words to tell me what I see there."

Should Manlius intervene, explain how there are many ways of understanding even a simple passage? Teach him how such mysteries as the Incarnation, the Trinity, the Holy Spirit were given shape in our minds through the teaching of the Academies? Caius was one of those who gloried in his ignorance, called his lack of letters purity, scorned any subtlety of thought or expression. A man for his time, indeed. Once, and not so long ago, he would have fallen silent in embarrassment at his lack of knowledge; now it was the knowledgeable who had to mind their tongues.

"And you must remember, dear Lucontius," Manlius interrupted, "that there are many who consider that Plato had access to the wisdom of Moses, that he merely translated Our Lord's wisdom into Greek, not the other way around." He looked anxiously, and saw that Lucontius, dear sensitive soul, took the warning, flashing a brief apology with his eyes. The moment of difficulty was over; the dinner continued, harmlessly and without point.

Except that Manlius was discomfited. He took care in his invitations, actively sought to exclude from his circle crude and vulgar men like Caius Valerius. But they were all around; it was Manlius who lived in a dream world, and his bubble of civility was becoming smaller and smaller. Caius Valerius, powerful member of a powerful family, had never even heard of Plato. A hundred, even fifty years before, such an absurdity would have been inconceivable. Now it was surprising if such a man did know anything of philosophy, and even if it was explained, he would not wish to understand.

Manlius thought greatly of such matters after most of the guests had gone to their beds, escorted by servants with torches. He stared out of the great doors at the landscape beyond, once a park of perfection, now disfigured by the rough cottages of farmers whose dwellings were coming ever closer, huddling nearer his huge villa for protection like piglets around a sow. He could have razed them, but feared their inhabitants might take themselves off, go and find a new lord to protect them—one who would not honor the law if he demanded them back. Then he looked the other way, to the bathhouse now abandoned and turned into a barracks for the soldiers permanently needed to protect the estate.

All they wanted was to live in security, and all the harm they did was to spoil his view. A man like Caius Valerius was very much more dangerous.

"None of us truly chooses our family, I'm afraid." It was Felix who had walked up quietly behind him. "People like my dear cousin have always existed; even Vergil, I believe, had a brother-in-law who despised his poetry."

Manlius put his arm around him, and they walked slowly in the fading light. Of all the creatures in the world, Felix was the one he truly loved, whose company made him relax and forget his cares. For years now, decades even, he had relied on this short, powerful man, whose mind was as quick as his frame was bulky. A deceptive man, for he looked as he was—a soldier, used to the hardships of fighting and the simplicities of armies. Yet at the same time, he was supple in argument, quick in understanding, and the most honorable, loyal friend Manlius had ever encountered. Nor did he ever condemn; while Manlius frequently heard himself making waspish comments about others, Felix never judged, always sought to see the good even in those who had so little virtue in them.

"I know," Manlius replied. "And I tolerate him for your sake. But, truly it is a hard job."

"Rude, vulgar, and scarcely lettered. I know. But a great donor to the church and someone who has dispatched men from his own estates to help defend Clermont from the Goths. As have I."

"But I haven't, even though Sidonius is one of my oldest friends? Is that how you wish to end your sentence?" Manlius added.

It had been preying on his mind greatly in the past few months. The city of Clermont, far to the west, was under siege from King Euric, blocking his desire to grab a stranglehold on the whole of Provence. If it fell, they would all soon follow, and it could not last long without reinforcements; indeed it might already have fallen had it not been for Sidonius, who had put himself at the head of the defenses and was refusing to accept the inevitable.

For inevitable it was, in Manlius's view. For years now, the barbarians had been moving into Gaul; sometimes they were encouraged, sometimes resisted. Sometimes they were treated as enemies, sometimes as allies against a still worse danger. But every time they took a little bit more, and every time the power of Rome to stop them proved a mirage. Not many years ago, an army of thirty thousand had been sent against Euric's father: none had come back. His own father had conceived the great strategy of the emperor Majorian to beat back the threat; but was undermined and killed by his enemies among the Roman aristocracy of Gaul even before any army could move. Now here was Sidonius, brave, foppish, foolish Sidonius, who had decided to take a stand where emperors had failed. He had always had a weakness for lost causes, for grand, heroic but empty gestures.

"I had another letter from him begging our help," Felix continued. "He says that a few thousand troops now could make all the difference."

"He said that six months ago as well. It made no difference at all. Has something now changed?"

Felix shrugged his shoulders wearily. "We must try, surely? The whole of the civilized world is at stake."

Manlius smiled. "We are the civilized world, you and I," he said. "A few dozen people, with our learning. As long as we continue to stroll through my garden arm in arm, civilization will continue. Euric or no Euric. And I fear that you may provoke worse anger than you imagine."

Felix shook his head. "You would not have spoken so cravenly a few years ago."

"A few years ago everything was different. When I was young we could travel without fear along well-maintained roads, through well-administered cities, and stay at the villas of friends stocked with labor. There was an emperor who wielded real power rather than being a plaything of warlords. Those days are as distant now as the age of Augustus."

"It is peaceful enough here."

"All illusion, my friend. We have been attacked by marauders at this villa three times in the last six weeks. It nearly fell to looters on the last occasion. Two of my other villas have been destroyed and now produce nothing. This tranquil scene you see here this evening depends on six hundred troops hidden in the background. They consume near a third of everything we produce and could turn on us one day. There are fewer people to tend the fields, fewer still to buy our diminishing surplus. In a way, we are under siege here as well, and slowly losing the battle, just as friend Sidonius is losing his. You must know all this from your own experience."

"I do, of course." Felix paused, and they walked some more before sitting at the edge of the pond. "And I am grateful to you for inviting me, as ever. I, too, grow lonely for company, even though I am surrounded by people."

Manlius leaned over and kissed his friend on the cheek. "It is good to see you once more. But however restorative, that is not the sole reason I invited you, of all people. I need to tell you something. Something important."

It was the moment when he had to test a friendship that had endured for nearly twenty years without argument, without dispute, with perfect amity. Manlius was aware that he was trespassing on something sacred.

Felix turned toward him, drew his arm away. "Such gravity and seriousness! Whatever can it be? You are publishing your letters at last?"

"This is not for laughing. I have been thinking as you have for some time. That we must try. That all we value may indeed be destroyed but it should not be given up so easily. I have received a letter from Bishop Faustus of Riez."

"Good heavens! You are going to pray! You are going to start going to church! Truly, this man is a saint and a miracle worker. All that I hear about him must be true."

Manlius grunted, and for a while they talked about the pond they were sitting beside, clogged now with weeds. They swapped aphorisms about water, played with quotations from Pliny about his garden, inverting grammatical constructions so that the neatness and order of the original became the clogged and unkempt reality of the present. Then, as old friends do, they said nothing, but looked at the lilies still growing and the insects hopping across them in the evening light.

"Faustus wrote to ask me to become Bishop of Vaison," Manlius said eventually.

Felix knew immediately the importance of what he said, but still tried to cover it over with a joke. "Not Bishop of Rome? How about emperor, too? You'd look handsome in the purple. Truly, the man doesn't know you very well, or he wouldn't have wasted his ink."

Manlius threw some dust into the water and watched as the perch swam toward it in the hope of food.

"I have decided to accept," he said quietly.

TO A SCHOLAR of Julien's generation, it almost seemed as though there were two Manlius Hippomaneses. On the one hand there was the bishop mentioned occasionally by the chroniclers, the miracle worker whose cult was still vaguely remembered; the man who converted the Jews of Vaison, whose shrine produced miracles long after his death and who protected his people from the depradations of the barbarian invaders. On the other hand, there was the man of letters who existed in the correspondence of his aristocratic friends and in the manuscript of the *Dream*. One was admired for his piety, the other known for his sophistication and learning, his disdain for the vulgarity of the world, his aloof contempt for the age in which he lived. Julien's article, the one that brought him to the attention of the authorities in late 1940, sought to reconcile these two.

This he did by arguing, in an essay published as Europe collapsed into war once more, that there was nothing to reconcile. That Manlius's two reputations were reflections of the same man seen through different perspectives. The bishop who looked after his flock was the same as the aristocrat who wrote dilettante poetry while the rule of Rome in Gaul crumbled into dust. The activist bishop, loved by his people for his good works, was identical to the languid man of literature, so consumed with degenerate idleness that he failed to block the advance of the Gothic Burgundian tribes down the Rhône in the year 475.

For, in Julien's daringly revisionist view, Manlius's hidden achievement was titanic, driven by a vision of breathtaking clarity. Because, he explained, Manlius did not fail to block the Burgundians, he deliberately handed over a portion of Provence to them, swapping the nonexistent protection of Rome for the coarser but more effective shield of a barbarian king. Roman Gaul did not fall; it was put out of its misery by the last embodiment of its cultural glory. And because Manlius did this, King Euric's Visigoths were blocked in their expansion up the river, which would have given them command of the heart of Europe. Manlius, he insisted, saw that the Burgundians would be a powerful protector for the church and ensure its continued communication with Rome long after the last emperor of the West had been deposed. Christendom could not have survived without him; the West would have split between Romans and Arians in religion. The power of the papacy could never have grown. And he ensured that the new rulers governed by law, Roman law transferred into a Burgundian code.

All because Manlius was able to take the imaginative leap to see that Roman civilization was more than Roman rule; he protected the essential while being ready to jettison the appearance. He possessed an intelligence lacking in his peers, for he grasped that the days of the emperors had drawn to a close, but that what it meant could survive, if the ground was well prepared, if the newcomers were taught carefully to guard their inheritance.

Thus an argument that even Julien realized was colored by the somber hues of his own times. He wrote his article and moved on to a more hopeful theme, choosing the literary aspect of Manlius for further investigation, looking at his later influence and slowly focusing on Olivier de Noyen as a key figure in transmitting Manlius's heritage to the modern age. For the extraordinary clarity of Manlius's vision had to come from somewhere; something had to make him stand so much higher, think so much more dispassionately, than the others of his generation who, it seemed, scarcely even noticed the end of Rome until fifty years after it had happened.

The crucial document in this later argument was the one he found in the Vatican, *The Dream of Scipio,* showing the bishop's grasp of Neoplatonism, that most sophisticated of philosophies. Of all those still capable of action, it was a philosopher who combined deeds and insight into a decisive intervention. Could someone like Julien have resisted such an interpretation? The secular Julien, concerned with literature and thought and history, did not consider the other part of Manlius's reputation, the part that spoke of him as a miracle worker. This he didn't even bother to dismiss as the superstitious nonsense of the credulous. He merely ignored it entire.

WITHIN AN hour of his death around the year 486, Manlius's body was torn to pieces by those who had gathered in the far courtyard to await the event. When it became known he had breathed his last, the crowd—which numbered perhaps two hundred people—surged into the building, demanding to see the corpse. As there were no longer any guards, nor any people capable of resisting such a force, the chamber was soon filled with mourners, singing, praying, and leaning forward to touch the human remains of a man who, everyone knew, was already a saint. It might, perhaps, have been a relic hunter, a type of creature already in existence, who first leaned through the throng to cut off a piece of Manlius's shroud and take possession of the sanctity residing in a cloth that had touched his mortal flesh. Perhaps it was a townsperson or a neighboring deacon who wanted to possess some part of him to bring glory to his church. Certainly it was not one of his family or friends, all of whom were pushed out of the room by the weight of numbers, or retired in disgust.

The action spread panic and prompted a second, then a third person to pull at the cloth. Within a few minutes the body was naked, but even that was not enough, as men and women alike began tearing at his hair, then his hands. A scuffle, then a fight broke out, and a sort of holy blood-lust developed in the room, with men screaming in rage, and sobbing in ecstasy, departing only when they had a part of him, bloody and jagged, wrapped in their cloaks, or held—still seeping warm, red liquid—in their hands.

What remained when the storm had passed was bathed, redressed, and anointed before being borne on a bier to its last resting place in the church he had so finely decorated in Vaison. Already a mason of the town was planning a shrine, for Manlius's family was still rich, and would dig deep in their pockets to have the honor of one of its number shown to the world. The deacon (now head of the church until Manlius's successor could be found) placed the strongest men he could find on guard, then thought more deeply.

Might not the relic hunters come back? They had been known to strip a saint's house in their ravening hunger for the holy. Besides, Manlius (despite his past) had given himself to the church, yet he was a rich man. Mindful of Our Lord's injunctions, the deacon did not want his bishop to have died wealthy. Had his death (an apoplectic fit, which came on him suddenly at the age of sixty-two, shortly after he had risen that morning) been more foreseeable, he was sure Manlius would have given instructions that all his wealth be transferred to the church, for its greater glory, and so he might die in proper poverty.

Once the body was secure inside the church, therefore, he gave the orders. By evening the next day, Manlius's great villa was empty; the gold and silver plate (remarkably little of it, in fact, for the deacon did not realize how often his bishop had paid from his own funds to repair roads and walls and waterways) were locked in the church, the furniture also, the lead and tiles stripped from the roofs to be transferred later. Four of the great stone columns from the colonnade were marked for reuse, when a team of bullocks and cart could be found strong enough to pull the load. The statues were left, but the workers, simple townsmen all, were shocked to see that nearly all were pagan imagery, foul and disgusting displays of impiety. These they toppled from their stands and broke with mallets, lest anyone see and scorn their patron. They were determined to guard his reputation in death as well as he had guarded them in life. It was the very least they could do, for they relied on him to guard them in the afterlife as well, and did not wish to risk his anger by neglecting to protect his good name.

Most of Manlius's great library was burned as well; the old rolls, the newly copied codices alike, were taken into the courtyard and destroyed; an extravagant gesture brought on by haste, for many were on vellum and could have been scraped and used again. The bonfire burned brightly for more than three hours as his precious Ammianus, Tacitus, Ovid, Terence, Plautus went up in the flames so their owner's purity would burn more brightly to posterity. Also consumed were his treasured Greek texts, his Plato and Aristotle, his two copies of Sophocles, his Xenophon. None were needed, many were scandalous, all should go. Only Christian texts were preserved, winnowed out like wheat from the chaff, lovingly wrapped in cloth and taken back to the church in Vaison, where they rested on a small shelf until, a hundred years later, they were transferred to a monastery outside Marseille.

Here they remained for two centuries until they, in turn, were consumed by fire. By then, however, some had been copied and, just as Manlius's commentary was preserved by mere chance after his death, mistaken for a Christian text, so it was by accident that, when a copyist came from a new foundation near Montpellier in 723 to acquire sacred works, one of his team of scribes transcribed it as well, writing so fast that he barely noticed what he was jotting down.

There were mistakes, bad mistakes, in this version, but the delicate thread that began before Manlius and stretched across the centuries held still. For though this version was, in its turn, destroyed by Protestants during the wars of religion, by then Olivier de Noyen had seen it and copied down most of it, errors and all. The voice that Julien Barneuve heard, when he picked up the manuscript in the Vatican library, was by then weak and feeble but in the echoing sound, and the chatter of other men's words and opinions, it was still just recognizable, and through it the words of Sophia, half understood or not understood at all, passed down the centuries into his mind.

 WHEN OLIVIER de Noyen found the manuscript in the library of a monastery near Montpellier, he suspected it might be of importance, but failed to understand anything of its arguments until he came under the painstaking tutelage of Rabbi Levi ben Gerson. He did not even realize that it was not original. He knew little of philosophy except for the poor versions of Aristotle that were so much a part of the church that many men were virtually unaware that he had been a pagan. Plato was to him but a name, a mysterious, half-legendary creature all but forgotten. Olivier was a clerical courtier and something of a poet, and had as his private goal the purification of letters, the casting out of the corruption of his times; in this he had more similarities with

Manlius than he ever realized. By Julien's standards, however, his knowledge was limited, his understanding meager.

The love of letters was an affliction that had seized him when he was young. His father, it is said, was a vain man, made bitter by his own lack of success in the world, for he was a notary in such a small, bedraggled, insignificant town that he knew no fortune would ever come his way. Vaison, so people said, had once been a great city, but so long ago no one really knew whether this was true or not. Certainly, farmers ploughing their fields often turned up huge lumps of stone, carvings, and even metalwork, but far from being interested, they cursed these lumps for the trouble they caused. Only occasionally were some of these salvaged, to be used to build a barn or a house high up on the hill where the inhabitants had retreated a century or so before for safety's sake.

In this little rabbit warren of dingy, dirty streets, looking out across the river and the fields that covered Manlius's city, Olivier de Noyen was born in 1322, to the delight of his father, who transferred onto him all his ambitions. Olivier (he believed) was destined for great things. He would become a true lawyer, go to Paris and rise to a position at the court of France itself, that foreign barbaric land to the north where men could become vastly rich and powerful. He conceived this idea almost at the moment he conceived Olivier in a hurried, dispassionate bedding of his wife, and the simultaneous creation of idea and subject struck him so forcibly (when his wife told him the news some fifteen weeks later) that he decided it must be guidance from the saint on the hill, a lady known for the goodness of her advice.

Such heavenly sanction was not to be cast aside, and Olivier was informed of his future career so early in his life that "lawyer" may well have been one of the first words he comprehended. He was sent to the school close by the cathedral, learned his letters and was beaten for his mistakes, then, at night and even on Sundays he was coached by his father for the great career that lay ahead of him after he had been to university in Montpellier. His father had few contacts, but assiduously cultivated those he did have in search of both bride and patron for his son. Through a distant cousin, he felt he had the right to correspond with Annibaldus di Ceccani, a monsignor at the papal court in Avignon with a great future before him, for his connections were as powerful as the elder de Noyen's were weak. By that stage, indeed, his father was beginning to grow alarmed at his son's demeanor, for the child seemed bent on obstructing his father's wishes in countless little ways. He would disappear for days, even though he knew the scale of the thrashing he would receive on his return; he deliberately refused to learn; was noisy, constantly asking questions his father—a good, but uneducated man—could not answer. He stole birds, mushrooms, fruit from other men's land, so much so that complaints were made. More beatings followed, with no result. The letter to Monsignor Ceccani, soon to be cardinal, was an act of desperation as much as anything else, a desire to hand the boy over to a greater authority who might bend, and if necessary break, a spirit too resilient for a father's will alone.

Why Ceccani agreed in 1336 to take on the fourteen-year-old Olivier that he might work and be surrounded with the sophistication of court life and ecclesiastical learning is not known. Perhaps he simply needed a servant; perhaps, when he met Olivier, he saw a spark in the young boy's eye that intrigued him; perhaps fortune took a hand, for if Ceccani had not agreed to the request then he would certainly have triumphed in his struggle with Cardinal de Deaux and changed the course of Christendom. Whatever the reason, Olivier shortly afterward packed a small bag, bade farewell to his beloved mother, left Vaison, and went to Avignon, where he remained for the rest of his life, a period in which his father's aspirations were destroyed.

For Ceccani was a man of some cultivation, and though he never became one of those fascinating, erudite philosopher-cardinals who redeemed the otherwise corrupt church of the next century, he read as widely as was possible in those days and had the beginnings of a library. To this collection of some one hundred fifty manuscripts Olivier was eventually given access. Not that Ceccani initially took a great deal of interest in the boy; he was no teacher and had little human warmth about him. But neglect was exactly what Olivier needed, and he flourished under the new regime. And he fell in love for the first time, the most enduring and consuming passion of his life. He began to read. He arose at four in the morning and read until his duties began; ate his meals quickly so he could run back to the library and read some more, if only for ten minutes at a time; read in the evening with candles stolen from the kitchens until he fell asleep.

There was not such a wide range of books available; some Aristotle, in a Latin translation of an Arabic version of the Greek; the church fathers; Boethius, whom he loved for his wisdom; Augustine, whom he admired for his humanity. But it was the day he discovered Cicero that changed everything. The beauty of the prose, the noble elegance of the ideas, the lofty majesty of the conceptions were like draughts of strong wine, and when he first discovered, then read, the one manuscript Ceccani possessed, he wept with joy for a full twenty minutes before immediately starting again.

Some six months later, he began his new career as a collector when he was in a shop to buy some sweetmeats for the household. This was not his task; rather it was something he often asked to be allowed to do, as the errand gave him the opportunity of leaving the dark, forboding palace where he now had quarters in the garret, and wander the streets of Avignon at will. Every time he went out he was transfixed by wonder, overwhelmed by the bustle of humanity, the noise, the smells, the excitement. For Avignon had transformed itself in a matter of a few years from a minor city into one of the wonders of the world. The arrival of the papal court, forced to leave Rome by civil strife and now showing every sign of staying forever, had sucked in merchants and bankers, priests and painters, goldsmiths, petitioners, lawyers, cooks, costume makers, furniture makers and masons, woodworkers and silversmiths, robbers and whores and charlatans who came from all over Christendom to jostle in the streets and compete for favor, influence, and fortune.

The city was not big enough for them all; it was bursting at the seams and men had to put up with being squashed, exploited, and robbed, but few found they were unprepared to pay the price. Bees around a honey pot, flies around dung; those were the common verdicts. Olivier had no opinion on the morality of it; all he knew was that a simple walk in the morning during the market, in the afternoon when the big religious processions took place, or in the evening when the city was taken over by drinkers and diners, singing and dancing, left his mind dizzy with excitement and all his senses tingling with joy.

And there were buildings as well; hundreds of houses, churches, palaces all being thrown up as quickly as possible, new land being leveled, old dwellings razed to make space for bigger ones. The first time he went into the papal palace he could not believe his eyes; he felt sure he was walking into an immense cave in a mountain; no man, surely, could dream of a building so vast. And yet even that was not big enough; the new pope, Clement, had deemed it all too small and was beginning again, doubling the size of the original, with decorations so sumptuous and so costly they would have no equal in the world. Sometimes, late at night when he lay on his bed wondering at all he had seen and smelled that day, Olivier could hardly stop himself laughing at the thought of his little Vaison, its few hundred inhabitants tucked up on a hill, which, until he came to Avignon, had seemed so grand.

The shop he went to was his favorite; shelves groaned with all manner of delicacies, some still hot and steaming from the oven, some cool and flaky with fresh pastry, stuffed with spices he had never heard of, and sold at prices that made him incredulous. He picked up what he had been told to collect, and as there was a risk his fingers might make dents in them, the shopkeeper took some pieces of paper to wrap them more firmly.

There was writing on them. Olivier read it and gasped; there was no possibility of mistaking that limpid, fluent voice that, once truly heard, could never be forgotten. In his excitement and eagerness to unwrap the paper, he let all the expensive foods drop to the floor, where they broke into crumbly pieces. He scarcely even noticed, although the shopkeeper was shocked.

"You'll get a beating for that," he began.

Olivier ignored him and waved the piece of paper in his face instead. "Where did you get this?"

His reddened, earnest, young face had such a look of intensity that the shopkeeper forgot his anger. "There's a little pile. I found them on a rubbish heap outside the church of Saint-Jean," he said.

"Give me them. I'll buy them."

A shake of the head. "That's the last one, young man. I've been using them for days."

The realization made Olivier almost choke, but he retained enough self-possession to get the names of the last dozen or so customers the shopkeeper had served. Then he spent the rest of the day trailing around the town, knocking on kitchen doors, suffering cuffs to the ears and insults, and the occasional pinch on the cheek in his quest. When he got back home in the evening—having spent an entire day in truancy—he was, as the shopkeeper had predicted, soundly beaten.

But it was well worth it, for carefully tucked away in his tunic he had most of a letter by Cicero, now known to be one of the letters to Atticus.

By the time his father came and paid a visit two months later, he had read his discovery so often he knew it by heart. Still, merely touching it— for he mistakenly thought it must be original and written down by Cicero himself, so little learning did he have at this stage—gave him the greatest possible pleasure. He even slept with it by his side at night. Nor could he comprehend that anyone would not be as excited as he; so, when he presented himself to his father and was asked to account for the past six months, he pulled the sheets of old paper out of his tunic to show them off.

As his story continued his father's countenance darkened. "And you have spent your time on this, to the neglect of your studies?"

Olivier hastened to tell him that he had studied hard and well, omitting that he detested the work and did it out of duty alone.

"But you could have studied harder, spent more time with your proper duties, had you not wasted so much energy on this."

Olivier hung his head. "But Cicero was a lawyer, sir . . ." he began. His father was not impressed.

"Do not try and trick me. That is not why you read this. Give it to me."

He held out his hand, and Olivier, after a moment's hesitation that his father noted all too well, gave the precious manuscript into his hands. Already he felt the tears welling up in his eyes.

His father stood up. "I will overlook your disobedience, but I must teach you a lesson. You must resist such foolishness. Your job is to become a lawyer, and fulfill all the hopes I have of you. Do you understand me?"

Olivier nodded mutely.

"Good. So you will see the wisdom of what I do now." And his father turned around and put the manuscript onto the fire, standing back to watch it burst into bright flames, then turn black as it curled up and disintegrated.

Olivier was shaking so much, concentrating so hard on making sure that no tears fell down his cheeks, that he didn't even flinch when his father gave him a friendly tap on the shoulder and delivered another homily about his obligations. He even managed to bid him farewell in a dignified fashion, received his blessing with humility, before rushing back to his home, climbing the stairs to the little attic room he shared with six others, and bawling his eyes out.

He had learned his lesson, although not the one his father hoped to inculcate. From that moment Olivier de Noyen determined that never would he become a lawyer.

A TOUCHING TALE, attributed in different forms to many different people. It was Julien Barneuve who realized that it had originated with Olivier, then had been transferred to Petrarch when Olivier's reputation collapsed in disgrace and scandal later on. The anecdote then took on a life of its own and became part of the legend of the early Bach. Either early genius is encouraged, with elders astounded and amazed by such infantile virtuosity, as is said to be the case with Giotto or Mozart, or it causes alarm, and the parents try in vain to block the torrent. None of the tales may be true, in fact; the stories are perhaps no more than a conventional way of signaling the birth of greatness, of the solitary purpose pursued throughout life.

Barneuve himself was not touched by the gods in this way, but merely studied those who were. The world needs only a few geniuses; civilization is maintained and extended by those lesser souls who corral the men of greatness, tie them down with explanations and footnotes and annotated editions, explain what they meant when they didn't know themselves, show their true place in the awesome progression of mankind.

For this task he was perfectly trained, and had been so for twenty years or more, decades of work that he had spent patiently and meticulously accumulating the resources required for his chosen task. His, too, was a labor of passion and of love, for he was no pedant, no dry scholar cut off from the world. Far from it; he considered himself in a small way a crusader for the true values of civilization, burning with the love of life and of learning in an age that valued neither.

In his youth he had attempted some poetry, but was too stern a critic of others to fool himself. He was happy to abandon any such pretensions, and prided himself on a maturity that enabled him to stop wasting time while others of his generation frittered away their hours in artistic dreams. Or died; for Julien was fifteen when German troops swept across Belgium and into northern France; twenty when the carnage that all but eliminated an entire generation came to its end. It was not the time for romantic verse, or psychologically acute expressions of decadence. He rarely talked about this period of his life; he had no wish to revive memories of events that had so shaken him. He had volunteered early, rather than waiting to be conscripted, for he felt a duty and an obligation to serve, and believed that not only fighting, but also being willing to fight for his country and the liberty it represented, would make some small difference. He was injured twice, decorated twice, and took part in the terrible conflict around Verdun; that in itself is enough to indicate something of what he endured. His idealism was one of the casualties of the carnage.

Millions died; Barneuve survived. When he was finally discharged in early 1918—his injuries rendering him unfit for further military service— he came home to the house in Vaison, a solid house of substance in what is now the rue Jean Jaurès, and resumed his former life. His father never discussed the experience, and Julien felt no desire to mention it either; he might have done so had his mother still been alive. The only slight hint of his feelings was that, one morning, just after the armistice, he was to be seen in the garden slowly taking the decorations and campaign medals he had been awarded and throwing them all on a bonfire. They had been earned by someone he no longer knew, indeed by someone he considered already dead, full of dreams and aspirations he could scarcely understand. From then on, Julien conceived of his duty in a different fashion. The medals themselves were hardly damaged by the heat, but they were dirtied and covered in ash, so much so that later the gardener unknowingly dug them into the ground where, presumably, they still remain. As for his father, Docteur Barneuve threw himself into organizing the public subscription for the huge monument to the dead that was cut into the mountain supporting the old town; it was the closest he ever came to telling his son of his relief that his name was not also inscribed on its panels, that he was not the dying soldier carved so vividly onto its white marble.

Three months to the day after he came home—a period mainly spent sitting in the garden of his maternal grandmother's house at Roaix a few kilometers to the west, for after a short while he found living in his family home irksome—Julien got up at five in the morning, took down the books he had been reading the day he left for the army, and began once more, picking up at exactly the page where he had inserted his bookmark three years previously. He worked silently, efficiently, and hard, showing the powers of concentration that he had always been able to summon. After he had drunk a coffee with a piece of bread from the previous day dipped in it, he sat and read and annotated until twelve, when he would put on a hat and walk into the village and eat some soup at the café. Then he worked again until six, ate, then worked again until midnight. This pattern of study he kept up, year after year, until he was ready: he sat, and passed with ease, the *agrégation* in history and geography, an intellectual marathon and obstacle race that, until it was reformed in 1941, was perhaps the most fiendishly demanding examination the mind of man has ever devised.

It says much of Barneuve's character, and of his intellect, that he emerged near the head of his year. His career in a sense was already made; he had now merely to collect the fruits of his labors. After doing his time in a provincial lycée in Rennes, sent there by the French state to teach him humility, he could reasonably look forward to spending the rest of his working life in Paris. A model academic career was already laid out, one of steady accomplishment, a continual drip of honors and rewards, and the quiet respect of colleagues and pupils. He was, by this stage, already working on his *thèse,* a vast work on late Neoplatonism in the West, which took him much of the next two decades to complete.

It was not to be so perfectly smooth, nor so easy; he had embraced self-satisfied complacency too young. The simple life of predictable, safe accomplishment was not, it seemed, what he truly craved. For in 1924 he won a greatly sought after scholarship to spend two years at the École de Rome, and as a preliminary took a cruise around the Mediterranean to celebrate, paid for by his father. On it he reacquainted himself with Olivier de Noyen, and he, in turn, eventually introduced him to Manlius Hippomanes.

IN SOME WAYS, though, Manlius had already reached out and touched him before his Mediterranean cruise. Even though the name had changed, Julien was a native of the same town and showed a precocious intellectual interest in his region, his *pays,* and it was this curiosity that attracted the attention of Canon Joseph Sautel.

Père Sautel has only an incidental role in this story; he is, in some ways, no more important than the plague bacillus that ultimately killed much of Olivier de Noyen's generation; an agent acting unknowingly for his own reasons and unaware of any of the consequences. But the effect he had on the young Julien was of such magnitude that he deserves to be considered, lest his brief intersection with him be misunderstood as either trivial or coincidental. There was, in fact, an inevitability about their encounter; it had been likely since Julien's parents married in 1892, his wife contributing to the family the peaceful little house in Roaix, which she adored so much that she went there every summer to avoid the oppressive heat of the town. It became probable when the youthful Sautel developed a passion for archaeology and won permission from his bishop to indulge it. It became certain when Julien, to escape the solicitudes of his mother, took to long walks during the otherwise empty afternoons when he was alone with her during the summer months.

He was ten in that summer, the age when children are the most impressionable, and Sautel was an impressive man. They met late in the afternoon, when the boy was tired and thirsty. He had gone a long way, along lanes and tracks, crossing the nearly dried-up Ouvèze, then walking in the direction of the bois de Darbaux on the other side toward the hills that rose from the river valley, dark and threateningly against the brilliant blue sky. Then he got lost, and turned back, cutting across fields to save time while also thinking of his anxious mother—who had told him not to go for more than half an hour—to give form to his mounting panic.

The freshly dug mounds of earth, dark in parts, sandy in others, mottled where the sun had partially dried them, attracted his attention first of all, and made him hope that there were some workmen in the field beyond, perhaps building a barn. He clambered through the ditch, scratching his leg on the brambles as he climbed up, then walked past the huge earthworks to see what he could find.

There was no one there, or no one he could see. Signs of recent activity were all around—wheelbarrows, picks and shovels, black circles of ash where trees had been cut and burned. But no people, just the swallows wheeling in the air. Julien stood uncertainly, then walked to what looked like a ruined building in the hope that someone was about.

There he entered a world of magic. The walls were only a few feet high, of rough stone and pebbles and crumbling mortar, nothing to look at, but as he walked past one, then another, he saw a sight that made him catch his breath. Before him, laid out on the floor, was an enormous, beautiful bird, picked out in tiny stones, its blues and golds and reds glittering as the fierce afternoon sun reflected off the water that had been used to clean it. Almost as though it was alive. Better than if it had been alive; no real bird could ever attract the eye like that, or nestle so beautifully in the stone foliage as this one did.

Utterly transfixed with wonder, and scarcely daring to breathe lest it hear him and fly away, he took a step closer, then bent down to run his hands over the irregular, almost sharp surface.

"Get off!" An angry, urgent voice broke the peace and the spell. The bird did not move. Julien stood up sharply and looked around him.

"I said get off, you little wretch! Hurry. Do as you're told."

Julien took a step backward, caught his foot on a loose boulder, and fell heavily, sprawling over the pavement.

"Dear heaven! Stay there. Don't move."

Then the owner of the exasperated voice appeared from behind one of the walls. A big man, only in his twenties but seeming much older to Julien, with a bushy beard and wearing a white shirt and loose, baggy trousers. In his hand he carried a notebook, which he put carefully on top of the wall before stepping over the bird to help Julien up.

"Are you all right? You didn't hurt yourself?"

Julien said he hadn't. The man smelled of sweat. A nice, comforting smell, Julien thought.

"Can't you read? Didn't you see the sign on the road? 'Private. Keep out.' I suppose that just made you even nosier."

"I'm sorry, sir," Julien said timidly. "I didn't come by the road. I came across the fields. I'm lost and my mother will be worrying about me. I hoped someone could tell me where I was."

The big man studied his face carefully, saw no signs of impudence or deceit, then grunted. "Very well. I'll take you to the road and show you."

"No!" Julien cried desperately, though he didn't know why he was suddenly so afraid. The man raised an eyebrow.

"I'm sorry," Julien continued. "But please tell me, what is this place? I must know. Why's that bird there?"

"Do you like it?"

"It's beautiful," Julien said reverently. "The most beautiful thing I've ever seen."

The man smiled. "Yes," he said gently. "I might well agree with you."

And he told Julien that it was a mosaic, which had lain unseen for many hundreds of years, until he had come along and uncovered it. Then as the boy evidently hung on his every word, he led him through the rooms of Manlius's villa, pointing out what he knew, or could guess, about each one, showing him the fragments of broken statues his workmen had discovered, the few roof tiles that had fallen to the floor when the timbers gave out, the remains of the colonnade by the great entrance-way, gap-toothed with four of its columns completely vanished.

Julien listened wide-eyed, completely captivated, for Sautel was a good storyteller and a natural teacher. He told Julien of the legend of the phoenix, its death and rebirth. Julien understood little of it, but was rapt with attention. In his imagination, he saw the men walking through the rooms, the vanished paintings on the walls mysterious in the candlelight, heard the waterfalls in the gardens as they moistened the air on after-noons such as this. He almost heard the conversations, and thought how wonderful it must have all been. Better than any fairy tale, like the bird was better than any real bird.

"You see," Sautel continued, "an example of how an archaeologist works. That mosaic you like so much. Look near its beak. What do you see?"

"A patch," Julien replied promptly.

"Quite right," he said. "Now, this was a rich man's villa. A very rich man, I'd guess. The mosaic is Italian work, third century. All the different stones brought from the corners of the empire. The villa was destroyed suddenly in the fifth century, I reckon. And in the middle of the center-piece of the entrance hall, there is an ugly patch. Where a worn spot was filled with concrete. What are your conclusions?"

Julien stared at the mosaic, momentarily angry that the bird should be discussed in such a dry way, that he should be robbed of its perfection by having its faults so clinically pointed out. He shook his head.

"The owner was short of money, couldn't pay to import new stones for a proper repair, couldn't afford the workmen, if there were any left to hire," Sautel continued. "The whole place was crumbling. The fields were overgrown as there were no workers. The great estates were breaking up. Trade collapsed, the cities, too. In that little patch you can see the decline of an entire civilization, the greatest the world has ever known. I see you were cross when I pointed that hole out to you. It makes me angry, too."

"Why, sir?"

"Because civilization depends on continually making the effort, of never giving in. It needs to be cared for by men of goodwill, protected from the dark. These people gave in. They stopped caring. And because they did, this land fell under the darkness of a barbarism which lasted for hundreds of years."

He shook his head, then glanced at Julien to remind himself he was talking so intently to a mere ten-year-old.

"Anyway," he said. "You're lost. And I am meant to be showing you the way home. If you'll wait a few moments while I pack my satchel, I'll take you to the road."

It wasn't far. His newfound friend was walking in the same direction, and Julien padded alongside him, taking two steps for the big man's one, trying to think of ways to make him keep talking. Sautel needed little encouragement; to every question, he gave a thoughtful, considered, serious reply. He talked to Julien as if to someone his own age, and listened to his responses in a way his brusque, unapproachable father never did.

When they reached the house, Sautel spoke to his mother, saying the delay was his fault, not Julien's, and asking if he might be allowed to come to the dig once again.

"Surely you don't want him, Father," Antoinette Barneuve replied. "He would be so much trouble."

"On the contrary; he is a lad of sense, and I have a high opinion of his views. He also has a pair of strong arms, and I could do with all the help I can get. I have little money to pay laborers, and if he is prepared to work for free, I will be happy to make use of him."

"I don't know . . ."

"Please, Maman," Julien said desperately, scarcely believing that she could even consider rejecting such an offer.

"I'll think about it," she said eventually. "We'll see."

Sautel knew he had won; as he turned to go, he gave the boy a wink. Secretly. Between friends.

Julien watched as the big priest disappeared down the road, whistling to himself, then until he disappeared out of sight around a corner. He thought of nothing else for the rest of the evening, and went to sleep dreaming of him.

THAT SAUTEL was a priest caused little concern to Julien, who was at the age when it is still possible to judge people according to how they behave, nor to his mother, whose faith was strong though hidden from view. It enraged his father, however, and when he heard of Julien's summer occupation, he wrote from Vaison demanding that the connection be severed instantly. For he—a doctor and a freethinker—prided himself on his liberation from superstition and his rigorous attachment to the modern. He detested priestcraft, and one of the major causes of his distance from his wife was his contempt for her weakness in this regard. The Barneuve family, indeed, was defined by this difference between husband and wife for, although it was never mentioned, both were at war, and the object of the conflict was Julien's soul.

At any other time, the elder Barneuve might have agreed; the scientific excavation of the past was something that, ordinarily, would have appealed to him. But that summer was not ordinary; he was in no mood to brook the slightest opposition. Merely because his wife wished it was enough reason for him to say no.

It was not cruelty that led to this decision; rather, he was looking after the welfare of his family, that of his wife as well as that of his only son. For that Easter, while his wife and child were once more staying in the little farmhouse, he had arrived to pay a surprise visit, clattering out on the horse that took him around the large area containing his patients. One was nearing death, and the good doctor—for he was such—came to give such comfort and ease as he could. The patient lived in the same village, so he turned out his horse and set off. As he trotted past the village church on his way to his patient's bedside, the door into the sacristy opened and out came some children from their catechism lesson. He looked, and saw Julien amongst them.

Julien only faintly discerned what followed; he was sent out of the room, out of the house even, and did not witness his father's cold rage, his fury not only at the lessons but also at the disobedience. He heard his mother crying, and tried to comfort her, but she turned away from him.

He did not understand what had happened; for him the lessons were a way of playing with the other children in the village; only rarely did the solemnity of the exercise descend on him. For the most part, he remembered the way he giggled with Elizabeth, the grocer's daughter, then his particular companion, and the way they would go afterward back to her house and be given a cake by her mother. But his father stopped all that; no more lessons, no more sunny, careless afternoons. Julien was never received into the church and for much of his life was inclined to attribute to this lack his slight aching sense of something missing.

His father had no regrets about his action; he would not tolerate disobedience in his own household. Circumstance, a certain fear of ambition, had brought him to be a country doctor in an isolated town, but in this small universe he was determined to rule. And for him, saintliness was hysteria, miracles naturally occurring phenomena misunderstood by the simple, belief mere self-delusion. A rigorous education in science was the antidote to all such afflictions, and to strengthen this medicine, he added a healthy dose of derision, sarcasm, and contempt.

Had anyone suggested that the violence of his dislike seemed excessive, that it suggested fear rather than confidence, he would have reacted with disdain. Few educated people in that region, after all, disagreed with him, and Vaison was in an area that had thrown off the shackles of the church long ago. Even his wife submitted quietly and humbly, never questioning his decisions, never answering back to his barbed remarks even though the hurt they caused was obvious on her face.

Yet there was fear in Pierre Barneuve's mind, a deep knowledge of the power of the beliefs he so detested, a fear that one day the tentacles of superstition would reach out and ensnare his son. His wife's passivity, her refusal to argue, made her all the more dangerous. He knew that one day Julien would have to decide between them. Was he to be his mother's or his father's child? He knew he had manliness and rationality on his side. But he was also dimly aware in a corner of his mind that Julien loved his mother. The idea that he was afraid of his son and had been ever since he was born was absurd, of course, but it was true nonetheless. He had, with his customary incision and lack of sentiment, dismissed all possibility of eternity for himself. The decisions the child took would confer or deny his immortality.

When he heard of Sautel, the fear within him awoke, and he moved swiftly. Julien was not to go to the excavations. He was not to associate with a priest. If there was any deviation from his wishes, the boy was to be sent back to pass the summer under his father's watchful eye. It never occurred to him that his wife would disobey him, nor yet that the child would disobey his mother. Nor did either do so, nor did they need to: the damage was already done. Our lives can change direction in an instant, and it is possible that an entire adult can be determined by only a few such moments, sparkling like gold in the dross of everyday experience.

Lodged forever in Julien's mind was the memory of that bird, brilliant in the summer sunlight, and the magic of the moment of discovery was linked completely to the kindness of the young priest. Set against both was the brooding authority of his father, never questioned but now suspected to be dark and lifeless in contrast to the brightness of what it forbade.

It would not be too much of an exaggeration, indeed, to claim that Julien's entire life was spent seeking to recapture that sensation, that his progression and thoughts and decisions constantly had this unknown goal in mind. It was the phoenix that led him, at school, to concentrate on the classics, so that by fourteen he had a knowledge of Latin and Greek that surpassed that of many a university student. The words of Père Sautel led him to volunteer for the trenches in 1916, and it was the phoenix again that gave him the quiet determination necessary for the *agrégation,* and sustained him in his career thereafter.

His father, who tried to be as kindly as duty allowed, encouraged and supported his son throughout, little knowing how much of the child's drive came from resentment of him. He got a quiet pleasure from every examination his son passed, every glowing report that came from school, every time someone mentioned the boy's undoubted talents. Certainly, he would have preferred that Julien had wished to become a physician like himself, or pursued a career in law—for he dreamed of his son as a deputy, even perhaps a minister in the government—but he contented himself with excellence in any field, and the prospect of a son one day as an eminent professor—the Sorbonne? The Collège de France?—was more than sufficient to satisfy his desires.

And when Julien excelled, he was rewarded, each gift bestowed with care, and received dismissively. His father was hurt, doubtless, by this coldness and could not understand why, as Julien grew into manhood, the closeness he had so often dreamed of seemed further away than ever. But each time Julien accepted a present with only perfunctory thanks, his father persuaded himself that this was manly restraint in a youth commendably reluctant to show emotion.

The grand cruise around the Mediterranean—the presents ever more generous, but no more effective—was the reward for success in examinations. Had his father called him in and said, "I know your mother would have been as proud of you as I am" or, "I wish your mother had been here to see you now," then his heart would have softened so easily. But he wished to claim Julien for his own and said nothing of his wife. And all Julien could say in reply was:

"Thank you, Father. That is very kind."

WHAT WAS Olivier's influence, his reputation, when Julien first began to study him seriously in the 1930s? Not that of a great poet, by any means; he was hardly mentioned in the same breath as Dante, Boccaccio, or Petrarch. He was known to only a few interested in Provençal literature, and although those who had read him knew his importance, his little piece of eternity was guaranteed mainly by the horrors of his crime and punishment. Only when Julien came across Olivier as a bibliophile and collector, an early pioneer of the renaissance in learning, did he reconsider the man and the poetry. Julien was drawn to him for obvious reasons: he, too, was struggling to ensure that, in the madness that afflicted all humanity, some little spark of purity would continue. He, too, had a debt to honor, one owed to both Manlius and Olivier, to continue the great task they had begun. In his own mind, Julien's life as teacher, and later as censor, complemented his labors in the library and archives, each an aspect of the greater project to allow thought itself to survive, even if it was a guttering candle rather than a ferocious blaze. From 1940 onward his study became an obsession in the same way that women became obsessed with ensuring that clothes continued to be washed on a Tuesday, that men became enraged if their game of boules was disrupted on a Saturday or if they could no longer sharpen their razor. The continuation of normal, civilized existence became the goal of daily life, to be attained through struggle.

Understanding the poetry came later; he initially conceived of Olivier as a man of the greatest promise destroyed by a fatal flaw, the unreasoning passion for a woman dissolving into violence, desperately weakening everything he tried to do. For how could learning and poetry be defended when it produced such dreadful results and was advanced by such imperfect creatures? At least Julien did not see the desperate fate of the ruined lover as a nineteenth-century novelist or poet might have done, recasting the tale to create some appealing romantic hero, dashed to pieces against the unyielding society that produced him. Rather, his initial opinion— held almost to the last—was of Olivier as a failure, ruined by a terrible weakness.

He took the lesson but could not help himself. Julien was still attracted to the Provençal's poetry precisely because of the incandescent passion he considered so dangerous. Olivier's words stirred his blood, created in him images of a different history. It was an effort to subjugate the lyrical, magnificent poems of love to the full force of critical reason, to disregard the expressions of desire and seek out the meanings that surely must lie underneath, to see longing as allegory, the beloved as metaphor, the love as a reflection of faith in the divine.

At least, the pure physicality of the poetry proved one thing beyond doubt. However much he may have collected the classics of philosophy and joined them to the theological masterpieces he must have read as well, Olivier de Noyen perfectly failed to understand them. While Manlius argued about the need to maintain the supremacy of reason in the face of the irrational that was eradicating all he held dear, Olivier embraced the opposite, unable to subdue his passions and falling victim to his weakness.

MANLIUS DID not lie to his friend; Bishop Faustus did indeed write to him, asking if he would consent to become Bishop of Vaison. But he did so only after Manlius had spent several months courting the saintly man, slowly convincing him of both the need and the appropriateness of such an appointment. He had acted because of the discomfort that came over him as he saw others, of lower origin, less education, and smaller ability, lording over the region with so little skill and foresight. For many years he stuck to his determination to turn his back forever on public life and live quietly on his estates. He was, after all, one of the richest and most powerful men in the province even when he did nothing but write poetry.

He had been destined for great things at one stage, but the fate that overtook his father filled him with contempt for a world he considered no longer worth saving; when the body was returned, he swore he would never succumb to such an end, remembered the look on the older man's face as Manlius cleaned away the blood, washed the caked mud from his hair. Women's work, usually, but far too precious to be left to them. He would take no obvious revenge; rather, he would stand by, cultivate those things that really mattered, and watch as the consequences of their deeds became clear.

For his father had attached himself to Majorian, a good and virtuous man, only to see the last competent emperor the West produced abandoned by those who most needed his help, then cut down by the warlord Ricimer, the man who had built him up in the first place. And his father had fallen victim to the purge that followed, set upon in the streets of Arles, butchered and left to die in a gutter. Manlius never discovered who was responsible; there were too many people who might have ordered such a thing. His father had been foolish, too trusting, too merciful. He had not moved fast enough to eradicate those who disagreed with him. "It is what is different about us," he had said. "We argue, and convince. We allow disagreement. If we no longer allow that, we might as well be Goths ourselves. What do we have a senate for in this poor little region of ours? It is to hear the opinions of those who disagree with us. What is the point of holding council, if we do not hear different opinions? It is our strength, not our weakness."

He paid heavily for his faith. Majorian had been the last hope for Gaul. He had a chance of putting together an army that might push the Goths back, rebind Gaul to Rome, and strengthen the frontiers. And he had sacrificed it, thrown it away through his delicacy. The constant bickering and disagreement had so weakened this brave, good man that he doomed himself. Manlius's father, charged with governing Provence and keeping it sound, had been part of that failure. Manlius knew that he would not show that same weakness; his retreat to his estates stemmed in part from the fear that realization caused in him. He did not wish to know what he was capable of doing.

Even so, the discomfort remained; the distaste clouded his idyll and drove him, eventually, back to Sophia to see if she could restore his tranquillity with her wisdom. He might have expected that she would do no such thing.

"So tell me. Why do you continue to live in idleness?" she asked once his salutations were presented. "What is your justification beyond that of natural lassitude?"

What was it about this woman that made him feel so confident and content? How was it that her mere look, the way she smiled, could banish all his fears and persuade him that all problems could be understood? How was it that, when faced with a difficulty, he always thought of what she would say or recommend? The first thing he had done after burying his father was to go south, to Marseille. She had comforted him, reassured him, stilled his heart. It was because of her words that he had not brought out his troops and let them loose for an indiscriminate revenge that would have convulsed the province into civil war, because of her again that he did not allow his inactivity to grow into a cancerous hatred of humanity. For twenty years now she had been his mentor, his teacher, his guide; never had she failed him. She had criticized, scorned, bullied, but never withdrawn her love. And he had risen to meet that challenge, always seeking to live up to her expectations, even though he knew he must always fall short.

Her question was a shock, even though it was put in her normal fashion, with the inquiring neutrality of a teacher probing her pupil, forcing him to consider unthought-of questions that he knew only too well once posed. They were in the house he had given her, although it was as unfurnished as the day she walked up the hill and into its door; her way of life was as ascetic as a desert anchorite's. She never had possessions; a few clothes and her books were all that she had or wished to have. In this she remained thoroughly Greek, although almost as archaic as she was in the Attic she still sometimes spoke in homage to her masters, already dead for nearly eight hundred years.

"Are you urging me to abandon a life of contemplation and take up public affairs? After all you have told me about the virtues of the philosophic life? Which side should I take? The bad, or the worse?"

She cocked her head to one side and looked at him dreamily, in the way she always adopted when teaching. As usual, she was a mess, a disgrace. Her dark hair was cropped short and looked as though it had been shorn by a slave with a blunt knife; her dress was of coarse linen, short in the arms and not very much different to the sort of thing shopkeepers might wear. Her nails were rough-cut, and her feet bare. She wore no decoration; her eyes were her only adornment, but these so far excelled all artificial baubles in their beauty that any jewel would have seemed tawdry in comparison. And her voice, which had not changed in all the time he had known her, still dark and throaty, seductive and commanding, amused and critical by turns; once heard, impossible ever to forget. Blind men could fall in love with Sophia, just as Manlius did, despite his usual fineness of discernment in the matter of female beauty.

"An example," she said. "You may comment on it when I am finished. According to Aristotle, one of the earliest laws of Solon, the great lawgiver of Athens, said that if a society split into strife and civil war, anyone who refused to take sides should be exiled and outlawed when order was restored. Your opinion?"

"An absurdity," said Manlius, with a sigh of contentment, for this is why he came to her, to have his mind tested and strained; it was what he lived for, almost, and what she had always unselfishly given. "It's obvious that the more people join in, the worse the conflict. It seems designed to

increase dissent, and spread the chaos of faction even to those who would ordinarily preserve something of civility in a period of violence."

"Your beliefs are so thinly held that you think your grasp on reasoned behavior would collapse under such conditions?"

"I hope not. Not least because of the training I have received at your knee, dear lady."

She acknowledged the compliment with a faint smile; she had banished vanity in most things, but not in this. "Then you must think that what I have taught you is so feeble that it can only be examined in the quiet of a sealed library, or with friends who are already of your opinions?"

"No; at least, I have never heard anyone refute an argument you have presented."

"Then there is only one conclusion; you think all men are unreasoning beasts."

"Most are; but you tell me all retain the faintest remembrance of the divine, and are able to respond to it. Even the worst of men can be persuaded."

"Then surely, if reasoning men do not abandon the people when they are in a state of frenzy, but ally themselves with factions, then they can begin to direct through being men of more than ordinary influence? Would not that soothe the passions, and guide men back to harmony? Would that not be the wisdom behind Solon's law?"

"Perhaps," Manlius said. "And it was no doubt good advice for Solon's time. But I do not see how such balm might be applied now. Which public office should a man take now? A senate seat? There is no one else to talk to. Command the military of the province? There are no soldiers. Oversee an administration and give orders which no one obeys? Perhaps become a tax collector? At least that still functions all too well. Rome will not abandon us as long as it can squeeze a few extra coins out of us. It is too late. There is only an empty shell, all the goodness sucked out and wasted. Majorian was the last chance. Now we must await King Euric's pleasure."

"You are making windy speeches when you know the answer," she said impatiently. "When Socrates was accused of corrupting the young he was also accused of contempt for the gods of Athens. He replied that he honored all the city's deities. And it was true; he sacrificed assiduously. Did he believe they were anything but stories, to comfort the unlettered and present the great ideas of the divine to the simple? Of course not, but as they were so believed, then he maintained a necessary decorum in public. And so must you do, to the gods of your time."

"Are you serious?"

"Very much so. Worship the three gods of the Christians, the father, son, and holy ghost. Make them the sacrifices they require. The church has a power that the old offices no longer have. If you do not fill its grand positions, others will do so. Why do you live, Manlius Hippomanes? Why do you walk this earth, if not to show virtue in your deeds, and how can you do that except by exercise of public office? For generations your family, and your friends' families, have brought honor amongst themselves with these baubles, and convinced yourselves that honor and virtue were one and the same. You have been what, in your time? Procurator, Comes, all these things. Your father had more such offices before you. What do they mean, except that you have vaunted yourself above rivals? You have been like children with toys, fighting over little bits of painted wood. Once upon a time all these places were worth something; their holders ensured good government and gave good advice. That has not been the case for generations now, and still you squabble for the outward show, thinking it distinguishes you from others. It does; it shows how much greater a fool you are."

"I hold no such office any more. Not since my father was killed."

"Even worse. You give delicate dinner parties and entertain your friends, and write letters and verse which get cleverer by the day. But what when there is no one left to read those letters? No friends to invite, no food to put on the table? What then? The schools of Marseille are long gone. No teachers, no pupils. The schools of Bordeaux, even, are growing feeble. Do children care anything for philosophy, for letters, for thought? Will their children even be able to read?"

"And you think joining the church will help?" he asked, scarcely keeping the amused incredulity out of his voice.

"Of course not," she said scornfully. "I think *running* the church will help. Perhaps even that will accomplish nothing, but at least learning will die with a friend by its bedside, rather than abandoned in a ditch. Virtue comes through contemplation of the divine, and the exercise of philosophy. But it also comes through public service. The one is incomplete without the other. Power without wisdom is tyranny; wisdom without power is pointless. Who, for example, is likely to be the new bishop?"

"Caius Valerius."

"And will he do a good job?"

"No. He is a contemptible fool." He did not mention that he was also a cousin of his friend Felix.

"So do a better job," she said simply. "Take that authority and use it. Defend all you hold dear. Use your skills and your intelligence, for you have both. Can Euric be stopped? If not, can his rule be moderated, or put under constraint?"

"Perhaps," Manlius said.

"'Perhaps,'" she repeated. "A possibility, with no guarantee of success, but said without hesitation. You have thought of this already, I see."

"Of course. I see a possibility."

"And yet you do nothing about it. Shame on you."

He looked at her. "I am concerned about what would be necessary, about what I might have to do."

"Then double the shame on you, and double it again," she said sharply. "You are like a general who will not send his troops into battle for fear they will get their breastplates dirty. You have your mind and your soul, Manlius, trained and honed, and will not act for fear of tarnishing them. You should be afraid; you are vain and arrogant, full of error. But I never thought you were a coward as well."

The next day Manlius summoned Syagrius and dictated a letter to Bishop Faustus; there followed a lengthy exchange of views, and a visit to the bishop a few months later. During this Manlius was perfectly honest. He could not claim to be a good Christian, but he was perhaps the most powerful man in the region. The church could have his help, or not. With heretic barbarians to the north and the west, with most of Gaul already gone and the ability of the emperor to protect what remained all but nonexistent, could the church do without him?

Eight weeks and three days later he was baptized, ordained, and elevated to the bishopric of Vaison, taking charge of a diocese that was already some two hundred years old and becoming, in effect, the sole authority in a region in which all others had crumbled into uselessness.

THE BISHOP'S manscript came to Julien's attention because, at the age of fifteen, Olivier de Noyen stole some money. He was working in the cardinal's chancellery, carefully watching the money coming in, the money going out again. Counting the gold and silver pieces, marking it all down in the ledger. There were twelve of the cardinal's people, all sitting at little desks, working from dawn to dusk to keep the great engine of the cardinal's power running smoothly.

It was not work to which he was greatly fitted; he was sent there as a punishment, and as he was constantly offending against the rules of the cardinal's household, he spent much time there, being bored to tears and failing to learn anything at all about the need for discipline. He ran too fast and collided with a cook carrying the cardinal's meal; one week of tallying figures. He disappeared for several days; two weeks. He went out late one night and had his first experience of drinking to excess, leaving the evidence of his debauch on the floor of the great entrance hall of the cardinal's palace; one month's hard counting resulted.

It was after this last adventure—of which even Olivier was ashamed—that he noted that a remittance from one of the cardinal's benefices in England was too great by one gold piece. At that time, he considered himself something of a dandy, delighting in the company of a band of fellows who dressed in the finest clothes they could find, and thought themselves grand indeed when they marched down the street singing, and making fun—normally good-humored—of passersby. Most bore their merriment well; only the Jews did not when they were taunted. They were not agreeable objects of tricks; they hurried by, their heads down, cloaks bundled around them, never answering back or replying with some remark. It was why comments turned to insults, insults to stones. Olivier sometimes joined in, just as he had, on occasion, tormented stray dogs and cats in his youth. He saw little difference, and stopped mainly because he found it poor sport.

His holiday outfit delighted him; it was scarlet and blue and well sewn. But he had no shoes, and the whole appearance was (he thought) spoiled by the wood and cloth sabots that he wore on his feet. What woman of elegance—what serving girl even—could ever be fooled by a man who clattered down the street, making as much noise as donkey and cart? Who could take seriously someone who had to dance barefoot, and often was forced to retire when a stamping boot crunched down on his toes?

The lack of good shoes tormented him, the gold piece tempted him. He took the money and bought a fine pair of leather-soled slippers, soft and so comfortable they scarcely seemed to have any weight at all. He sat in bed looking at them, and delayed a month before he would risk wearing them out of doors, in case they got dirty.

They were his delight, and when he turned from such pleasures they stayed, carefully wrapped in cloth, in his chest. It is shameful to admit, but his love of his shoes was so great he did not once feel in the slightest bit guilty about his wickedness. On the other hand, he knew that one day restitution would have to be made. So it was that when he found *The Dream of Scipio* he handed the copy he made over to Ceccani rather than keeping it for himself. The gift, he considered, more than paid for the delight he had felt for his shoes. From there, it made its way to the papal library after the cardinal's death, and lay, waiting, for the young French scholar to come in one morning in 1925, sit down, and read.

MANLIUS HAD first met Sophia in Marseille, after the death of her father, the philosopher Anaxius from whom he had taken instruction. He had gone there to attend the schools in a city that was still functioning, although the ever more intermittent water supplies, the inability of the authorities to prevent crime, and incursions of brigands into the outlying suburbs caused much grumbling among the populace. The schools were among the best in Gaul; for a better education, an earnest student would have to travel very far indeed: to Antioch, or Alexandria. A generation ago young men did this; now no longer. Even going to Marseille produced expressions of astonishment and incomprehension amongst his family.

It was not a happy experience. The schools received little subsidy from the city anymore; that was reserved for the administration or was swallowed up by the greedy maw of the church. The teachers were old and tired, discouraged by the dwindling numbers of students and the constant abuse of those who denounced them as pagans. One day, as Manlius sat and listened with three others to the old man discoursing on the poetry of Horace in a hall capable of taking near a hundred, there was a dull cracking, rumbling sound that echoed through the room. Anaxius took no notice, but droned on in a monotone that completely contradicted the points he was making about rhythm and rhetoric.

Then, in a cloud of dust and plaster, a portion of the roof collapsed onto the podium. Manlius, then seventeen, thought it hugely amusing, the punishment of the gods for having bored him so completely, until he realized the seriousness of the event. Anaxius collapsed under the pile of plaster and heavy concrete, more than a century old and now weakened beyond salvation. The cracks had been all too obvious before; no one had paid any attention to the way they had been growing for weeks.

He was dead; a fragment of concrete as long as Manlius's arm had pierced his body like an arrow, driving into the top of his shoulder with such force it penetrated deep down into his body. He expired with scarcely a groan as Manlius stood above him, wondering what to do.

And when he turned around, his two colleagues had left. They had packed up their books and walked out. One, Manlius learned later, threatened legal action to cover the costs of a course paid for but never completed; he threatened to sue the daughter for the funds. Manlius arranged a small demonstration that she had powerful friends, not to be trifled with. While the student was still nursing the bruises administered by Manlius's servants, he completed the lesson by visiting the sickbed and hurling twenty times the amount claimed, in gold, onto the floor all around him. It was a gesture from which he gained far too much satisfaction.

So it was Manlius who found a janitor, arranged for the body to be removed from the wreckage and taken to be cleaned and prepared. It was he also who went to inform the household of the tragedy, and discovered that the old Greek philosopher had lived alone with his daughter, Sophia, who was, perhaps, about twenty-five at that time, and still unmarried.

He was impressed, first of all by her reaction: no tears or sorrow, no manifestations of undignified grief; she listened and thanked him, asked where the body was, then offered him a cold drink, for it was a searingly hot day. Her self-control, her nobility was striking in a period much given to lamentation and ostentation in emotion.

"He will be happy now," was her only comment.

Later, after the funeral rites had been conducted by Sophia herself, a pagan rite ending with a cremation, he asked her about the remark. She considered, and then told him something of her philosophy, weaving an explanation that captivated him and left him slightly in awe of her. It was his first instruction in Platonic thought, pure and unadulterated by Christian admixture. The way she talked, what she said, hypnotized him and fascinated him. He once remarked that had her father spoken of such things, he would have had a throng every day, beating at his door for the honor of hearing him.

"Ah no," she said. "My father was a much greater philosopher than I could ever be; and when we came here from Alexandria he had high hopes of teaching such things; but few wished to hear, and many were afraid of what he had to say. So he fell silent, and taught the mechanics of giving speeches empty of meaning. You have been too polite to say what we both knew too well, that he had no skill at this at all; his words reflected the dullness of his heart. But Manlius, if you had only heard him talk of true philosophy! His voice was music, his thought the purest beauty. All gone now, and all silent forever."

"Not while you are alive, my lady," he replied. "And you are wrong that no one wishes to hear. I know myself of half a dozen people who would fall at your feet and worship you, if they were only allowed to listen."

Over the next few weeks he proved it, gathering together those whom he considered trustworthy and bringing them to her. All aristocrats, all young, all ready to be captivated. For the next two years, they met twice a week at Manlius's house in Marseille, for he was by far the richest of them, and heard of marvelous things. When he was finally summoned away, to accompany his father to Rome in the entourage of the new emperor Majorian, others had joined the group, and for the next twenty years Sophia was able to live out a penurious existence in the manner he had created for her. It was unusual, of course, but there were enough precedents in the past to go by. Was not Hypatia the greatest philosopher of Alexandria, and a true martyr to the old values of learning? She was torn to pieces by a mob of incensed Christians not because she was a woman, but because her learning was so profound, her skills at dialectic so extensive that she reduced all who queried her to embarrassed silence. They could not argue with her, so they murdered her. And Sophia's father had been one of her last pupils, and when she died had fled to Marseille, a city less under the sway of religion, for fear that the same punishment would be meted out to him.

For Sophia, Manlius's efforts were a mixed blessing, as not all he summoned to her feet were moved solely by the love of philosophy. Many dressed ostentatiously, gave dinner parties modeled on the banquets of old, sneered at the vulgarity of Christians, the coarseness of the rabble unable to appreciate the delicacies of true thought. They stood around in the street, loudly talking of the nature of the divine. Her philosophy, so jealously protected and cradled within her, became their youthful defiance, spitting in the face of the world. She even had to reprimand them on occasion.

"I do not wish to become like Socrates or Hypatia. I do not wish to be accused of corrupting the morals of youth and be murdered because of my pupils' behavior. I do not wish my teaching to be nothing more than a costly garment, to distinguish you from others. More decorum and modesty, if you please. There is no virtue that I know of in giving offense. And today, as a punishment, we will talk of the beauties of Christianity."

And so she did, shaming them, cowing them with her arguments, awing them with the immensity of her knowledge, for she could see good even among absurdity, and wisdom among the dross. They all loved her, it was impossible not to do so; and she knew she took far too much pleasure in their reverence and punished herself with lengthy fasts and days of meditation.

AMONG BARNEUVE'S POSSESSIONS, sorted out by a cousin after his death, was a photograph discovered in a volume where it had been used, evidently, as a bookmark. It meant nothing to the cousin, who had scarcely known his relation and performed the task out of family duty. Barneuve's goods passed to this man, who had little need for the vast number of books and papers Barneuve had accumulated during his life and which were stored in several rooms of his capacious apartment on the rue de la Petite Fusterie in Avignon. Some were offered to his university, which took what it needed; everything else he sorted through, selling what was valuable and throwing out the rest. This photograph fell into the latter category; a few hours after it was found it was put into the refuse bins in the courtyard, then taken away the next morning.

There was no reason not to throw the photograph away; there was nothing to identify the person shown and it could never have illuminated any dark corners of history. Only Barneuve himself could have said who it was, and even the careful observer could discover little from the image alone. It was square, in black and white but faded into those sepia tones that creep over old photographs with the passage of time. The subject, a woman of about twenty, leans against the rail of a ship in a conventional holiday-cruise pose, the sort of snapshot that must have been taken tens of thousands of times. Had the photographer moved a little to the left, the name of the ship might have been known, for there was a fraction of a life buoy to be seen on the rail. Beyond, in the background, was a port and what seemed to be a minaret—enough evidence to suggest the eastern Mediterranean.

Of the woman, still less could have been said. She was dressed in a light cotton dress, down to the mid-calf, a sun hat on her head, but didn't seem to be in a holiday mood. She had her own beauty, but it was not a conventional appeal. It was the intensity of her expression, staring determinedly and unflinchingly at the camera, which caught the eye. She stood like someone issuing a challenge. The more fanciful—filling in the gaps with imagination when firm conclusions cannot be reached—might have detected an impatience. Look, she is thinking, why are we wasting time here when there are so many fascinating things to be seen and done on the shore?

More, she was alone. On a crowded ship, brimful of people, she stood alone, waiting. Perhaps she had difficulty making friends? Maybe she needed none? She had the expression of someone searching constantly, yet never finding it. She looked, indeed, just a little cautious, but determined that no one should suspect her weakness.

Nothing else could be gleaned from the photograph, ripped out of its context in such a brutal way, the book that contained it upturned and shaken, so that it fluttered down onto the old worn carpet where it rested until swept up with all the other debris. In this way, the vital connection was lost, for before Barneuve's relation so rudely disturbed it, the photograph had rested in a small book on Provençal church decoration, tucked up on the page that contained a reproduction of what Julien had come to believe was a portrait of Olivier de Noyen's true, unknown love.

Anyone who chanced to see both together—had they taken the trouble to look, if they knew both faces so well they were engraved in the mind as they were in Julien Barneuve's—would have had to agree that the resemblance was extraordinary.

ONCE HE HAD turned away—in his heart, if not yet openly—from the career of a lawyer, Olivier de Noyen for many years assumed that he would become a priest, despite his evident lack of capacity for the life, and accommodated the idea in his mind so completely and with so little thought that he never truly gave it up. It would have been more surprising if this notion had not occurred to him. He was, after all, surrounded by priests, living in a clerical household, knowing mainly priests or others destined for the church in one form or another. The priesthood was the most certain route of patronage as well—stay within the fold and he could count on the support of Ceccani and others within his circle who would willingly advance a personable, if wayward, young man of intelligence who would bring credit on them in return. And Olivier would have risen high indeed—Ceccani held immense resources in his gift. Even though Olivier could scarcely expect great advancement, for the necessary instincts of a politician were as strange to him as they were fundamental to his master—he would undoubtedly have come to a position of some power within the curia, and servants are often more influential than the masters they serve.

A life of plenty, power, and obscurity. How many names of papal bureaucrats are known to us today? How many engage the attentions of a Julien Barneuve? The Romans (before they became Christian, and probably thereafter as well) held Renown to be a god, and sought out her harsh attentions, even though her blessing might be bought at the price of death and disgrace. Some part of Olivier was attracted to that same altar in a way a man like Julien could never understand. And if (as the Romans also held, although they contradicted themselves often on this point) immortality is conferred by the continuous memory others hold of us when we are dead, then Olivier was the only one to win everlasting life.

Not that he ever thought all this through, weighed the pros and cons of the various options open to him, then made up his mind. Had he proceeded in this way—had he been more reasonable—a priest he would have become, for he did not know he sought fame nor did he ever understand why he sought it.

Rather, his life developed on the surface in the way necessary to indulge his passion for the old learning. Once his father had left him and his tears had dried up, the first thing he did was to go to his master's scriptorium, take pen and ink and sand, and copy out the now destroyed manuscript. Word for word, with no errors. He had read it so often—and indeed had the gift of phenomenal memory, so that a text, once read, stayed with him forever—that it was not even a difficult task. And then he had a small inspiration. The hatred of his father, which he did not allow himself to feel—such things were unnatural and could not be admitted—he transformed instead into admiration and regard for Ceccani. And to express this admiration, he decided to make his patron a gift.

It was, in its way, his first publication, the nearest that could be reached in the days before the printing press. In his best, still-adolescent hand, he copied out the secret treasure that he had held to himself for so long and, to present it in an appropriate fashion, added a separate sheet of paper on which he wrote an epistle dedicatory praising the cultivation of the recipient, describing the gift as best he could, and expressing how the joy of bringing both together was reward enough for someone who admired Ceccani as much as he reverenced Cicero.

And he wrote it in verse, although he had not intended to when he began. But the first two lines came out as natural hexameters, and once Olivier noticed this, he grasped that he could lay on another level of compliment, by repeating a classical form for a man learned enough to appreciate the style.

By later standards—his own, and that of the intellectual world he helped bring back to life—it was a pitiable performance, gauche and inelegant, and this was no doubt the reason he refused to let it be reproduced later. But there was also a freshness to his efforts, a touch of spring in his words. The imagery, the grammatical constructions, were no doubt unsophisticated, but they also lacked the arch mannerism, the self-referential cleverness of a later and earlier period. What he wrote instead was a poem of simplicity and directness, a fresh morning after a long cold winter, with a faint aroma of rosemary and lavender in the air suggesting the warmth to come.

It was also a remarkable performance by a boy of sixteen, and Ceccani's greatest talent as prelate and politician was to spot ability and harness it to his own purposes. Olivier was too shy to present his gift in public, at dinner in the hall or on some other occasion when others might see and perhaps also witness his master's scorn should his effort not be well received. Indeed, he carried the roll of paper in his tunic—neatly tied with a piece of red ribbon he had stolen from the seamstress, and sealed with wax bearing an imprint from a seal he had fashioned himself from a small piece of wood—for several days, always hesitating whenever an opportune moment presented itself.

Nor could he draw strength and encouragement from any of his fellows, for although Ceccani had some twelve boys in his household, the rivalry between them was too great. All knew that patronage and advancement would come to only a few lucky ones, and the eldest, furthest up the pecking order, were more concerned to portray their juniors in a bad light to prevent them becoming rivals. Olivier knew instinctively that no one must know of his gift before it was delivered; it would be either stolen or ruined if anyone so much as suspected its existence. Few secret letters of state, fewer treaties of alliance between popes or emperors or kings were of such importance in Christendom as his few sheets of paper in the world of the boys' dormitory, for they had the power to turn all upside down, to break alliances, shift the balance of power, exile some, and shower others with gold.

Did Olivier realize this? Was his the innocent gift of a young boy consumed by the love of learning and intoxicated by the half-sensed awareness of his abilities? Or was this his first offering to the god Renown, a move in the great game of power and advancement? Perhaps both; perhaps he knew that both are necessary, that his desires could only be satisfied if he won the support of men like Ceccani, and that his gift was a route to that support.

Either way, he carried his roll of paper with him for many days before courage and circumstance combined. He saw Ceccani walking along a hallway of his newly completed palace, so great that only the pope's excelled it in size and magnificence. Merely possessing it gave Ceccani power, no one could enter it, even glimpse its high walls or fortified tower from the street, without being overcome by awe. He had only a secretary with him, and Olivier, knowing that no better chance would ever come his way, stepped forward, then bowed and did not take a step backward to allow the cardinal to pass.

Ceccani paused, a look of surprise on his face, one of those ambivalent expressions that could turn into anger or amusement in an instant.

Olivier bowed again and reached into his tunic, utterly oblivious of the look of momentary alarm that passed over the stocky man's heavy and powerful face. For it was not unheard of for men like him to be struck down by an assassin, nor for youths as young as Olivier to carry daggers in their clothes. This was the papal court.

"My Lord, ah . . ." Olivier began, then paused, overcome with doubts and worries and the overwhelming self-consciousness of youth. Ceccani's expression began to turn wrathful; he considered such grotesque inelegance of expression to be insulting to his person and position. Olivier saw this all too well, and knew that he had but a fraction of a moment before his fate, his entire life, perhaps, was decided.

"My Lord, I have been most graciously permitted to live in your household, and in your presence, for many months, and yet I have never given proper expression to my gratitude. I have prepared this gift. It is a poor thing, inadequate, and I hope only that you do not find it an insult. But if you will read words of the author, rather than those of the giver, I believe you cannot be too displeased with my presumption."

And he handed over the roll of paper—to Ceccani, not to the secretary, which was itself presumptuous—bowed sagely, then came close to ruining everything by turning tail and fleeing down the corridor.

The last sounds he heard before he turned the corner was a gale of laughter from the two men, as their sudden tension and alarm dissolved. His ears burned for days. And that night, after the other boys heard of his *démarche,* he received the most savage beating of his life. They knew that, if his petition was well received, they would never get another chance.

EVER SINCE MEN began to study themselves, the gift has attracted the fascinated attention of those who see the practice as one of the strangest and most complex forms of communication—particularly, but not solely, human. When to give, how to give, what to give; these are complex matters, and getting the practice right requires subtlety and care if it is not to miss the mark. In many ways Olivier, though still so young, had the easiest task, as he lived in an age when the language of gift giving was understood, with a straightforward grammar and simple syntax. His position in relation to Ceccani was perfectly clear to both, and there was no possibility of confusion. He did not need to ask for anything in return as it was taken for granted that this was what he wanted, and the request (and its fulfillment, should he succeed) would be to the honor of the donor, rather than placing a burden on him. The boy did not mind the prospect of being under an obligation, perhaps for the rest of his life, since every man was obliged to someone (if he was lucky), and all were obliged to God.

The only doubt was the response: kind words that would be translated by all to mean "I appreciate your request, but do not feel it is worthwhile to do anything for you; your family is not important, and you have little prospect of repaying me by bringing credit on my patronage." Or alternatively: "Your request is granted. I take you under my protection; in return you will bring credit on me, for I intend that what you do and how you behave will be a small—very small—aid in my perpetual ascent in men's esteem. And perhaps in God's as well."

No such words would ever be exchanged, of course; there was no need. The joy in Olivier's heart when he received back a letter from Ceccani himself, *in his own hand,* asking him his opinion about the form of gerundive used in the seventh sentence knew no bounds. His petition was accepted, his way was assured; within a matter of hours everyone in the household knew it.

By the time Olivier's father saw him again—and it was nearly a year before he passed through Avignon once more—it was instantly clear there would be no more burnings of books, and no more instructions about becoming a lawyer. The boy had passed forever beyond the older man's control. It says much either for Olivier's character or for the formal reverence in which fathers were held, that this new situation was never alluded to directly, and there was no glorification in the triumph. It also says much about the father that, while he grieved that the desires he had nursed in his heart for near seventeen years were now extinguished, he allowed himself to be consoled by the prospect of the favors that might descend upon him from a son in papal service. Children exist to safeguard their parents in old age; it is their entire purpose. Instead of a bleak, mean old age (should God allow him to live so long) living solely on the small rents of his little estate, de Noyen's father could now bask in the prospect of security, perhaps even a pension, which would descend to him from the court and through his son. This expectation (which in a later, crueler age would excite only resentment in the younger generation) was fully shared by Olivier, and while he rarely thought about it, when he did consider the prospect of being a good and dutiful child, the idea brought him great pleasure.

THE TRIUMPH was on the same scale as Julien's achievement in passing the *agrégation,* although the Frenchman would never have seen the parallels; rather, he saw his success as the legitimate result of a meritocratic examination, rather than the exercise of a fickle, personal favoritism. The element of patronage—the fact that he was under the protection of the great Gustave Bloch, who had decided to advance him and, by doing so, would augment his own already prodigious reputation and power—never occurred to him. Nor, when he left the ship at the end of his cruise and gave Julia Bronsen an old book he had found (at a good price) in a Palermo bookshop, inscribed with an oblique salutation in his own hand, he never for a moment considered any great subtlety in the gift, nor considered that he signaled a desire for something in return.

A few words, yet so many meanings. The choice of book—Vergil's *Eclogues*—recognized the young woman's intelligence and education, suggested that the giver appreciated her interests and shared them. The edition, an Aldine, indicated a commonality of taste and discernment, for how many people truly understand the difference between one edition and another, see beyond the cover, which in this case needed a good deal of care and attention?

The inscription, a fragment of the second line of de Noyen's poem that begins "my soul, completed, rises to God . . ." was a curious choice. It was hardly appropriate; a bit jarring, a little excessive in a gift otherwise so restrained and refined. Yet of all the phrases in all the poems, this one came to Julien's mind and remained there when he pondered the inscription. It was, he later discovered, Olivier's first real love poem, when he passed beyond singing of an ideal and fell into the grip of a real passion.

AND MANLIUS, penning the *Dream* that encapsulated all of Sophia's teaching, how can his gift be understood? It was not given in the same spirit as his first offerings, presented in the full flush of his youth, when his exhilaration had rendered him foolish. For in Marseille he offered her two things; both were rejected. On the first occasion he had tried to express his esteem for her by giving her money, enough for her to live in security; he had presented her with a small casket filled with gold—a vulgar, ostentatious gift, full of the coarseness of youth and the arrogance of his position, which he had not yet learned to control.

"Why do you give this to me?" she had asked calmly. He replied that it was because she was the only good and noble person in the world.

"Then let me remain so," she said, handing it back.

And the second occasion, he offered his entire soul, and declared his love for her. Again, a crude gesture promptly rebutted, for it meant he had failed to learn anything from her at all. So she turned it into a lesson, starting again the long and arduous process of teaching him something so utterly hidden from his sight.

"Come with me," she had said. And she had led him from the room where they had their conversations—Manlius had nervously paid a call to her alone, outside the hours she normally held for public speech—and took him outside to the midden.

"Look inside," she said. "Smell. What do you see? What do you smell?"

Manlius did not know what to say. The cubicle smelled, and looked like all such.

"Only I use that," she continued as she shut the door. "Do you love it as well?"

"Of course not."

"Yet it is me, part of me. The natural product of my body. And yet you turn from it, wrinkling your nose in disgust. You say you love me, but do not love what is part of me. Or are you lying, and is your love just an adolescent fancy?"

"I love the idea of you." This from their lessons.

"My beauty is a reflection of the divine beauty?" she said ironically. Manlius hung his head in shame; being mocked was not something he could ever accept.

"No. The love I feel is the reflection. As you say, madam, you are not beautiful, although I find you so. If I were as useless as you imply, I would surely have fallen in love with the pretty young serving girl who draws the water at the end of the street every morning I come here. I would have drowned in her black eyes and her beautiful hair. But I do not. I lie awake thinking of someone much older, who turns no heads when she is not known but fascinates all who have heard her speak. You say that, at its best, the physical craving is a reflection of the desire of the soul to reunite with the ultimate beauty, with God. And can only be justified as such."

"But I said it was only a reflection. Not a reality. As real as a glass reflected in a pond."

"But a reflection of water in a mirror can make you thirsty."

"That is true. And is what you should work towards. You should not bend your mouth to the imaginary glass and try to drink."

"I know all this. I have learned well. And yet I cannot stop."

"That is the corruption of the body, its triumph over the soul. The soul is imprisoned, and what you feel is the same as the prisoner in a dark cell who sees nothing but shadows and thinks these are reality. You must study to escape the cell, let your soul contemplate what causes the shadows. That is the purpose of philosophy, and why it is suited to only those few who wish to escape. In the moment of love, when we escape ourselves and become united with the lover, then we have a hint of the joys to come when the soul rejoins the divine; but we think it is a reality of itself. And we lose sight of our aim. That is why it is dangerous."

Manlius looked at her. "You never feel such things?"

She looked serious. "Often," she replied. And for the first time her gaze dropped, and would not meet his.

N O   D O U B T a psychoanalyst, excited with his new knowledge in Julien's epoch and convinced that his skills could be applied universally and eternally, would have made much of this.
Had he been able to read the letters that the two exchanged over the next
fifteen years, some three hundred in all, he would have dissected their
souls and their lives, turned over Sophia's thoughts about her father, analyzed her views on eternity and death, and rested content with a conclusion of extreme neurosis. Celibacy, suppressed desire, the search for the
mystical could now only be seen in such terms.

Sophia was spared such analysis because, as with so much else, the letters did not survive; Olivier de Noyen almost discovered them, as the last
remaining copy sat for hundreds of years in a church in Aix-en-Provence,
which he visited in 1344. But he had, by then, found one version of a
poem by Horace and concluded, wrongly, that there was nothing else in
the little bookroom except for theological texts of no significance for him.
Besides, he was hungry and tired, and wanted to go home; a cold was
coming over him and he felt the need to get to bed as quickly as possible.
Or perhaps it was because the wind was blowing strongly that day and
sapped his patience and dulled his spirit.

No one else passed by to rectify his mistake; in 1407 a baker in the
house next to the church overfilled his oven and allowed burning embers
to fall onto the floor. Half an hour later his house was ablaze; an hour
later the entire street was in flames.

It was a great loss, for they were the finest things Manlius ever produced. Sophia had no use for artifice in speech and was impatient with it
in literature. Clever allusions, apposite quotations, delicate metrical struc-
tures excited in her only contempt. Manlius consequently dropped all
those devices that he considered obligatory for good writing in all other
spheres and wrote directly and simply. What they produced together
might well have been considered the finest collection of love letters ever
written, had the baker been more careful. A mingling of the emotions and
the intellect, the desire suppressed but forever bubbling near the surface,
barely under control. A complete communication of two people founded

on the respect and affection of one, and reverence of the other. What the analyst would have cooed over was the eroticism of the images presented as abstract philosophy, although he would probably have missed the playful, affectionate lilt of the language. He would have assumed both writers were unaware of the feelings that saturated the prose, although each was, in fact, all too aware of them. He would probably not have considered the possibility that this great passion was the more fulfilling for each because of its abstract nature, that for Manlius sex was something all men had with their servants when necessary, that for Sophia it was a reminder of a position in the world that bred resentment rather than release.

HAD OLIVIER not been on the church steps that day and fallen in love, he and his family might not have suffered such ignominy; that, at least, is the conventional view, one which all who have heard of him have accepted without demur. The disease of love would not then have infiltrated his mind, and her husband would not have avenged his honor by attacking him in the way he did.

The conventional interpretation is, in fact, entirely incorrect. Had he not seen a particular woman *then,* in those precise circumstances, he might have remained either unaware of her existence or indifferent to her appeal. It is no longer fashionable, or even respectable, to talk of fate or destiny taking a hand. Love is a random matter, no more than that, in a universe governed by chance, which has swept aside all other deities and taken on a power that is all but supreme. But what a dull deity Chance is in comparison to those it has vanquished. Dressed up as cool rationality—how rational it is, after all, to assert that there is no reason for anything—it appeals only to the impoverished of spirit.

This stricture applies even if Olivier did not fall in love with a woman. He fell in love, rather, with an idea as it was mottled with sunlight on that warm morning. Sophia would have said that he was touched with a remembrance of the divine, a faint recollection of the soul's origins before it fell to earth and inhabited a body. It seemed a breathtaking idea, but was not as unique as he believed. Dante's Beatrice was scarcely a real person by the time he had reduced her to verse; Petrarch's Laura might not have existed at all except in his imagination. Both loved their lovers the more after they were dead, and could not disturb their imaginations with the onset of wrinkles or the annoyance of opinions independently expressed.

The result is well enough known, at least to scholars acquainted with the poetry of the period and the language of the time, for Olivier wrote in Provençal, which had come back into vogue in the generation of Julien Barneuve's father, and the son learned the language as well. For such people, the surviving poems—about twenty of them—fall neatly into two categories, called the juvenile and the mature. In this categorization, the earlier poems are considered *essais,* apprentice works where the young poet has not yet mastered the art of expression he was hewing from the rough stone of language. There is an imprecision about the verse that is redolent of the formality of the Middle Ages, the slightly coarse troubadour style that went before. Olivier in his youth did not have the means of expression or the confidence to cut through the inherited mannerisms and speak straight from the heart.

And then there are the last poems written, it seems, shortly before his downfall, when he finally throws off all artifice and speaks with a vibrancy unheard of in poetry for more than a thousand years. Even in translation and over half a millennium, it is hard not to be touched by the way he talks of his overwhelming joy at love realized and the poignant knowledge that it can lead to nothing. Not that this was the only reaction, of course; for others, the final poems were evidence of a mind disoriented by the Black Death or falling prey to some innate madness.

What was not considered, because it was not even thought of until Julien surmised it, was that this sudden maturity of expression, this shift toward a heightened emotional intensity—accompanied by a new solidity in imagery and sureness of approach—was because Olivier truly fell in love, this time with a reality, not an abstraction that existed only in his imagination. Nor was it known that this love was not for Isabelle de Fréjus, the commonly accepted subject of his poems; Julien established that this particular association began only after he was dead.

Isabelle did come down those church steps that day, but Olivier scarcely noticed her. He was looking in the other direction, staring fixedly at a girl in a dark woollen cloak, neatly but obviously patched, hurrying by alone on the other side of the street. Until he saw her again and discovered her name, Olivier searched for her with an obsession that can be seen in the lines he wrote in that period. Every day he went out he hoped to see her; on many occasions he followed a figure in a dark cloak, only to be horrified when at last he did discover whose face lay under the veil.

JULIEN GLIMPSED Julia on the first day of the cruise, as he walked up the gangway carrying the small bag he was unprepared to entrust to the ship's crew. She was leaning against a rail, high up, staring at the bustle of the port, talking to a man whom Julien correctly assumed to be her father.

She was as beautiful as her father was ugly; in her the darkness, the fullness of the lips, and the slight elongation of the nose produced a result that a painter like Modigliani would turn into a classic image of the age, a hint of unplaceable strangeness. In her father those same features could be stretched, twisted, and caricatured also into another classic image of the age, but with none of the subtlety of a hint.

He met her that same evening at the cocktail party to celebrate the start of the voyage. They were all in first class, which had been taken *en bloc* by the organizers for the learned party of professors and writers and intellectuals who had banded together to take the leisurely cruise around the Mediterranean, some giving lectures or leading tours when the ship came to the part they had studied, others listening. Most were French, although there was a scattering of Europe across the tables, mainly from those countries that had so recently fought together. Julia Bronsen and her father, travelling alone, were of uncertain nationality; France was a flavor in a complex recipe, but an expert concerned to analyze could also detect a touch of Italian and a suggestion of Russian about her. Julien never knew how important this was for his love of her.

Initially it was the father, Claude Bronsen, who struck up an acquaintanceship, and when Julien joined him and his daughter for dinner one evening, he was astonished once more to realize that such an ungainly, unhandsome man could possibly have produced such a beautiful daughter. He responded to the way Bronsen drew him out, asked him questions about himself, congratulated him on his success—which he was vain and young enough to mention before the first course was done—and talked about Paris and Rome and London. They brought a touch of the sophisticated to Julien's world, for despite the war he had seen little of society. He had long dreamed of such surroundings, of being welcome at soirées and receptions, of counting writers and artists and diplomats and men of power among his circle, or at least to be part of theirs. The Bronsens were his first taste of such things, and he would have found it delightful even had they been less pleasant, less amusing, less friendly than they were.

"And you are going to Rome, is that right?" Julia asked.

"In September," he replied. "To the École de Rome for two years."

"I congratulate you on your good fortune," she said. "I have only been once. And that was when I was fourteen. But who knows? Maybe I can persuade Father to let me go again. It is even possible that he might one day let me go without him watching over me all the time."

From some mouths such a comment might have been sarcastic and even cruel; Julien at that stage would have talked of his father in this way. But Julia mingled the criticism with a loving acceptance of his weakness that still did not manage to disguise the way his need weighed on her. Her gentle, rich voice had all the resigned, partly amused affection of a daughter for a doting parent, who had separated from his wife when Julia was young, and who had done his best—according to the temper of the times—to bring her up alone. He had never remarried, never even considered it; Julia was his beginning and end, and she accepted this with only a small protest at the cost to herself.

"And what will you do there, Monsieur?" the father asked. "Become dissipated and steep yourself in idleness? Or waste your time in honest labor?"

He had this way, which his daughter inherited, of turning remarks upside down and presenting them in a humorous fashion that, if analyzed properly, spoke volumes. Was Julien a mere bookworm? Or was he sensitive to the outside world, could he absorb time and place, feel history in the stones and use this to make his work more sensitive and more subtle? Are you a mere pedant, Monsieur? Or do you have the spark of vitality inside you? Will you do something with your life? Answer my question with all the wit at your disposal and let us see.

"If I do not labor, I cannot be idle," Julien replied. "There are constant supervisions and I would be sent back if I didn't perform well. After nine months we are allowed to live in the city and begin to work more on our own—or not, as the case may be. But I may not have much encouragement in corruption. Everyone at the École, who will be my comrades, will be people like myself."

"Which means?"

"Earnest, hardworking, and dull," he said. "We cannot help it. Dissipation is not on the curriculum."

"In that case," the father said, "you will miss what is most charming and educational about Rome. We must come and rescue you. I have to come to Italy at least once a year, and I offer you an exchange. You show me Rome, which you will no doubt know better than I in a short while, and I will show you the Romans. They, at least, I know well."

"I accept with great pleasure," Julien replied happily. "And you must keep your word. I shall now be looking forward to your arrival and will be greatly disappointed if I don't hear from you. Might I ask why you come to Italy?"

After near an hour of conversation, this was the first initiative he had taken, the first time he ventured to move the conversation away from himself, partly aware that he must be seeming terribly self-centered, but more because the two people were making him relax in their company.

But the father waved his hand. "Neither important nor interesting," he said. "But merely work. It will take a generation to replace what was destroyed in a few years. Perhaps longer, as the politicians seem determined to waste as much time and money as possible. It is my job to make sure they have no excuse but their own lassitude. But it is not exciting, not in comparison to what you do."

Was that a joke at his expense? Julien thought so, but Julia translated for him. "Father is a scholar *manqué*," she said gently. "He always wanted to write books. But he became rich instead, so is not allowed."

"And you, Mademoiselle?"

"She is an artist," Bronsen said, smiling at him.

"Are you really?" He addressed his question back to her, and noted that she was scrutinizing him carefully as he spoke. False admiration? Disdain for the rich hobbyist of no talent? Incomprehension and slight disapproval of the possible bohemian? "What sort of artist?"

"A painter," she said, but gave no more away.

"A good one?" He persisted.

Again, her father answered for her. "Yes, she is. She is exceptional."

Julien's smile, understanding but with too much insight, prompted her to respond a little more fully. "No, I am not," she said. "Not yet." She said it with such care that Julien, who could easily have changed the subject then to pursue matters less obviously sensitive, was minded to probe further.

"I sense a little divergence of opinion here."

"Father speaks from hope. I speak from knowledge. I am not being self-deprecating. I have the ability to be a good painter. More than that, perhaps. But I am a long way from that point yet."

"And what is required? What is missing?"

"Work," she said. "Labor. The sweat of my brow. A great painting is not genius with a paintbrush. It's years of concentrated effort. A journey without maps, with only a faint idea where you are heading."

"She is being disingenuous," Bronsen put in with a smile, patting her affectionately on the shoulder. "You should not be fooled by her modesty. She has none, in fact. She is perfectly aware of her abilities. As are the committee at the Salon d'Automne, which chose three of her pictures for hanging last year."

"Now it is my turn to congratulate you. Although without seeing something for myself, I will have to suspend judgment," Julien said. "I would like to see what you do. If you have no objection. Although I warn you in advance that my opinions are worthless."

Julia gazed at him carefully. "We'll see. Perhaps."

ABOUT HALFWAY through the cruise, Julien began talking amiably and purposelessly to a middle-aged man—a jovial, good-natured, kindly fellow, the sort who is instantly likeable. They had just left Athens and were heading for Palestine; the weather was beautiful, all had relaxed into complete pleasure in their shared experience.

"I am surprised to see you spending so much time with those two Jews," came the remark. "If you're not careful, people will think you're one, too. Personally, I think it spoils the atmosphere, having them on the ship."

A pointless, casual remark, made even without malice. For the flickering of a second the comment nestled in Julien's mind, and made him anxious, but the brilliant, hypnotic glittering of the water was too magnificent for him to worry too much and he soon forgot it. He said nothing in reply to either justify himself or praise his companions' qualities. Rather, he shrugged with feigned indifference and looked out over the sea; he understood the comment. It was a moment, he realized later, that summed up his whole existence in a tiny moment, like the world reflected in a tiny bead of water as it falls to earth.

JULIA WAS sitting cross-legged on the ground, sketching, in the hills above Jerusalem, where they had gone for an overnight stop. Brown arms and a concentration so perfect even a wasp—the one thing that made her genuinely terrified—could walk up her leg unnoticed. Julien watched, enamored of her self-possession, recognizing something in her, a faintly stirring unease about him as he did so.

This image lodged in his mind like a photograph, and stayed with him until his death. Such things happen; the entire voyage, the wonderful things he saw—cities and towns, ruins and pyramids, temples and churches—were slowly effaced from his memory, or became the sort of memory that can be summoned when necessary but, for the most part, rests undisturbed. This one vignette had a life of its own. It nagged him, called him, imposed itself on him. As he went to sleep, sometimes when he was buying a newspaper or walking in the street or sitting reading by a warm fire and his mind drifted off, it would take him back to that precise moment—always unvarying, never changing.

Everyone has a glimpse of paradise in their lives; this was Julien's. All he had to do was reach out.

Later, he decided he had been constrained by the morality and timorousness of the provincial bourgeois; the man who returned from Rome in 1927 would have been subject to no such doubts and hesitations; he would have become Julia's lover then and there, and given the magical moment a fleshly guise. He knew, however, that the explanation was a false one, designed only to disguise and reassure. He was not afraid of being rejected but rather was afraid of being accepted. He knew that she was the one person he would never manage to let go. He was afraid of falling in love with her.

A few moments later she sighed and began packing her paper back into her bag. She didn't know why she sighed, she did not do it often. Perhaps she, too, realized something had been missed at that moment.

And Julien came away with his shard of memory, forever glinting in the hot Mediterranean sunlight, as a reminder of something offered but turned down. It stayed with him until he had learned more and was ready. Until then he had that moment instead, that look on her face as their eyes met.

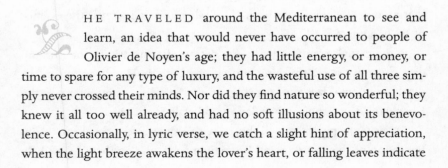

HE TRAVELED around the Mediterranean to see and learn, an idea that would never have occurred to people of Olivier de Noyen's age; they had little energy, or money, or time to spare for any type of luxury, and the wasteful use of all three simply never crossed their minds. Nor did they find nature so wonderful; they knew it all too well already, and had no soft illusions about its benevolence. Occasionally, in lyric verse, we catch a slight hint of appreciation, when the light breeze awakens the lover's heart, or falling leaves indicate a love that is dying, but in general the works of the age are quiet about nature's beauty except as metaphor.

Even Olivier thought he traveled for a purpose on his endless crisscrossing voyages across what is now Southern France, Italy, and Switzerland. There is even a hint that he once visited England in the retinue of the Bishop of Winchester in 1344, although there is no solid evidence and, indeed, it seems unlikely. Ostensibly, he voyaged either on those little missions of informal diplomacy and administration at which he proved adept and useful—delivering a message, paying a compliment, finding information—or he was in search of those manuscripts with which he became ever more obsessed.

And yet Julien did not entirely impose his own values and opinions when he fancied that Olivier took pleasure from the journey as well as the destination, and that he often took a less than direct route and dallied unnecessarily in places with no other interest except their charm. Much, again, was supposition: The poet was only known for certain to have taken two trips, one to Dijon, which produced his great allegorical letter on Saint Sophia, the other to Bordeaux. Nonetheless, others must have been made, for the list of manuscripts he acquired implies considerable travel.

Certainly Olivier saw the world in a novel and strange fashion. Manlius contemplated the landscape and forced it into the conventions of the Vergilian eclogue, making it a confirmation of a literary tradition that was by his time almost dead and imbuing it with the melancholy of a nostalgic futility. Julien responded with all the orthodoxy of a man brought up on Rousseau, but Olivier's response was more wayward and indeed more original. For he felt he was tasting a private, personal pleasure; the fact that no one else could—or wanted to—share his delight was the essence of his happiness.

Some casual comment led to the detour after his trip to the Burgundian court in 1346. Refreshing himself at a household obliged to the cardinal about two days outside Avignon, he heard someone mention the Chapel of Saint Sophia, which lay a good walk to the east.

"A very holy place," said his host, "with great powers, thanks to the intercession of the blessed saint. Women in particular go there to ask help when faced with difficult decisions. There is also a little hermitage, I believe, of very great antiquity, occupied by a few people who look after the shrine."

Olivier was intrigued immediately, and the mere name of the saint almost guaranteed that he would cancel all his plans the next day, leave his small band of servants and friends—much to the irritation of his host, who was faced with the prospect of feeding them for an extra two days— and set off the next morning. That the chapel lay only a short while from his hometown, and he had not seen his family for nearly two years, perhaps also aided his decision. Besides, it was well known, he said to justify himself, for such places to contain all sorts of treasures.

And all that was part of the reason; the other part, which he scarcely even recognized himself, was the delight of walking through the fresh country air, entirely on his own, never knowing what might be around the next bend. To sit halfway up a warm hill in the sunshine, listening to the birds and eating some bread and an onion, to doze off in the shade, then wake up to the sight of the light glittering through the thick trees above him. And to be quiet, to hear no man's voice, make no conversation, to let his thought flit hither and thither.

What a paradise it was, as well. For if that region of France delighted Julien Barneuve's heart, and made him rush to return there whenever he was in need of solace, it was still more so for Olivier, before building works and deforestation had cut into the landscape and robbed the hills of their trees and soil. Although settled for two thousand years already, mankind had yet made only a small impact on the landscape; most was still untouched and uncaring of his presence.

At the end of his journey lay the little chapel; a tiny thing on top of the hillside looking down the valley of the Ouvèze, only partially cultivated and the rest given over to woodlands; by Julien's day the trees on the western side would be cleared and replaced with vines and olive trees, as they had been during Manlius's lifetime. The chapel itself was stone, and a more educated eye than Olivier's would have categorized it as Romanesque, built on an earlier foundation. A semicircular archway framed the door, with a space for a bas-relief that was never executed. The roof also had an unfinished air to it, despite the small shrubs and treelets growing up between the stone tiles, but its lack of completion did not bother Olivier at all; he was more transfixed by the way the trees had grown around it, giving it shelter from the sun and the winds of autumn, the way it nestled in the landscape. He felt joyous the moment he saw it, and it was this feeling that he tried to capture and turn into first prose and then poetry.

The walk took two days and—because even poets tend to reduce their experiences to a conventional and often literary form—became in retrospect a pilgrimage. Julien knew of it because Olivier wrote a letter to his patron on the tour that was also filed away by the clerical bureaucracy. The letter was partly an excuse, to explain why a simple expedition to deliver a letter had in fact taken five months and cost a small fortune—but also one of those occasions where an attentive reader could discern the first glimmerings of something new. He used the allegory, describing the long journey as the journey of his soul, the ascent of the hill as the climb toward God, the arrival at the chapel as the embrace of truth. Within this form—not novel—was a realism of description without parallel either in Dante or Petrarch, a feel for nature that the others reduced to conventionality. The confusion then very much present in Olivier's mind produced a remarkable effect, a mixture of pilgrimage and tourism, spiritual yearnings and physical desire, all expressed in a form that was part troubadour, part a revival of classical form, and as a result entirely novel. Julien translated and published it as an appendix to his *Histoire,* although the troubles of the times meant that it received little attention.

WHATEVER THE beliefs of the inhabitants nearby—and many still hold that the saint came with the Magdalen and lived the rest of her life as a hermit once she had converted the area—the shrine of Saint Sophia had more ordinary origins, which Julien first glimpsed when he noticed the relationship in name between the saint and the female guide in Manlius's manuscript. For Sophia did indeed live out the last years of her life in this place, but scarcely as a Christian evangelist; rather, Manlius Hippomanes placed her there when he plucked her out of a Marseille that was becoming too dangerous. Without his support, her future would have been bleak indeed; she had never had much in the way of family fortune, simply the rents from a few houses and shops and some land in the hinterland, but these now produced next to nothing. The population was dwindling, the trade drying up, and the rental was all but vanished. Only the tax assessment remained the same.

So great was her distress that Sophia, for the first time in her life, knew true poverty. That such a woman—once revered and even feared for the power of her thought and the nobility of her soul—should be reduced to such a pass touched Manlius deeply when he heard about it, even though by that stage he had not seen her for some years. To be able to help her was the greatest, proudest moment of his life, which gave him more pleasure even than the moment he stood before all the senators of Rome to speak, and was rewarded for his words with a ceremonial high office. Little else occupied his mind until he could deliver that help.

The news was brought by a Jewish merchant of Vaison, who came to his villa to inform him of her plight. A quiet, softly spoken man, not unworthy to be treated as a guest and given hospitality, if he would only have accepted it.

"You know the lady?" Manlius asked after the refreshments were brought. The Jew—politely and unostentatiously—declined even to touch them, and drank only water. A small, neat man, with precise movements and a face that only rarely changed expression. Calm rather than cautious; Manlius would have found him intriguing had he been closer in rank to himself.

"I have known of her for some years," he said. "Although I cannot claim to know her, of course."

"You say she is in some distress."

"She can barely afford food and dresses in rags, although she finds this of no great importance. But her health is not good and her spirit is diminished by her troubles. She is alone there, and has no family to turn to. Some people have tried to assist but"—he spread his hands wide in a gesture of hopelessness—"every day there are fewer people capable of assisting. She is a proud and haughty woman, My Lord, and is somewhat feared by the population. She would not ask for help, I think, unless she was truly desperate, and yet she asked me to deliver this message to you."

Manlius scarcely thought of what to do; he had no need to. The obligations that bound him to her had not lost their strength merely through the passage of time, and his position was such that he was perfectly equipped to assist. Not that it would be so easy; the days when a simple letter to the authorities would have sorted all were past; there were scarcely any authorities left, and those who retained their positions were no longer able to do anything.

But he still had vast resources. "She must be brought to safety so she is troubled no more," he said. "I am in your debt, sir, for being so kind as to bring me this news. When will you be returning there?"

"In about two weeks, assuming my business goes well."

"In which case, I trust you will do me the great favor of carrying a letter to her, and perhaps of rendering me some more services on her behalf."

The Jew agreed readily, and left. He returned, as good as his word, exactly thirteen days later, and Manlius handed him a letter and a leather bag.

"The letter is for the lady, and the bag for her taxes. I would like you to take care of the matter for me; you will of course be rewarded for your goodness."

"Thank you, sir."

"The letter to her explains everything, but lest she refuses to accept what she so obviously needs, then I will explain it to you as well. Please carry out the instructions whatever her opinions in the matter. Find the owner of the tax revenues and pay whatever debts she may have. Sell the properties for the best you can. Then I will come as swiftly as possible to take her to my villa. I will be there in three weeks."

The Jew nodded and prepared to leave.

"One last thing," Manlius said. The Jew turned.

"Yes?"

"What is your name?"

The man smiled. "Strange how rarely I am asked that," he said. "My name is Joseph, My Lord."

"Thank you for your kindness, Joseph."

"Odd," he said with a smile to Lucontius later when he recounted the meeting, "that the world depends on him."

"I wasn't aware that it did."

"Oh, indeed. My deep researches into all things Christian show me so plainly. They fully accept it. The resurrection of the body, which I understand to be a stage in the second coming, cannot take place until all the Jews embrace Christ. Saint Paul says so, I think. Judging by my friend Joseph, it seems that greatly longed-for day will be some considerable time a-coming. He shows no sign of doing any such thing."

"Did you point out that he was being a little inconsiderate, keeping everyone waiting like that?"

"Ah, no. He is an admirable fellow, honest, kind, and diligent. A sense of humor was not easily detectable in him, though. It may be that he doesn't find it funny. And, truth to say, these Christians believe the absurdity so strongly that there have been occasions when their efforts at persuasion have gone beyond mere argument. My dear friend, it makes me sad."

"What does?"

"To see the triumph of something so crude and coarse. Think of Sophia, and the wisdom and elegance of what we learned from her. Think of the beauty of her philosophy and the completeness of the contemplative ideal. The sophistication of her conceptions and demonstrations of God. Then think of this smelly rabble and their beliefs. These poor Jews being screamed at simply because these vulgarians think it a way of getting into heaven."

"You could hardly explain her doctrine of the soul to the Christians," Lucontius replied. "Let alone instruct them in the formal nature of her logic."

"I know. They want results. They want someone to come along and say, 'Repeat after me, and live forever. The less you know, the better it is.'"

He smiled. "It's not that I plan to invite Joseph for dinner. He is a merchant, after all, and would not accept the invitation in any case. But I talked to him a bit, and he seems decent enough, if as strange as most of his people. He, after all, doesn't insist that his salvation lies in anyone else's behavior. He just believes, in a perfectly polite way, that everyone else is wrong about everything."

He stood up and took a cup from a servant. "Long may he do so, say I, for it is worth it just to see the look of outrage on the Christians' faces at the very thought of such people."

And, smiling ironically, they drank a toast to Joseph the Jew.

MANLIUS THOUGHT carefully before she arrived, and prepared one of his houses in Vaison for her use, a building near the forum and one of the areas that remained busy and fully occupied. It was a compromise; as simple as she wanted and as grand as he required, for she would be under his protection and could not embarrass him with her frugality. The slaves, however, she insisted be removed.

"I have my one slave, and that is enough for me," she said. "What would I do with a dozen?"

He tried to answer.

"I know. You are worried. 'There goes a protégée of the great Manlius and he only gives her one slave.' You are concerned about your reputation. Take them away, my boy. There must be better things for them to do."

So he did; also, he removed nearly all of the furniture, shut off many of the rooms, painted over the frescoes (thus preserving them for Père Sautel when he began to excavate), and let her be.

Eventually, she came to him again. "I am weary of town life," she said. "It weighs on me, this provincial little place."

"You told me that philosophy could only exist in the society of men."

"Cities, my boy. Not small towns. And certainly not towns so shrunken they are scarcely more than villages. Do you know, they call me the pagan, these worthy citizens? They spotted in a day that I do not go to church, and actually came to ask me why. I thought I might give some lectures here, but I might as well try to instruct a herd of goats."

He knew what she saw, she whose father had come from Alexandria, one of the greatest cities on earth, who had grown up in Marseille, still a city even though diminished. Vaison was a poor thing now, though once rich and prosperous. Several quarters had been sacked a century before and never rebuilt; slowly they were being quarried as the fitful work to build a wall continued. Even this project was not complete; the town could not even act with dispatch over its own defense. The builders would not work without pay, and there was no money. The citizens would not do the job themselves, for they considered it unfitting. There were not enough slaves and servants left to be forced to the task. The public buildings were small and crumbling; houses once great were divided up, or abandoned or dismantled. He felt the conflicting loyalties of a man who belonged here, a member of the tribe of the Vocontii, which had occupied this land when Rome itself was still a few huts on an Italian hill, and of a Roman aristocrat who had seen better and greater things.

"I was told you have established a reputation for yourself," he commented.

"As a giver of good advice. People come to me with their aches and their worries. I pour balm on both. Do not misunderstand me; I am happy to do so. But all they are really concerned about is the state of the roads, the level of taxes, and how long the water supply will remain fresh."

"All pressing problems."

"I know. But sometimes the noise of their chirruping and gossip drives me close to madness."

"So what do you want?"

"Somewhere to be quiet. Peaceful. Where I can meditate without being interrupted by the rabble, or harangued by a deacon about the love of Jesus. Do you know, the only people I can have a conversation with are the Jews? At least when they quote scripture at you they are not merely repeating something some priest has babbled in their ear. They have the great merit of disagreeing with nearly everything I say. In fact, they disagree with almost everything they say themselves. And most importantly, they don't think that shouting strengthens their argument. They just talk loudly out of habit. I have been entertaining myself by reading the Bible with one of their priests or whatever you call them. It has been most instructive."

"You astonish me."

"I astonish myself. But fascinating though I find Moses, I still want a little peace and quiet. Do you have anywhere in the country I can go to?"

Manlius laughed. "My lady, you know quite well that I own nearly all the country. According to the tax collectors, I have some forty-nine villas, many of which are now unoccupied and falling into ruin for lack of labor. Not that they take this into account."

She sighed. "Don't you start. I would like to borrow something small, about two days from here. As isolated as possible."

Manlius thought. "I know just the place," he said.

A fortnight later, the repair work had been carried out, a dozen serfs transferred to provide basic services, and the lady Sophia was escorted to the villa he had in mind about four kilometers from his own principal residence. It lay among a group of hills that provided coolness in the summer and protection from the winds in the winter. It was much too grand for her, consisting of some twenty-five rooms, and she hated it on sight. But, as she was leaving, she saw the tiny dwelling on the hill—with a clear view over the countryside, a copse of trees to provide shelter—and on the instant decided this was perfect. Clean water nearby, a path for bread and other supplies to be brought from the valley. Fresh air, and the simplicity she desired. Once the family of farmers had been ejected on Manlius's orders—for Sophia never thought that philosophy should bow its head to equity—she took it over and achieved something of the tranquillity she had long sought. When she finally decided that this was where she would stay, he gave it to her, along with the neighboring farms and about forty laborers. Within a few years all but six of the laborers had run away, and the farmland had turned back into scrub. What did he expect? That she was going to turn farmer? Fret about the wheat? Examine the olive trees for blight? The waste annoyed Manlius, he who worked so hard to keep production going on his own lands, but he said nothing. Nonetheless, she was a difficult, impossible woman, sometimes.

She lived there, on and off, for near twenty years before she died, and much to her annoyance, she became genuinely respected by the rough country folk who lived nearby and adopted the habit of coming to her with their illnesses and concerns. She even outlived Manlius himself, and on his death, the tax revenues of the land passed to a Burgundian soldier, who collected them, every quarter, in person.

They even came to have a grudging affection for each other, this representative of Greek sophistication and the rough, unlettered barbarian who was now her effective overlord. She was lucky, and she knew it; her new master—such he was, although only she, with characteristic bluntness, ever referred to him in this way—wished to be more polished, and had a crude, rough sense of fairness that made her life more fortunate than many enjoyed. Ordric—middle-aged, fat, and powerful—was one of the better men in an age with few shining examples of virtue left. It was strange to find such qualities in such an unlikely place, but the times themselves were strange. She taught him nothing, he did not wish to learn; rather, they learned only to appreciate the kindness of the other, and in the end, she left him all her remaining lands in her will, not merely the taxes of them, as she could think of no better person to take possession. In return, Ordric built the little monument to her over her grave, to remember someone to whom he had become quietly devoted. The story of his respect survived, the memory of her advice gathered miraculous overtones, and eventually a small chapel grew around her tomb as people came to pray there for help.

CARDINAL CECCANI kept Olivier's letter about the shrine, which was constructed from the Burgundian's respect, for it gave him an idea that nagged quietly at him in the months after he read his protégé's words.

By 1347 Ceccani was a star in the ecclesiastical firmament, and had become so powerful that he was richly detested. He had accumulated so many offices that he was all but indispensable for the good running of Christendom. And he had absorbed so many benefices that many whispered he had an annual revenue rivaling that of Pope Clement himself. He was, consequently, a focus of real hatred for all those who either wanted more for themselves or genuinely believed that the gentle shepherd of men would have been appalled to see what he had created.

Ceccani, of course, was as aware of this as he was aware of everything that went on around him. And he was wounded by it, for he was, in his way, a man of the utmost piety and duty. He wore the richest, costliest garments made of silk and cloth of gold because it was necessary to impress men with the majesty and power of the church; underneath he wore a shirt of the coarsest hair, crawling with lice, his flesh covered in suppurating sores. He gave banquets of such cost and magnificence that they endured for days and attracted the disgust of those excluded, yet himself drank only water and disdained the roasts and sweetmeats and fine wines that he pressed so liberally on his guests. He entered church like a prince, carried on a bier and attended by at least a dozen servants, generating more condemnation from those revolted by his arrogance, yet prayed alone three hours every night, on bare knees on the stone of his private chapel, carefully locking the door so no one would see him. He was the greatest lover of learning, using men like Olivier to rescue priceless texts and his money to restore them to humanity, yet condemned all deviation from the orthodoxy of the church and, on two occasions at least, ordered the burning of heretics. Like the church of which he was a faithful servant and perfect reflection, Cardinal Ceccani was a contradictory, inexplicable creature.

He was, moreover, the embodiment of the corruption that had settled on the church like a thick fog since it had fled Rome and come to Avignon, and yet no man in the curia was more aware than he of the dangers of its presence there, nor more desirous that the pope should return to the Eternal City. But he had been too young to stand a chance in 1342 when the Frenchman Pierre Roger instead had ascended the throne as Clement VI, and Clement could live for many years yet. Other means of restoring the head of Christendom to his proper place, accordingly, began to come to his mind.

The chapel of Saint Sophia and the story of her life appealed to him greatly, not least because when he prayed to her for guidance as the papacy was being drawn into the English wars, he found her assistance valuable. He was a man of many vows, and he offered her at that time a gesture of thanks, should her intercession be efficacious. Her name meant wisdom, and wisdom, he considered, had been granted him; the chapel was in his diocese—one of his many dioceses—and it needed a reminder of his power. The area was not entirely quiescent; although the heresies of the previous centuries had not badly infected the region, it had been touched; to have a saint of such antiquity revealed to them in their very midst was a gift from heaven. That she was all but forgotten was better still, if Ceccani could restore her to proper attention.

All these reasons combined to make Ceccani one day summon Luca Pisano and commission him to decorate the chapel with as much speed and grandeur as he could manage. For his part, Pisano was overwhelmed with gratitude until he learned just how isolated it was; for he was only just beginning to be a master of works, and craved attention more than anything. He knew that Martini was unwell, and would either shortly die or return to Italy; the post of chief painter was there for the taking, and although history has largely forgotten him, at that time he was coming to be highly regarded.

But a commission was a commission, and one from a man like Ceccani was doubly valuable; everyone thought he could well be the next occupant of St. Peter's chair, if the French could be persuaded not to meddle for once. And then, perhaps, the papacy might return to Rome after its long exile in Avignon. Pisano bowed deeply, expressed his profound thanks to His Eminence, and backed out of the chamber to go and organize some money with the cardinal's pursekeeper. He came away from that encounter somewhat disappointed.

"I think I have you to thank for this, my friend," he said to Olivier later that day. "It is your doing that I am now a fellow servant of the great cardinal, and must stand and fall with him."

"I would like to take credit for your good fortune," Olivier replied. "But I cannot see how I am responsible for anything."

By this stage, the two men were old friends; both were alone and without any family, having to live off their wits in a town where there were many men and few places. They had gravitated into each other's company mainly by virtue of sharing the same tastes and ambitions, but little opportunity as yet of realizing them. Each believed in the other, and each was convinced by the other that their abilities would surmount all obstacles.

"Nonetheless," he continued, "I congratulate you, for it is good fortune indeed."

"The higher they are, the further there is to fall," Pisano said.

Olivier laughed. "I do believe you are the most miserable person I have ever met," he replied. "You have gained work from one of the most powerful men in the world, and all you can think about is that he might not remain so. Even if he does fall, so what of it? A brief spell in his favor is better than never to have been favored by anyone. Besides, you might even do a good job of it, although considering your utter lack of ability, I doubt it very much. But should a miracle occur, then others will want you, too."

"Why should they?" asked his friend. "No one except shepherds will ever see it. I will quite literally be casting my pearls before swine."

"But there will be great things to come, no? Decorate the chapel well, then there will be a basilica in the nearest town."

"Oh, yes. Thirty years' work, no doubt. And meanwhile the pope will go back to Rome, and I will be stranded here."

Olivier burst out laughing. Pisano was always superstitious; whenever anything good happened to him, he would spend at least the next day seeking out every possible misfortune that might result from it, on the reasonable grounds that a disaster imagined never occurs. As indeed was the case here; one thing the painter did not foresee was the plague, which ambushed him late one night as he was sleeping beside his donkey on the road back to Italy.

"You can be certain that this pope will never go back to Rome. He listens to Cardinal Ceccani on most things but on this he has cloth ears. My lord will have to chain him up and drag him there. He is a Frenchman, remember, and they do not like to go far from home. Even being in Avignon makes him feel homesick. You must pray for his health and longevity, I think."

"But I am serious," the painter protested. "I am to paint a series of pictures which no one will ever see, in a chapel hidden from everyone, about a saint I have never heard of."

"In that case you can paint anything you want."

Pisano frowned. "Just because I am frivolous sometimes does not mean you can take liberties, you know. To honor a saint is a great thing. A life of holiness is precious, and to retell it is a heavy duty."

Olivier studied him, surprised by the somber voice. "I suppose so."

"And you are my only source for the story."

"I know very little."

"That is more than anyone else."

"I can barely tell you enough for a sketch."

"That will be enough. Tell me what you know, and prayer will supply the rest."

"Are you sure of that?"

"If you are sincere, yes. I will pray to the saint and, if my wish is granted, then all the details I need will come to me. If they don't, then that will mean she does not want her life commemorated, and I will have to tell the cardinal so."

And so Olivier settled down and retold the story that he had heard from the shepherds on the hill.

"A FEW YEARS after the crucifixion of Our Lord," he began, "when men were beginning to embrace His teaching, the priests became angry and fearful, and started persecuting the faithful. Mary Magdalen, so privileged that she was the first to hear of Christ's resurrection, was hounded and spat on, as were the group of women she had gathered around her. A plot was hatched to kill them all, but an angel came to her in her sleep and warned her. 'Rise up, Mary,' the angel said, 'and leave quickly. Gather your friends and depart.'

"Mary did as she was told, gathering half a dozen companions, and went to the shore. Waiting for them was a miraculous boat, empty of sailors, its sails of silk and its hull of pearl. The moment they got in, the sails unfurled and the boat slipped into the water, just as their enemies ran up to stop them.

"The voyage lasted weeks, but no one was afraid. When it rained they did not get wet, when there was a storm the boat scarcely rocked. Angels brought them food and water every day, and kept them cool in the sun by carrying a great silken awning over them. When the time came, the boat turned inshore, even though the wind was blowing strongly in the opposite direction, and came to rest on the beach of a strange land. Again an angel spoke to Mary and said they were to travel throughout the land and tell everyone of Christ's coming. But some were afraid, and refused to leave Mary's side, knowing that she was beloved. Only Sophia obeyed, bidding farewell to Mary and converting town after town so that everywhere she went became Christian, tearing down temples and building churches in their place.

"Many miracles attended her; on one occasion a great nobleman called Manlius who had been blind for years came to her.

"'You say God is love and cares for all his creation, yet I am blind,' he said. 'How can that be?'

"Sophia took him to one side and instructed him, then passed her hands over his eyes, and instantly his sight was restored. He fell at her feet in gratitude, and the crowd was so amazed that they all did the same. This man spent the rest of his life preaching, and established himself at Vaison, converting the whole area around. He, too, became a saint.

"One day, when Sophia was preaching in a town, the people, incited by the priests, began to shout and threaten her; they took her to jail and sentenced her to death. But her work was not yet done, and an angel appeared to the man she had cured and told him of her plight. Straightaway he was transported to the spot and held up his arms; the guards all fell asleep and the jail doors opened. He then escorted her away from the town, and they walked until they came to a hill. When she died she was buried there, and so many wonderful things happened at her grave that all realized she was a saint. So they built a chapel, and came on pilgrimage."

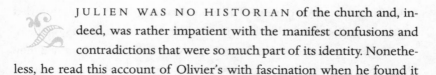 JULIEN WAS NO HISTORIAN of the church and, indeed, was rather impatient with the manifest confusions and contradictions that were so much part of its identity. Nonetheless, he read this account of Olivier's with fascination when he found it

amongst Ceccani's papers, in the same dusty bundle as the *Dream,* not least because of the correspondences with the other manuscripts he discovered at the same time. It would have taken someone very much slower than he not to have noticed that the philosophical discourse by Manlius Hippomanes used its Greek personification, Sophia, as a guide. Nor that Manlius was Bishop of Vaison while the shrine to Saint Sophia lay only two days' walk to the southwest.

Initially, though, he did not pursue it, not really knowing how to do so. And, in any case, he was distracted by some of the other fragments in the same folder, one of which appealed more to his youthful sense of drama and flair. To begin with he was mainly interested in the mention of Gersonides, as he sat in the Vatican archive one spring, dressed in suit and tie and waistcoat, sweating in the heat, taking endless notes in his neat, precise hand. He never hurried, never skipped a page, but wrote methodically and steadily. It was his technique not to think too much about what he was transcribing; he had discovered that this made him careless.

Rather, he emptied his mind entirely and copied, storing up impressions that he refused to dwell on during his working day. The pleasure of analysis he kept for later, for the evenings when he returned to the École and, after eating with his fellows, went for a walk or for a quiet drink in the Piazza Navona. Here he would sit, watch the world go by, and let his mind wander over all his day's reading.

Shortly after his discovery, he was taken to dinner by Julia's father. Julien was pleased by the invitation; he was intrigued by the older man and he was, in any case, kept on a tight financial leash by his bourse and the supplement given to him by his own father, an allowance that was generous by his standards but pitifully small when set against Julien's Romanized tastes. For he began there the interest in art that was to become a passion for the rest of his life. He spent every lira—a drawing here, a painting, a print—and on several occasions he visited the *monte di pietà* to pledge his watch or his ring to get the cash he needed for another purchase. Every couple of months, more or less, another letter went to Vaison, and his father grumbled, criticized, moralized, then sent the money required, just in time for him to recover the articles he had pawned. Julien never felt any gratitude for the generosity, although he knew he ought to do so.

In Rome also he discovered those more sensual pleasures to which his inner turbulence made him all too susceptible. The series of mistresses he acquired began in Rome and did not end for some fifteen years. Unlike his pictures, he took few pains to retain them once the initial pleasure had faded. He discovered he could be charming, was generous with his time and his money, listened well, but could not be held, always moving on before the slightest hint of disappointment or true intimacy could taint the pleasure.

He wondered about this in only the most superficial fashion. His parents had not been happy; he did not wish to experience the same unhappiness. He met no one who could tempt him. His work and his paintings held his attention more securely. For the most part, these affairs were conducted with decorum; Julien perfected a style of courtly pursuit, loved lavishing expensive dinners and presents and holidays—none of which he could truly afford—on the women he had chosen for his attentions. Even more, he was meticulous in the little details, always noticing clothes, perfumes, the way their hair was set. Nor was this merely a strategy; he could not help noticing such things, and took the greatest pleasure in being in the company of beautiful women.

Throughout these pointless dalliances he was aware of a sense of avoiding something important, and his constant pursuits had less of the sensual and more of the desperate about them. For every time he was charmed or fascinated or smitten, he was made aware once more of part of him that was detached and that stood aside in disdain. He had no idea what he was looking for, except that he always knew that he had once nearly discovered it; that on the hills outside Jerusalem he had come close to unlocking a secret so deeply buried he might well have lived out his entire life without even suspecting its existence. It was why he was more than a little afraid of Julia.

Instead he occupied himself with those whom he could never be close to, or who could never be close to him, diversions high or low who had no interest in either his work or his pleasures. He invariably pursued those who were unattainable, married, or unlikely to regard him as anything other than a temporary entertainment. At one time he spent several months with a woman slightly younger than himself who worked in one of the great department stores that Rome was at last acquiring. When he bade a final farewell, he could not recall a single conversation he had ever had with her, not one remark that had struck him. Afterward he seduced the wife of a notary a decade or so older than he was, listened carefully to her sadnesses and concerns, enjoyed her company, and took an odd pleasure at the necessary secrecy and subterfuge that enlivened an otherwise empty involvement. It was not insensitivity or cruelty that meant that, some months afterward, he could barely remember her name; both were of the moment, and their moment had passed.

He knew, of course, that not loving them was part of the attraction; Julia was the only one to whom he had ever responded in that manner and with her he had held back. But in contrast to all the others, she remained in his thoughts almost daily; he dreamed of her and could recall every word she had ever said to him. Even more, he could imagine whole conversations he had never had, but knew what she would say nonetheless.

He welcomed the arrival in Rome of her father, for he brought news of Julia, and also provided a good dinner and sympathized with his passions for paintings and ruins. The conversations they had were delightful and fitted in perfectly with the Roman life that Julien had fashioned for himself. Indeed, the sojourn in Rome ruined him. He went there as a bright star, destined for a glittering career; he left it almost a dilettante, unwilling to settle down, determined that the drudgery of teaching would never claim his soul. Rome has destroyed many a character; in the period 1924 to 1927, it claimed Julien's as well.

An alternative explanation: During this period the impact of the war finally swept over him, and accounted for the sleepless nights, the distraction, the refusal of what was expected. He became dissatisfied and as eager to embrace new experiences as, in the previous few years, he had shunned them entirely. But the frivolity masked the continued seriousness that showed up in his work; the sheer volume of notes he took in this period, squeezed in between the meals and the excursions, the elegantly empty conversations and the charming women. For Julien had seen into the darkness and felt in himself what could happen.

He dreamed of it still, a face he had seen only for a fraction of a second as a flare lit up the area around, and the German soldier turned. He remembered the look of foolish concern as they stared at each other, neither knowing what to do next. And Julien had reacted first; he had been on patrol, his nerves were frayed, while the other had only just come on duty and was slower. A slight frown, the impression that Julien was behaving badly, rudely, when the bayonet went into his stomach. And then nothing else at all; the rest was in total darkness; Julien heard him fall, remembered pulling the bayonet out and ramming it in again and again. More than anything, he remembered the satisfaction. He remembered that he had continued to stab long after he knew it was necessary, that he did so for pleasure. The moment turned him into a barbarian, exulting in his triumph. That was what he dreamed about, and which so frightened him. He knew how easy it had been to surrender to those feelings. Even worse, his dreams played dreadful games with him, and confused themselves, so that when another flare lit up the landscape and he looked down, he saw the deathly pallor on Julia's face; the blood flowing from her body in the mud; her lips, moving inaudibly as the rattling of gunfire drowned out her words like a train passing through a station and extinguishing all conversation on the platform. He had killed her, and the nightmare came to him fitfully and without any reason he could discern.

"How is she?" It was the question that he asked as soon as was seemly.

"Splendid," her father would reply, as he always did, even when the letters she wrote to Julien suggested differently. Julien never discovered whether Bronsen was unaware of her travails, the difficulties she had in painting something she was proud of, or whether he was reluctant to admit that she was not perfect. If the last, the aim was laudably paternal, but even when he first met the Bronsens he considered that it made her life that much more difficult, and in one burst of correspondence he mentioned it. Once a month on average, Julia wrote him a letter, once a month Julien wrote back—long letters on both sides, funny and touching, although neither fully appreciated how much the other waited for them, opened them eagerly, and read them with breathless delight.

"Of course you are right," came her terse reply. "He wants so much of me and how can I deny him anything? It's hard to work with someone looking over your shoulder all the time. It would be easier if he thought I was a bad painter, if he discouraged me rather than being entranced by every piece of rubbish I produce. Sooner or later, though, I must find some room . . ."

"She is doing wonderful things, wonderful," Bronsen said at the dinner in a magnificent restaurant near the Spanish Steps shortly after this letter arrived. "She must keep going with it, I think. I do hope her marriage will not distract her."

This was said with a slightly arch look, as though he was well aware of the impact the words would have. *What, young man? You presumed to my daughter? Don't be so ridiculous.* Julien froze for a moment, and had to make an immense effort to try to hide the effect of the news.

"I didn't know . . ."

"She's very private, of course. She will marry a diplomat, a man with the greatest potential, from a good family and the sort of connections which will help her immensely with her work. They will be very happy together, I'm sure."

So that was the escape she had decided upon, Julien thought. He was not quite convinced by the story; her father seemed too satisfied and content, but he wrote some formal congratulations that omitted all the little intimacies of earlier letters. And back, in due course, came an equally formal reply. There their friendship lapsed for some time.

"Perhaps Mussolini will manage something. Who knows?" The conversation continued, as did the dinner, and Julien tried to enjoy himself, or at least to appear to do so. "Everyone else has failed. He has the support of absolutely everyone from cardinals to avant-garde sculptors, so there must be something to him."

Bronsen had turned to politics now. He had that morning been at a meeting at the finance ministry and two days previously had met the new Italian leader for the first time.

"What did you think?"

Bronsen paused, enjoying himself. Julien had learned that there was no point expecting an even conversation on such topics; Bronsen believed firmly that the person who knew most should dominate. To give him credit, he deferred to Julien on the subject of ruins and paintings, but would brook no interruption on more worldly topics. It made conversations with him sometimes a bit like miniature lectures. "I was impressed," he said. "Truly I was. He looks like a bit of a fool, but clearly isn't. He knows what he's doing and what he expects everyone else to know as well. That clarity is refreshing. It makes a change from the normal squabbling and bickering. Decisions get taken and acted upon. You don't know how rare that is. God knows this country needs it. France could do with some of the same, I fear. Someone like Mussolini would make mincemeat of the corrupt incompetents we manage to put into power."

Julien shrugged and looked away. "Politics bores you?" Bronsen said.

Julien smiled. "It does. Apologies, sir, and it is not that I haven't tried to be fascinated. But careful and meticulous research has suggested the hypothesis that all politicians are liars, fools, and tricksters, and I have as yet come across no evidence to the contrary. They can do great damage, and rarely any good. It is the job of the sensible man to try and protect civilization from their depradations."

"And how do you do that?"

"Me? In particular?"

"Yes."

"My contribution is to go into the archives and read old manuscripts. To collect paintings—one of which I would like to show you later on to get your opinion—and try to communicate the importance of such things to other people. To persuade people that politics is the waste product of the ferment of civilization, unavoidable but dangerous if not properly contained. To be a teacher, in fact, which is probably what I will end up doing when I go back to France."

"That'll frighten them, no doubt," Bronsen said with a smile.

"I mean it," he said, trying to cover his earnestness with a worldly smile. "Civilization needs to be nurtured, cosseted, and protected from those who would damage it, like politicians. It needs constant attention. Once people stop caring, it withers and dies."

"So? The world burns and you sit in a library?"

"The world did burn," Julien replied. "I was at the cremation. And it would have been better if I had stayed in a library. One person, at least, would be alive now who is dead, because I wouldn't have been there to bayonet him."

Bronsen grunted. "I admire your clarity—though not the experiences which brought it to you. My horizons are bounded by making money, because it is something I know and am good at. I become thereby something of a caricature, which distresses me, but not enough to deter me. I am all too aware that a Jew without money is even more vulnerable than a Jew with money. Not that any of this is so very interesting. I would much rather hear what shape your defense of civilization is taking these days. So tell me. What news from the archives?"

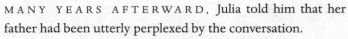 MANY YEARS AFTERWARD, Julia told him that her father had been utterly perplexed by the conversation.

"He was so pleased with himself. He had just signed the biggest contract of his life, to build two factories outside Rome and Milan, and was bursting to tell someone. And you never asked what he was doing."

"I thought I had," Julien replied. "But he had just dropped into the conversation the little detail about your getting married. I don't think I was quite so keen to gratify his vanity after that. I did give him a chance to tell me, though. At least, I gave enough hints."

She laughed. "Oh, dear. Did you never notice that he didn't understand the meaning of the word 'hint'? That subtlety was not part of his makeup?"

"I thought it would be rude to ask."

"And he thought it was rude that you didn't. Therein lies a lesson for us all."

"Is this a characteristic you've inherited?"

She considered. "I am, perhaps, a little bit more civilized than he is. But only up to a point. You may, perhaps, have realized that now."

THE MAIN THINGS preventing Claude Bronsen and Julien Barneuve from becoming close friends were Julia, and their different ages, a form of separation that the ever more egalitarian twentieth century found no means of overcoming. In other respects, a deep and abiding amity should have been possible. But the reserve that attends a span of years, building disparities of experience and vision, was too great. Over the few days following the meal the two saw each other frequently, talked incessantly. They shared many small experiences, and many pleasures. But the distance remained, and in the end Bronsen left to go home and Julien returned to his archives. Insensibly the friendship, otherwise so promising, lapsed because neither of them saw its potential, and because Bronsen was a constant reminder of his now unattainable daughter.

No such possibility even arose with Ceccani and Olivier de Noyen, although each had a genuine though ill-defined affection for the other. There the distance was much too great. It was impossible for a man such as the cardinal to have friends; there was no one with whom he could share. He was bound by the strictness of his relations; disparities of power were evident in all his dealings with his fellow men. Popes and kings required deference and respect, which shrivels friendship like vinegar on the oysters he loved so much he stopped eating them. His fellow cardinals were also his rivals, requiring constant watching. Others were his clients and his servants, and the rest of humanity simply did not exist.

Similarly, the gap between Manlius and Syagrius was too great, because Manlius regarded his secretary as a son, and no true friendship can exist between fathers and sons. Indeed, in the *Dream,* he excluded such relationships specifically from consideration when he touched on the subject of love. There duty took pride of place as the great motor; children

fulfilled their fathers' wishes, ensured that their names and fame continued. There was no room in such a vision for anything more tender. It was
because of this that his treatment of the young man was also so harsh and
distant, for Syagrius was his opportunity and his reproach.

Manlius had no children of his own, and it is possible that this lack determined many of his actions and decisions. For the twilight of the culture
he held so dear was paralleled by the extinction he himself faced. The
Christianity he affected, and which others of his age adopted with greater
conviction, had no power to conquer such fears. When his name ended,
there would be no one to take offerings to his grave, hold an annual feast
in his honor, give him the eternity he craved and which he did not believe
his new religion would confer.

The night his wife miscarried for the fourth time all his training as an
aristocrat and a philosopher left him. He went to the cemetery and
poured oil on the grave of his father. It was the only way he could apologize for his failure and the looming end of his entire line. When he slept,
he saw the tombs crumbled on the ground, the low-born taking them to
build their barns, the weeds growing all around.

He accepted his fate nonetheless. He did not divorce her, although he
could easily have done so and few would have blamed him. Even she
would not have minded so much, coming from a family that knew the importance of continuity. She would have gone to a woman's house to pray,
and been happy. But he kept her with him, made plans to adopt Syagrius,
and soon afterward turned back to public life.

He knew that Syagrius would carry on his name only; nothing of true
value, for the boy was kindhearted but utterly stupid, dull in conversation
and simple in thought. He never read and, in all the time he stayed in Manlius's villa, never said a single word of any interest; nothing beyond the
commonplace ever dropped from his lips. No cliché, no imbecility was too
hackneyed for him, it seemed; the most trite remark would cause him
to nod his fair head in agreement, any phrase of elegance or profun-
dity would elicit only puzzlement. He tried hard, certainly, was keen to
please, was liked by Manlius's wife, had many merits. But Manlius could
not but compare him to what his heir should have been, and the difference

made him curt, and unjustifiably rude. Syagrius put up with it; indeed, he had little choice and still got the better part of the bargain. For in return for earning Manlius's disappointment, he got his name, and would in time have his estates as well. He had been lucky; had Manlius waited a few years until his character was more formed, he would not have chosen him, but he had been misled by his flaxen hair and open smile into thinking that a beautiful face must indicate a refined and noble soul. This was Manlius's mistake, for the boy was kind and honest and tried to please. But he was part of a different world, and could see nothing of value in the refinement and cultivation that lay at the core of Manlius's being.

When Manlius turned back to public life, it was not with total enthusiasm, for he was also mindful of other aspects of Sophia's teaching, which appealed to him on a more profound level. Her eternity was different, a search for completion without ever knowing the goal until it was attained. She taught by parable and by discussion, as her father had before her, using the simplest of forms to begin the task of approaching the most complex ideas. One of her favorite techniques was to examine the myths, to discuss them and dissect them through the lens of philosophy to seek out the truths that lay therein. One day, Manlius found himself talking of Hélène, who fell in love with Paris because the Trojan shepherd had won a promise from Aphrodite. It was a matter of moments for Sophia to dismiss the story as nonsense, of course; the divine does not intervene in the life of men in such a way, either by entering beauty contests or, she said with a smile, by parting the seas or turning water to wine.

"But can we see anything more here? As we have concluded that the higher does not intervene with the lower, does this mean the story is foolish and without merit? I remind you that literature is full of such tales. Why do Dido and Aeneas fall in love, an event which Vergil also attributes to the gods? Why does Ariadne betray everyone she holds dear for love of Theseus?"

"I have read," Manlius said, "that it is sickness, a disease of the blood. Is that not what Hippocrates wrote?"

She nodded. "But why do we contract this illness? The way the lover is drawn to the beloved, suffering sleeplessness, sweating, a loss of reason, an overwhelming desire to be united with the other person that can cast all normal behavior aside? An illness, I grant you. But we must go further. Why a *particular* person? Why this person and no other? Why only one person at a time? I have heard of many strangenesses in man's behavior, but I have never heard of lovesickness for two people at once."

And she went on from there, weaving in the speech of Aristophanes in the Symposium, in which he says that men were once spheres but were cut in two by the gods to punish them. Thereafter, they must search for their other halves, and can never rest until they are reunited. And the myth of Er in the Republic, in which men must be reborn time and again until their soul learns to ascend to the heavens and escape the prison of the body. Again not to be taken literally, of course—nothing she said was literal—but a metaphor for the quest that the soul must be engaged upon if it is to embrace the transcendent. In its dissolution lay the immortality Sophia had to offer, and which Manlius chose to pursue through his deed.

Manlius avoided so long his public duties because he was afraid of how he would discharge them. His father had known he had enemies, but did nothing until it was too late; he was killed by those he was trying to save. Manlius knew that he would not make such a mistake. He would then be faced with a decision, and a conundrum: Can one act unjustly to achieve justice? Can virtue manifest itself through the exercise of harshness? He did not know how he would answer these questions. All he knew was that his father had answered wrongly and paid heavily. Whatever virtue he had possessed was dissipated in failure.

WHETHER THE CONVERSATION about Saint Sophia between Olivier de Noyen and the Siennese painter ever took place is merest supposition; Julien surmised the existence of something like it because of the strong correspondence between Olivier's narrative in Ceccani's archive and the iconographic sequence on the walls of the chapel. Something of the sort must have occurred, and to suppose that Olivier repeated to the painter of the chapel the tale he put in his letter to Ceccani is reasonable. By the time Julia Bronsen had grown so familiar with his work she might almost have painted it herself, it seemed even likely.

She had told Julien she was potentially a good painter, and her self-confidence was not misplaced. By the late 1930s she was beginning to be known as such, although her reputation was still small. She had, it is true, studied in Paris at the Académie Colorassi—the Mediterranean cruise with her father was to mark the end of this part of her apprenticeship, and the beginning of the period in which she truly began to learn to be a painter—then was an early student of Matisse, a man she admired and who even attracted the approval of her father. After this she went her own way; she did not follow the necessary route to fame, was disdainful of the associations and connections that artists must have to make their mark.

Someone once said that being wealthy had been her ruin as an artist, and in her heart she agreed. Not because it had stunted her vision, or affected what she painted, but because she could afford to ignore the dealers and the critics who make artists great. She paid little attention to them; they returned the compliment. Had she worked at it a little harder, the posthumous reputation that began to form in the 1960s around her surviving work would have crystallized earlier.

She worked obsessively, and generally in solitude. It was a life she had chosen at some cost to herself, for no husband could fit into such a schedule for long; there was not enough room. The marriage that so distressed Julien when he heard of it was a foolish mistake, partly a desire to escape the overpowering presence of her father, and partly a desire, for once in her life, to do the expected, to be like everyone else. Jacques Menton was, as her father told Julien, a diplomat with a great future in front of him. A good family, not too high, not too low. A man of intelligence, kindness, and even some wit. A Protestant originally from Alsace, with more than a bit of German in him. Not wholly French, as she was not, but in his case the sense of not quite belonging made him more conventional, straining constantly to be and appear perfect.

But he loved her, in a diplomatic, cautious fashion, and she believed for a while that she responded. She felt a wish to belong, and he could show her how to do so; curiously her father said nothing against the match even though he found Jacques's company tiresome and never for a moment believed it was based on any great love. Julien saw this and later remarked on it in a letter to her. "Of course he was unsuitable as a husband," he said loftily from his desk in Avignon. "Your father didn't mind him. You must make it a rule in the future never to fall in love with anyone unless Claude Bronsen detests him. The more he detests him, the more suitable he will be. If you are not prepared to meet your admirable father's jealousy head on, then you will have to wait until he is dead. He is a healthy man, your father. Good for many years yet. You'd better get on with your painting, I think."

His instincts were right, for while her husband indulged her painting, and judged it a fine thing to have an accomplished wife, she thought that he understood why she painted, and mistook his indulgence for something more profound, his silence on the subject for an instinctive understanding.

"I'm not going to stop painting. It's my job. It's what I do." This astonished comment replying to a casual remark he dropped into a conversation after they had been married for some six months, during which his disappointment grew that she had not changed her way of life one jot since their wedding. He had pointed out—perfectly correctly—that she did not have time to paint ten hours a day and fulfill her role as hostess at the parties he needed to give in order to rise in the diplomatic service. Let alone fit in children, which he wanted quite desperately.

It was his light laugh that killed the marriage, stripping away all the make-believe. One slightly high-pitched whinny from his mouth, half choked off in the way he had learned, imbued with a cynical tone, lasting only half a second. He mistook her passion for an amusement, and her deep concentration for empty-headed vacuousness. Worst of all, he had no idea how good she was. That was something she would not tolerate.

Perhaps she was wrong in her reaction; she never discounted the possibility. From a diplomatic point of view—her husband's point of view, indeed—the unrestrained rage she let loose was unforeseeable, excessive, even a little coarse. But there was no forced melodrama, no striving for effect in the way her hands trembled and her voice shook as she tried to explain—to someone who could no more understand than a deaf man could understand Bach—why she did what she did, and why it was important.

"Why *are* you people always so hysterical?"

Centuries, if not millennia, were squeezed, dessicated, and distilled into that one offhand comment made merely to fend off her anger; the implications could write, and had written, many books. The words themselves, the tone of contempt, the mingling of distaste with a slight fear. All these could have been unraveled at enormous length. But there was no need to; Julia needed no interpretation and could see by the alarm in his eyes that he needed none either. He knew what he had said.

She never talked to him again; there was no point. Nor did she ever divorce; there seemed little point in going through such a complicated ordeal, and for her husband's career even an invisible wife was better than none at all. He had been, and remained, a decent, honest, simple soul; loving in his way, and once the anger passed she could see his many fine qualities. But she had also glimpsed a darkness that, although she could forgive, she never wanted to be close to. Still, she had no desire to harm him. She was not vengeful and eventually felt somewhat apologetic. The fact that her rage had faded so swiftly convinced her she had never loved him in the first place; the whole messy business was her fault.

By the time she told Julien, she could even laugh about it. He had been her confessor during this period, as she reopened the correspondence with him shortly after her wedding, ostensibly to explain why he had not been invited. She wrote him letter after letter justifying what she was doing, and he replied, sometimes consoling her with idle anecdote, sometimes giving reassurance, sometimes criticism. It was, Julia realized, the worst form of betrayal, an adultery of the mind and of the emotions, and the pleasure she gained from his letters was one of the main reasons that she ultimately decided to walk out.

"You spend too much time trying to find a reason for things," he said gently in one letter. "I suffer from the same fault myself, so I know what

I'm talking about here. Listen to an expert. You want to run away. You have made a mistake. And that is the end of the matter. After all, no one around you will ever manage to be happy while you are not."

"Do you know why I'm a painter?" she said when they met a few months after she had finally packed her bags and moved into an apartment. "Do you know why I cover myself in brightly colored oil like some ancient Pict? It's my sign. It's so that people know immediately that I belong to nothing and don't waste their time trying on me. My mother was as Jewish as can be, my father has cast all that off and regards religion as superstition and tradition as cowardice. So I am nothing. Thanks to him even the outcasts cast me out. So I have to do it all myself."

"Do what?"

She laughed. "I don't know. If I did, I probably know what I was looking for. And I wouldn't have troubled poor Jacques by marrying him."

He smiled gently at her, and watched as she ordered another drink. A whiskey this time, her second since they'd come into the dingy bar that she had adopted as her favorite after a day working in her studio on the boulevard Montparnasse.

"Why do you never ask me questions, or try to understand me? I always feel a bit of a failure with you. I try to be elusive and mysterious, and you seem quite uninterested."

He shrugged.

"Don't you find me fascinating? Strange? Wonderful? Quixotic? Exotic? Aren't you concerned about where I come from, where I'm going? What makes me tick?"

He looked puzzled for a moment. "Not really," he said eventually.

She sniffed. "I don't know whether that is charming or the most insulting thing anyone has ever said to me."

"At least I haven't said you're hysterical."

"That's true. But I've never thrown a vase at you either."

"You threw a vase at him?"

She nodded, an impish, childish look glinting in her eyes. "Missed him though," she said. "Dammit."

Their eyes met in mutual appreciation, and they started to laugh. It was a delightful meeting. And Julien was aware once more that he had never tried to charm or impress or compliment her. He was also aware, of course, that Claude Bronsen quite liked him.

HER REMARK was not true; not entirely true in any case. Julia had determined to become a painter at the age of ten, in 1913, when she had a tantrum two hundred yards from the family apartment in the boulevard Haussmann. She was with her nanny, an Englishwoman of the sort the wealthy Parisians preferred at that time, a kind woman but with the emotional subtlety of a cavalry officer, reluctant to admit what sort of family she worked for but who loved Julia after her fashion. She was not destined to remain long; she tried to impose order and discipline, but had to battle against Bronsen himself and his indulgent whims. Julia at that stage had spent only a short while in school, for her father was forever taking her with him on his voyages around Europe, sometimes for a month, once for six. They would go where his business took him, and while he knew he should settle her in some pension and give her proper schooling, he could not bear to be parted from her. He had, after all, worked hard to keep her from his wife and, having won her, would not easily let her go again.

Julia had many relations, but was brought up almost alone, for the way her father had ended his marriage had been bitterly criticized. His wife, thought sweet and obedient, known to be so gentle, had been clearly wronged, had been driven into illness trying to understand the fiery and aggressive man she had married, so given to titanic rages and bursts of angelic kindness, each as unpredictable as the other. All agreed that he was impossible, and in revenge for the condemnation, Bronsen had cast off much more. He never accepted his guilt; far from it, he believed he had defended his daughter from a woman whose dark moods and violence were insupportable. He never put forth his side of the case; he was either too proud or still too loyal to a woman he had once loved; never detailed the innumerable doctors, the times she went supposedly on holiday but in reality to clinics across Europe in a fruitless search for a cure that eluded even the most famous of psychiatrists. He never told of the screaming, the times she disappeared and he had to call the police to find her, the times he had to bundle Julia into her room and stand in front of the door to protect her from her mother's rage over a trivial wrong. Only Julia knew; in her memory she kept those dark days hidden and spoke of them only once, when Julien came to her after her father's death. But she remembered, and she remembered lying on the floor, the bruise growing on her cheek, and her brusque, rude, ill-mannered father kneeling by her to comfort her, stroke her hair, and carry her to her bed. He stayed with her all that night, to keep her company and to reassure her. The next day her mother left forever.

Claude Bronsen took the blame, but he also took his revenge on those who were quick to judge and condemn him. He walked away from his family, his religion, his entire society, eradicated all memory of the language he had spoken as a boy before he had left Germany to escape the cloying attentions of his parents. He knew, as early as ten, that he had to leave the hardworking, solemn atmosphere of their house, where his father labored as a commercial traveler and his mother kept a traditional Jewish home in a pinched and joyless fashion. He took pleasure in little that they—such respectable people, so timid and cautious, but also disapproving and demanding—found valuable in life. But he did his best to mollify and reassure them, tried not to make them ashamed of him when he was still poor and unsuccessful, guarded his tongue meticulously when they came to admire the life he had built for himself from his own labors and abilities in the sparkling world of Paris at the turn of the century. His wife, Rachel, was the prize of this hard work, a German-Jewish beauty, blonde and cultivated, with a haughty, almost aristocratic air.

His parents' criticism, the way they assumed that his fine wife must have been unbalanced by his treatment of her, or by the birth of Julia—a difficult, painful birth, for she did not enter the world without a fight— was a betrayal of trust which he could never forgive. Even in the 1930s he refused to be reconciled with those who had, in his view, ostracized him so unjustly. Now they needed his help; they were being buffeted by economic chaos and political malevolence and they turned to him. He did not respond and felt little concern for their persecution. Bronsen indeed scarcely considered himself Jewish; he was French, naturalized many years before, and a man of business and of culture. That was all the identity he needed.

It was his greatest pleasure that Julia resembled him and had almost nothing of her mother in her, either in looks or in temperament. When she grew up to be both beautiful and accomplished, his pride and gratitude were so great he could barely contain them. His reward for her achievement was to offer her the world: He gave her books and museums and foreign cities and a sense of never-ending inquiry. He denied her ritual and offered her freedom in exchange. Anything she wanted was hers, and only once did he lose his temper with her, and that was when she said, at the age of fourteen, that she wanted to see her mother. They had their only serious fight, which Julia won. But she only did it once. The meeting was not a success; she had had an adolescent dream of making everything right, of healing injuries, and of having both her parents. It was not possible; her mother's illness had grown rather than diminished and had turned into a deep and violent hatred of the man who, so everyone told her, had been so cruel, so heartless and so unjust. Julia, by then, had so many of her father's mannerisms that even the way she stroked the side of her cheek when trying to think of something to say became a provocation. She was thrown out, told to leave and never come back. She obeyed completely and ran away crying into the arms of her father, who had been waiting, anxiously, at the end of the street. They never met again, and Julia learned only through a gruff comment from her father when she was eighteen that her mother had died. "Go to the funeral if you want," he said.

And she had; she went alone and was confronted with the baleful glances of her family, none of whom offered her any consolation or understanding. It was her first and last brush with her religion, and from then on, she associated it with the disapproval that suffocated her in the synagogue that cold March afternoon.

In bringing her up, Claude Bronsen knew that Julia should learn to be more polite and refined than he was, cultivated in a way he could never be; his own appetites created in him a sort of disdain that he hoped Julia would share but learn to control better. He knew exactly what sort of child he wanted, could see her growing up in his mind, and the results of his labors bore their first fruit that day in the boulevard Haussmann. The nanny was completely perplexed by the outburst and smacked the child to make her hurry up. Julia screamed even more, and kept on screaming until her face was red with a mixture of outrage and despair. She was dragged back, still screaming, to the apartment, and sent to her room until she learned to behave. She never knew how much this frightened her father, how many nights he stayed awake, unable to sleep lest the affliction that had destroyed his wife had also been visited on his beloved daughter. Out of this terror came the overwhelming, stifling concern for her that too often turned into a swamping solicitude that allowed her little room to breathe.

Her performance that day, however, was mere petulance and rebellion, not a sign of incipient insanity. Julia did not behave; indeed it might be argued she never really behaved again; a moment transformed a polite, amenable girl into the paint-stained outcast she described (with some pride) to Julien much later. The outburst was triggered by a picture just visible through the window of a not particularly respectable art dealer; she wanted to stop and look, but the nanny was in a hurry and wanted to make tea. She made tea every afternoon, and Julia was expected to change her clothes, sit politely, and make proper conversation for thirty-five minutes about her day.

She had always done so; after that afternoon she never did again. The nanny left to go to a more civilized family a few months later. She refused Julia's request to go into the little gallery and look at the picture that was not even in the window, but partially glimpsed on the wall on the left-hand side. Julia pointed to it. The nanny laughed. "Look at that thing; why, a monkey could do better."

The incident opened the floodgates in Julia's developing personality. Here was something around which she could organize all those confusing, confused thoughts and feelings that swirled through her mind. Here was a reason not to make polite conversations, not to change her clothes and sit with her knees touching. Here was a reason to disobey.

The next day she slipped out of the apartment when she should have been reading quietly in her room, tripping out of the maid's entrance, then down the stairs, past the concierge and into the street. It was the first time she had ever been outside on her own, and she was frightened by her daring for the first dozen steps, and exhilarated thereafter. She walked brazenly into the gallery, affecting the manner of those grand women she had witnessed buying cosmetics in the faubourg Saint-Honoré, and went to look at her picture.

It was a pencil and wash of a woman with a firm mouth and chin, a streak of hair falling down the right side of her face from where it had been bundled up on top of her head. She looked tired, mournful even; Julia felt a pang of recognition.

In the background two men were talking, and their voices got louder and louder, so Julia could not help hearing as she stood entranced before the picture.

"You goddamned crook," one was saying in heavily accented French. "You cheat. Why should I have anything to do with you?"

The unsuppressed rage was frightening; he was small, undistinguished-looking but with dark eyes and an air of compelling power.

"I do what I can. What do you expect? I keep this gallery, pay an assistant, pay the rent, give parties to try and drum up clients and get little in return for it. It is not as if these paintings are snapped up the moment I hang them on the wall, you know."

"You don't even try."

The older man spoke softly, trying to conciliate. "I'm sorry. I do my best. And if you know a better dealer I will be happy to let you go. And wish you all the success you feel you deserve. But I speak the truth. And, if I may say so, your own attitude to the people who do think of buying your pictures does not help."

"My attitude? My attitude? I am charm personified."

"When you want to be. Which is not often. For the most part you are gratuitously offensive and overbearing. You talk about yourself without a break, and the first thing you ever do is inform your clients that you are a genius and you will first have to determine whether they are good enough to own one of your works."

There was a long silence, then the little man burst out laughing and embraced the other. "And why not? It is all true." Julia was thoroughly perplexed. She thought a punch on the nose might have been more appropriate. Then she noticed that both men were looking at her; she blushed and started to retreat.

"Stop, little one," cried the painter. "You see, someone likes my paintings. She came in just to look at it. Did you see? Did you see the look on her face? I know that look. Ha!"

He walked over and knelt down beside her. "You do like it."

She nodded, cautiously. The little painter put his arms around her and kissed her chastely, but full, on the lips; it was the first time anyone had ever done such a thing. She wished she could stop blushing.

"So? Tell me what you think."

Julia panicked, then forced herself to respond, trying to think of something sophisticated and worldly to say. She could think of nothing at all.

"I think you must love her very much," she said eventually, and felt ashamed of her reply.

But it delighted the painter, whose dark eyes bored into her in a way she found disturbing. She did not want him to take those eyes off her, ever.

"Yes," he said. "I did."

Julia looked sad. "Did she die?"

"In my heart, she did." He cocked his head to one side and smiled impishly. "She was my mistress, some years ago. I gave her to someone else. She began to tire me."

"For heaven's sake," said the dealer, appalled, "don't talk so to a young girl. What a shocking thing to say."

The painter laughed, but Julia looked at him very seriously. "I think she was unhappy already, when you painted this. You made her unhappy, then painted her sadness. That was cruel of you. You can love someone and make them unhappy, I know."

"Do you now?" he replied uncomfortably. "Then maybe you know too much for someone of your age."

The owner of the shop looked satisfied. He had never seen his most difficult client made uncomfortable, never heard him challenged so effectively. He would retell this story often.

"She was looking for something I could never give her." Again his dark eyes bored into Julia's mind. "You have something of the same about you, young woman. Take my advice: Don't think you will find it in another person. You won't. It's not there. You must find it in yourself." Then he stood up.

"So that's me unmasked," he said. "But at least you like it. Eh? Don't you?"

"I think it's the best thing I have ever seen," she said.

He bowed. "And that's the best compliment I have ever received. Are you going to complete my happiness and buy it?"

Julia gasped. "I couldn't possibly. Why, it must cost at least a hundred francs!"

"A hundred francs! Oh, dear me! It is worth millions of francs, my child. But my—dealer—here tells me that in fact a picture is worth only what someone will give for it. How much money do you have?"

Julia took out her purse and counted. "Four francs and twenty sous," she said, looking up at him sadly.

"Is that all the money you have in the world?"

She nodded.

"Then four francs and twenty sous it is." He took it off the wall. "And in return I can say I have a patron who bankrupted herself, gave me every penny she possessed, just to have one of my works. Besides, it's more than this greedy little pig will ever get for it."

He handed it to her, taking the four francs and twenty sous, counting them carefully before pouring them into his pocket. "You see?" he said over his shoulder. "You see how charming I can be with a real client? A worthy client, rather than one of these self-assured morons with too much money who lecture me about what is wrong with my paintings. Now, my child, you must have a proper receipt. What's your name?"

"Julia. Julia Bronsen."

He paused, and looked at her. "A Jew, are you?"

Julia thought carefully. "No," she said, looking at him carefully. "My father says I am not."

"A pity," he said. "Perhaps you should pay less attention to your father.

Never mind." And he scribbled on a piece of paper, which he handed to her with a flourish.

Julia looked at it. "Received, from Mademoiselle J. Bronsen for a portrait of Madeleine, four francs and twenty sous. Picasso." He signed it with a prideful gesture, which Julia tried to emulate on her own works for months afterward.

 I N   1 9 3 8 , Julien read an article published in an English journal of that year on the Italian banking house of the Frescobaldi, who dominated European finance in the fourteenth century. It was not his usual sort of reading, far from it, but a colleague remembered his quirky interest in Provençal poetry and passed it on to him: the story of Olivier de Noyen's end was well enough known, but the reference to the Comte de Fréjus, Isabelle's husband, caught his eye. The article was concerned with laying out something of the network of the bankers' interests, trying to show how international and sophisticated its operations were before it was brought to ruin by impolitic lending to the English king to finance his wars: The king defaulted, and the Frescobaldi, together with most of the international banking system, went down as well, adding extra misery to people already battered by the Black Death.

As part of the argument, the author was at pains to show how important the Frescobaldi were for the smooth running of the church across Europe and, in one example, cited the business they did with Cardinal Ceccani. This included a loan given to the Comte de Fréjus on his behalf, to finance the purchase of land in Aquitaine.

The implications were fascinating and not only because Aquitaine was then owned by the English, against whom de Fréjus had fought only three years previously. More, it demonstrated that de Fréjus, like Olivier, was within the network of patronage controlled by Ceccani; by attacking Olivier the count had attacked one of his own. Initially this confirmed Julien's suspicion that Olivier must indeed have murdered Isabelle de Fréjus as legend said, for only such a dreadful deed could possibly have prompted such internecine violence. Only later did he reconsider this comfortable conclusion.

The first stage in the events that were ultimately recorded in the article was in fact perfectly simple; the comte came to Ceccani's great palace for a loan. And in his brusque way, he indulged in no elaborate phrases.

"I have to pay two thousand crowns to the king of England to complete the payment of my ransom and gain the release of my cousins," he said. "We were all taken captive at Crécy, and the king of France refuses to help us. So we must fend for ourselves. And I do not have the money."

There was a defiance in his voice that suggested that he anticipated a rejection, that he was used to such rebuffs already. He was a big man, trained to the horse and the sword, used to commanding. He was not one who had ever had to plead. He had no objection to priests, but had never been in their power before. The fact that circumstance had given someone like Ceccani a dominance over him incited him to defiance and petulance. He had in fact been in captivity in the English castle in Aquitaine only a few months, scarcely enough for his pretty young wife to realize how pleasant his absence was. But the cost of his release had been high, and he had promised those relations captured with him that he would not rest until they, too, were set free. He was a man of his word, too straightforward and too uneducated to be anything but honorable. This was why he so bitterly resented the fact that those for whom he had fought had not stepped forward to help him in the same way that he had so dutifully gone to fight for them. In this lay Ceccani's opportunity.

The cardinal's eyes narrowed. He had taken the precaution of discovering much about the comte's finances before the interview took place and knew quite well that he was desperate. Five banking houses had already turned him down, and if he did not find the money within a month, he would have to return to Aquitaine. Those were the rules; no one broke them readily.

"That is about five years' income for you," he said. "I would guess. I would not, could not, charge any interest, of course. But a donation to the bishopric's finances equivalent to, say, one twelfth of the total each year would be in itself more than you could easily support. How would you ever pay down the principal?"

"You talk like a banker, not a man of God."

"I talk, I hope, like a man who takes due care of the funds entrusted to me," Ceccani said severely. "You are not asking to borrow my money, but the church's. I am charged with its good governance. I have many requests, most of them worthy, still more of them desperate. It is my regrettable task to have to choose. And, sir, I must say you do not seem like the best or most secure way of laying out money."

The comte was not a man to beg; his dignity was too great to allow such a thing. But the way his jaw tightened; the look of despair that passed over his flaccid, somewhat stupid, face; the set of his shoulders; all these confirmed what Ceccani already knew: This was a man waiting to fall into his hands.

"Surely," the cardinal said, delicately putting his touch onto the most painful of wounds, "you must understand that the king of France has many difficulties at the moment. You cannot expect him to trouble himself over such matters."

"I can, and I do. I fulfilled my obligations to him, even though I had my own troubles. I left my new wife, raised a mortgage on my land to pay for my soldiers, marched the moment I was summoned. I served him faithfully."

"Then if he does not reciprocate, your duty to him is the less, is it not? He is defeated in battle, yet will not repay the help you offered him at that time."

"He is still my lord."

"But so are the counts of Provence. Perhaps the Lady Joanna might be prevailed upon?"

"I think not. I have in the past rendered her homage, but not service. She owes me nothing, and has troubles of her own at the moment, I believe."

The cardinal sighed. "Of course, we all have troubles. And any man who might help with those would earn the blessing and indulgence of many. If, for example, you chose to ally yourself to the countess, and found some means by which you could dissociate yourself from the king of France, then you might find yourself amply rewarded and compensated for any loss."

"I would forfeit all my lands in France."

"Which produce about seven hundred livres a year, as I understand. That could be rectified."

"And my ransom, and my cousins' ransom?"

"Those would both be forgiven you. Indeed, you might well find yourself compensated by double their value."

"And what service, exactly, would be required of me?"

The cardinal smiled. "Nothing."

The count smiled back for the first time. "No countess or cardinal is ever so generous for nothing."

"A word then. I believe you have in your service a man who is currently seneschal of Aigues-Mortes?"

"That is true."

"Bring him to Avignon. And make sure he does as he is told. His obedience will pay your ransom."

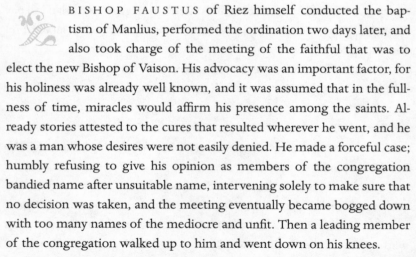

BISHOP FAUSTUS of Riez himself conducted the baptism of Manlius, performed the ordination two days later, and also took charge of the meeting of the faithful that was to elect the new Bishop of Vaison. His advocacy was an important factor, for his holiness was already well known, and it was assumed that in the fullness of time, miracles would affirm his presence among the saints. Already stories attested to the cures that resulted wherever he went, and he was a man whose desires were not easily denied. He made a forceful case; humbly refusing to give his opinion as members of the congregation bandied name after unsuitable name, intervening solely to make sure that no decision was taken, and the meeting eventually became bogged down with too many names of the mediocre and unfit. Then a leading member of the congregation walked up to him and went down on his knees.

"Gracious sir," this man cried, "God is not with us. We see it all around us, and we see it here today. We are without guidance, and we need a shepherd to show us the way. Help us, sir. Tell us your opinion. Help us make a choice."

Still Faustus dissented. "I would not presume to interfere," he said. "I have no right to do so. The choice of bishop is your own, and must be taken by you. But I must disagree when you say God is not with you; you must learn to see. For His ways are often hidden from man's sight, and are not easily discerned. Rather than interfere, then, I wish only to give you succor by showing how what I say is true. For I have recently witnessed a miracle, a great sign of the Lord's care for all his sheep."

The crowd rumbled with excitement at this, as all were in awe of miracles.

"There is a man among you known as a great sinner, careless of God. Throughout his life he had given himself up to the things of this world only, and turned his face from the faithful. And yet the Lord cared for him and gathered him in. He had a dream in which he saw a man weeping, and asked, 'Why do you cry so? What can I do to stop your sadness?' And the other said,

"'Save your soul, for I weep for you.'

"And he looked up, and this sinner saw the marks of the crown of thorns on his head, and saw the wounds in his hands, and, in his dream, fell down before him and said, 'Lord, I believe.'

"The next day this man came to me on hands and knees, begging to be baptized, and so I did. And here he sits with us now. His name is Manlius, servant of God."

The tale caused all except Manlius to rise from their seats and rejoice, and when they quieted once more, one man stood up and said, "Sir, surely this is a sign that the Lord has work for this man, that He should appear to him now? What is your opinion?"

"I do not know," said the bishop. "I simply rejoice at a sinner saved, a man of such skill and birth and wealth and learning now adds faith to all his other qualities. It may be indeed that the Lord needs him, or that He sees our needs more clearly than we do ourselves."

"He must be our leader," shouted another man. "This must be the meaning of this vision. Manlius must be our bishop."

Even then, after such careful preparation and such an allegorical inter-pretation of Manlius's embracing of the faith, there were doubts among many in the meeting, whose prevarications had been stoked well in advance by Felix's family, and particularly Caius Valerius, who saw what he considered his bishopric being stolen from under his very nose. There was no split in the meeting, but even Faustus's great authority had to be deployed to the full to achieve the result he desired. And he, afterward, had a sense of foreboding. He knew, of course, that raising Manlius would not be easy; he had not realized that the Adenii clan would object so much. He was a bishop. But a politician enough to realize that if Manlius was to be effective, he would have to deal with what threatened to be a constant thorn in his side.

He could have retreated, of course. Announced that the will of God was not with the meeting, called an end to it all in order to reconsider. But this man of great qualities and high ability had one fault: His belief in his judgment, and belief that his judgment and the will of God were one and the same, was all but complete. For his recommendation to be rejected was the same as the entire congregation throwing off the word of the Lord; it could not be allowed. He pressed, and insisted, used all his skills, and finally prevailed. Manlius, weeping with dismay, was dragged from his chair and brought to the front of the meeting.

All his plaintive cries about his unworthiness were brushed aside in the enthusiasm for what was now accepted as God's will. He cried with humility, threw himself at Faustus's feet, and begged to be relieved of this terrible burden for which he was entirely unfitted, and by his behavior began to confirm his suitability for the position.

At the end, only Manlius himself was unhappy, disgusted by his own actions and even more contemptuous of the vessel he had chosen to save everything he held dear. It was necessary; that he saw all too well. But the utter vulgarity of it, the stink of the congregation in their enthusiasm, the incoherent babble of their voices, the way they had been so easily led, left him in a misery so profound it endured for days afterward.

ON THE OCCASION of his thirty-first birthday, Julien gave a dinner party at a small restaurant near Les Halles, for he was leaving the life of the Lycée and had won a position teaching at the University of Montpellier. It would be a new life, far from Paris, and deserved to be marked with some style. As he did not care for large gatherings, he invited three friends only: Bernard Marchand, Marcel Laplace, and Julia Bronsen. The friendship between the three men was a strange one, for neither of his two friends liked the other, and endured each other's company only for his sake. Both knew the moment they saw Julia that she was different to Julien's usual women friends, with the result that the evening, inevitably, turned into a hunt to discover why.

The times had strained even old friendships that would have endured easily had no pressure been exerted on them. The Great Depression had arrived, and with it had come hardship for many and worry for most. It had not greatly affected Julien; the modest fortune left to him by his father he had guarded with the utmost conservatism, and the residual provincialism that showed up in a profound suspicion of anything to do with high finance meant he had still had a comfortable addition to his salary every month to provide those luxuries that he now considered mere necessities.

Others had fared less well. Claude Bronsen's business empire, he gathered from Julia, had been devastated; factories had closed, businesses dwindled, thousands he had employed had been dismissed forever. He was still rich, certainly, but not nearly as wealthy as when Julien first met him, and the reverses he had suffered galvanized him into a second youth. No sooner had a plant closed down in one place than he was laying plans to make the rest more efficient and profitable. Julien could imagine the fanaticism he brought to the task, for being more successful than others was part of his being, and he would labor at it until it was reestablished, no matter how difficult the bleak economic climate made his task.

"It's like being an orphan," Julia said in one of her letters. "I haven't seen him for months. It is oddly liberating. And now I know he's coming back in a week or so I find myself apprehensive. I don't know why; it's not as if I will see him if he is in Paris any more than if he is in Milan. But I have decided to rent myself a little house by the sea for the summer. Somewhere in the Camargue, I think, where I will see no one, and be able to pretend there are no such people as fascists or communists, and no such things as depressions or gold standards, strikes or riots. I'd invite you, but I know you won't come, and to be frank, I don't want even you to disturb me. I have done no useful work for months and am dreadful company."

Between Julien and Bernard there was an amity of relaxation; between Julien and Marcel, a friendship of interest. Both were loyal in their way; both believed fervently that the course they took was correct. Both Bernard the *résistant* and Marcel the collaborator were engaged—to borrow the lofty phrases of Manlius Hippomanes—in the business of salvation, and both were prepared to abandon humanity in order to achieve their aims. Both were, or became, accidental fanatics; circumstance brought out tendencies that otherwise would have remained hidden. That evening over the dinner that Julien had carefully crafted, from entrée to dessert, the first signs were there to be seen.

Bernard was amusing in a way that Marcel could not imitate, and did not wish to imitate. He was too serious; devoted to books and his religion. In place of skiing holidays, Marcel went, every year, to Lourdes, to help the sick and the poor and to bathe in a faith that was never shaken, and which Julien envied, remembering still the faint loss he felt when he was removed from his catechism lessons. He endured the sneers of Bernard with stoical fortitude as confirmation of his faith.

For Bernard was not only a freethinker, he was an ostentatious atheist, and took a perverse delight in insulting those with any religious sensibilities whatsoever. All were fools or cowards, often dangerously so, wedded to lost causes like the monarchy, believing in some lost idyll of order and rank that had never existed. A century and a half previously he would have sent people to the guillotine. A century and a half previously, Marcel would have been one of his victims.

Curiously, they were not dissimilar in appearance, although character obscured the resemblance so much that both would have been shocked at the idea that they looked alike. Both had fair hair, and both had green eyes. But, where Marcel cut his hair short and oiled and combed it so there was never a hair out of place, Bernard's grew long, hanging just close enough to his collar to indicate a bohemian soul. Marcel's eyes gazed steadily at whomever he was looking at, giving an impression of calm and consideration; Bernard's never rested in one place for more than a few seconds. Even when studying Julia, he seemed to absorb her in fragments, while also examining the food, the way the waiter served, the diners at the other tables, all details Marcel scarcely noticed. But the greatest difference of all lay in their expressions: Marcel somber, always serious, often with a frown; Bernard always smiling, leaning forward into the conversation, managing to suggest fascination with whatever was being said.

Julien's later dilemma could be seen in microcosm at that dinner, indeed Julia did see it; she was more perceptive because she saw with fresh eyes. She noted without commenting how Bernard interrupted the other two ceaselessly; interpreted Marcel's seriousness and the frivolity of Bernard's replies. And she saw how Julien took upon himself the role of pacifier, steering the conversation this way and that, trying to avoid the pitfall of open argument. It was a mistake to invite both of them to sit together; they could not help battling for his sympathy and her interest, even though both knew that Bernard would win, if victory there was to be.

In other circumstances, Julia would not have been so determinedly polite; she had not the patience. Rather she would have encouraged a brawl, or at least permitted it; it would have been good for Marcel, at least, to lose control of himself so utterly. She also noted that although Bernard was the more genial, he was the more ruthless, prepared to use his quickness to impose all manner of tiny humiliations to win his point. Marcel doggedly plodded on, severely and seriously arguing in a straight line. "But really, you must see what I am saying."

Bernard did, of course; saw it long before Marcel did, but that was of no concern. He did not argue from principle; he argued to win. His delight was in tripping the slower one up, of demonstrating his superiority in countless little ways. Julia saw also what Julien did not, that there was the seed of true hatred there, deep buried, one expressed in the barely concealed contempt, the other in the detestation that the slow must develop when the quick strive to humiliate them. Perhaps Julien was right after all; it was only the thin crust of civility that kept these more dangerous emotions in check.

Because Marcel was polite, and because Julia was beautiful, he refrained from discoursing on the malign influence of Jews in France; he never got to the point where belief could overwhelm courtesy. Rather he talked about art, which served as a more civil cloak for the same thing. In Marcel, the conventionality of his tastes matched the orthodoxy of his religion and the conservatism of his politics. Julia, and people like her, infuriated him.

"It is not a question of *understanding*," he said at one stage during the dinner. "I am talking about responsibility. People like you have turned away from responsibility. Instead, you suit yourself."

"I don't think I understand," Julia said.

"Artists should be servants. That is their glory. Either of kings or priests. You have broken that association and exist only for yourself. What was it that man said? Can't remember which one. He painted some pictures in a church and the priest thanked him and said God would be pleased with such a gift. And he snorted and said, 'Who cares about God? I've pleased myself.' You are unrooted and egotistical, and you call it the search for beauty."

No one at the table needed the meaning of the statement explained. Everyone knew what "unrooted" meant.

"I call it nothing of the sort," Julia replied, not even considering getting angry, so foolish was the attack, dismissing the implications as not worth contesting. "I do not think I can please God—if there is one—if I do not satisfy myself. Am I supposed to give things which aren't even good enough for me? I paint. Some think quite well, others think badly."

"Why?"

"Because it pleases me. And it provides me with a small income which keeps me from feeling totally dependent on my father."

"You might as well be a typist, then."

"That wouldn't please me."

And here Bernard broke in. "She is misleading you, dear Marcel. Telling you lies to put you off the hunt. She is not saying why it pleases her."

"It pleases me because when I am working well I am aware of nothing. Because when I have done something good I know it is good, and no one else's opinion is of any consequence. And occasionally, not often, I do manage to do something good. What is more, I know I can do better. So I keep on trying."

"What do you mean by 'good'?"

"Oh, I don't know," she said impatiently. "Has anyone ever managed to say what it is? A catching of some idea. Reflecting it, pinning it down."

"But it is rubbish, what you do. No technique, no skill. Just self-indulgent daubs on canvas. And the less people understand it, the happier you are. And you're mistaken. I think people understand it all too well. That's why they don't buy it."

Even his expression seemed stupid, for Marcel's tendency to frown as he spoke gave the impression that thinking was an effort for him. It was a mistake; many people underestimated him, as Julien told her later. In both intelligence and determination he was a good match for Bernard.

"And you?" she asked.

"I don't compete with either of them," Julien said. But with a little smile that gave another answer. He did not feel he needed to.

"Personally, I've always found that the less people are interested in art, the stronger are their opinions about it," said Bernard smoothly. "In my case, I would like actually to see some of your work before I pass judgment. If, that is, you won't mind me denouncing you as a self-indulgent fraud the moment I clap eyes on the ridiculous rubbish you try to foist on the public."

Julia laughed; Bernard had sapped the implicit violence from the conversation and forced Marcel into awareness of his offensiveness. He had not the slightest intention of looking at her pictures; it was something in which he had absolutely no interest. He was curious about her, mainly because he picked up Julien's fascination and would have tried to capture her for himself had he suspected for a moment it was possible. But even he—

generally insensitive on such matters—could grasp that there was something perfectly untouchable about her. And Julien realized he had been outwitted—he should have intervened, not Bernard.

"I am always happy to show anyone who is interested," she said.

"Splendid. Next week, perhaps. Now, if you don't mind, I will finish the story of my extraordinary skill on the ski slopes."

After the meal, Julien walked her home. "I'm sorry about all that," he said. "My mistake. I imagined a jolly dinner with everybody getting on tremendously well. I hope at least you don't take Marcel seriously."

They were crossing the Seine and paused to look along the dark cavern of the river to where the towers of the Conciergerie could be seen against the lights of the city. "I'm used to people like him. And I don't suppose he will ever do me any harm. If you disagree with him about the way I am sapping the vitality of the French race, you could always say so, you know."

He snorted. "I have. But it's a complete waste of time; he will rabbit on about discipline and order. I sometimes think he should have gone to Rome, not me. Then he could have seen the new society in the making. He would have had a lovely time singing the praises of Mussolini. Although I don't think he could ever bring himself to march around in a black shirt. He would find it too ostentatious. Besides, his abstract beliefs have never to my knowledge got in the way of perfect kindness when dealing with individuals. He is a good man. It may surprise you to hear it now you've spent an evening in his company, but he is."

"And Bernard isn't?"

He thought about it; she had picked up a parallel he had never bothered to consider. "No. He isn't. He has many fine qualities—he's intelligent, funny, dynamic, capable of good advice if he doesn't have a personal stake in the outcome. But he is not a kind man. He has no time for people, and doesn't understand them. He loves the working class, but the workers revolt him. Marcel, in contrast, likes the workers but loathes the working class."

"And these are your friends?"

"I'm afraid so. If I confined myself to friends who were perfect I'd only be left with you."

She gave him a push. "Stupid thing to say," she said, and began walking once more.

"I mean it," he said, catching up with her and walking alongside her, close but not touching. "I put up with their imperfections, and they put up with mine."

"And what are yours?"

"Mine? Oh, dear, where can I start? Pride, excessive caution, unwillingness to take risks, a general disdain for humanity masquerading as humanism. An inability to love what can be loved, and a fascination with what cannot be."

He stopped, and she laughed. "You're letting yourself off very lightly this evening, if that's all you can come up with."

"I know you could do better. That's the trouble." He paused, sensing the atmosphere, and retreated once more. "Anyway, all three of us have many faults. Unfortunately they cannot manage to tolerate each other in the same way that they put up with me. It was a mistake to have invited them both. I should have just gone out with you."

"Why?"

He completed his withdrawal. "It would have been cheaper. Did you see how much both of them ate?"

FOR FELIX, the elevation of Manlius was an attack on his family. Moreover, he knew perfectly well that the election—presented here in mimicry of the bishop's own version—was only partially true. While a holy man might be pressed to become a cleric by a grateful village or rustic town converted through his influence, or under the impact of a miracle wrought before their very eyes, a town as old and as sophisticated as Vaison was not to be overwhelmed in such a fashion.

Manlius and his family had undoubtedly worked hard at securing the position, setting up contacts long before the previous bishop had died, dropping hints about his availability, laying out policies to be pursued should the prize become his. What he had offered was unclear. His wealth was certainly a factor. His estates were large enough to build the walls and man them should the need arise, and few doubted that soon it would. His granaries could feed all the poor and still have enough left over for others. His influence across Gaul and into Italy might be of use if help was needed—although whether anyone had any help to give was a matter for debate.

But his action was a slight against Felix's family nonetheless, pushing them into a subordinate position in a region that the two families had shared. For four generations the Hippomanes and the Adenii had competed for office, and in the region east of the Rhône, Manlius's family had come to dominate the secular positions while Felix's clan had taken the ecclesiastical ones. Manlius had broken the unspoken treaty; moreover, he was still young. He could be bishop for two decades or more, and the Adenii would have to watch their influence slowly but steadily wane.

Felix had no choice, in fact; the most important members of his family made that clear. During a heated meeting, he was informed by young and old that, although his leadership was undisputed, that position could change. He was expected to act in their best interest.

"We know that this man is your friend, has been your friend since boyhood," said Anacleius, a cousin of his wife's. "We applaud your loyalty to him. But we must remind you that your loyalty to us must come first. How will you be able to defend us, enrich us, look after our interests in a hundred and one ways if you are powerless, having to go to your friend and beg favors? I do not even doubt his friendship to you; I do him the honor of believing him an honorable man in this respect at least. But he has his own family. Will he put your interest above theirs?"

The question went unanswered. There was no need to answer it. Felix dismissed the meeting with sweet words and reassurances, then went to pray, for he was devout in a manner that Manlius could scarcely understand. In his youth he had grasped this problem and saw the disjunction between Sophia's logic and the faith of the church, and placed her reason in a secondary position. His faith was an area she could not penetrate, the more valuable because it defied her rationality.

And when he had finished praying he knew what he must do. He could not risk open enmity with Manlius, for that might lead to violence; rather he had to bide his time. Whatever Manlius wished to do, he had to be allowed to argue his case, and it was not inconceivable that he would deserve their support. Justice demanded that he get his hearing. Their friendship was gravely wounded, but he could not bring himself to dispatch it yet.

This he told his family, noting that Caius Valerius, the cousin who otherwise might have won the bishopric had Manlius not intervened, fortunately seemed willing to accept his disappointment.

In fact, Caius Valerius stayed quiet because Felix's reticence gave him an unparalleled opportunity, and he had resolved to make the best possible use of it. For years he had smarted under his cousin's leadership of the family, and saw a chance to take what he considered his due; he considered himself the better Christian and the better man, for all of Felix's accomplishments. He would now outclass Felix in the area where he had been unchallenged: in that of action. But not yet; like Felix, he saw the virtue of waiting.

SHORTLY AFTER this family gathering dispersed, Manlius traveled the seventy kilometers to the south and west to Felix's principal villa. He arrived on his own, with no attendants except half a dozen guards. He was astonished at what he saw, for the great, elegant building he had known since his youth was transformed beyond recognition. He stood and gazed at what had happened, the arching columns vanished as dark, heavy walls were built around, the baths abandoned and plundered for stone, the immaculate lawns and flower beds dug out to make defenses. And all around the noise, the shouts of laborers, pulling stones and fitting them in place. The workmanship was terrible; great gaps were filled with rubble and concrete; it seemed like something children would make with building blocks, and seemed as strong, as well.

Felix came out to greet him, and saw the look on his face. "Not a decision taken easily," he said sadly. "This place has been in my family for two hundred years, grown and added to and nurtured."

"Are you sure it is necessary?"

"You know it is. If Clermont falls and Euric moves east into this region he will inevitably have to take this area. Like you, we have been attacked already by brigands. Lawns and ponds are for a time of peace. These walls are as weak as you think, but the skills to do better have gone. We have run out of choices."

"Are you sure?"

"Or we roll on our backs and pray for mercy. That, I suppose, is another option."

"Have you forgiven me yet?"

Felix sighed. "You insulted my family and our friendship. You should never have acted without talking to me first of all."

"I know. I'm sorry. I did not fear you; only your family, who I was sure would put you in an impossible position."

"They did anyway; I have persuaded them to wait and see. If you serve us all well, they will accept the situation. But you must not presume on friendship too much. You have made a great enemy of Caius Valerius. He will not readily forgive you, although I imagine I can rein in his anger, and he is too stupid to do anything on his own. But enough of all that. Do you want to see what I'm doing here?"

And for the next hour, they climbed over the new fortifications, surveyed the walls and the countryside beyond, pointing out weak spots, giving and taking advice. Manlius almost found it thrilling, and reveled once more in the friendship of a common purpose, however temporarily it might last. And he was impressed as well; Felix was in his element, he was a natural soldier, and needed war to give of his best. That was what worried him. He desired a solution that would enable him to win fame, to justify himself. In that lay the center point of their difficulty.

"Very fine," Manlius said eventually. "But you remember Diocletian's remark: that a defense is only as good as the soldiers manning it. What quality of soldiers do you have here? Old men and women with scythes?"

"Better than that," he replied shortly.

"How much better?"

"If they are properly led, and sufficiently frightened, they will do well. But all I can do is defend. To counterattack, to take the battle to the enemy . . ."

"You need mercenaries. Money. And help."

He nodded. "Exactly. And are you going to get them for me, Manlius? For if you do, I will show you wonders in return. Together we can accomplish extraordinary things; things men will talk of for generations to come. So tell me. You have your power now, My Lord Bishop. Faustus, and through him all the other bishops, seem to have placed their trust in you. They must have done, for you cannot have been elected for your piety. What are you going to do with that trust? What is it for, this sudden irruption from your study into the world of affairs?"

Manlius thought and was aware of the difference between them. Felix, as ever, was openhearted, straightforward, and spoke with the most total sincerity. And Manlius composed his words, trying to turn them into the music his friend wanted to hear. He did not lie; but he knew he deceived.

"I am going to try and get you something even more precious at the moment than either men or money. I wish to buy you time. And I wish to avoid the war you are preparing for here. It is the one thing we cannot afford. Whether we succumb to an invasion or beat it off, the result will be the same: ruin and devastation that will be almost total. Look at this villa of yours; you see what even the threat of war has accomplished? What will be left if you have to defend it? How many laborers will there be afterwards, or fields able to be cultivated? How many sheep and cattle? And what about the towns which depend on your produce? Who will live in them then except ghosts and memories of what once was? If I can avoid that, I will. So I will weave words and fine phrases and try to make your valor unnecessary. But if it comes to war, my old friend, I will pick up my sword and die with you shoulder to shoulder, like the sacred band of the Thebans did before Alexander."

Felix bowed his head, so Manlius could not see his tears. "Thank you, my friend," he said in a choking voice. "Do this, and our friendship will last forever."

FROM THE MOMENT he arrived back in the south, Julien's life continued smoothly until war came and disrupted it once more. He saw his friends every now and then, continued his correspondence with Julia, heard occasional news of her father and his successes and setbacks. He had not particularly wanted to return; for him, as for all academics, anywhere but Paris was a defeat, a backwater. To abandon the idea of the capital was a wrench, even though he never accustomed himself to the northern climate, the long wet drizzly days, the overpowering grayness of the skies, the coldness of people and climate. That was not his idea of France.

In Paris lay everything he needed. The professional and intellectual context, the new ideas, the constant necessity of striving. In Provence lay peace and tranquillity—calm, reassuring, and stultifying. But the choice was not his; his career was guided by others. It was Bloch who had raised him so high, and now it was Bloch who cast him adrift, or so it seemed. In the great man's mind was a question of strategy as he neared the apogee of his own career. He needed no one in Paris to ensure his reputation; although he was not so foolish as to believe that his reputation would last forever. No; in Paris he had dozens of others raised by him and placed by him. It was beyond Paris that his hold was weaker; it was the outlying defenses of his reputation that needed to be bolstered. So one pupil was sent to Rennes, one to Strasbourg, one to Clermont, and Julien to Montpellier, to establish their sway over departments and educate pupils themselves, passing on an ever fainter but still palpable echo of the great man's method and style. It was another form of that eternity so greatly desired by those who believe in it the least. None of these chosen apostles had any say in the matter; this was not the way things were done. And the strongest would claw their way back to Paris eventually.

So, in 1932, Julien had packed up his apartment, rented a smaller one to maintain at least a foothold in Paris, and headed back home, going initially to the big empty house in Vaison, which he had maintained as an act of thoughtless filial piety ever since his father's death. He realized how much he hated the house, and was suffocated by the heavy furniture, the velvet curtains, the dark wallpaper, the ponderous pictures on worthy themes. In the end he sold it, sent the furniture to a brocanteur and took instead a large apartment in Avignon opposite the church of Saint Agricole. A curious, whimsical decision, for it would have been so much easier to have lived in Montpellier, but he decided that if he was to come home, then he would do so properly, and be in the city he had known since he was sent there *en pension* as a schoolboy of twelve. He refused to live in Montpellier itself; rather he travelled there by train when necessary, lived in a guesthouse when teaching, and always returned to his true home the moment his liberty was granted him.

The apartment he lived in for the rest of his life was not in the most opulent part of the town—that already lay beyond the walls, in the grand suburbs that had been spreading since the latter part of the previous century—but he considered it to be by far the best, on a circling avenue of handsome eighteenth-century buildings, alive with shops and bars and restaurants and people, not so large that it attracted the motorcars that were beginning to clog the streets with their smells and impatient raucous horns. His building was light and airy, angled to avoid the whine of the winds in winter and the excessive heat of the summer. Into this he put his eclectic, judiciously chosen collection of furniture and pictures—his little Greuze, the Cézanne he had bought at a street market in Avignon for a few francs, the drawings he had acquired in Rome, the picture of the hills of Jerusalem, which Julia had given him—and they fitted as if they had all been designed for the pale green walls and the soft gray of the delicately carved woodwork. Over the years he added to his collection, carefully buying works that few others liked. By the time of the war, he had a substantial number that were beginning to be of some value. Among these were four paintings by Julia, which he had selected quite ruthlessly, returning to her studio each time he went to Paris, coming away empty-handed on nearly every occasion.

"You are very hard to please," she said dryly once, after he had examined carefully one work she was proud of and yet again shaken his head. "What do you like?"

"I don't know. Something special. There's a vacuous reply for you."

"Yes," she agreed. "An intellectual like yourself. You should do better. Why don't you like this, then?" She pointed at one painting, a seemingly rough sketch of a woman in a boat, the form of the woman blending into the shape of the water. She was pleased with it; she remained pleased with it despite him.

"I don't know," he said.

She grunted. "Go on. You'll have to try harder than that."

"You've looked at too many pictures, you know too much. You are too aware of what you're doing and of the past. That's what's wrong with it."

"Hard words," she commented. "And being too aware of the past seems a strange criticism from a classicist."

"True." He thought, then smiled apologetically. "I don't mean to criticize. I meant it as a compliment."

"Really? Heaven help me if you decide to be rude."

"I am never rude. What I mean is that you really are very good. And that is not simply because I adore you without reserve. Although it helps. But look: You have Matisse and Cézanne and a bit of Puvis there. A touch of Robert, perhaps, as well. I look at that picture and I can see what you've built it out of. That's what's wrong."

"Derivative and second-rate, you mean?" She was not in the slightest bit offended; it was one of her best qualities and one Julien could never share.

"Not at all. I mean you are being too careful. That's what I mean. This is a perfectly good picture. And if I didn't know you I would be impressed and charmed. But I do know you."

He thought some more, wondering whether he dared say precisely what he felt, for he knew he could never explain exactly why the idea came to him. "It's the painting of a dutiful daughter," he said eventually, looking at her cautiously to see her reaction. "You want to please. You are always aware of what the person looking at this picture will think of it. Because of that you've missed something important. Does that make sense?"

She thought, then nodded. "All right," she said grudgingly and with just a touch of despair in her voice. "You win."

Julien grunted. "Have another go, then. I shall come back and come back until you figure it out."

"And you'll know?"

"You'll know. I will merely get the benefit of it."

"What if I get it wrong?"

He shook his head and grinned. "Believe me, I know what I'm talking about."

THE CONVERSATION summed up much of his appeal for her. Alone of anybody she had ever met he allowed her room to breathe. He wanted nothing from her. Merely knowing that she lived was sufficient for him. He did not wish to live with her, marry her, did not become jealous or fretful for her. He did not watch her or live through her. Did not swamp her with attentions or drown her with excess adoration. Above all, he did not make things easy for her. All negatives, all things she was unused to. He admired what she did, but was brutally honest when asked his opinion. Where he found the resource for this neither she nor he knew; it was a far cry from the self-confident pretense he learned with many of the women he pursued over the years, or the detachment he formed for the world in general.

Both Bernard and Marcel—neither of them particularly acute in such matters—realized that Julien and Julia were deeply in love with each other. Julien was afraid that if they became lovers now, Julia would turn into another woman, one to be consumed and discarded, and so he held back for fear that showing his love would extinguish it. Julia, in contrast, was not yet sure enough of herself for the battle—with her work and her father—that would result. She knew that her irresolution would seem pathetic and childish to many, that a stronger person would dispatch the looming, overbearing presence of her father and demand the right to a life untrammeled by his needs. He was an impossible man, and placed her in an impossible position. For most of her life she had had no one but him, and she was afraid not so much of his hurt if she fell in love, but of what it would say about her. Her life had been utterly selfish, she knew; she had allowed no one in to disrupt it; was she now to hurt so desperately the one person who had always meant something to her? She had to put someone's interests and needs above her own in order to remain human; and the only person she could do this for was her father.

So she was contradictory and difficult, with him and with Julien, hard to understand; often irritable, veering between affection and criticism, drawing close then pulling away again. She knew all the while that she did indeed love Julien, needed his existence in a way that she had never known with anyone else. When she was depressed or frustrated with her work, she thought of him, constantly concerned herself with where he was and what he was doing, felt incomplete without him, and anxious when he was there lest a mistake ruin everything. If he had only forced the issue that day in Palestine before she could consider all the complications, then, she sometimes told herself, all would have been well. She even felt slightly insulted by his rejection, but knew that such disdain was unjust. Julien could not make it so easy for her; he wanted her soul as well, and must bide his time until she was ready to give it.

So, instead of each other's physical company, they had their letters, which crossed the country in a constant flow, month after month and year after year, continuing even when Julia went to Vietnam, then on to Japan for nearly two years to seek inspiration and escape there, or when Julien returned to Rome, something he did as often as possible. For much of the 1930s they were not even in the same country, but the letters continued nonetheless, creating something far stronger than mere physical closeness could ever approach. In between the letters, both burrowed down into their work to hide from the world, which was becoming ever more terrifying.

That there was going to be another war they both knew, as did everyone else; sometimes Julien was even sure there was going to be a civil war, with the streets of France again running with blood and echoing with screams of faction. Almost any little incident, it seemed, could set off a disaster, either in France or in Europe as a whole, but no one knew when it would actually happen. The threat contaminated everything they did and felt long before it actually erupted. Men like Marcel and Bernard took their sides and seemed to make it the more likely, sowing rancor and blame in advance for a defeat that, strangely, everyone knew would come this time. Even those like Marcel, who once lectured Julien on the extraordinary military achievement of France's defenses, could talk in the next breath of what would happen when the war was over and the Germans had established their grip on the whole of Europe. And as the day grew ever nearer, and the continent sleepwalked its way into a conflict that threatened cataclysm on a scale no one could imagine, his opinions became the more extreme and the more vengeful.

Julien once pointed out the contradiction to him. "If the defenses are so good, why do you talk of defeat?"

"All the defenses in the world will be useless if we are led by fools. We've built ourselves a wall, but we are crumbling behind it. Our politicians are corrupt, money-grubbing rabble-rousers, obeying the orders of the moneylenders and the masons. Will you fight for them? Give your blood so they can continue to stuff their pockets with money? Sweep them away; then we can start again. Build something new."

"You want to be beaten?" Julien asked.

"Of course not."

And Julien returned to his books, turning in these years to the subject that had been in the back of his mind for so long: to describe the resilience of civilization, its enormous strength, the way that even when near death it could revive and regrow, bringing its benefits to mankind once more. It was a lyrical conception, his own defiance of the blackness of Marcel, or the gleeful cynicism of Bernard, who derived much humor in his newspaper articles from describing the confusion, incompetence, and corruption of politicians at work. He imagined civilization as something lying outside the individual, a spirit that only required a little care to survive. It consoled him; as it had sprung up again after the Romans, and again after the Black Death, so it would now, after the darkness to come. His great book on the history of Neoplatonism thus became his plaintive song in the falling light, and gradually he worked in more and more commentary on Manlius's manuscript to illustrate the points he was making. He, too, expected defeat.

OLIVIER AND PISANO had little in common during their daily life save their joint adherence to the camp of Cardinal Ceccani, but nothing to divide them either. No faction, heresy, or dispute over politics ever clouded their amity; they were both too lowly to have any interest in such matters, which were solely the concern of the great and the powerful. Their job was to live, although that was not necessarily such an easy thing to accomplish. They shared their food, their hopes, their worries, and sometimes their shoes and clothes and money. Gave each other advice, drank together, and knew that, sooner or later, they would part forever. It was Pisano's ambition to go back to Siena one day, for he daily suffered the pangs of homesickness and saw himself in exile. Olivier knew perfectly well that he would probably never go there. Nor would their friendship continue by letter, for while Pisano could write, he did not like to do so.

Indeed, had the commission for the chapel of Saint Sophia not suddenly descended on him, Pisano might have gone already, as until that moment all favor and income had been denied him. He had been in Avignon for two years or more, waiting his chance. He had worked as a journeyman for that fat, smug dauber Matteo Giovanetti when, by rights, the old-fashioned, harebrained scribbler should have worked for him. Pisano was young, but not without confidence, and held within him the conviction that he could do something the world had never seen before, if only he was given the chance.

He had received the best possible training, under Pietro Lorenzetti himself; the only man in the world for whom he had total reverence and unquestioning devotion. He had seen the quiet, great man racked with the agonies of doubt and indecision about what he did, and seen that uncertainty convert like magic into calm assurance the moment he picked up his brush. For what he was doing was remarkable, unique. He did not try to paint nature; he made his paintings part of nature, as real as the birds and the trees in the countryside all around. The endless possibilities made a head as young as Pisano's giddy with delight, and after he made

his way to Avignon—to seek his fortune, as he had heard of all the building works going on there—he sometimes physically ached with desperation and yearning to show what he could do.

For Pisano had an idea, an idea of such boldness that he scarcely dared
mention it. It first came upon him one day when he had brought his master a drink of water from the fountain after a hot morning's work at Assisi.
He'd found him sitting idly on the ground in the shade, with a young boy
before him. They were talking, as Pietro delighted in the company of the
young, never turned away any child who came to see him work, spent
long hours talking to them, and always gave them a little present when, at
last, it was time for them to go.

The two were talking as he approached, the child laughing and telling
the master a story, unaware of his greatness and importance—as, indeed,
was most of the world still, despite the prodigies he had created. Pietro
was listening and encouraging him to continue, but kept on glancing
down at a piece of parchment that he was drawing on with a lump of
charcoal. As Pisano put down the water, Pietro laid the parchment aside
and told the boy it was now time he went home to his mother. Pisano held
out a hand to help the aging, arthritic man up—his hands the only part of
him still unaffected, it seemed, either by the grace of God or the sheer determination of willpower—and also picked up the sheets of paper as they
were about to blow away on the wind.

He had drawn a portrait of the boy in the act of tossing his head as he
had done when talking and laughing. It was so perfect in the way it captured the child's spirit that Pisano was astonished and cried out in delight.

"Something I learned to do when I was young," the older man said.
"Before I was trained and forced to forget it all again. I began with sheep,
then shepherds."

"It is wonderful."

"Ah, but it is but a boy. Our job is to paint the divine."

Pisano must have looked confused, not knowing what to say. Pietro
clapped him affectionately on the shoulder and laughed gently. "Come
with me."

He led the way back into the church, then slowly and ponderously climbed the scaffolding that covered the choir of the building, working his way up then across with an agility that left him the moment the day's work was done. Eventually he reached a scene he had painted himself a few weeks previously; gestured at it, then stood back.

It was of the Last Supper and, though the face of the Jesus conformed absolutely to what it must be, he had given the figure a similar gesture, that toss of the head, the movement of the shoulders, the slight upward glance and flash of the eye. Half in jest, Pietro held his finger to his lips.

"Our little secret," he said. "But observe it well. Something of God is all around us, perhaps. All we need is eyes to see and a hand to capture."

Lorenzetti dared no more, however; or perhaps that was the wrong word, for in his craft he was as absolute in his determination as any pope or emperor. He saw no need to. Still his figures for the most part needed to have something of the divine about them, needed to be recognizable as well. He would give them a gesture, a movement, an air that he had seen in the street, but could not go further. His art and his pride would not allow it. Knowingly or not, he turned from that last step, fearing it might lead to blasphemy, that he might be drawn into the conceit of making God, rather than humbly representing Him. Give the Blessed Virgin the face of an anxious mother? Have Saint Peter resemble a fisherman? Make Our Lord look like a carpenter? Thus formulated, Pisano had his answer, and the secret he took with him when he left for Avignon. He would take that extra step, or try to.

His first essay came when he was given the opportunity to do a whole painting himself in the entrance to the Cathedral of Our Lady in Avignon. Close by the doorway, but in a dark corner, a space of wall that needed filling but that no one would ever see unless they peered hard in the gloom, the contrast with the light flooding in through the door making it all but invisible. Too insignificant a spot for Matteo himself to bother with, so he farmed it out. And there Pisano painted a Virgin high up on the wall, being approached by a prince of the church, an appropriate scene for what was fast becoming the main cathedral of all Christendom. The Virgin was conventional, seated, with the child on her left arm; here he dared little. But with the figure before her he allowed himself to experiment. He painted this as a real man, standing rather than kneeling, giving an impression of power, almost of equality before the divine. And he gave it the face of Cardinal Ceccani, conveying through it the strange mixture of deference and command that that man had so perfected.

He was not pleased with it; he could do better, he knew. And Matteo was outraged and wanted it erased. It was he who sent word through the corridors of what Pisano had done, hoping to cause a scandal; the result had been that Ceccani himself, the next time he came to the cathedral, stopped and looked, peering up in the candlelight to see his own features flickering on the wall.

He stared, his eyes narrowed, he grunted. Then he turned to a priest standing nearby. A few weeks later, Pisano was summoned to the cardinal's palace and given the commission to paint the chapel of Saint Sophia. So cryptic was his benefactor that Pisano could not be sure whether it was a reward or a punishment. Nonetheless, once the dismay and disappointment faded he realized the chapel would give him his chance. There were no conventionally understood notions of what any of the characters in the tales looked like, apart from the Magdalen; the chapel was isolated and unlikely to attract too much attention; he could experiment at will and see what resulted.

But whom could he choose? How could he decide? This practical detail had gnawed at him. He could not choose anyone; he had to find someone who, in some way, resembled what the saint must have looked like, which meant he had to know in his mind what that was. Hence his reference to prayer, for he was convinced that God would show him the way.

He had the face of the Magdalen easily, although he did not know where it came from; he sat down one morning and this handsome, tranquil face drew itself on the piece of slate he habitually used for idle jottings. It was not what he expected, certainly, but the pious painter was not one to query the will of Heaven; he had prayed and had then settled down to draw: this had been given him. A pretty face, young and charming even after the necessary artistic improvements had been made to make it conform, just a little, to what such a woman must have looked like. He knew well enough that it was probably the face of someone he had seen, someone glimpsed in the street, for he had an extraordinary memory for such things. But he had not the slightest idea who it was, or when he had seen her. His mind, or God, had joined the face with the subject; that was all he needed to know.

For the blind man, he decided he would allow himself a small jest— nothing impious—but painters were habitually permitted a little leeway in the matter of sinners. He used Olivier for this figure, a piece of whimsicality that made him smile throughout the business of transferring his sketches onto the chapel wall. For Olivier was, surely, such a person, forever seeking wisdom so he could see more clearly. But even he, this man he saw daily when he was in Avignon, he could not get right. He could draw his face, of course, that was easy. But he could not get the pair of them, the saint and the blind man, Olivier and this unknown other, to look anything other than two figures placed side by side, and he wanted more than that.

For Saint Sophia herself would not come to him, and as she was to occupy all the first panel and was to be a major figure in all the others as well, the lack reduced him to despair. He could, of course, have used a conventional image, but knew he must not; he had set out to do something new, and refused to retreat into the ordinary merely because a difficulty came to interrupt his progress.

So Pisano went to the chapel, then came back to Avignon having accomplished little, and there he moaned to Olivier and all the friends who were prepared to listen, prayed incessantly but to no avail. Even renewed visits produced only the barest outline of a face, until one day he was walking through the streets and saw the Blessed Saint Sophia, shopping at a market stall. He noticed nothing at first, and only became aware of her when Olivier turned pale and gasped in surprise.

Pisano noticed and followed his eyes, saw what he saw, and knew that his search was over. That was what the saint would look like, and that was how a blind man given back his sight would react, not with joy, not with a happy smile, but with something close to anguish, with a piercing cry and an expression of something approaching terror.

"Yes," he cried. "That's it. Perfect."

Pisano began to dance up and down in his excitement, making so much noise that passersby turned to look, and the woman herself glanced around in fright and then hurried away.

"Hush, my friend," Olivier said urgently. "Calm yourself."

"Why should I be calm? You're not. I've never seen anyone turn so sickly in my life. Who is she? Are you in love with her? You must be. Is this the woman you've been putting in all that doggerel you produce?"

"Be quiet," Olivier snapped, so violently that Pisano for once ceased his otherwise endless babble. "I do not know who she is. But I am going to find out. Stay here. Don't move, and above all, don't talk."

He pushed his friend away and told him to wait quietly at the corner of the street, then walked up to the seller of herbs she had bought from.

"Who was that woman you were talking to?" he asked.

The woman chuckled at his attempt at innocence. "The fat one?" she asked.

"No."

"The old one with the warts? I have lots of customers."

"No."

"It couldn't possibly be the beautiful one in the old cloak."

He grinned.

"The one wearing the yellow star," she added with a smirk as she saw Olivier's face freeze.

"Fallen in love with a Jew, have we, dearie?" she said with a cackle.

Olivier looked shocked, and stared at the grinning woman. "No," he said hesitantly. "It could not have been her." And he retreated before her jeering, contemptuous look.

JULIEN NEVER admitted to himself that Gustave Bloch had done him the greatest service in packing him off back south, that he came alive again as the memory of the northern fog was replaced by the southern early morning mist, burning off as the sun rose, fresh and clear each morning. Despite his profession, despite the fact that he had to spend most of his life indoors, in archives, libraries, or classrooms, Julien was an outdoors creature. This was where he read best, thought best, and worked best, given the chance. As he ate breakfast each morning, the housekeeper bringing him his fresh bread and jam and coffee, or sat on his broad balcony in the soft warmth of the evening looking down at the people below, or when simply walking in Avignon or Montpellier, past the soft, crumbling stone of the buildings, and the ivy and plants that grew along the walls so luxuriantly in the heat, he knew he was content. Still more so when it became too hot or oppressive and he packed a few things and left, taking the train that then still operated to Vaison, and walking the last ten kilometers to his mother's old house outside Roaix, where he would stay a few days, or weeks or months, reading, talking to old friends he had known all his life, even occasionally helping pick the grapes as he had done as a child. And when he went back to Paris so he could spend necessary time in the libraries, or commune with colleagues, he noticed how his heart shrank, just a little, as the train chuffed north, and how it had shriveled into an inhumane lump by the time he stepped onto the platform at the Gare de Lyon.

He kept tabs on his dinner party friends, though their differing trajectories meant that he saw them only infrequently. The occasional letter, a meeting every year or so, sometimes a holiday skiing with Bernard. He went to Marcel's wedding—a staunchly Catholic girl from a respectable family of lawyers, just right for him—and again a year later to become acting godfather to their newborn daughter. The world outside the library detained him only a little; the rash of strikes that paralyzed the country in 1936, the riots in Paris he read about; the way the streets became dirtier, voices more harsh and raucous, tempers shorter. He noticed, but his only reaction was to find his work the more comfortable. He was sheltered from the storms, and felt they could never touch him.

Only Marcel, solid and dutiful, had anything that could be called a career in this period. His grandfather had been a prosperous corn merchant, his father an ever poorer miller, whose love of drink exceeded his devotion to duty. Of the three friends, only he had known poverty, and from the age of fourteen, when he had found his father covered in his own vomit with his neck broken at the foot of the stairs, he became determined never to make its acquaintance again. His father had debts, and his creditors, who had long indulged him, were harsh when he died. Marcel came away from the experience with a fear of insecurity and a hatred of those who lend money. Big business, banks, financiers, men like Claude Bronsen, were his natural enemies, who exploited the humble and honest who could not defend themselves. For him the civil service was the perfect home— warm, comforting, and secure. His achievement in rising within it was an immense one, too easily discounted by the likes of Bernard, whose own father—a landowner and *rentier* whose wealth had begun to form with Napoleon—had protected him from too much reality until the economic hammer blows of the twenties and thirties turned his fortune also to dust.

Bernard indeed forever made fun of Marcel's sense of duty, his belief in the goodness of governance, the dogged, dull way in which he made his way in the world. The aspiring civil servant was sent hither and thither as opportunity, carefully cultivated contacts, and friendships brought promotions that took him, inch by inch, up the ladder to the point where he even began to be allowed to make decisions. He became a sous-préfet in Finistère, enduring purgatories of weather and food to learn the arcane craft of administration; attached himself to a rising politician and went to Paris with him when his patron won his ministry; was all but unemployed for a year when the Popular Front came to power. His patron worked tirelessly to bring the government down, and was reputed to have strong contacts with those bands who took to the streets to demonstrate against bolshevism, radicalism, and Jews. Marcel took little active interest in any of this: his religion had become administration, paralleling and completing his Catholicism; the belief that, whatever the law, the country had to be carefully and firmly governed.

Indeed, so discreetly did he manage himself that in 1939 he won a better position in a department on the Loire. It was a deserved post, for he was able and diligent and experienced. But by then he had seen how politicians worked at too close quarters, and the sight had bred not a safe cynicism but a holy and much more dangerous disgust that reinforced his belief in the bureaucracy, the sole institution that could save the country from the rabble on the one hand and the politicians on the other.

Bernard, in contrast, did not have to see and learn in order to become disenchanted; Julien thought he had been born so. He was an only child, yet absorbed nothing of the father's seriousness of purpose or the mother's sweetness. He drifted, becoming first a poet interested more in the life than the words, then a casual journalist. When the first war came, he avoided any fighting, delaying his entry into the military until 1918, then opted for training as a pilot. He arrived on the front line in October, and never saw an enemy plane.

In his subsequent writings he was scathing of the generation that had caused the conflict, and even—no one knew exactly how—began to acquire a reputation as a hero, responsible for all sorts of bravery talked about yet never actually detailed. His career by the 1930s was successful, and lucrative, for he applied himself to the business of earning a living when his father's impoverishment required it and even enjoyed the liberation that self-reliance provided. He was engaged in—or at least engaged in commenting upon—all the major political issues of the day, his opinions sought after and valued; in Julien's view the amount that many were prepared to pay him for his views was remarkable. Marcel had a much less polite response and considered that the constant criticism and cynicism that came from people like Bernard was one of the fundamental symptoms of the weakness in the country. Given the slightest opportunity, he would silence them all, so that men of goodwill would be able to build something worthwhile, rather than seeing all their efforts pulled down and destroyed by those who delighted merely in destruction.

It was, perhaps, inevitable that Bernard should support the left-wing Popular Front as much as Marcel detested it; equally inevitable that he should rail against the feebleness of a government that refused to help the republicans of Spain, and that he should go there himself, although as an unofficial observer and informant for politicians rather than as a combatant. He returned once more as a man with a glowing reputation, so that his opinion was still more valued, if not directly sought after, when the war he had predicted finally erupted once more.

PART TWO

CLAUDE BRONSEN was trapped in France when the invasion of May 1940 came because, like most people, he did not believe that disaster could hit so completely. He had taken precautions, as his confidence in the French military was far from total, and had transferred money out of the country in case of necessity, but underestimated how quickly he would need to move. And he could not bring himself to leave; his businesses, swiftly converting to war production, needed him, and he did not trust anyone else to run them properly. He was patriotic, more French than those who had been born in France, though born in Germany himself, and had a strong sense of duty. For years there had been sniping and criticism about people like him—businessmen, financiers, Jews—and to run away at such a time, he felt, would merely have provided more ammunition. Besides, the war came and nothing happened; a sense of calm descended after the initial panic. A perverse faith in the ability of diplomats to fend off catastrophe grew, people began to laugh again and think they had panicked for no reason. Their enemy was more timid than they feared; their own defenses as strong as they had hoped.

When catastrophe did strike, the shock was all the greater, and even a man like Bronsen, normally so canny and prepared, was caught by surprise. He delayed, not able to accept that the defeat was as total as all his

intelligence told him. Besides, Julia was not there, and he would not leave
without her. She was in the south, somewhere in the Camargue in the little house close to the coast she rented every summer she was in France, as
reassured as everyone else. As usual, she had gone off without saying
where she was; she guarded her solitude and privacy jealously on such
occasions. So, rather than leaving himself, taking one of the last cross-
channel ferries before they were cut off, he stayed behind, hoping that she
would turn up, and having nightmare visions about what would happen if
she arrived and found him already gone.

When it was clear that disaster was looming, his reaction was typically
defiant and indeed perverse: He went to the restaurant, the Grand Véfour,
with half a dozen friends whom he managed to round up, and had a valedictory meal. One of these friends was Julien Barneuve.

A grand and fine meal it was, although the service was patchy; the
waiters' minds were distracted. Fortunately, the chef's professionalism
held out and supplies of food had not yet run low. Bronsen made a short
speech at the end; the mood was immensely, almost hysterically, good-
humored.

"All around you, my friends, on this table, you see the best of what two
thousand years of civilization has to offer. We have the finest damask
cloth, its origins in the Middle East, amongst the Semitic nations but actually, I believe, made in Lyon. This rests on a table cut from a mahogany
tree, hewn in the Americas, transported on a ship manned by a crew such
as those who have been carrying the goods of the world for millennia.
The table rests on an Aubusson carpet, worn and dirty perhaps, but in a
design which dates back to the reign of Louis the Fourteenth and which
has been produced by craftsmen in the same factory ever since.

"And all this to support, to bring close to us, the food, which we eat
with our knives and forks in a fashion we learned from the Ottomans,
served, course by course, in a style we used to call the Russian manner.

"Here we approach the foothills of civilization; I chose everything
carefully for this reason. We began, did we not, with foie gras from the
Dordogne, perfectly produced in some farmer's basse-cour, fatted on
cream and corn, taken to the railway station, and transported on a train

line paid for by the British. I pay tribute to them. Whatever one may think of our allies, no one can deny that they make fine railways.

"Then a fish, a fine fish, a glorious fish, a Dover sole. Caught in the Atlantic by sailors who can in a day sweep in enough to feed the five thousand. You see that, despite my own origins, I am not averse to using Christian imagery to make a point. It is brought to us, lightly sautéed and served in a delicate sauce that was first tasted by the great Cardinal Mazarin himself.

"Then we had a tour of France, the very heart of France. Lamb raised on the salt flats of the Vendée, with potatoes in the manner of the Dauphiné, and a great platter of beans grown in a kitchen garden near Paris and cooked, Provençal style, in olive oil from the Lubéron. A simple meal, with little enough finery, for we must say goodbye to the extravagances of our past.

"We have then the cheese, brought to us from all the corners of the country, perfected over the decades to remind us what the greatest civilizations can do when they turn their minds, wholeheartedly, to the arts of peace. Think of those shepherds, herding their goats and sheep and cows; the farmers milking them day after day. Think of their wives and sons and daughters, carrying the pails and separating and curdling and setting. Think of the good women of Normandy preparing this fine Camembert; pay tribute to those people whose cheese went moldy in a cave near Roquefort but had the sense to realize that the delicate blue stains which resulted were a miracle, not a disaster. Then consider the ribbon-like trails of the carters, their routes like veins across the entire country, coming to collect the result on behalf of the merchant, who has already used his elaborate network of contacts, his financial tentacles, to find a price and a buyer. All so that we can eat it, here, as the armies march upon us.

"And all along, gentlemen, we have had the wine. The Gewürztraminer, which we drink here as our own for the last time. I hope the vintners who produced it will forgive me if I say it will not taste as good tomorrow, when we must drink it—or not—as a German wine. The champagne, a product unique in civilized history, dependent on mixing the very best techniques of fermentation with the creation of the glass bottle and cork, and mixing these with a dash of divine inspiration. The Burgundy, that hearty, earthy, refined wine which has a trace of our soul in each bottle, so that when we drink it we become, all unknowing, more French than before.

"And now, as we begin our cigars—brought from Havana, docked at Le Havre, and stocked in a shop which prosperity has allowed to become so specialized it sells nothing but cigars—now, gentlemen, we begin on our cognac.

"Here words fail me. Nothing in the annals of literature can capture the essence of cognac, drunk amongst like-minded friends, after a fine meal. You know this, all of you; I am telling you nothing you do not know. Did Racine ever succeed? Did Hugo capture its essence? Did Voltaire or Diderot pin it down? They did not. They were too aware of their limitations even to try, and who am I, businessman that I am, to presume where men of genius have failed?

"I will merely point out to you that all of this—food, wine, and even cognac—are nothing in comparison to what they permit, which is the easy and unrestrained exercise of friendship manifested through conversation. We have been sitting here now for near three hours in perfect amity, as we have known each other for many years—many decades in a few cases. We have managed, I am glad to say, not to talk of the war, as this last supper—my imagery again, I apologize—is to celebrate civilization, not to mourn its passing. We have talked here of literature, I believe. Some of you I heard discussing the performance of *Tosca* canceled last week, taking consolation in having seen Furtwängler conduct it in Milan three years ago. One person I heard complaining about the way Cézanne is now considered to be a good painter. My friend Julien, who owns a Cézanne, was polite and restrained; it is as well my daughter is not here, as she would have been more forceful in her reply.

"Such refinement, gentlemen! Such delicacy of address, such sophistication of tastes. But not, for me, the essence of civilization. No; instead I heard the goddess brush her soft lips over my ear when I heard my friend over there lean across the table and ask whether it was true that a mutual acquaintance had separated from his wife.

"Gossip? you say. Idle chitchat? Yes, gentlemen. Men in trenches, men starving, men in chains, do not have the leisure to gossip. Gossip is the product of spare time, of surplus and of comfort. Gossip is the creation of civilization, and the product of friendship. For when my friend here made his inquiry he passed on the information necessary to keep the delicate fabric of friendship together. A question about a friend known for decades but hardly seen, an acquaintanceship which would fall into the past unless its shade was sustained by the occasional offering of gossip. And think again: My friend, an Alsatian businessman, was asking a question of a half-Italian writer about the marriage of a Norman lawyer and a Parisian lady of faintly aristocratic origin. All this at a dinner given by myself, born a Jew. What better distillation of civilization is there than that? Gossip binds three people—the gossipers and the subject of their gossip—together. Repeated often enough it binds society together.

"I fear, my friends, we will not have much time to gossip in the future, and we will be too far apart to have anyone to gossip about. So, with this meal, I must declare civilization closed. It was the finest product of the mind of man, too fine, perhaps, to survive long. We must mourn its passing, and turn ourselves into beasts to survive what awaits us. Gentlemen, I bid you rise. The toast is: 'Civilization.'"

Three hours later, Claude Bronsen got into his car—well stocked with petrol, cans on the backseat, for he had prepared as well as possible for emergencies—and struggled south down roads already choked with refugees. He had arranged in advance to meet Julia in Marseille, had told her to go there if something dreadful should happen. It never occurred to him that she could be safe without him, nor did it ever occur to him that he could be content without her nearby. Six weeks later, in Marseille, he was detained by the French police as an alien Jew and sent to the internment camp at Les Milles. Three months after that, in the middle of a cold winter, he died of pneumonia brought on by malnutrition. He was buried the next morning, in an unmarked grave.

JULIEN WAS TOUCHED and rather surprised by the valedictory; he had not expected a man like Bronsen to be capable of such a speech; the times, it seemed, wrought the strangest effects. He was invited to the meal because he had been summoned to Paris to examine a thesis, and had taken the opportunity to see if Julia was at her apartment. When he got no answer there, he visited Claude Bronsen's house in Neuilly-sur-Seine and found him packing furiously and, for the first time, uncertain about what to do. Julien counseled him to leave for England while he could; he would find Julia and ensure she followed.

"If she is in the south, then she is not in immediate danger. Your position is more perilous, I think. If you stay she will worry about you and not look after herself properly. So go. Head for Normandy and you might get to a port that is still open."

But he would not. He would not have Julia beholden to anyone but himself. It was his greatest weakness, a trait that came close to erasing all the good he had done as her father. Even in such circumstances he would not let go, would not allow anyone else to protect her; he did not want her depending on Julien, of all people.

"No. It is better that we're together. I'll find her, and we'll go to Marseille. I've told her this already. I have a hotel booked, have contacts at a shipping company. All we need is a few visas. She's probably waiting for me there already." Julien renewed the offer, then gave way and accepted the invitation to lunch instead.

The very mundaneness of the task that had brought him north, the fact that it could go on at such a time, in itself testified to the confidence that was felt in the French military up until the last moment. He arrived two days before the German assault to listen to a defense of a work on the late antique city—a revision of Fustel's work, with little originality but showing promise—as the tanks began to enter the Ardennes forest, thought impassable and left virtually undefended. By the time the candidate had been congratulated, the outflanking of the French forces, defending their country from an army that was not there, was all but complete. In an afternoon, between the time Julien donned his robes to the time he shook the candidate's hand, the war was effectively lost—although full realization of this would take a few more weeks. Even the German commanders were worried, unable to believe that some trap was not waiting for them, certain that the foolhardy valor that had stopped them in their tracks the last time would sooner or later inspire resistance.

When the full enormity of the debacle began to hit home, Julien did not submit to blind panic as so many others were doing, but did earnestly desire to get back to the south as quickly as possible. This was a common reaction that summer; many people fled the oncoming armies but very soon the overwhelming desire was to go home. Julien thought initially he could simply take a train, then realized this was a foolish idea; trains belonged to civilization, and that had, at least temporarily, stopped. He did not have a car, and even if he had, there was no petrol. Ultimately he escaped and managed to flee south because of Bernard. Nothing worked anymore except family and connections; it was an indicator of what was to come. Julien went to see him at the newspaper he was then working for, partly to get the latest news, but mainly because friendship at that time became so much more important. They embraced with a warmth neither had felt for the other since they played in the main square of Vaison as children. Both were relieved to feel something fixed and secure. Old friendship substituted for nationality, place, and position; it was all there was left.

Bernard, as usual, was well informed, a man who seemed as though he could understand the inexplicable. A train was being put together in a marshaling yard in the south of Paris to take junior members of the government and civil servants to Tours, he said. There was talk of a new defensive line on the Loire. And also talk of an armistice.

"Why are they going?"

It was strange; the building seemed nearly deserted. In the middle of the greatest crisis that the country had ever faced, the newspaper had all but closed down; once before, Julien had visited him here, shortly before the war broke out, and the scurry of activity, the noise of work, was intense and exhilarating. Now there was silence as though events were too stupendous for a mere newspaper to report and explain.

"If they stay they'll be captured in days. It's all over here. The only choice is to retreat and start again. The Germans are not prepared for a massive advance; it wasn't part of their plans. Their lines of communication will be too stretched. They'll have to pause to regroup, and then we can counterattack."

He stopped, then looked at Julien, a curious half-smile on his face.

"But we won't," Bernard said softly. "The generals and the politicians have already given in. They had before it even began. They're going to a place where they can surrender. They will call it an armistice. More peace with honor. How much honor do these people have? It seems they have an inexhaustible supply."

"And what are you going to do?"

"I don't know. I thought of going to Brittany. Rumor has it that the English may try to hold it, although I can't imagine they will do so for long. On the other hand, the government is going south. Perhaps I should go, too." He laughed. "Extraordinary, isn't it? Four days ago, we were convinced we could withstand anything the Germans threw at us. All the talk was of attack, the offensive. Now look. We don't even know who is in charge of the government or what it plans to do. So we must follow our instincts, and we must do something, even if it is only with a gesture," he continued, thinking aloud and quite oblivious to Julien's presence. "I will go to Brittany, I think. I must be on the Germans' list of undesirables, so I can't stay here." As ever, vanity had its place in determining his understanding of the world.

He turned to Julien. "Come with me?" he said. "You'll get no thanks from anyone for it, not from the government or from the English, I suspect. But it will be a lark. You and me together against the world, just like when we broke the window of the church."

"What good would a forty-year-old classicist be to anyone?" Julien asked.

"What good will a thirty-eight-year-old windbag journalist be?" came the reply. Bernard was, in fact, the same age as Julien, and both knew it.

Julien shook his head. "You like gestures too much," he said. "Besides,

I've fought my war. I can't do it again. It accomplished nothing last time, and won't this time either."

"A pity more Germans are not of your opinion. And that fewer French generals are. But I can't blame you. You are right, after all. Go home then. At least no one will bother you—assuming you get there."

Bernard turned and took Julien's hand. "Go to the Ministry of the Interior this afternoon; I'll talk to contacts and make sure there is some suitable piece of paper to get you onto the convoy. But after that you'll be on your own."

Julien nodded, and stood watching as his friend strode off down the corridor to the newsroom, suddenly purposeful where he felt no purpose whatsoever except for the need to get home. There was something in his friend's step, a bounce almost, that hinted that Bernard was actually enjoying all of this, that he sensed an opportunity. More than anything else that day, that made Julien uneasy.

 THE OUTCOME of the chance meeting was laid out in miniature thirty years previously, during the summer of 1911, when a group of children were playing in the square of Vaison. High up, in the medieval hill town to which the townspeople had retreated long before Olivier's day, and where they stayed until half a century before Julien's birth, when they began to move back down to the plain that once had held the bustling city of antiquity.

Bernard, the youngest by a few months, is the most exuberant, jumping off walls recklessly, laughing loudly. Every now and then, a head appears in the window of one of the houses, and a voice—old or young, male or female, angry or amused—tells them to keep the noise down. They try, for a few minutes, until Bernard finds something else to laugh about.

Marcel, the eldest by a year, uncertain whether he is too old to be with such young children, stands aside, then is drawn into the play. They throw stones at the splashing water fountain, just below the window of the church. Their faces reflect their characters. Bernard tosses the pebbles with abandon, joyfully seeing if he can lob his missile into the water trough, but not caring whether he succeeds or not. His pleasure is in the movement of his arm, and in seeing the stone curl through the air. He tries different ways of throwing—fast, parallel to the ground. Slowly and elegantly, curving upward in a great parabola. Standing with his back to the target and closing his eyes before throwing it over his shoulder, whooping with as much pleasure when he misses as when he doesn't. He lands his pebble in the water fairly often; he is a natural sportsman.

Julien has no such frivolity, and much less ability. He concentrates hard, trying to overcome nature. He misses, time and again, but keeps on going, methodically working the stone nearer and nearer to the target, until at last he drops one into the trough.

He laughs with pleasure, and Bernard cheers him, dancing around him and clapping.

Marcel is displeased at the attention. He throws his pebble hard, and incautiously. It smashes through a window of the church, scattering slivers of glass and noise across the little square. He runs, leaving Bernard and Julien standing alone. When the priest comes out of his house, Bernard claims ownership of the deed, knowing that if Marcel's father—a brutal man—hears of the event, he will be savagely beaten.

Marcel never thanks him, although he is not ungrateful.

THIS WAS THE event Bernard had referred to, one of those moments of childhood from which the whole of adult life can be projected. Julien, nervous, innocent, but standing fast. The insouciant Bernard, making the grand gesture in the name both of friendship and of self-aggrandizement, his actions extravagant but generous. And Marcel, a little cowardly and frightened, afraid of authority, not wishing to take on the ownership of his deeds, content for others to be punished instead of him. The resister, the collaborator, and the vacillating intellectual. A vignette of later events, whole histories condensed into a small square of a provincial town.

Except that Julien remembered it like that only because Bernard retold the story many years later and brought it back to his mind. Imposed his narrative on what had become the faintest of recollections; created memories by his skill as raconteur. Julien did not query the account and even came to remember the look of panic on Marcel's face, the quirky little smile of bravado as Bernard stepped forward.

But, on a few occasions, he was almost certain he remembered that it was Bernard who had thrown the stone and run away, and Marcel who had been beaten.

DESPITE THE MANY little tasks that Olivier had to perform to guard his place in Cardinal Ceccani's household, and the position within the papal administration that guaranteed him his stipend, he still found a considerable amount of time to indulge in his passion of searching out old knowledge. The understanding with his master on this point was clear. Whenever something of particular importance turned up, Olivier was to obtain it for the cardinal's collection if possible; if this could not be done, then he was to make a copy to be lodged in his library. Over the years, Olivier obtained some forty original manuscripts; most he purchased, either with coin or with the promise of favors or intercession. Four he stole, because they were uncared for, in danger, and because he took a dislike to their supposed guardians. As far as he could tell, he could have absconded with many more; certainly no one ever noticed the thefts.

The Dream of Scipio, Manlius's philosophic testament, was one that he copied himself with diligence, declining to slip the original into his bag simply because the old monk who let him see it was so kind and, in a strange way, so respectful of those manuscripts he had never troubled to read for himself. A short little fellow—old, but with a wiry resilience—he had, it seemed, been put in charge of the library because he was held in some contempt by the others in the monastery. Olivier did not understand why; he was, certainly, a little vague, a bit of a dreamer, absent-

minded, occasionally gruff and ill-humored, but easily placated and responsive to any show of interest. Initially, when Olivier showed up—brought
by the abbot who had read Ceccani's letter of introduction—he had been
indifferent, even hostile, putting innumerable obstacles in the way. The
second day, after Olivier had invested many moments in conversation, he
brought manuscripts himself for Olivier to see. The third day he gave him
a large key and told him to help himself to whatever took his fancy.

And, although many, perhaps most, of the old documents had never
been read, he yet had some pride in his domain; all the shelves were clean
and dusted, the manuscripts neat and well ordered. There was no way of
telling what was there—the only works identified were the ones that were
used. Olivier offered to make a list as he went through, so that all would
know in future what was where, but the suggestion was turned down.
Cardinal Ceccani's servant was welcome to inspect and read whatever he
wished; the monk did not anticipate anyone else being so foolish, and for
his part he had no desire at all to know what he guarded and tended so dili-
gently. He had his task and that was enough; its purpose did not concern
him in the slightest.

Initially Olivier thought the manuscript was another copy of Cicero's
essay that bears the same name. As it was one of the best known classical
works in existence, finding another version was of little excitement. Perhaps it might enable him to correct a mistake or two—for Olivier hazily
saw that the constant comparison of differing sources could lead to the
purification of errors that had crept in in transmission, although he never
proceeded very far along this route—but it would be a labor of duty, not
of love, to copy it down. It was only when he read the first few pages that
he realized that this was something else altogether.

Still, his excitement was limited, for his concern was above all with the
golden age of Rome, the age of Catullus, of Vergil, of Horace and Ovid,
and, above all, of Cicero. Even this period was perceived only dimly, but
everybody knew that it was the most valuable. The dying songs of the Roman world were secondary, interesting only insofar as they cast a light
back still further to the glorious days of Augustus and Athens. This is why
Olivier copied, and why, perched unsteadily on his horse the next day, he

found his mind wandering back to what the manuscript had said. He knew little enough of ancient philosophy, and these words he had been reading were scarcely comprehensible to him.

"A man worthy of God would be a god himself, and can achieve this state through death alone; the man dies when the soul leaves the body, yet the soul dies a sort of death when it leaves its source and falls to earth. Man's striving for virtue is the soul's desire to return whence it came. Until the soul achieves virtue, it must remain below the moon. Pure love is a reminiscence of the beautiful and a striving to return to it. Only through its accomplishment is the soul freed."

In word, clear enough perhaps, but there were many things Olivier found disturbing. A man becoming a god himself; souls dying when they are born; love a reminiscence; all these were turns of the mind he found baffling to the point of being nonsensical. Perhaps indeed they were ravings, but there was a lyricism to the writing and a sureness to the prose that made him hesitate to dismiss the manuscript so readily. He said as much to his cardinal when he handed the work, and seven others, over to him. They were the payment, at last, for his shoes.

"And who wrote this?" the cardinal asked.

They were sitting together in Ceccani's summer study halfway up the great tower, a room dark and dank in winter, but perfectly refreshing in the fierce brilliance of June, a blissful refuge from the overpowering heat of the day. Ceccani had a jug of fresh water on his desk, kept cool by being collected as ice from the hills in winter, brought by cart to his palace, and stored deep underground, far below the cellars, until it was needed. This precious, delicious liquid he poured by himself; he enjoyed his conversations with Olivier and wanted no interruptions to them. Every time his wayward protégé came back from his travels, Ceccani cleared at least an hour or two from his busy schedule and looked forward with the eagerness of a schoolboy to hearing about the young man's adventures and discoveries. It was, indeed, uncertain who had infected whom with the passion for manuscripts, or indeed which of the strange couple most envied the other, for while Olivier saw the cardinal's power and glory, Ceccani saw only Olivier's freedom and exuberant youth.

"It begins, 'Manlius Hippomanes, servant of philosophy, to Lady Wisdom, greetings.' There is also a reference to deeds done in the reign of Majorian, who was, I think, one of the last emperors."

"But not a Christian document?"

"There is not a single reference to Christianity in it. On the other hand, Saint Manlius is still revered and lived in the same period; he is a saint from the town where I was born. It is not a common name; they must be one and the same person. And if that is the case, then Lady Wisdom, Lady Sophia as he calls her, may well have some connection with the Saint Sophia you know well. That is only a guess, of course. And it makes it all the more perplexing."

"Why?"

Olivier thought, trying to explain what were little more than feelings. "It stays in my mind, although I don't know why," he said eventually. "Parts of it I am sure I have heard before somewhere. Others I feel I understand but when I think more carefully, I realize I don't understand them at all. And I do not know how to find out whether it contains sense or nonsense."

"What is it about?"

"Partly it is a commentary on Cicero, hence its name. Partly it is a discourse on love and friendship, and the connections between those and the life of the soul and the exercise of virtue. That much I can understand. But not much more. Then there is the last section, in which the teacher takes this Manlius into the heavens and shows him all eternity. This is the most baffling part. All I know is that anyone who wrote this sort of thing down now might find themselves in grave difficulties. So I don't know who I can talk to about it."

"You will have to go and ask Cardinal de Deaux's Jew," said Ceccani with a smile. "He might know. And he will hardly denounce you. I will ask Brother de Deaux to give you an introduction. He will not deny me the favor, I think, despite the fact that we loathe each other cordially. Knowledge is neutral territory in our warfare."

Olivier was half surprised, half excited by the prospect. He had, of course, heard of the cardinal's Jew, but had never met him; few people had. How he had attached himself to Bertrand de Deaux no one knew, although it was known that even the pope brought him in, on occasion, for some form of advice. When he arrived in Avignon he talked to no one, and those curious who tried to engage him in conversation were met with a quizzical sort of disdain, a polite but utterly distant response that suggested that their good opinion really was not necessary to him in any way. Many, not surprisingly, found this offensive, considering that such a person should be flattered and honored by their willingness to converse with him at all, but their opinions seemed to count for little in his mind.

Olivier had always assumed that this Gersonides was, if not a money changer, then a physician; such being the most notable occupations that Jews followed, and because the law forbidding Christians to use their services was universally ignored. Certainly the curia had need of the former; not to lend money, for its revenues were titanic, but to channel that great river of gold throughout Europe, so that it reached the right people with dispatch. Well-connected Jews were ideal for such purposes and, in return for protection, could be relied on to perform such services honestly and cheaply. Such people, however, were not obvious choices for the elucidation of obscure manuscripts from the evening of Rome.

"Oh, he is not a money man," said Ceccani with a chuckle. "He is as poor as can be, and has no sense in that direction at all. I have consulted him myself on occasion but have long since stopped giving him gold; he only gives it away before he is a dozen paces outside the door. Asceticism and poverty are noble and holy things, but I confess I do find them annoying in a client."

"So? What is he?"

"He is a man of learning, my dear Olivier, and his people value this so much that they give him money merely to make himself more learned. You, no doubt, would appreciate this habit of theirs. He is what they call a rabbi, and what we would call a philosopher, as he seems to exercise no priestly functions at all. He lives in Carpentras and rarely leaves his house. Even the pope almost has to beg him to answer his letters. You can take it as an indication of his worth that His Holiness is willing to do so. I will get you a letter of introduction and you must go and see him. He will talk to you if de Deaux insists. Do not expect to like him, however, for he tries hard to make himself disagreeable and generally succeeds very well."

IT IS HARD to believe that so little is known about one of the greatest philosophers of the Middle Ages that no one is even sure within thirty years when he died, and yet this is the case with Levi ben Gershon, also known as Gersonides and, to those with a cryptic turn of mind, as Ralbag from the Hebrew letters of his name. Officially he died in 1344, as this is the last time his name appears in the archives and in 1352 he is referred to as being already dead. Others, however, dismiss this and point to evidence that suggests he was still alive in 1370. No one, however, has devoted much time to the mystery, as his life is such a blank page that discovering when he died would add little. Apart from the fact that he lived his entire life in Provence, and was known to the curia of Avignon, almost nothing remains of his daily existence.

Instead, there is his work, one of the most extraordinary outpourings of his, or any other, age. Gersonides was a polymath who turned his mind at various stages to astronomy, chemistry, the Talmud, ancient philosophy, medicine, and botany. Only politics, the art of statecraft, did he leave well alone, perhaps a wise decision considering his position. Few people would have thanked him for his thoughts. Instead he turned his particular situation—utterly isolated from the society around him, devoid of any influence but rather vulnerable and subject to any of its whims—into an aspect of the philosophic position that he painstakingly created over so many years. In contrast to his great predecessor Maimonides, he advanced the proposition of the superiority of the contemplative life to the active one, dismissing the notion of an ideal balance between action in this life and preparation for the one that comes after. For one of his most important works was on the existence of the soul, a matter that had also concerned Sophia but which Christian thought rather tended to take for granted as something that needed no demonstration.

He had once—with some considerable reluctance—set out his line of argument to Ceccani, who had struggled to grasp the concepts that the Jew had brought to bear on the problem, and it was because of this conversation that the cardinal, a few years later, dispatched Olivier to see him. It should not be thought that Ceccani had befriended him in any way; both were much too proper for any such connection, and in any case, Gersonides belonged to Cardinal de Deaux. Ceccani would no more have broken the law by breaking bread with Gersonides than Gersonides would have accepted any such invitation. Ceccani, equally, did not hurry to let anyone know of his occasional contact, even though he consulted him on matters such as medicines and astrological forecasts—another area in which the Jew had a more profound knowledge than anyone except, perhaps, a professor in Paris fully in the pay of the king of France and hence somewhat unreliable.

Nor did Ceccani like him much, although he was intrigued by the man's demeanor, a sense of his own worth that was haughty and unflinching. Other Jews he had met—not that there had been many, and even these had always been purely business meetings—had been well mannered, excessively so. Ceccani knew that it was insubstantial, this persistent politeness, a mask to disguise their nervousness at dealing with one as powerful as he, but did nothing to discourage it or set them at greater ease. With the rabbi there was no such uncertainty.

"Why," he said to himself after one of their earlier meetings, "I do believe the man feels sorry for me! He talks to me like a backward pupil." It was a measure of the cardinal's qualities—one which Gersonides also sensed—that he was faintly amused, rather than outraged, by the realization.

As for Gersonides himself, he found the assorted prelates who badgered him a distraction, not quite an irritant but certainly an honor he was quite ready to do without. He did not wish to be consulted by princes of the church, and took no satisfaction from their attentions. It was a service that might, perhaps, do some good one day. He did not wish to turn away anyone with a genuine desire to know, and both cardinals de Deaux and Ceccani—though no philosophers, and too much men of power to cultivate any true passion—perhaps had some spark within them.

So, every time he was summoned, he sighed wearily, put on his cloak,

and made his way to Avignon, a monument to greed and excess he detested. And there he gave answers and opinions as best he could. His reward in 1347, three years after we are told he died but in fact a year that
saw him still in rude good health, was a knock on the door and a visit from
Olivier de Noyen. It was a fateful meeting for reasons even more important than the explication of an obscure text in the tradition of late Neoplatonism. In Olivier, Gersonides felt the flame burning brightly, the same
one that Sophia had felt in Manlius when he, too, had come to her door.
Like her, he could not resist. Unlike her, however, he cursed his ill fortune.

The phrase of Manlius that led Olivier to the rabbi was at least a considered one, and one of the greatest importance. Indeed, it was at the
summation of nearly eight hundred years of thought on the relationship
that must exist between the physical and the metaphysical. "The soul dies
when it falls to earth." More Christian heresies were contained in this
statement than in almost anything else in the entire document. It contradicted the idea that the soul is created *ex nihilo*—at birth, at quickening, or
at conception, a question never precisely answered. It contradicted the
idea that man is born and dies once only; it contradicted the idea that salvation lies through God alone; indeed it suggests that man is responsible
for his own salvation, but through knowledge, not through deeds or faith.
The idea that birth is death and death is life again hardly sat easily with
contemporary Christian doctrine, although it echoed all too readily with
the heresies of the Cathars.

More important, it did not accord at all with the ideas that Olivier had
learned so far from his readings of Cicero and Aristotle, containing a mystical, magical element entirely absent in their works.

In truth, they were ideas all but dead in the West when Manlius put
them on paper, although they survived in ever more feeble form in the
East until the emperor Justinian closed the Academy of Athens and ended
nearly a millennium of teaching that began with Socrates. It was a long
time since anything of the sort had been taught in Gaul, and Manlius and
his circle only came into contact with it when they encountered Sophia,
the intellectual legatee of Alexandria.

It was a duty, not a labor of love, that made her teach, for she could not
but be aware that each newcomer to her door, however curious, knew less

than the one he replaced. The ability to argue diminished; the grasp of basic concepts weakened; and the knowledge that comes from study grew perpetually less. Christianity, which spread over men's minds like a blanket, put faith above reason; increasingly those brought up under its influence scorned knowledge and thought. Even those with a spark given to them by the gods wanted to be told, rather than wanted to think. Getting them to accept that the goal was thought itself, not any conclusion at the end of thought, was hard indeed. They came to her for answers; all they got instead were questions.

But she continued, because every now and then, just often enough, someone like Manlius came to her door and she tasted the joy of guiding someone whose curiosity was boundless, whose desire to approach truth inexhaustible. As Manlius grew into manhood he came to disguise this under the sneering façade of gentlemanly idleness, but it was only ever buried, not extinguished. And she felt an urgency that slowly changed their relationship from teacher and pupil into something more complex and dangerous. For after a while it was not simply that he wanted to learn from her; she also felt the desperate need to teach him, to pass on to him something so that at least it would be preserved awhile longer. For the first and only time in her life she put aside all doubts, and almost willfully refused to see him whole. She knew that Manlius had his weaknesses, knew that the regime of contemplation she offered could subdue but not quell his pride and his desire for renown. She suspected that the Manlius who retired to his estates and the Manlius who emerged to impose himself on the province were in opposition to each other, not two facets of a harmonious soul. But she ignored this, because she needed to.

There were some illusions she could not hold onto; she saw clearly that whatever he took from her would not be philosophy in any pure form. Yet through him, something might survive, and Sophia desperately wanted it to do so. She spent her life in thought, and held that thought was its own end; yet she was still sufficiently of this world to wish that something would outlast her. She scorned the body, rejected marriage, and was past the age of children; the ideas and concepts that she deposited in the mind of Manlius would be her only legacy, her only memorial. Without realizing it, she came to depend on him more than she ever dreamed possible, and this need, which rose from the depths of her soul, often showed itself in a hectoring, lecturing, critical harshness that revealed little but her desire. She loved him because he was all she had; and worried about him for the same reason.

"The soul dies when it falls to earth." It was not a literal belief; nothing she taught was to be held literally; this was one of the most difficult concepts that her poor pupils had to grasp. For Christians had taken from Greece the idea of the *logos,* the word, simplified it, stripped it of its meaning, and then identified it with the God they worshiped. Sophia taught that the divine was not only beyond words but beyond meaning; only the process of thought could give an approximation of it. The phrase was a metaphor, an illustrative myth to show the magnitude of the thought journey the individual had to travel to grasp the essence of the divine and approach God in the mind. After many months' study, much reading from Sophia's library of texts, and detailed discussion, Manlius began to understand, and when he did, the fatuousness of Christianity was borne in on him all the more.

Olivier, however, had no such advantages; the context had vanished, the associated texts were destroyed or buried in monasteries scattered around the Mediterranean. All he had was this one text, without the means of decipherment.

And so, with great trepidation, he knocked on the door of Rabbi Levi ben Gershon. The door was opened by his servant, Rebecca, whom Pisano wanted as his model for Saint Sophia, and whom Olivier had first glimpsed two years previously hurrying along the street in her brown cloak, as the Christian stood on the steps of the church, thinking about love.

HE DID NOT make a good first impression; only the clipped recommendations of cardinals de Deaux and Ceccani persuaded Gersonides to allow the young man to return, for Olivier was so flustered after his unexpected encounter on the doorstep that he could scarcely speak. And being in the presence of the learned Jew made him distinctly uncomfortable. He had never talked to such a person before, only spied them in the street; Gersonides's manner also was intimidating: gruff and ill-humored, rude and excessively critical in his remarks, but only partly managing to disguise a humanity that showed through in flashes of dazzling insight. Olivier was both admiring and repelled and did not know how to react or behave. All he did know was that after the meeting he could remember every word the old man had said, and had in his mind dozens of other questions he needed answered. And knew, also, that only Gersonides could help him find those answers.

Only toward the end of their initial meeting, when he began to talk of the things he had discovered, of the manuscripts he had read, did his speech become animated and his face light up. Even so, the old man remained in a bad mood, for he was feeling his age that day, and was crotchety about being interrupted from his work. Olivier's youth reminded him of how little time he had left to study.

"You talk too much about the language, and not at all of the content," he said with annoyance at one stage. "Is that all you think matters? You think ignoble thoughts become less so if they are phrased beautifully?"

"I assume ugly things cannot be disguised."

"Then you think wrongly. Indeed, you are scarcely thinking at all. I have spent my life in study and have witnessed all too often the words of the devil coming from the mouths of angels. You bring me this manuscript—which I must confess I have never seen before. I am grateful for that. It is, as you would no doubt say, written beautifully. Elegant. Charming. Even witty. But is what he says beautiful? And what do you know of the author? Is he therefore elegant and charming? You suggest only good people can write beautiful things."

"You do not agree?"

Gersonides levered himself up from his chair with a groan, then leaned on the table in front of him as he felt his head spinning. Olivier jumped up to support him. "Sit down, sir, please. I do apologize. I never realized you were ill. I'll go away and come back when you are better."

"Stop fussing over me," said Gersonides more sharply than the young man's consideration deserved. "I cannot stand it. I am an old man. This is what happens when we grow old. It is neither unexpected nor unwelcome. Go and get me that book you see on the shelf over there."

It took some time to pinpoint which one he meant, but eventually Olivier found it and brought it to him. Gersonides flicked through it.

"Aha," he said. "Here we are. At least my memory still serves me. Now, then. Manlius Hippomanes. Your philosopher-bishop. Do you know how he seems to Jews?"

Olivier was not meant to answer, so he kept silent while Gersonides read: "I will spare you the preamble," he began. "The essence of the matter is this. 'Manlius sent a letter to the leader of the Jews in that town and said, "I wish to live in peace with you, but your deceit and stubbornness has been the cause of violence. My patience is thus at an end. If you are prepared to believe what I believe, then become one in my flock. If not, then depart. And if you will do neither, then you must look to yourselves." Most did embrace the truth, although some fled. The rest were killed by the mob, to avenge the stain on their bishop's honor caused by this stubborn refusal.'"

Gersonides looked up. "Remember, young man, when you wax lyrical over his beauteous prose, that this man also killed my people. Not only that, he set an example for others to emulate or surpass. In this lies his sanctity. Do not expect me to admire the elegance of his thought without reservation."

Olivier could hardly say he found it no great shame to have done so, that no one had even suggested that such a deed was to be condemned, but he could not let the matter pass silently. "Caesar was a general who killed far more people, but he is praised for his style."

A grunt. "Caesar writes of battles and of armies, not of virtue and beauty. There is a difference. Not that we have time to talk anymore. Go away and think of this. Think of what sort of virtue this Manlius might have had in mind when he wrote about the need to embody virtue in activity. And consider also that what seems untrammeled virtue to one person may seem total iniquity to another. The task of the philosopher—your task if you so desire—is to see beyond such subluminary deceits and grasp the comprehension of virtue entire." Gersonides waved his hand. "Now, go away. Leave me in peace. And shut the door when you leave."

"Can I come back tomorrow, sir?"
Gersonides peered up at him. "You want to?"
Olivier nodded.
"Very well, then," he said reluctantly. "If you must."

HE WAITED in the street afterward, the main thorough-
fare of the Jewish quarter—neat, tidy, well tended though
far from prosperous, noticeably cleaner than the streets all
around, for fewer people used it, and the women swept outside their
doors nearly every day and washed away the mud and filth. He was conscious of the fact that everyone who passed him—an obvious Christian—
stared. Some suspiciously, some with mere curiosity, all a little warily. He
waited because he had heard Rebecca go out during his discussion with
her master, and what goes out must, he decided, sooner or later come
back in again.

He didn't know what he was doing; he did not want to see her, he told
himself. Now he knew for certain who she was and what she was—a servant, a Jew—he did not want anything to do with her. He was furious with
her, indeed. For near two years now he had held this woman in his imagining, written her poetry, turned her into his muse. Every day in his mind
he laid flowers at her feet, kissed her hand, more than that. And then he
discovers her. And she is a Jew, a servant. He hated her, never wanted to
see her again, of course not. The feelings she had aroused in him disgusted him, the poetry he had written, in praise of a Jewish servant,
would make him mocked by all who learned of it.

Yet he stood waiting, pacing up and down the street as these thoughts
went through his mind. He should not even talk to her. He would treat
her with the utmost disdain, not even notice her next time he went to see
Gersonides. It would be good for him, even a mortification of the soul, to
be confronted with his error. The moment he went back to Avignon, he
would burn all his silly verses, and thank God that he had read them to
only a few.

And still he stood there, looking up and down the street, telling himself he would move on in a minute and go back to his lodging. But a part of him rebelled already. Those lines he had written were good, he knew, even though he could hardly bear to think of them. No matter. They would be destroyed. He would write an epic instead, celebrating noble deeds. The death of Cicero, he thought; that would be a topic, worthy of the times. Not foolish love poetry deserving only scorn and derision.

Then she was there, walking down the street, and his heart stopped and his hands began to tremble. It was a mild evening, but he felt burning hot, then an icy chill crept over him. He would not talk to her; would walk straight past her.

But she would see him, might smile at him. He could not have that. Quickly, he pressed himself against the wall, hoping she would pass by without seeing him, and hoping as well that she would not.

"Sir, are you sick? Are you not well?"

Oh, that voice, so gentle and delicate, reassuring and caressing, so inviting and so soft. Of course she spoke like that; he had had dozens, thousands of conversations with her already and knew her voice better than he knew his own, long before he ever heard it. It had its own music, and he had borrowed it for some of his songs, written down by his hand, in her voice. They could only be read by her, and sometimes, when he read them back to himself late at night, he heard her so sweetly speaking his words.

"Sir? Is something not right?"

Of course it isn't, he wanted to say. I am in love with a Jew. How can anything be right?

He shook his head.

"You must come in. Sit down by the oven. I will give you some food." The concern was real. She reached out and took him by the hand to gain his attention and the touch burned through his skin like flame.

"No," he said, and snatched his hand away, looking at her as though he had seen a devil.

She paused and frowned. "Then I will leave you. If you do not require any assistance."

And she turned, and Olivier's fine resolution crumbled. "Please don't go."

She turned back again, very patiently.

"Who are you?" he said.

She looked puzzled. "My name is Rebecca. I am the rabbi's servant. You know that already."

"Yes, but . . ."

"What?"

"I've seen you before," he said in a rush. "I've seen you twice. Once, two years, three months, and twelve days ago. You were walking past the church of Saint Agricole in Avignon. The second time was five weeks and three days ago, in the market. You bought some herbs."

He said it with such intensity, such seriousness, that she looked slightly frightened, then smiled. "Possibly," she replied.

"Definitely. On the first occasion, you were dressed in an old brown cloak, which you had up over your head. You were not carrying anything, and you seemed in something of a hurry. You were alone. You only slowed to walk around a puddle on the ground. I don't know how it got there, it hadn't been raining at all. You were not wearing a star. The next time, you were wearing a blue cloak, with a patch by the right shoulder. No one talked to you. You bought the herbs and paid for them with coins that you took from a little purse you carried in your right hand."

"You remember a remarkable amount."

"I remember very little, usually. Whole days go by and they are blotted from my memory. I cannot recall anything that I was doing yesterday. For daily events I have a terrible memory. These were not daily events. My life has not been the same since. I have had nights without any sleep, when my head has pounded. I could not concentrate on anything. My friends and my master have criticized me for my rudeness, all because of you."

"I don't see—"

"I never want to see you again," he said, growing angry as he thought of it. "How dare you."

Had she grown angry in response, or been frightened, or turned away saying no more, then all would have been well. Olivier was sure of it. Instead she smiled at him, not mockingly, but with such sympathy and understanding. I wish I could help you, but I cannot, she seemed to be saying. And was there something in her glance that was a response, or a reflection of what he felt? Olivier recoiled from that smile, turned and stumbled, then ran away, oblivious to the strange looks the few other people in the street gave him.

He ran through the town and out through the gates, past the scattered houses and workshops outside and into the open country, then walked steadily and purposefully but without a destination. After an hour or so the effort calmed him, his feet slowed and his breathing returned to normal. He was not free of her; if anything, he had made his situation even worse. But slowly his mood lightened. He did not become happy, but a sort of peace came on him, and his mind began to wander, trying to think of everything and anything except for the way she had smiled at him. He mingled his lesson with Gersonides with the encounter in the street, blending what he had heard with what he had felt, the one turning into a metaphor for the other. "Woman of darkness, wisdom touching the light." The line came to him, and he was pleased with it. The next one followed, then the next; soon the whole poem—short but so tightly packed—was in his mind dancing over his thoughts.

He shivered, though it was not cold. He walked back into Carpetras as quickly as he could, found a quiet spot in his lodgings, and, by the flickering light of a tallow candle, wrote the poem down. Then he slept, better than he had for months.

REBECCA DID NOT sleep well; she lay on the straw pallet beside the cold grate, wrapped in her blanket, her mind turning over what had happened that evening. But what had happened? A deranged, bizarre young man had spoken to her in a way that was hardly understandable, then had run away. That was all. Nothing to be concerned about.

But she was frightened nonetheless. Not of the young man—that would be ridiculous—but because of the reaction he had caused within her. For two years now, she had secluded herself in the rabbi's household. No man had even looked at her or spoken to her. She had felt safe for the first time since she had become an orphan, forced to wander the world looking after herself. She had made herself forget that time; the loneliness of it all had been banished from her mind. Anything outside the cocoon she had built around herself was dangerous, and reminded her of fear and hunger. She knew far too much of the cruelty that lay just beyond Gersonides's hearth, and away from his quiet, unquestioning protection.

For the old man had found her wandering the streets bedraggled and bruised from the evening she had been attacked—by whom she knew not, nor for what reason. She had asked him for money, as the Jews had often been generous to her, and they didn't frighten her. He had looked carefully at her and seen her despair.

"I have no money with me," he said sadly.

She had shrugged. It didn't matter.

"But I believe I have some at home. Walk with me, and I will see if I can find it."

She got up and walked by his side. He said nothing, but did not seem embarrassed by her company, did not want her to walk behind him to guard his reputation. And when they got to his house—this house, the first she had been in since she had left the empty place her parents had occupied—he ladled a bowl of vegetable soup onto a plate for her and made her sit and eat. Then gave her some bread and water. Then some more soup. And some more.

"The woman who looked after me has decided she can stand my habits no longer," he said when she'd finished. "I am too messy for her, and always shouting when she tidies my papers away for me. She could not grasp that what seemed mere chaos to an unlearned eye was in fact carefully arranged and designed. Just like the world, no doubt, seems to men who cannot understand the complexity of God's creation."

She smiled at him. His face was wrinkled and severe, and would have been forbidding had it not been for the vivacity of his eyes, the slightly amused way he had looked on as she had (no doubt) eaten up both his dinner and his breakfast for the following morning.

"So I am a desperate man, you see. Abandoned, and alone in the world. Do you know how that feels? I see you know all too well. Will you help an old man in his hour of distress? That is the question."

"Help you, sir? How?"

"Stay here awhile. Cook me some more soup. Do all those mysterious tasks which women do so easily, and which send me into a panic. My people bring me food, which is kind of them, but they are forever bothering me. They expect to be paid in conversation. You could not only keep body and soul together, but you could defend my sanity from their constant chattering. Be warned though; I am a dreadful man. I shout and grumble almost without ceasing. My habits are considered all but impossible. I sleep little and often talk to myself in the middle of the night. I am, as you see all too well, horribly untidy, and become quite ill-humored if I am disturbed while I am working or thinking. You will no doubt come to hate me cordially."

She had scarcely left his side since, and loved him like mother and father combined. Despite his warning, his ill temper consisted of little more than a tendency to complain about lost papers or a bad back. He had no violence in his soul whatever, only gentleness and immense patience, for to begin with she made many mistakes. But bit by bit, they became indispensable to each other. The dark little house settled down to a reasonable level of organized chaos that satisfied them both; she worked all day— preparing food, cleaning and tidying, chopping wood—and it was not hard work, as the house was scarcely more than one room on top of the other, and the upper room was reserved for his papers. Occasionally, as a special treat, he would let her up there to sweep the floor under his supervision, clucking over her anxiously lest she tip over a pile of papers or disrupt his personal universe of manuscripts. And once a week she would prepare a special meal, get out the candles, and sit quietly with him, and they would talk; wonderful, fascinating talks, for he was a magician with words and could do anything with them. She learned much from him and through careful, discreet questioning, he learned much about her. She knew this, and saw that he did not mind what he knew.

And then Olivier arrived, made his incoherent profession to her in the street, and immediately this life she had built herself began to crumble and shake. He had said little, but she read into his words much that he had not intended. This will not last forever; the old man will die and you will be on the streets again. You are living in a dream, and dreams all end sooner or later. You are young and he is old; do you not want more?

For the first time, she did want more. She did not know what she wanted, knew that it was dangerous and that she should rest content with what she had, but she knew an emptiness deep inside her, which began to ache.

OLIVIER WENT BACK the next day, and the day after; the week's absence from Avignon stretched into a fortnight and then a month. It was only when Gersonides could stand him no more that he was dispatched back to face the wrath of Ceccani and make a groveling apology for, once again, having disappeared without notice. In that time he changed irrevocably. He became a poet, a true poet, rather than a youth penning verses for his amusement or to explore the classical forms of the long-dead heroes he so admired. He went beyond his models and created something new in that month, at the same time that he wrestled with Gersonides's elusive answers and tried to pin down Rebecca's irresistible appeal. He did not know, at the end, which of the two was the more important for him; both complemented the other, for eventually the old man abandoned his caution and reserve and allowed himself to be seduced by Olivier's boundless curiosity and desperate desire to understand.

He was unlucky, he knew it, even cursed. Why, after all, should he have found himself in this predicament? He had fallen in love with an idea of a woman, then had that idea made flesh. Had her voice, her face, and her character been different—had she been any other person in the world— the disease might not have taken hold in such a way. More than this cannot be said; there is no reason to explain why someone like Olivier may love someone less beautiful, less agreeable, less fortunate than those more favored but who left him utterly indifferent. He tried not to speak to Rebecca; she tried to avoid him. It would have been easy to do so had each truly wished it. But on almost every occasion he came, she was there, preparing food or sitting on the step outside the house. And on nearly

every occasion he stopped, and found some reason to talk to her and become engaged in a conversation neither thought they wanted. Both then
went their own ways, determined that it should not be repeated, and then
Olivier spent the rest of the evening seeing her dark hair and hearing her
soft voice, and as she chopped vegetables or swept the floor, she thought
about his awkward, endearing grin, or the way he spoke to her more
gently each time they met.

Gersonides saw it all, and worried for her.

IT TOOK FOUR weeks to get back home, and by the time
the trip was over, Julien was, if not exactly a changed man,
then at least profoundly affected. Like most of his generation,
he had experienced war before, directly and brutally. But he had never experienced defeat, nor tasted the chaotic panic of blind flight. Even at Verdun, order had held, just, and he had maintained the illusion at least that
the outcome depended in some minuscule manner on his own contribution. Such a thought had given him solace as he froze during nighttime
watches, as he shivered with fever in the caverns below the fortress, and as
he had bayoneted the one enemy soldier he had killed with his own hands.
But the memory of his flight home did haunt him; it was far worse, in his
mind, than anything he had experienced twenty years previously. He traveled through a collapse; everywhere he went he could see an entire society, a civilization, even, coming apart. It gave him much to consider as he
traveled—first on the train that inched forward then stopped for hours,
heading for a destination that was supposedly Bordeaux. He abandoned it
at Clermont-Ferrand to let it go west while he began to walk east, uncertain whether the blistering summer heat would be worse than the cold of
winter for such a trip. The train was still immobilized long after he was
out of sight of the station.

What was he flying from? The chaos and panic in Paris were obvious,
the emotions on the faces of those who got on the train, and those
roughly ejected from it, were clear. And yet neither he, nor anyone else,

had even seen a German soldier, nor had a single enemy plane yet flown over Paris. No newsreels reporting the debacle had come in from the front. They were all flying from an idea, nothing more concrete than that, and as they fled, the delicate tissue of society came apart. There was no one to ask for information, as no one knew anything. No one to ask for help, as few could even help themselves. Nowhere to buy food; there was none to be had and no one wanted money anymore. A millionaire was poor compared to a peasant with half a loaf of bread. In the space of a few days, the citizens of one of the most sophisticated nations on earth, which ruled a good part of that earth, which had a history of continuous growth stretching back to Clovis the Frank, had suddenly been propelled into a state of nature, knowing no rules except survival and no law except self-protection.

Men reacted as they always did; some with an extreme of generosity, giving what little they could spare to strangers; others behaved with an equal and opposite extreme of harshness, demanding outrageous things in exchange. Honest men became thieves, honest women prostitutes, criminals became saints, all driven onward by an idea of what they were leaving behind. Home was the only certainty left, and Paris, the great city of immigrants, disgorged all those who realized that they had never belonged there, that it had never given them a sense of place. Hundreds of thousands were on the move, walking down the roads carrying suitcases, abandoning cars that had run out of petrol, scavenging in fields for food.

The train at least allowed Julien to leapfrog over the great wave of people who were not fortunate enough to get such transport; from Clermont onward he was in the vanguard, a pioneer taking the plague of panic and despair with him, communicating it to all he encountered through his ever dirtier, scruffier clothes, the increasingly gaunt expression as he walked twenty miles a day on little food. But he at least found compensation in it all. He saw his France through fresh eyes, and marveled once more at its extraordinary, overwhelming beauty and variety. He tasted, for the first time, what it must have been like for someone like Olivier de Noyen, traveling so slowly and registering every minute change in landscape and vegetation. Being without a map and having to take directions from passersby. Doing without any assurance that there was a bed or a meal to be found at the end of the day. Sleeping under trees in a forest, wrapped up in an old blanket he had found by a stream, picking fruits and mushrooms and making a fire to roast some potatoes he stole from a field. The parching heat of a shadeless road along a valley that he walked along after Issoire, the sudden torrential downpour that made him sit and shiver in a cave a few kilometers before Allegre.

And in the deepest valleys, farthest away from the towns, the less people were interested in the war, and the less they wanted to know. They or their children had been taken last time, many never came back; every village had its monument with the names on it. All Julien saw was relief that it was already over, that more names were not to be added to the roll call. Quick defeat was better than lengthy victory. The Germans would come, drink champagne, then go home again. That's what they did. Perhaps the old woman who told him that was even right. Julien did not know, and after nearly two weeks without any news or any reliable information he found that he didn't even care. The war was to the north, the concern of others. It did not touch those who ploughed their fields and tended their goats. He was more concerned with the way the soles of his shoes were giving way.

He arrived home, at his mother's home, strangely rested. Montpellier had been in chaos; the university closed, every building, it seemed, crammed with refugees, food running short. Avignon was worse. He stayed there for only a day, then packed a bag, wheeled out his bicycle—now the fastest means of transport available—and pedaled slowly to Roaix, feeling safety wrap itself around him the farther he left the big city behind. He had learned much and was fitter than he had ever been, burned dark by the sun, with the walk—near three hundred kilometers, more or less— having triumphed over the effects of years in libraries. He had a beard, which he kept for a week before shaving it off, burned his clothes and bathed, then waited to see what he should do next.

The little house in the country had scarcely changed in the past thirty years; he had not bothered to put in electricity or any of the other conveniences of modern life. Its whole purpose, after all, was to escape from it; now it served its purpose better than any well-equipped house. He had water in the well outside, a good supply of candles for night, an endless store of wood, which he chopped himself, and had spent so many years playing with the farmers' children, now the farmers themselves, that there was never any chance that he would be denied food. There was one comfortable chair, a stout oak table, and all the books he might need. In a cupboard there was an old shotgun, which he oiled carefully and regularly, hiding it when possessing such things became illegal, and cartridges so that he could shoot birds or rabbits. How to skin and gut an animal was something he had learned as a child from the local farmers.

He stayed for nearly five months, moving between bursts of anxiety, during which he would pedal into Vaison and try to telephone Paris, or send off letters to find out what, if anything, he should do, and an indolence that permitted him to shut out the world and live the simple country life. He had enough money, and his needs, he discovered, were minimal; he could pass almost a week at a time without spending any at all. In the countryside he lived as he always did, rising at dawn and going to bed at dusk to conserve his dwindling stock of candles, and managed to behave as if nothing had happened. And he wanted to hold onto that feeling for as long as possible.

Of the outside world he had little, and only sporadic, information. The humiliating armistice filled him with despair, as did the exile of the government to Vichy. The treacherous way the English suddenly attacked and sank the best of the French fleet outraged him, and made him think of England's own imminent, inevitable defeat with greater equanimity. The reestablishment of the government under the firm, reassuring guidance of Marshal Pétain was the only thing that gave him hope, but so far it made little difference to him. He watched from afar, and distinguished little of detail. So he missed most of the vast influx of refugees into the south, was unaware of how slowly they flowed out again like a human tide when a sort of calm returned. He did not hear of the resentments caused by these people, the shortages and the confusion. He saw nothing of the bedraggled, miserable army struggling south then breaking up in hopelessness; heard only a little of the much vaunted new moral order that was to rebuild France, restore its pride in itself, and begin the titanic task of cleaning out the decades of corruption and decay that were responsible for defeat. For France had brought this calamity on itself; that was the feeling, and now France must rise from the pyre of its own making.

Like most people, he was overwhelmed by the magnitude of events, the way the world had fallen to pieces so easily and the obvious difficulties of making sure it did not get even worse. And he consoled himself with reading, and doing little tasks, and by reawakening his long-dormant friendship with Elizabeth, his partner in catechism of near thirty years before. Her presence recalled easier and simpler moments, when all that was to be feared was the wrath of his father, or the disapproval of the priest when they broke out in a fit of giggles in church. She was long since married, but unhappily, to the local blacksmith, a man of almost legendary dullness whose sense of duty just managed to hide a streak of cruelty that, every now and then, would come peeping to the surface. What happened was almost inevitable; Julien certainly should have seen the danger. They began talking in the lane one day as old friends, she came in for a glass of water, and they reached out for each other at the same moment. She stayed for several hours, and returned on many occasions over the next three months. It was a foolishness brought on by the times.

She was not beautiful, not educated, not refined in any way, but had a coarse sensuality that Julien had rarely experienced, and they were drawn to each other because warmth and affection became so priceless in those days. Both of them were starved of it, and both managed briefly to forget everything else in each other's company. But the world called him back to reality, and her dreams of escape vanished as he explained to her that he had to go, leaving her no alternative but to return to her rough, unsympathetic husband.

"But we can still see each other, when you come back here?" she said.

"I think it's better not to," he replied, as gently as he could but with a growing discomfort. "I don't know when I'll be back. It's better if you just forget all about me. It was a dream; a lovely dream, but nothing more than that. Besides, sooner or later your husband will find out, and then everyone around will know about it. What will happen then?"

"Maybe he'll throw me out," she said with a smile. "Maybe I'll have to come and live here."

It was the look of alarm on his face, a slight disgust at the idea that came through the carefully constructed regret and understanding, that did all the damage. Elizabeth's face turned stony, and she stood up from the little table in his kitchen.

"I see," she said.

"Please," he began, but she waved him away.

"Don't say any more. There is no need to. I don't intend to embarrass you, or make your life difficult. As you say, it would be best to forget it ever happened. I'm only sorry I misunderstood."

"So am I," he said, but could make no contact with her. She left a few moments later, and Julien breathed a heartfelt sigh of relief. The next day he packed a little bag and pedaled to Avignon, for all other forms of transport had vanished as if they had never existed

Someone knew where he was; one of his letters had been received somewhere and had been passed on, in that mysterious way of organizations, into other hands, for in late February 1941 a letter was delivered to the post office at Vaison and was held there until he came in one day to see, again, if there was any soap; one of his neighbors had said there was some, and though he found the country life suited his temperament, he did like to wash properly.

He bought his soap, one precious bar of it, then called in at the post office and was given his letter. Marcel wanted him, needed him. The idyll was over; it was time to return to life. He was being asked to work for the new government. As he told Elizabeth when he announced he was going, he did not know when he would be back, or what he was wanted for.

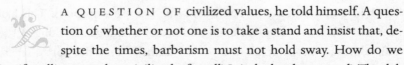 A QUESTION OF civilized values, he told himself. A question of whether or not one is to take a stand and insist that, despite the times, barbarism must not hold sway. How do we justify calling ourselves civilized, after all? Is it the books we read? The delicacy of our tastes? Our place in continuing a line of belief and of common values that stretch back a thousand years and more? All this, indeed,

but what does it mean? How does it show itself? Are you civilized if you read the right books, yet stand by while your neighbors are massacred, your lands laid waste, your cities brought to ruin?

Do we use the barbarians to control barbarism? Can we exploit them so that they preserve civilized values rather than destroy them? Was the old Athenian right, that taking any side is better than taking no side?

THE QUESTION CAME to Manlius's mind as he sat on his horse and looked at the devastation all around. His farm, one of the outlying dependencies to the north of his villa, had been attacked two days before. A band of brigands had come, murdered some of the tenants, and carried off the rest.

So he told himself, for he clung to some hope. But he soon learned it was worse than that, much worse. As he sat and looked, he saw a movement in the copse to the left; he sent off some of his bodyguards to investigate and they swiftly returned, leading a young boy with a rope around his neck. He was about seven, and he was crying in terror.

"Stop that noise," Manlius ordered. "Give him some food if he needs it, if it will shut him up. Then bring him back to me when he is quiet."

He turned away, got off his horse, and continued to walk around the burned-out buildings. Already he was beginning to suspect the truth. The damage was too neat, too orderly. Too little had been destroyed.

The boy was still crying. Manlius became itchy with his impatience to have confirmed what he already knew. He took his whip off the saddle and prepared it.

It took a long time to get even the basics out of the whining, blubbering child. But eventually he confirmed the bishop's suspicions. This had been no raid. His tenants had simply walked out, taking everything of use and value—his property, all of it—and marched off to the north, where softer conditions and better land had been promised them amongst the barbarians. They had had over a day's start and would be hurrying. They'd taken oxen and carts and donkeys and goats, all the supplies and tools he had lavished on them.

The worst of it all was that he had, as always, most earnestly asked their leader at the last tax collection whether they had any complaint or wish. He had professed utter contentment; desired no better master.

He had not said, however, that he desired no master at all.

"This cannot continue," the bishop said to himself. "It cannot go on."

He was about to gallop off, when one of his bodyguards called him. "Sir, the boy . . ."

Manlius looked at him kneeling on the ground, quiet now.

"Cut off his hands and give them to him in a bag. Then let him follow his family. Let him be a burden to them from now on, not a help."

He turned his horse, then hesitated. "No," he said. "We cannot waste anything these days, however justly. Bring him with you and put him to work in the granary. There's more than enough to be done there."

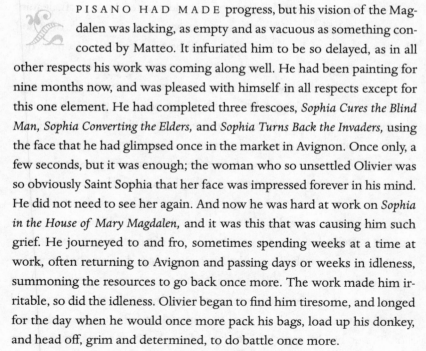

PISANO HAD MADE progress, but his vision of the Magdalen was lacking, as empty and as vacuous as something concocted by Matteo. It infuriated him to be so delayed, as in all other respects his work was coming along well. He had been painting for nine months now, and was pleased with himself in all respects except for this one element. He had completed three frescoes, *Sophia Cures the Blind Man*, *Sophia Converting the Elders*, and *Sophia Turns Back the Invaders*, using the face that he had glimpsed once in the market in Avignon. Once only, a few seconds, but it was enough; the woman who so unsettled Olivier was so obviously Saint Sophia that her face was impressed forever in his mind. He did not need to see her again. And now he was hard at work on *Sophia in the House of Mary Magdalen*, and it was this that was causing him such grief. He journeyed to and fro, sometimes spending weeks at a time at work, often returning to Avignon and passing days or weeks in idleness, summoning the resources to go back once more. The work made him irritable, so did the idleness. Olivier began to find him tiresome, and longed for the day when he would once more pack his bags, load up his donkey, and head off, grim and determined, to do battle once more.

The Magdalen would not come. What he had, he had done from

memory, and a strange forgetfulness came over him as he tried to recall her features. So he gave up once more and returned to Avignon. He was often to be seen wandering the streets. Pausing and making sketches of faces flitting past. Only once did anyone remark on this and draw attention to his strange behavior. It was in the open space near the ramparts, marked down for building but not yet filled up with new houses, the fruit trees still there, the little stalls where merchants sold bread and fruits to women of delicacy who were wont to parade in the evening with their maids and mothers even in winter, for the evenings were not so very cold. Isabelle de Fréjus was there, walking up and down, and there also was Pisano, sitting on the ground, pretending not to look, sketching away to get her face just so, pitched at an angle he had seen once before and which, he knew, would be perfect for the representation of the Magdalen descending from her boat with her entourage. It was not her face that he wanted, merely its expression, but he studied her carefully nonetheless, staring at her in a way that, sooner or later, was bound to attract attention.

By instinct he took the pose of his old master Lorenzetti, leaning against a wall, sheets of precious, expensive paper on a plank of wood, charcoals in his pocket where they could be found quickly if one broke. He did his best to be discreet, but it was impossible to remain there for long without being noticed. Too many young women and their chaperones passed by, sneaking a little look at the paper as they passed, then whispering to their friends. It was an event now; Avignon was a huge city, its streets normally full of entertainments, jugglers and dancers and penitents and musicians, vendors of all sorts of goods, beggars and mendicants, but the imminent threat of the plague had closed down most diversions. The smallest novelty was now seized on and subjected to ceaseless comment, and a young, handsome painter directing his attentions at Isabelle de Fréjus was too much of a curiosity to pass unnoticed.

In due course, Isabelle marched straight over and, with a boldness that often marked her, demanded to see what he was doing, together with an explanation. It was an encounter witnessed by everyone, who gathered around quite openly to hear what they hoped would provide much diversion. Pisano had his speech ready; he had prepared it for use many months before when he began his furtive thefts of other people's faces, but had never before had occasion to use it.

"Dearest lady," he began, "I must beg your pardon for acting in such a way. I am a painter, engaged in a work of the greatest importance, decorating a church with the lives of a saint and of the Magdalen. I wish to depict the Magdalen as she was, famed for her beauty, kindness, and sanctity, and yet have no model in my mind of how to do so. Then one day, a friend whose name I will not—need not—mention, told me of a lady he knew whose loveliness was such that heaven itself could scarcely contain anything of greater merit. I scoffed at him for a fool, and he led me into the street one day when you were passing.

"Once I had seen you, I fell on my knees before him, in the mud though it was, and begged his forgiveness for having doubted his word, rebuking him only for his restraint in his descriptions of you. For I saw in your beauty my Magdalen, and ever since, I have been unable to work. Your face appears in my mind whenever I try, and in my dreams I know that this lady must have had something of your charms.

"And so I have sneaked around like a beggar these last few days, with my paper and charcoal, snatching a little sketch here and a likeness there. It is unforgiveable in me, I know, but a heavenly command cannot be ignored so easily."

A little round of applause greeted these words, limited only by the fact that Pisano's accent was so execrable that some of his phrasing was lost. It didn't matter; he was playing with her, enjoying the attentions of a beautiful woman. It was meaningless; he would have said the same to any pretty girl he was caught sketching; someone whose face was worth sketching deserved such compliments, and would be forgotten the moment the next presented itself for study.

But Isabelle frowned, and tried to disguise her pleasure. "I would have thought, sir, that if my face was so much in your mind then you might have been able to remember what I looked like without following me around like a puppy dog. Or perhaps your mind is so weak it cannot hold an idea for very long?"

Pisano grinned at her. "This friend of mine tells me that the apprehension of true beauty is hard. We may approach it, and feel it, but we are too corrupted to keep it within us for long. This is my great tragedy, for however much I look, and however much I sketch, all I can take with me when I leave your presence is the palest reflection, as inferior to your beauty as man himself is below the beauty of the angels."

An easy reply, for Olivier had once talked to him of his manuscript, and used such an example to try to explain what it meant—or what Gersonides thought it meant. From then on, however, Pisano was on his own and had to do the best he could. He disguised the sudden drop in the quality of his eloquence by deciding it was high time that he was overcome with remorse and shame at his impertinence. This allowed him to give ever shorter replies and pack up his paper.

"May I see this sketch you have done of me?"

He was ready for that, as well. He had worked up a little miniature in colors, a few inches square, and a fine thing; it was oval, and around the bottom he had carefully written her name. It ended up in the *Musée des Beaux Arts* in Lyon, eventually, after passing through many hands before it was acquired at a sale in Paris in 1885. Isabelle gasped as she saw it.

"Keep it, my lady, if you wish. For now I have seen the original close up, I realize how feeble my hand is and cannot bear even to look at it."

Can anyone really resist the flattery of image-taking? Can, in particular, a young girl of scarcely eighteen, conscious of her appeal and disenchanted with her husband, remain cold when given a portrait that—despite Pisano's false modesty—was remarkably good considering the primitive nature of portaiture at the time, complimenting at the same time it remained true to the original? She ran home and put the little picture in a missal, where it remained until long after her death, and every time she prayed she opened it at that page and gazed again.

Was it in any way surprising that, as she prayed and looked and remembered, all at the same time, imagining that this was how she existed in the young Italian's heart, she was certain that at last she had fallen in love?

THE PLAGUE REACHED Avignon the following month, at the beginning of March 1348, when even near the Mediterranean there is little enough to be cheerful about, and when months of winds have already sapped the vitality of all those exposed to them, wearying their bodies and enervating their souls. The most likely direction was from Marseille, a sailor or a priest or a trader on a boat carrying the infection with him, then traveling inland, up the river to present a petition at the curia or hawk his wares around the market or merely return to his family. Had it not been this unknown person, it would certainly have been another the next day or the next week, for no place was immune; everywhere was touched sooner or later.

The records for the city are slim, but it is certain that almost everyone knew that the pestilence was coming. Travelers' tales from the Levant, from Sicily, and from Genoa or Florence had traveled a little bit faster than the plague itself, just fast enough to frighten or alarm, but not fast enough to allow anyone to do anything. And there were many who felt that nothing should be done, in Avignon of all places. Such a visitation was manifestly the will of God, his chastisement to a worldly city, a sinful church, and a corrupt population. Some felt almost a satisfaction at the prospect of punishment, as confirmation of their condemnation; others even prayed for such an event to sweep away the foul stench of worldliness and bring men back to God and their senses. Every cataclysm is welcomed by somebody; there is always someone to rejoice at disaster and see in it the prospect of a new beginning and a better world. Equally, however much an act of God, there is always someone ready to take responsibility for any event or, failing that, to have blame thrust upon them.

As the plague first broke out in the rue des Lices in one of the poorest parts of town—a grim street of leaky hovels that the nearby monastery wished to demolish if it could evict the occupants—and the first victim was an ordinary day laborer, the arrival of the death initially passed largely unnoticed. Not until twenty were already dead did the first priest come to the scene, and it is to his credit that, though his flesh crept and he was stricken with terror, and even though he had to leave for twenty minutes to throw up in the street outside, nonetheless he returned to the bedsides of those within and did his duty. What he saw was so revolting he could not believe he was truly looking at a human being. The body was so covered with eruptions and pustules all its form had been lost, the face had disappeared, leaving only a gaping mouth streaming with pus and blood, that still managed to cry out in agony. The stench of corruption and decay was unlike anything he had ever smelled before, gripping his guts and making him retch. His name was Rufinus, and even though he was a man of no other virtue and, indeed, was generally hated in his parish for his idleness and greed, this one act should be recorded of him. It was a noble deed, and the better for being performed in abject terror rather than in tranquil confidence. For Rufinus conquered fear, and the example he set was not so often emulated in the weeks to come. Moreover, his courage would have been tarnished had it come from confidence in divine mercy, for such magnitude was denied him; within fifteen hours he felt the first hideous pain that announced imminent death to its victim. Twelve hours after that he was dead, having suffered such agonies that his final release was, at last, a true manifestation of mercy.

Those few hours were more than enough to turn Avignon from a thriving mercantile city, full of self-confidence and bustle, of goldsmiths and jewelers, cloth merchants and sellers of food and wine, bankers and lawyers, into a mass of terrified humanity, each individual with no thought but of their own impending end. Twenty people died the first day; sixty the second, one hundred the day after that. At its peak, five hundred a day were dying, more than could be buried, and the rotting corpses piled up and became a source of disease on their own. Within a week, travelers could tell where the corpses were being taken from the thick black cloud of flies hovering overhead, the noise of the buzzing audible long before the smell could be detected. After that, the fires lit to consume the corpses threw up a thick column of smoke and deposited a thin layer of ash over the nearby streets.

The city collapsed; trade stopped, no food came in, the merchants packed their bags, the streets remained unswept and rapidly became filthy.

All those little services that enable huge numbers of people to live crammed together in a small space vanished overnight. Fresh water, bread, all the basics of daily existence became scarce until the pope himself intervened to order men back to their jobs. The rich fled, many priests and cardinals amongst them, but accomplished little except to take the infection farther afield before they, too, died. Others stayed, from lassitude or defiance, and died in their turn. The lucky ones were those who were already outside the city before the plague hit, and who had the good sense to remain there. But it was luck that decided who lived and who died; men were like soldiers ambushed in the night, not knowing who their assailant was, where it came from, how it might be fended off.

Ceccani was one of the few who was not afraid; his iron will and belief in divine favor rather led him to see the onslaught as an opportunity. What he wished to accomplish was perfectly clear in his mind; how to do it was less certain. He wanted to make sure the papacy went back to Rome, and had become the discreet leader of the faction in the curia that held that every day that the pope remained in corrupt, venal, greedy Avignon was an extra offense to God. As long as the papacy was there, it was subject to France, that barbarian nation from the north. The pope was French, as was his predecessor, and so would his successor be, in all probability. The cardinalate dare not even cast a vote without gaining the king of France's approval. Not that this implied disdain for the current incumbent, whose only sin, in Ceccani's eyes, was his country of origin. He admired Clement greatly, considered him a true prince, a man of stature who filled the throne well. Nonetheless, that throne was in the wrong place.

The plague itself was a sign of divine disapproval, a punishment meted out against the whole of mankind for this error. It was also the opportunity to restore the situation, and Ceccani realized this immediately. The theological and the political blended so perfectly it was impossible to tell them apart; there was, in fact, no distinction to him at all. It was the destiny, the right, the obligation of the papacy to reign supreme over all temporal rulers. This could not happen in Avignon, and so the pope must leave. It was God's will, and God had now provided the means to ensure his will was obeyed.

However, Clement VI did not want to leave; he had committed himself to vast building projects—his palace, churches, walls—that underscored in stone and gold an ever more likely permanency. So he would have to be persuaded and, failing that, forced to return. The Comte de Fréjus in his way became part of God's plan.

Necessarily so; for Ceccani was aware that his desires were in a distinct minority in the palace. The influence of France had been exerted for so long that far too many of the cardinals were French; the life was settled, prosperous, and more satisfying than that of Rome, that decrepit, violence-ridden, bug-infested ruin of a city. Such people, led by Cardinal de Deaux, held that the days of Rome were done and, just as the church had once thrown off the empire and emerged the stronger for it, so now it could discard Rome itself. Tradition said the leader of the church must be Bishop of Rome; it did not say he should live there, and as a man possessed of four bishoprics he had never visited, Ceccani might have looked more sympathetically on this argument than, in fact, he did.

For Ceccani, power-hungry and ruthless though he was, had a soul touched by the sublime; it was what led him to patronize Olivier, to collect manuscripts, to accumulate one of the first collections of Roman coins and antiquities. He was fascinated by Rome; he believed—and held that others should so believe as well—that the church in Rome was a greater thing than the church in Avignon. That only in Rome could it play out its allotted role as the true heir of the empire, and re-create that empire in a new form. He aimed high, higher than any man alive, and was prepared to stoop low to achieve his dreams. He would open Aigues-Mortes to the English, strip the king of France of his only Mediterranean port, strike a blow against him that could never be forgiven. And in so doing would set the French against the Countess of Provence, the owner of Avignon. She would cancel the lease the papacy held on the city, and the whole curia would have to leave. Where would it go then? Where could it go, but back to the place it should never have left?

IT IS A MATTER of record that Marcel had a good war. When the lightning strike of the German military hit France, he was a *sous-préfet* west of Burgundy, and took upon himself the task of organizing relief for the tens of thousands of refugees flowing through his *département* like a human river. He instructed the officials he did not need that they should fly, and took over the whole area when his superior disappeared as well.

On the evening of 21 June, four hundred soldiers took up a defensive position by the river Loire, another fifty mined and defended the main bridge into the town. From a hurried visit, he learned that these men—mainly Senegalese—had been instructed to hold the river crossing as long as possible, then blow it up. The captain in charge had not slept for days, and already looked like a man defeated.

"The Germans are about a day behind us. The division needs a couple of days to regroup so it can counterattack. We have to delay them. There are two crossings, and if both are held, the Germans can be stopped."

"They'll shell the town."

The captain shrugged without interest. "Yes," he said. "More than likely."

By the time he got back to his office, a delegation from the town council was waiting for him. The mayor had fled, and they knew nothing of what was going on. Marcel explained, and as he did so he saw the panic spread across their faces.

"They'll destroy the town," one said. "There will be nothing left."

Marcel nodded.

"Is there nothing you can do, sir?" another asked.

He made up his mind. "Leave it in my hands," he said. "Go into the country for a few days. Head south, not north. I will see what I can manage."

He went back to the soldiers. "You are not to stay here," he said. "Your task is hopeless, and all you will accomplish is the destruction of my town. The army is disintegrating. The war is lost."

The captain was not interested. "I follow orders," he said. "If I am told to stay here, here I stay. Win or lose."

Marcel left. Half an hour later, he took a step for which he was roundly congratulated by the whole town later on, although some also considered that it was as near to treason as was possible.

What exactly he did in the next six hours is unknown. He shut himself in his office and saw no one. All that is certain is that at five that evening— a beautiful, soft summer's evening—he went back to the captain and told him the Germans had been in contact and demanded their surrender or withdrawal.

"They say they are already across the river upstream, so your task is pointless anyway. If you withdraw now, you can rejoin your battalion and continue to fight. If you don't you will be surrounded and captured within hours."

The captain heard him out, then hurled the glass he was carrying against the wall in blind fury. "They said they would hold that bridge," he shouted at Marcel. "Come what may, they would hold it. They promised me. At least they promised me that."

He turned away, not wishing the civilian official to see him in his moment of shame and humiliation, but not doubting the truth of what he was told either.

Then he straightened himself up and called his junior officer. "It's all over. The bridge upriver has gone. We've got to get out of here."

The news traveled fast. The soldiers abandoned their positions as they had apparently been abandoned by their comrades. They knew, as soldiers do by instinct, that there would be no more fighting. Many left their weapons, some already were changing out of their uniforms, wanting only to go home. Only the Senegalese troops stayed armed and uniformed. They had nowhere to go.

Only they, also, were pursued by the Germans when they swept into the town four hours later. There was a brief fight. They were all killed.

After the war, when Marcel's career was being examined to see whether he should remain in public office, he said that the initial contact came from a phone call from the German forces, which were under orders to cause as little destruction as possible. During the six hours in his office, he was negotiating terms to save as much as he could from the wreckage of the country.

For this he received his exoneration, and was allowed to continue in the civil service. Long before that he had also received an official vote of thanks from the town council when they returned, and a tearful farewell from the townspeople when he was transferred south three months later.

The fact remains that no note of any phone call or other contact has ever been found in the archives of the German army, nor could any of its officers remember such a thing when questioned after the war. It is also a matter of record that the bridge upstream held out for another two days, until its defenders heard that the troops in Marcel's town had surrendered.

SHORTLY BEFORE the plague arrived, Olivier traveled to the west, into France. He often made such trips, voyaging on behalf of a master who sent him to sort out some quarrel between recalcitrant priests, reorganize the tax gathering, represent his master in a dispute with the secular authorities; all these things he did with care and some success, as his obvious desire to resolve problems rather than merely end them made him a popular and welcome figure.

This time, however, he was to be merely a messenger.

"A little below you, my boy," said Ceccani with a smile. "But I can trust no one else. Do your job well, and you will be rewarded."

"I need no reward, sir."

"This time you will get one, whether you like it or not. Because this time I forbid you absolutely to tarry. Not even if you come across the manuscript of the Republic in Plato's own hand will you delay for so much as a moment. Do you understand?"

Olivier nodded. The cardinal seemed unduly preoccupied, as though he was carrying an enormous weight on his shoulders. He had been like this for some weeks; short-tempered, refusing to respond to questions, drifting off in the middle of conversations to dwell on his thoughts.

Olivier knew nothing of what was going on, of course; even gossip was for once carrying no tales or rumors. But something was worrying the cardinal greatly; of that he was certain.

"I will do exactly as you say, My Lord," he said gently. "To whom am I to deliver this letter?"

"You will take this to the Bishop of Winchester, who you will find in Bordeaux. You will bring me the reply as swiftly as possible."

Olivier was not that surprised; the Bishop of Winchester was one of the most important people in England, known for the way he had sought to weave a tapestry of alliances to entrap the king of France and further his master's aims in the war. Ceccani, he thought, must be taking a hand in the business of trying to find a peace between the two sides. Certainly it was needed.

He bowed deeply and left.

He accomplished his task, traveled to Bordeaux and discharged his commission; and also controlled himself in the matter of manuscripts. Not that this is so important; rather, the one event that is of significance amid the tumult of war and diplomacy, overshadowing the march of armies, the letters of the great, and the march of pestilence, is that on his return, about two days' ride from Avignon, he met a traveling peddler.

Olivier was traveling simply, as was his wont, alone and on a horse, carrying with him a little food and water, a bag with the papers he needed to discharge his tasks, a thick woolen cloak to keep off the cold, and a wide-brimmed hat on his head to protect him from the rain. He had taken off the gold ring that was his one sign of position lest it tempt another into avarice and violence, and had slung his shoes around his neck so that his feet could be kept fresh by the air as he plodded along. He was happy; the weather was fine enough though chilly, the road good and empty; he was lost in thought and careless of the world—perhaps the state that gave rise to the couplet on forgetfulness in one of his surviving poems, for Olivier had an unprecedented ability to seize a passing moment and fix it in words, rendering the transient timeless.

As he rounded a corner obscured by a clump of trees, he came across an upturned wagon, a donkey lying on the ground and struggling to get up, and a man, not young, trying to loose it from its harness. He was cursing quietly; all around were the impedimenta of the traveling craftsman heading from village to market—his own stock, which turned out to be three pairs of beautifully made shoes, some uncut leather freshly tanned, and some baskets made by his family. The food grown by others in his village and surplus to their needs, and some small rolls of cloth, gray and ragged, for sale to whomever wished to buy such rough material.

Olivier stopped his horse and watched a moment, then leaped down and went to help. His assistance was needed, as the donkey was thrashing around and risking breaking one of its legs or snapping some vital part of the cart. The owner scarcely acknowledged him to begin with, but concentrated on the task of saving his livelihood, breathing a huge sigh of relief when, eventually, the beast was freed, rolled away, got up, and went carelessly off to the nearest patch of grass for a feed. Then he turned to Olivier and grunted his thanks.

He was, perhaps, twice Olivier's age, strong but not big, with the precise movements of the craftsman and a gaze quite unlike anything Olivier had ever noted in one of his rank. It was open and inquiring, seeing and assessing Olivier in one glance, and yet he sensed something cautious and watchful as well.

He left it to his savior to speak first. "Come, let us turn your wagon the right way up. It seems undamaged, and it will not take long if both of us are at the job. Some of your goods are a little muddy, I'm afraid, but most seem fine."

The man nodded, and they moved around the wagon, working out the easiest place to attack the problem. Then, under the craftsman's direction and taking care not to get his clothes dirty, Olivier and he lifted, pushed, and pulled until at last the wagon balanced precariously on one wheel, then crashed down onto the ground the right way up. His new companion inspected it carefully, then sniffed with satisfaction.

"Thank you," he said, speaking for the first time. "Grateful."

As if to make up for his lack of words, and not wishing to seem churlish, he reached inside a large cloth bag that had fallen onto the ground and brought out a flask. This he unstoppered and offered to Olivier.

It was water, fortunately, for the day was young for wine, and Olivier drank gratefully. Not that he needed it; he had more than enough of his own, but it indicated his acknowledgment of the thanks. When he finished, he wiped his mouth on his sleeve and handed it back. "The water of the soul," he said with a smile, unthinking, not even remembering where the phrase came from. It was simply the first thing that came into his head and he wanted to fill in the silence caused by the man's taciturnity. Or maybe he wished to establish who he was, a person of some importance, of learning, not to be treated with familiarity even though they had just heaved over an old wagon together. Helping a traveler in trouble was one thing, a good Christian act that also broke some of the monotony of the journey. But that didn't mean that he was encouraging presumption. Olivier was young enough and vain enough to want it known he was a man of mark.

If that was his aim, the result was quite other than the one he anticipated. The older man stared at him in surprise and suspicion, hesitated, then spoke himself. "Flows to the ocean of the divine."

And now it was Olivier's turn to stare, dumbstruck with astonishment. For the moment the man spoke, he remembered the source of the words. It was as well there was no one else nearby, for any casual observer would have been piqued by the sight. Two men, of clearly different ranks, standing close and eyeing each other warily. To the left a donkey, unattended, and all around the bric-a-brac of the market. All this in the middle of the countryside, several miles from the nearest habitation. It was a puzzle picture, which someone like Julia would have thought almost surrealist, the meaning there but hidden, needing an explanation that could only come from a particular vantage point. Not that she was never tempted by such things; her aim was clarity, not games designed to obscure.

"Why did you say that?" Olivier asked. "How do you know that?"

The man now looked frightened, as though he had made a mistake and suddenly realized it. He mumbled something that Olivier didn't catch and turned away, hurriedly throwing the rest of his goods on the back of the wagon and shouting at the donkey, dragging it away from its meal to hitch it up once more.

Olivier caught him by the arm. "Tell me at once," he said. "Where did you hear that phrase? I mean you no harm."

But he was not to be persuaded. "Nothing, nothing. It doesn't matter," he muttered, then, his task done, he got back up on the wagon once more and started to move off. Olivier ran alongside. "Stop," he called out. "I order you to stop."

It was no use. The man stared stolidly ahead, completely ignoring all of Olivier's pleadings. And after he had run alongside, shouting some more, Olivier stood in the mud watching as the wagon lumbered down the road. He could have caught him easily; he had a horse, after all. He could have jumped on the wagon and wrestled the man to the ground, for although he was powerful and strong, Olivier was the younger by more than two decades.

He did neither of these things. There was something about the man's sheer terror that made him stand there until the wagon had rolled over the next hill, giving the man time to get away, so that he wouldn't be frightened anymore.

He waited an hour before continuing; his horse needed a rest in any case, and while it was munching the grass, continuing the meal that the donkey had so abruptly abandoned, he sat down under a tree and thought. It was wasted time, a frustrating and pointless exercise, for he knew before he started he could not work out how a cobbler could have quoted a luminous phrase written down by the Bishop of Vaison more than eight hundred years previously.

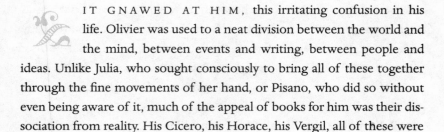

IT GNAWED AT HIM, this irritating confusion in his life. Olivier was used to a neat division between the world and the mind, between events and writing, between people and ideas. Unlike Julia, who sought consciously to bring all of these together through the fine movements of her hand, or Pisano, who did so without even being aware of it, much of the appeal of books for him was their dissociation from reality. His Cicero, his Horace, his Vergil, all of these were occult knowledge, whose existence and meaning was hidden from the world. His labors were contradictory; he wanted to recover such works, but to recover them for himself alone; he felt that at some level they would be tarnished if exposed to the generality, like silver when exposed to the air.

And yet there was this cobbler. . . . The problem exercised him all the way to his destination, which for that day was the town of Uzès, deep in French territory, but a duchy, whose overlord was of an independent frame of mind. Too lofty a business for someone like Olivier, however; he was not someone who dealt with dukes and kings. The seigneur, unaware of the poet's visit as well, slept undisturbed in his fortress that night, and Olivier stayed in a small abbey in its shade, where the cardinal's name ensured him hospitality, and he was surprised and delighted to discover that Althieux of Nîmes, passing through on his way to Tours, was also there, and ready to provide him with good company and conversation.

Althieux, the older man by some fifteen years, was not of Ceccani's family; he belonged to the entourage of Cardinal de Deaux, Ceccani's great opponent in the matter of Rome. The two friends had long since learned to negotiate the rocky shore on which one false word might cast all their hopes. Say, for example, that Olivier had let slip to Althieux that (as was the case at that particular moment) Ceccani was maneuvering with his usual skill to place his illegitimate son in the archbishopric of Dijon, a move that would have given an enemy of France access to the Duke of Burgundy—who was wobbling in the matter of England. If Althieux had spoken of this to his master, Olivier's career would have been ruined. If he had not and it had emerged that he knew about it in advance, then Althieux's own career would never recover.

Besides, Althieux was as devoted to his lord as Olivier was to Ceccani; both would have had to choose between friendship and obedience, creating a conundrum of irresolvable proportions. Better by far to avoid any such topics; to discuss matters of the mind alone, certain that both of those great princes were quite aware of the connection and smiled on it, as a discreet conduit for messages, should any such need to be sent from one side of the curia to the other.

All the more extraordinary, then, that Althieux should be so awkward, so strained in his company, he who was normally so easygoing. Olivier even asked him directly, but for some time was put off with a wave of the hand. "Nothing, nothing," he said impatiently.

"Come along, my friend. 'Nothing, nothing,' is not true. Something is on your mind quite clearly. Tell me what it is, if you can."

And eventually his friend began to talk. "I am doing this out of friendship, and against all common sense, but I have come to warn you to be careful as you travel the road back to Avignon."

"I am always careful," Olivier replied. "Anyone who has traveled more than ten leagues knows how important that is."

"I do not mean brigands and robbers. A group of men is waiting for you somewhere. They have been told to take a letter you have on you and kill you if necessary. They will probably find it necessary."

"Why?" said Olivier, quite astonished at the news, but not doubting it for a moment: his friend's demeanor was far too serious for it ever to have been a joke.

Althieux shrugged. "I do not know. Do you have some letter?"

"Yes."

"What is it?

Olivier shook his head. "How should I know? I haven't read it. Anyway, who has sent these men? Who gives their orders?"

"From the fact that I am telling you this, you may guess. May I count on your absolute discretion? You must never say how it was you evaded these people. If, indeed, you do so. "

"Of course, of course." Olivier fell silent, pondering what to do. Evidently the rivalry between his master and Althieux's was reaching some sort of crisis, if de Deaux was prepared to risk a direct attack on him. Whatever the letter said, it must be even more important than he imagined. But now he had the problem of delivering it, and staying alive. Obviously, he would have to take a different road, make a diversion. That would be the best thing. He could head north, pick up the river at Orange, take a boat down to Avignon. That would be easy enough. It would add several days to his journey, but better to arrive late than not at all. In the circumstances, even Ceccani could hardly complain.

"I am deeply grateful to you for telling me this. I do not have to say so, I imagine."

Althieux clapped him on the back. "One day perhaps you will have to do the same for me. Now, let us go and eat, and say no more of this gloomy topic. I hear this abbot keeps a fine table, and I haven't eaten properly for days."

FOR ONCE, rumor about monastic opulence matched the reality; both men were in a more mellow frame of mind when they retired to the special room reserved for the powerful and well-connected guests of the community, and called a servant to stoke up the fire and bring some warm drinks. Althieux was disinclined to revisit the topic of the ambush, and Olivier readily put the matter to the back of his mind. It would be easy enough to avoid them, after all. He did not pause to wonder at the coincidence of his friend being there to pass the warning on.

And Althieux tried to forget his last conversation with his master, the way he had begged for the opportunity to get this letter before the cardinal's soldiers were let loose on his friend. Anything, even a sacrifice of his company, to avoid bloodshed.

But he knew that, if he succeeded in his promise of taking it while Olivier slept, and set off for Avignon long before his friend even awoke the next morning, then this would be the last night of their friendship, and he wished to revel in the conversation, the comfort, of a true amity, about to be sacrificed for the sake of that very friendship. Why would he even consider doing such a thing to Olivier if he did not love him? For the number of people who could talk of the things in which both men were interested was small; to lose such a friend would be a dreadful hurt.

So they talked, and in due course, Olivier mentioned his encounter on the road that afternoon, and the way the man had echoed the words of his manuscript. His friend listened with fascination, savoring every drop of the tale: the way the manuscript was found, the time Olivier had taken to transcribe it, his inability to understand it, his meetings with the fearsome

Gersonides, and the manner in which it was brought back to his mind that afternoon.

"When I get back, I shall reread it more carefully," Olivier said. "And I will have a copy made for you, if you like. Then we can write to each other and examine what your cardinal's Jew says about it. He is a fascinating man; I learned more from him in a few weeks than I did from the most skilled doctors in Avignon in the course of several years. I hope to continue the acquaintanceship. I have scarcely scratched the surface of what he knows."

"I can think of nothing better than such a project with such a friend," came the reply. "My one concern, however, is that we might be led onto dangerous areas of inquiry. You must have suspected yourself that this cobbler was a heretic."

"I considered the idea. It is another area of the rabbi's expertise. How he became conversant with the details of the heresy I do not know. I thought they'd all long been destroyed."

Althieux laughed. "Oh, no. It was the usual thing. The soldiers and the priests and the magistrates all came. They attacked, and captured and tried and burned. Hundreds of villages, whole towns burned to the ground, tens of thousands massacred. And many good Christians among them, I think. Then they declared complete victory over the forces of schism and heresy, and went home. I am not saying that most heretics were not killed or forced to change their views; they were. But many were quite untouched, hiding out in the mountains to the north. They have learned greater discretion, that is all."

"I suppose I should have known," said Olivier simply. "But there seemed nothing especially dangerous about this man."

"I don't doubt it. They are perfectly ordinary people, for the most part. But dangerous nonetheless, every bit as much as the Jews. More so, I should say, as the Jews are plainly visible and use no subterfuge. Nor do they seek converts. These are quite the reverse. Your duty, as I am sure you know, is to report the matter to the magistrate. This man has undoubtedly come to market here. If he can be found and his village identified, then the entire settlement can be destroyed."

Olivier thought, and once more in a small way Sophia spread out her

protective cloak from the past; the man who carried her words, the anony-
mous messenger in the same way that Olivier was on occasion for Ceccani, was saved by his message.

Olivier shrugged. "I doubt we'd find him," he said. "And besides, I am
in something of a hurry. I think the cardinal would not be best pleased to
hear that his business was delayed because I chose to go a-hunting with
some friends. I must be off tomorrow. I have a long journey; thanks to you
it will be longer than I anticipated."

Althieux grunted; then the shadow over the conversation passed.

"You can, if you like, tell me why you are so sure this man is a heretic."

Althieux stretched, lazily, in front of the fire. "Something I heard. Have
I ever told you of my earliest meeting with Pope Clement? My brush with
greatness?"

"You told me that you had encountered him once. But not the circumstances."

"Ah, the circumstances. Indeed. I must say that when he rose to his current position I had high hopes for a moment. Not everybody can claim to
have assisted a pope in the days before he became so. And he remembered
me, as well. But chose not to advance me any further. He considered I was
quite well enough placed with Cardinal de Deaux, and needed no assistance from him. Besides, it may be that I brought back unpleasant memories, which he wished to shrug off once he exchanged the name of Pierre
Roger for Clement the Sixth."

They lay on the floor together beside the fire, as it was cold in the
evenings. There were no candles, no other light except for the logs sputtering in the large grate, and this gave off a fitful dancing light that made
Althieux's words seem the more resonant as he spoke.

"It was when I was very young, and a novice at the house of Saint-
Baudil near Nîmes. We had a new and dynamic young abbot, called Pierre
Roger, known as a favorite of the king, an advisor to the powerful, a magnificent preacher, and as a man learned and effective in disputation. He
turned out to be all of these; indeed, I have never met his equal before or
since. He only stayed a short while; it was obvious he was destined for
greater things, although we could scarcely guess how great they would be.

"The lay courts often used to hand over cases, or at least ask for our advice, when there might be a religious complication, and the monastery had habitually gone along with this, not least because all concerned wished to avoid the return of the inquisitors, who were always looking for an opportunity to intervene. One day, such a case came up, and as the abbot's secretary was ill, I was brought in to help and take notes for his personal record.

"There were six of them, three men and three women, although (they hastened to assure us) only two were man and wife; the others had never had any sort of union. They came from a village nearby and had been accused of fraud. This turned out to be a falsity, a charge brought up by a jealous neighbor who wanted their land, but it became clear as the hearing progressed that there was much more to it than that. These people were heretics, and up until then had kept themselves well hidden. Only the false accusation brought them into the light of day. They would not swear, or take an oath, and when the abbot asked them why not, they told him."

"As simple as that?" Olivier asked.

"As simple as that. They cannot lie. Anyway, they were quite unashamed of their beliefs and seemed to enjoy the chance to tell them to the court. I think they had accepted that their end was coming, but were completely unperturbed by it. They were asked why this was the case, and said that as their bodies were the prison in which they had been confined, the prospect of escape and return to their status as gods, alongside the Great God, could do nothing but please them. If they died well, then their next return to the material world would be the shorter."

"At which point," Olivier commented dryly, "our future pope leaned over and set light to them."

"On the contrary; he found it all fascinating and questioned them closely for a long time, so much so that the others began to become impatient with him. Also he hates that sort of thing, and tried desperately to get them to say something, anything, which would allow him to recommend leniency. He is a legist and a theologian, well used (dare I say it) to spinning strong arguments from insubstantial threads. Had they said anything at all with even the breath of orthodoxy or repentence about it, he would have jumped on it and let them go. And the rest of the court would not have protested, for they had little stomach for the task either.

"Nothing could be done. The more they said, the more everybody's jaws hung open. I have never heard anyone, not even a Jew, contradict so many fundamental doctrines quite so quickly or quite so willingly. They claimed to be gods themselves, they denied the resurrection of the body, they claimed the world was evil and man a prison rather than something created in God's own image. That God Himself, the god of the Bible, was but a meddling demon and had nothing to do with the true deity from which we all come. There was, of course, no mention of Our Lord, and they plainly believed in reincarnation. And, of course, no judgment, no hell—except for this world—no purgatory, no heaven."

Althieux smiled as he remembered. "And they were so serious, and so earnest; they spoke to us so intensely, as if they expected us to understand and even be converted by the sense of their words. On the other hand, they didn't seem that surprised either by the verdict. The abbot even gave them a stern talking to; said one last time that all they had to do was say something orthodox and they would be saved. But they wouldn't. Even then he would not give the order; he left the court to give them more time and went back to his monastery. But while he was there the local magistrates intervened. They all burned a couple of days later as thieves, for fear that the inquisitors would hear about it and come back. They didn't want another massacre in their area. It put Clement into a fearful mood for a week; he was sure he could have talked them round eventually, he said. He had been looking forward to the next meeting.

"It stayed with me; they turned to each other and smiled when they talked, so sweetly, and gave a warm embrace. Nothing ostentatious, you understand. Simple satisfaction and pleasure, quietly appreciated. You know, when I read the lives of the saints, sometimes I think they seem less graceful."

He paused, then shook himself and remembered that he had strayed far off his subject. "The point is, they referred to their soul as a river, flowing to the sea. Not individual, but coming from God and going back to God on death. That's why I am sure your man today was the same."

"Extraordinary," Olivier said. "But there is one problem."

"And what is that?"

"The person who wrote the words that I quoted to this man was no heretic."

"No?"

"No. He was a bishop and is still revered as a saint."

Althieux grinned. "Better not tell his parishioners, then. They'd be most disappointed."

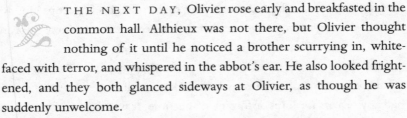 THE NEXT DAY, Olivier rose early and breakfasted in the common hall. Althieux was not there, but Olivier thought nothing of it until he noticed a brother scurrying in, white-faced with terror, and whispered in the abbot's ear. He also looked frightened, and they both glanced sideways at Olivier, as though he was suddenly unwelcome.

"What is it? Is there something which concerns me?"

"It is the plague. Your friend has brought it here."

Olivier's blood turned cold, both for Althieux and for himself. No details or explanations were necessary. Everybody knew the moment they heard the words what it meant. Some of those in the hall began looking around them, as though they expected death to walk through the door at any moment; others left the table and began to pray on their knees; most, though, sat still, looking at their abbot, silently begging him to do something, send it away and save them.

The abbot did nothing. He offered no words of consolation, provided no lead for the others to follow. Instead, he got up abruptly from the table and hurried out; Olivier thought he must be going to his friend to offer him the last rites—perhaps too late, but at least to do his job.

He stopped being frightened, for some reason that he did not understand. He should have been; this he knew all too well. He had no more idea than anyone else what the sickness was, but was sure that the air was infected around the sick man. As he had spent the evening with him, his chances of succumbing himself seemed great. But he would not leave. He knew he would not. The idea never crossed his mind. The plague happened to others, not to him. He was not destined to die of it. Even the realization that others had this naïve opinion and died nonetheless did nothing to shake his confidence in his invulnerability. He kept on eating, watching the hall empty, the monks break up into little groups. Some walked out sobbing in the direction of their cells, the chapel, or the gardens, then he got up himself and went to Althieux's room.

His friend was dead, and when he saw him Olivier realized for the first time why the world was so terrified of the plague. For what he saw was no longer a human being, just a mass of all-consuming sickness, his face wreathed in agony, his clothes stained dark with pus and sweat and vomit. He was lying on the floor, doubled over on himself, his fingertips bloody, the nails having come away from being dragged across the stone floor in agony.

And there was the smell. Not that of death, which he had often come across before, nor of sickness, which he knew still better. None of these had any terrors for him, or for any of his time. It was the sour sweetness of the odor that shocked him, a tantalizing, seductive smell, almost, beckoning the passerby, wheedling and reassuring. The smell of the devil, in fact, clever, powerful, ruthless, and truly frightening.

Olivier crossed himself and went outside into the morning sunlight to recover. He knelt on the ground and pushed his face close to it, to smell the fresh clean smell of the dew-soaked soil as it dried in the warmth.

"You, Brother, I need help," he said as one of the monks hurried by. The man didn't even pause. Olivier hailed another and another; they all ignored him. As he stood, he heard the sound of a horse, looked up and saw the abbot leaving through the main gate. Hurriedly, not looking back, urging the beast into a gallop the moment it was clear of the doors.

The order and discipline of the monastery collapsed in minutes; three hundred years of contemplation and prayer and blind obedience wiped out by terror. Nor did it ever recover; three of the forty-five brothers survived, but they went elsewhere, and the building was abandoned for years before it was finally taken over by the duke and used as stabling. In the eighteenth century a fire in a pile of hay burned down most of it, and the depredations of builders removed much of the stone for new houses. What remained was incorporated, in 1882, into a school, a fine monument to the meritocratic ideals of Republicanism. The spot where Olivier stood in the sunlight, and where Althieux died, is now a favorite haunt of adolescent boys, who come here to smoke when their lessons are over for the morning. Wildflowers grow where Olivier buried his friend, tipping him into the grave he dug himself, saying a brief prayer in farewell, and promising to have a mass said for him when he could find a priest to say it. They are picked, every year, and the boys give them to their girlfriends of the moment.

OLIVIER COLLECTED HIS bag and left as soon as he could. The speed of what had happened had shocked him, not only the plague itself but also the reaction to it. It was clear that the news had spread to the town; the silence, perhaps the most alarming of all the symptoms, had descended. People talked softly, looked frightened, moved as though they might be attacked at any minute. Only a few people were in the streets, doors and windows were being barred, and horses were whinnying as they were loaded with essentials.

Even the market had few people in it as Olivier walked through, only a handful of traders remained in their places, still hoping that someone would come and buy to reward their efforts in coming. As Olivier looked around him he saw, quite plainly, his heretic of the previous day.

The man noticed him as well. His eyes met Olivier's.

You know what I am, the glance said. What will you do?

The faintest ghost of a smile crossed Olivier's face. A half, even a quarter, of a wink. Then the meeting was broken. The man bent his head and saw to his pile of cloth. Olivier passed on his way, the bags bouncing against the side of his horse as he walked it toward the gate leading back to Avignon.

Even though he was mindful of Althieux's warning, and circuited so that he came into Avignon from the north, nonetheless the precautions were insufficient. As he stopped one night at a rough hostel for travelers on the far side of the Rhône, already back in Provençal territory, he heard two merchants talking.

"Don't know who they're looking for, but they must want him badly."

"What's this?" he said. "Trouble on the roads?"

"Soldiers," replied one of the men. "Don't know whose they are, but they're stopping everyone heading for Avignon. I'm told every way into the city has got blocks on it."

"Maybe they're after brigands," Olivier suggested.

"No, there's only a few of them. Enough to stop one man," he said, looking at Olivier carefully, "but not much use for anything else."

He thought as he lay scratching on his flea-ridden straw pallet that night. If they were searching everybody, then they could not know what he looked like. It must be that they anticipated the letter giving him away. Therefore, the solution was simple.

The next morning, after he'd had some bread and wine, he started off again, but instead of heading south to Avignon, he turned east inland and toward the hills that rose on the far side. Again, it added time onto his journey; in all, the detours took him a total of ten days, but as he did not want his throat cut, and as Ceccani would not have thanked him for losing the letter, he had no real choice. He headed straight for the chapel of Saint Sophia, thinking that by far the most sensible thing would be to consign it into his friend's hands. Ceccani could then send some of his own body-guards to bring the Italian, and the letter, into the city. His friend would like that; indeed, the prospect of being escorted into the town surrounded by an armed retinue in full regalia like some visiting potentate might well be the high point of his life, for he always had a grand sense of occasion.

It began to rain the day before he arrived, and kept up a steady down-pour for nearly thirty-six hours. He was soaked to the skin and shivering by the time he finally made it to the top of the hill, hoping desperately that he would soon see his friend, huddling over a fire in the makeshift en-campment he had once proudly described. But Pisano was not there, of course; he rarely was when he was needed. The chapel was deserted; only the mess all around—the poles for the scaffolding, the scorched patches on the grass where he had built his fires at night, the splotches of bright red and blue on the earth where he had washed his brushes after his work—suggested that anyone had ever been there. It was bleak, and desolate, half finished and with the air of something that never would be finished. Olivier stood uncertainly, gazing out over the thick woodlands that surrounded the hill, listening to the rain pattering down on tens of thousands of leaves so that the whole of creation seemed to be drumming with the noise. In the distance he could just see the smoke rising from the chimneys of Vaison, which he had not visited for years. He shook the rain out of his eyes, then turned miserably to the chapel, which offered the only dryness within reach. Once inside, in the gloom, for the darkness of the sky meant little light came through the windows, he shivered; he knew a fever was coming and that if he didn't get dry he would be in great danger. Even as the shivering grew worse and he had trouble standing, he still never considered the possibility that he, too, might have the plague. Instead he was as practical as he could be, knowing that he had little time before he would be too weak to stand. He took the warm blanket from his pack, his flask of water, took off his wet clothes, and, teeth chattering from the cold, wrapped himself up and huddled on the floor.

He had no idea how long he slept, possibly a day or more, and half the time he did not know whether he was asleep or not. Rather, he kept passing in and out of dreams, sometimes thinking clearly, sometimes only aware that he could hardly think at all, and luxuriating in the strange thoughts that passed through his mind without his bidding. At some stage the rains stopped; he noticed the sudden silence, then the skies cleared for the chapel grew light once more, and a shaft of sunlight streamed in through the windows to illuminate Pisano's unfinished work.

Olivier lay there and looked; for as much as half a day he looked at what his friend had accomplished, sometimes aware he was looking at artifice, sometimes thinking he was looking at real events. He was entranced and knew that all of the Italian's boasting, all his claim to be doing something the world had never seen before, were perfectly justified. He had created real people and endowed the story with life. Olivier saw how he used Isabelle de Fréjus to make his Magdalen, and wondered how anyone had ever considered that the blessed saint could have looked like any-one else. Even though it was unfinished, the panel of the saints arriving on dry land in their miraculous boat made him wonder at the glory of God who could protect such a frail craft on such violent seas. He even noticed that Pisano had given the blind man his face, and saw that Sophia was Re-becca. That darkness, with the radiance shining from her, the kindness of her gestures, the sometimes rough way she spoke, the twist of her head and the fall of her hair. Who would not wish to see such a person? Who could not love her?

He dozed again, and heard her words as she addressed the sinner who came to her. "You will see when you understand what love is," and she passed her hand over his face—an imperious, commanding gesture, not something mannered as some fairground charlatan would do—and the sunlight streamed into his eyes and woke him with a start.

The fever had gone, but still Olivier lay there, trembling in the mem-ory of the dream, rather than from the illness. Eventually he got up, his bones creaking, his stomach protesting from hunger, his mouth dry and foul-tasting from the lack of water. His head hurt abominably, and he cried out in pain as he stood up, then knelt down again to stop the dizziness.

And then he remembered why he was there. He checked his clothes to make sure they were wearable—they were still damp and clammy, but would dry swiftly enough once he got moving. He drank thirstily and forced himself to eat some of the bread, now green and moldy, that was in his pack. Then he reached in and took out the cardinal's letter. After hesitating for a moment, he slipped his finger under the grand seal of the bishopric of Winchester and opened it up, still unsure whether he was do-ing the right thing or making the biggest mistake of his life. He began to read. He read it six times, concentrating as much as his weakened state al-lowed. When he was sure he had got it, he put it down and recited it to himself, finally picking it up once more and correcting his errors in recol-lection. In an hour he had it entire, not a word out of place, the message hidden in the one place soldiers could not pry.

As for the letter itself, there were few enough places to put it; eventu-ally he decided that the rough stone altar would have to do. He put his shoulder against it and heaved until it leaned over just far enough to create a gap at its base. He slipped the letter underneath and let it down, then sat down himself once more to steady his head.

Ceccani could send some soldiers, or Pisano could bring it next time he came out here. It and its contents were safe from discovery, at any rate. He had done his best.

Still sniffing, still unsteady, he went out into the daylight and was dazzled by the sun. The rain had long gone, leaving only the smell of sweetness behind it. A heat haze was already forming in the far distance, and the birds, grateful for the rain and happy also it was over, were singing their songs with a vehemence Olivier thought he had never heard before. Perhaps because of Pisano, he noticed the colors of the landscape properly for the first time, the extravagant purples and browns and yellows and greens covering the hills and the valleys as far as the eye could see. He looked the other way, across the broad plain of the river valley toward the Rhône, dotted with tiny settlements and fields. He relaxed in the warmth and the peace, and went down on his knees to give thanks merely for being alive, and for being allowed to see such sights and smell such perfumes.

WHEN MARCEL ARRIVED to take up his duties as préfet in Avignon at the start of 1941, he came as something of a hero. The way he had put on his full dress uniform to give the Germans a cold but unimpeachably correct welcome. The way he had himself lowered the tricolor and insisted that no German hands touch it. The way he had protected the town from destruction and prevailed upon the German authorities to punish any looting. The way he had even gone in person to the general in charge to demand that German vehicles be used to bring food into the town. All these had won him a reputation as a humane man who kept his head in a crisis. Such men are rare in the best of circumstances; in late 1940 they were beyond value; he swiftly had his reward. He was needed badly.

There was much to do, a whole society to rebuild, an entire regime to establish. Simple things, normally taken for granted, required immense effort and labor. All his tasks he accomplished with efficiency and dispatch. He never complained, never made excuses, seemed to sleep in the Préfecture, was an inspiration to all around. He was the perfect product of the system, almost its justification.

It was some time before he turned his mind to the minor matters and, on the recommendation of the Minister of Education, wrote the letter that summoned Julien Barneuve from his exile to see him.

"People have been making inquiries about you, my friend," he said, and was gratified to see Julien look slightly alarmed. A little joke, which was also a small exercise of power. "I have had two memos about you."

Julien looked puzzled. "I cannot think why," he said.

"We have been drawing up lists of people who might be pressed into service. You wrote an article a year ago, it seems. About a bishop. It has been noticed by people who think it has the right attitude. Which shows how thorough they are being. Combined with personal recommendations . . ."

"I published it a year ago," he interrupted. "I wrote it several years back."

"Yes, yes. The point is that it is just the sort of thing we need at the moment. The context. A model, if you like, of how relations with our—what shall we call them?—new friends—may develop. That's why your name has come forward. It is a small consequence of having a classicist as Minister of Education."

Julien looked thoroughly puzzled. "What are you talking about?"

"The Germans, Julien, the Germans. Remember them? Those people who have occupied half our country? You argued that although the barbarians conquered Gaul, the Gauls civilized them. A greater victory and in the end beneficial all round."

"I did nothing of the sort," Julien replied. "And I can see no parallels between then and now at all."

Marcel looked slightly irritated. "That's how it seems to people in Vichy. Goths and Germans, rebellious serfs and communists. Very neat. Don't expect politicians to pick up subtleties. The point is, they want you to help. Do your bit to steady things. Your duty, really."

"I'm really not with you."

"Give lectures. Write articles. Check the newspapers aren't being un-helpful. That sort of thing. Radio, now. We could organize a few talks on the radio as well. Immensely popular, those are."

"I don't think that's something I'd be very good at. Or inclined to do. Peddling vulgarized half-truths is not something that would appeal much."

Marcel paused and sat down at his desk. "Listen, Julien my friend. Let me give you a little lecture. You, after all, have given me enough of them over the years. Do you know what the situation is here? In this country? Probably not. We have been beaten. This you may have noticed. Even you. Definitively and completely, this time. We are in a new world, one which has changed forever. The Germans have won, so comprehensively they cannot now be defeated. There is no one left to fight them. They have complete control over Europe. England is hanging on by its finger-tips and will inevitably be destroyed sooner or later. Eventually, no doubt, there will be a war on Russia and it will suffer the same fate. Our govern-ment, meanwhile, is in the grip of an old general surrounded by men of often doubtful motives. The people are dazed, confused, and prey to any convincing charlatan who might come along. They have to be protected from false hope and expectation. . . ."

"People like Bernard, you mean?"

"Exactly like Bernard. I hear he has fled the country. That was the best news I have heard for a long time. Think what he would be writing now. Sniping criticism from the sidelines, assaults on those who lost the war—all justified, no doubt. Worthy articles on democracy and freedom. Con-stant bickering about every piece of legislation. Character assassinations of ministers and politicians. A never-ending stream inciting hatred against those people who have just driven their tanks all over our country and divided it in two. Again, justified no doubt. But that is not the point. We cannot look back. We dare not. The people have to be consoled and encouraged and protected. We cannot afford a people divided, or a gov-ernment hampered by internal bickering. Not at the moment.

"And there is another point. *I* need help. Me, your friend. Another thing you do not know, I imagine. Have you heard of the Legion of Com-battants?"

Julien shrugged. "Of course. What of them?"

"A group supposedly of old soldiers. Very virtuous. Heroes of the last war, although how many actually took part in it is doubtful. They have attached themselves to the president, got close to him. Do you know what they are doing? 'The bureaucracy will not carry out your orders,' they whisper in his ear. 'You cannot rely on them. Let us help. Let us be your eyes and ears, tell you what is going on, do those jobs which otherwise will not get done.' They are dangerous people, Julien. If they are not stopped, they will bypass people like me, all the usual balances of administration will collapse, and it will fall into the hands of old street fighters. Do you remember we were both in Paris in 1928? When there were the riots, when the right battled the communists on the streets? You said you couldn't decide which was worse, you were merely terrified either would ever come to power?"

Marcel paused. "They are nearly there, Julien. Marshal Pétain is a fine man, a hero. But he is easily influenced. And these are the people who are influencing him. And unless I can surround myself with people I trust, then they will take more and more of the administration here into their hands. And that is why I need you, a decorated soldier, a renowned scholar, a respected figure, by my side. I need my friends, now more than ever. And, as I say, you cannot sit on the sidelines talking about your inclinations. If there was a war on, you could go off and fight, if you wanted. Very noble. Very simple. But the war is over. Now the really dangerous part begins. You have to see, Julien, what a chance we have. To renew and rebuild this country, give it good government, get rid of all those people who do nothing but criticize and weaken us. All those people who lost us the war. Look at the Germans; look at how they run things, and look at the shambles that we became. I don't like them, but we must learn from them if we are ever going to get off our knees. But we must keep it out of the hands of the thugs as well. A balancing act. If you do not help me, you are helping them. Here ends my lecture."

Julien gazed at him, saw that he had considered this speech, written it in his head for this moment, and was absolutely convinced that what he was saying was correct. Nor could Julien disagree with him. His friend was talking little more than common sense. But he was still reluctant to take the step Marcel seemed so desperately to want.

"I just don't see how giving lectures will help," he said.

"Oh, that. Useful. Keeps spirits up, explains what we're doing. Keeping an eye on the newspapers and publishers is the more important part. Making sure no defeatist, critical nonsense is spread about. We can't afford it. The government, no doubt, is not perfect. But it's all we've got at the moment, and it has to be given a chance. And at the same time you must fend off criticism of me from within. Do a good job, use all that intelligence of yours."

"What do you mean by keeping an eye on things?"

"Which journals and papers get allocations of paper? Which books should get priority for printing? All that sort of thing."

"I am completely unqualified."

"Who isn't? You are an academic with a good reputation. Aren't you?"

"I think so."

"There you are. Trustworthy, to me and to the people who will be benefiting from your fatherly advice. It's for the general good, you know. We have to keep things calm. If you don't do it, someone else will. And, frankly, you have no choice. You've been sitting on your backside for years talking about the need to defend civilization from the barbarians, and now's your chance. The barbarians are here."

Marcel stood up and brushed his lank hair back across his head. His face—now slightly pudgy from age, scored with lines from work and worry—was flushed from the intensity of his speech.

"Go away and think about it," he said. "And when you've thought about it, go to the Hotel Continental. I've requisitioned a floor for the new censor's office. You start work on Monday."

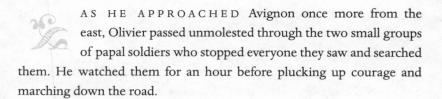 AS HE APPROACHED Avignon once more from the east, Olivier passed unmolested through the two small groups of papal soldiers who stopped everyone they saw and searched them. He watched them for an hour before plucking up courage and marching down the road.

"What's this?" he asked as they grabbed him and made him stand while they searched his clothes and bag.

"Orders," said one. "Nothing there. Thank you."

"Come on, tell me. What's this about?"

"Sorry."

And then he was through, and went safely on his way. Just outside the city, on the approach to the great bridge that led over the river to its gates, he came across a sight that initially made him laugh out loud, and he rushed to Ceccani to recite his letter and tell him of what he had seen.

"Fifty men and women," he said later, "all roped together, beating the hell out of each other with rods and ropes, singing psalms while they did it. Not very well, I must say, as they weren't hitting each other for show. They were really hurting. What is going on that we have so many madmen on the road?"

Ceccani did not smile. "They call themselves flagellants, for reasons that are obvious. They believe they can fend off the plague through self-mortification."

"Judging by the state of this town, they are not succeeding. Is it as bad as it seems?"

"Worse," Ceccani said grimly. "And by all accounts there is still worse to come. Do not laugh at these people, Olivier. Much has changed in your absence, and you will not find anything so amusing when you see what is happening."

"I saw some things on the way across town, my lord." And he had; never would he have thought it possible that a city could change so quickly and so drastically. Not the buildings, of course; the town looked exactly as before, every house and church and palace was as it had been. But the streets, denuded of their people, the stalls, the noise, the movement, were like ghosts. Olivier had never thought about it before; only now did he realize how much he had come to like, even to love, this greedy, corrupt, sinful, excessive town, a byword throughout the world for its extravagance. To live in Avignon, survive amid the cruelty and venality, mingle with Italians and French and Germans and Flemings, was to encounter the whole world at once. And now, it seemed, it was gone forever; all that was left of the pageantry were the bells of the body collectors, and the harsh rumbling of their carts as they pulled another load of corpses to the river; it was difficult to imagine it would ever come back. No city, he thought, could recover from such a blow.

"How many are dead?"

"So far? About seven thousand, maybe ten. We thought that perhaps it was abating, that the miasma was heading elsewhere, but it seems not. There will be many more deaths yet. There is nothing to be done, Olivier. No human assistance has had any effect. Nonetheless, I wish you to do me a service, when you are rested."

"Willingly, my lord."

"Go to these people you find so amusing, they must have a leader, and bring him to me. I do not know whether they are dangerous or not, and we must find out what sort of men they are."

He had already told Ceccani about his voyage, and apologized profusely for having taken such a long time. Ceccani listened, silently, nodding as he spoke.

"And he's dead, this Althieux?"

"Yes, my lord. I buried him myself."

He grunted. "You tell me you read the letter?"

"Yes, sir," he replied a little nervously. "I did not intend to or want to. But I decided the only way of bringing it to you safely was in my head."

Ceccani thought of this, then smiled. "You did well. Very well indeed. I am pleased with you. So tell me."

And like a schoolboy before a master, Olivier recited, calling up every word from his prodigious memory. How the proposal was acceptable to the king. How it would take some time to get troops into position. How the English needed eight weeks before any action could be taken, but that they would be ready outside the walls of Aigues-Mortes by the end of May. And how they undertook to provide any and all assistance to Cardinal Ceccani when the time was right.

Ceccani nodded. "Do you understand this letter?"

"I believe so, my lord."

"And?"

"I believe the English wish to wrest control of Aigues-Mortes from the king of France, to take from him his only port on the Mediterranean Sea. And that you intend to help them do so."

"Go on."

Olivier looked perplexed. "That is all, sir."

"Your opinion?"

"I have none, sir."

"Do you not find it shocking? Fascinating?"

"No, sir."

"Why not?"

"Because I am your servant, my lord, indebted to you for everything I have. And because the doings of princes are not my affair. Whether Aigues-Mortes is French, or whether it is English, or whether it belongs to the emperor of China is of no matter to me. I serve you to the best of my ability. What else should concern me?"

Ceccani rose and gave him a warm embrace, the first time he had ever done such a thing. "By God, I choose my servants well," he said. "Now go to my chancellor and get the money to buy yourself some new clothes. Get enough for expensive ones. And go and see if there are any clothes merchants left in this town. If you choose to buy modest attire and spend the rest on a manuscript or two for yourself, then—then I'll bless you anew."

 THE FOLLOWING DAY, Olivier did as he was told, although with some foreboding. The group of penitents were not hard to find; a considerable crowd had gathered around them and the noise of screaming could be heard from some distance. Olivier indeed had to push his way through to reach the front.

What he saw revolted him once more. There were about fifty of them, stripped to the waist, dirty, filthy men and women all drawn from the dregs of society, uncouth, loud, and vulgar, standing in a circle. Time and again one would step into the center to be set upon by the others, all of whom carried weighted scourges. Evidently Olivier had missed much of the spectacle, for the ground was as red with blood as the sand after a bear baiting. Several had collapsed, and when they did so, the others rejoiced and ignored them, turning their attention to the next. Olivier could barely contain his disgust, then slowly realized that he was alone in the crowd in feeling this antipathy. Many of the others were on their knees, singing. Others prayed with tears in their eyes, others ran up with handkerchiefs to wipe the blood, which they carried away reverently. He saw one woman grab one of the men and lick his wounds before collapsing in a heap on the ground. A tall man with a thin, wispy beard, his face covered in scabs, walked over to her, picked her up, and gave her a blessing.

Olivier called out to him. He had to repeat himself several times before he was noticed. "Are you the leader of these people?"

"I am their captain," he replied. Alone of the group he did not seem taken with a madness. Alone, Olivier noticed, he did not submit himself to a beating either.

"I have a message for you. Cardinal Ceccani orders you to attend him."

"I take no orders from a priest," the man replied with a sneer.

Olivier turned and indicated the ten guards he had brought from Ceccani's palace. "Then perhaps a polite request would be honored with a reply?"

The man eyed the troops, who looked nervous and unready to do their duty, but decided not to risk it. "You may tell the priest," he said, "that I am desirous of saving all souls, even his. I will come to him this evening."

And he terminated the interview, walking back to the center of the circle, and continued. Olivier retreated; he heard the snigger of the crowd as he did so.

STRANGELY, Ceccani was not offended by the response when he reported it. He laughed, merely.

"But, my lord, these people are shocking," Olivier hastened to tell him. "And they are dangerous. They do not acknowledge the church; they wrap the people round their thumbs and could make them do anything. Believe me, I am not joking. I saw the effect they were having."

"I'm sure the same was said of Saint Francis and his followers," Ceccani said evenly. "And who knows, perhaps these people have been touched by divine grace. Let us see, when this man arrives. Did you get his name, by the way?"

"He calls himself Peter."

"Peter? Well, well."

"You are taking a great deal of interest in a few lunatics, my lord."

"A few?" Ceccani replied. "Dear me no. If there were only a few I would ignore them. A few would be no danger, and no use either. But we have had reports in from all over Provence, into Italy and France, of bands of people like these. I need to know whether they are truly dangerous or not. As you have seen for yourself, they capture the minds of the populace. But what will they do with those minds? That is what we must discover. Please go and wait for this Peter, and bring him to me the moment he arrives."

So Olivier retired to the gatehouse and passed the next three hours working hard, reading the manuscripts that Gersonides had lent him, rereading his own ever more confusing document by Manlius Hippomanes. The contrast appealed to him: the limpid, clear thought of Manlius and the confused, noisy outpourings of the flagellants told him much, suggested to him why the old Roman had written these words. For the first time he picked up and truly understood the tone of regret, the fear in the text, how Manlius must have intended this work to be a bastion against the darkness of ignorance, and a valedictory to an age he knew was dying all around him. But he remembered also Gersonides's words at the meeting when he had tentatively suggested that his assault on the Jews of Vaison might have been motivated by faith. "Oh, but this man was no Christian when he wrote this. And he was a bishop, as you say. So go and think yet again; what sort of man can persecute others in the name of a faith he clearly does not profess?"

He read, then reread, the section on friendship in the light of the death of Althieux, and there at least found much to comfort him. The bishop had understood about friends, loved his friends, advocated forgiving them if they erred. "For nature gives a man two eyes, two hands, two ears. If one eye weakens, the other becomes stronger in its aid; if an arm is injured, we do not cut it off; rather, the other does its work as well as its own until it is whole once more. So it is if a friend falls from virtue."

He was thinking on this passage when Peter arrived. Olivier had to intervene, for the guards on the gate wished to deny him entrance. Then, walking ahead of him, being careful not to talk to him, Olivier led him across the vast hall and up the stairs to Ceccani's chamber.

"I did not give you permission to sit," the cardinal remarked as Peter placed himself on a chair, carrying it over from the wall where it stood.

"And I did not ask it," Peter replied, sitting down anyway. "You wished to see me, not I you."

Olivier smiled, and waited for Ceccani to erupt. His anger was a terrible sight, and he felt a small tingle of anticipatory glee at the thought of what must come next.

But it didn't. Ceccani did not react, merely nodded and thought. "You addressed the crowd this afternoon, I gather. I heard reports of it, but not enough to make sense of it. Would you care to repeat it to me?"

Even Peter found this mild-mannered response surprising, but was not a man to turn down an opportunity to talk. "I told them that the plague is a punishment from God for the sins of the world. It is only through repentance that his vengeance can be deflected. We are penitents. We urge others to repent as well. So doing may show we are sorry for our sins, and may assuage divine wrath."

"You are not a priest, I think."

Peter snorted. "I come from Marseille. When the plague arrived there, the priests were the first out of the gates on their donkeys. I spent a week going round houses no one else would enter, giving comfort to the dying. They asked me for blessings, thinking I must be a priest. At first I refused, but then I knew that I had been ordained by God, if not by men. I was sent by Him, to comfort the sick and save the healthy. Who is the greater sinner? A man who gives the sacrament though not ordained, or a man who is ordained yet refuses it through his cowardice?"

Even Olivier knew the answer to that one. Many a man had been hanged for less. But again, Ceccani smiled, almost as if encouraging him to continue.

"And while this continues, what do priests do? They sit in their castles, blockaded in their towers, and give themselves over to debauchery and lust. That is why God has struck, because of the evil of the church itself, which dissipates itself in this town."

Ceccani nodded cautiously. "You feel that the plague would abate if the pope returned to Rome?"

"The church must mend its ways and repent, and it must take action," Peter said, looking at Ceccani with level, steady eyes. "All the world knows how this plague is being spread. Everyone knows that it is the doing of the Jews, and that as long as they exist we are all in danger of our souls. And what does the church do? Nothing. What does the pope do? Builds himself great buildings and seduces women in them. Go back to Rome? Yes. But in a spirit of repentance, vowed to sin no more. And that would be only a start. This is God's warning, and we must do as we are told."

Olivier almost broke in to point out that either the plague was God's punishment or the Jews' evil, but could hardly be both, but kept silent. It was all too incoherent to be taken seriously. And the remarks about the pope . . . many men thought such things. Few were foolish or rash enough to speak them out loud.

The interview went on for some time, Ceccani using all the formidable power of his character, skills normally reserved for princes and cardinals, to win over this filthy beggar. And when it finally came to an end he stood up and embraced him, then offered him his ring to kiss. "You have been touched by God, my friend. There are many who think as you do, but do not have the courage to act. You must be strong, and faithful. You have great work to do. I offer you my protection, and do not think you will not need it in days to come. There are many who fear you, and who hate to hear the truth."

Peter bowed, and kissed the ring, tamed at last. "Thank you, My Lord."

"It would be as well if you were prepared to take advice, on occasion. I will send messages to you, giving you my opinion, making suggestions. Consider it well, when you receive it, for we have the same aims in mind, and together, who knows, perhaps we can bring mankind and his church to his senses before it is too late."

He nodded that Olivier was to show him out. As they left the room Peter said, "You are lucky, friend."

"How so?"

"To have such a man as a master."

Olivier said nothing. He thought Ceccani had taken leave of his senses.

IN APRIL 475, the day after his encounter with the abandoned urchin on his estates, Manlius Hippomanes traveled to Arles and summoned a meeting of all the bishops from areas threatened by the barbarian armies. His insolence in doing so was extreme; the most junior of them all, and a priest who had never yet given communion, did not even know how the service was conducted; he should have spent the next decade in humble supplication before his superiors.

And yet this was why old Faustus had chosen him, and why Faustus wrote, quite independently, a covering letter to his fellow bishops instructing them to obey Manlius's summons. So, over the next month, they assembled, some twenty-four of them in all, finding lodgings of assorted quality in the town—some severe and austere, others aristocratic and opulent. Manlius himself stayed as a guest in the house belonging to a relation, and it was in this still impressive residence that the meeting—or rather the series of meetings—took place.

For although they were leaders of their flocks, they were desperate to be led themselves through the maze of this dark and troubled world. They were now well used to raising and spending charitable donations, to looking after the poor, to getting hold of corn in times of hardness, to raising work duties to repair roads and water supplies; all the things that the civil government had once done and could do no longer. They maintained, on the whole, good relations with their brother priests and bishops both nearby and far away. But dealing with the secular powers, with generals and armies—with politics and diplomacy at a high level—was something of which few had any experience, and they were worldly enough to know that skill and dexterity in such matters was now vitally required. They were Romans and they were Catholics; the barbarians—Euric to the west, the Burgundians to the north—were neither.

So they turned to Manlius, who had been to Rome, who had even accompanied a member of his family to the court of Euric's father at Toulouse, and who, as a result, was considered to have an unrivaled insight into the barbarian mind. Such was the poverty of the empire at this final sputtering moment that this judgment was correct.

To Manlius, looking around the table, it seemed like a sad parody of the great days of the past, when the emperor would summon ministers and councillors to give advice and take orders. Such meetings, glorious and full of pomp, perhaps still took place in Constantinople, although no one was certain anymore; no one he knew had ever been there, not even Sophia. Here, instead of emperors in their purple, senators, generals, and councillors, there was a group of dowdy and anxious men, most of them old, whose main remedy for any political problem was prayer. So let them pray, he thought; it might do some good. It would give him more freedom of action.

Despite their trust, the look of happy confidence in him, he found it hard to keep the brusqueness out of his voice, to remember that he was supposed to be taking orders, not giving them. "Remember," Faustus had told him, "you are their servant, selected to do their bidding, to translate their wishes into action. They are good and holy people, for the most part, but have a sense of their dignity, which it is unwise to offend. You will not insult them; it cannot be done. But you can so easily insult their office, and the church itself, and they will not easily forgive you for it."

A wise old man, this Faustus; someone who would have made a place for himself in whatever world he was born into. Even half a century before, he might have advised emperors, perhaps even become one himself, for he had a quick and active mind coupled with membership of a powerful family. Such were the times, however, that he had turned his back on the world that so desperately needed his talents, and crossed the sea to the island of Lérins, there to spend near twenty years as a virtual hermit. He had come back to the world quite against his will, for Riez had appealed to the abbot for a bishop, and he had seen that Faustus had the skills to manage such a disputatious bunch of people. It was the first and only time he had rebelled and disobeyed, refusing for a whole week to accept the order, begging that it be withdrawn, praying to God for a deliverance that the Almighty, in His wisdom, had no intention of permitting. God needed Faustus for more than contemplative prayer, and eventually he had accepted his fate, leaving the island monastery at the age of forty-five for the first time in nineteen years.

His sanctity—news of which arrived before he did—made him a resounding success; his very shadow, it was said, could make the infirm whole once more should it fall on them. Such holiness was held in awe, and few dared to question the authority of such a man. On top of this, he was wise, not just in matters of theology, but also in the ways of the world; he had no need to think that all men were naturally good to believe in the goodness of his Lord. Thus, he knew the efficacy of prayer but also when God required men to help themselves. It was his decision to push Manlius forward. The church had many good men already, he reasoned; it could afford to have a few effective ones as well.

In his quiet and efficient manner, it was Faustus who managed the meeting, just as he had managed the diocesan assembly that elevated Manlius to the chair. He said little; just a look now and then, a quiet murmur, a raised eyebrow, and a suggestion or two. Only Manlius saw the skill, and he was grateful for it, as he knew he had no understanding whatsoever of such people and could easily make a mistake. Indeed, Manlius had a better understanding of the minds of barbarian chieftains than of these people. He knew already what was necessary, but had no idea how to persuade them of it.

"Perhaps," Faustus said after a while, "we should see in what direction the Spirit has moved this meeting so far; then its wishes might be all the more clearer. We are agreed on the need to restore order in the region . . ."

Here at least was general assent; all of the bishops controlled lands, given by the pious, whose output was declining month by month and year by year as slaves absconded, making their way to lands outside their control. And that was the best that could be hoped for; some stayed and went to the uplands, banding together into marauders and sweeping down to take what they wanted. Bagaudae, they were called in the far north where they first appeared, and the name had become commonplace.

". . . and that we should proceed to raise the siege of Clermont. For both these ends, it is desired that the Bishop of Vaison should travel to the emperor to request an army . . ."

A murmur of assent.

"This army to be dispatched immediately, and without delay. We accept the full burden of payment, on condition that a general of suitable merit is put in command. Funds to come out of church resources, donations, and taxation. Should this fail, our brother will investigate any other means to salvage the situation."

Manlius sighed; he knew the purpose of this was to give him as much freedom of action as possible, but the woolliness of it all made him despair. The bishops seemed to think that all you had to do was tap the emperor on the shoulder, point out that an army was needed, and it would suddenly arrive. At least when you negotiated with the Goths or the Burgundians, you knew who was in control, and that any agreement would be kept. And that thought, which had been with him for some time, niggled at him still.

"You must bear in mind," said Manlius with as much restraint as he could manage, "that any army is likely to cause more damage and chaos than it prevents. I do not know much yet about the finances of the church, but I know something of the tax revenues, and I can tell you that this whole region will be strained to pay for one campaign. Any more than that and there would be precious little left worth defending."

"Nevertheless, something must be done," said the Bishop of Orange. "The situation is intolerable. I have lost two hundred slaves in the past six months, and another three hundred serfs have run away as well. Last season two farms were raided just after the harvest and all the corn taken, as well as animals. This cannot go on."

Everyone nodded, and Manlius could hardly dissent. He was uncertain himself which was worse, the abstract prospect of Euric's troops—who certainly would be terrible enough if they ever arrived—or the steady wasting away of civil society that the slow attrition of labor meant. Both, certainly, had to be dealt with.

"I must point out," he said, "that gold can only be spent once. It can bribe Euric, pay for troops, or be spent on supplies for Clermont. But not all three."

"Which is why you must find the emperor . . ."

Manlius shook his head slowly.

"I really do not think that is the right course," he said. "Not only because the emperor is little more than a puppet. Even if he were truly in command of himself, I doubt I could prevail on Rome—or Ravenna, or wherever he is—to help."

"Why is that, brother?"

Manlius winced. He hated being addressed as brother by anyone, and certainly resented the implication of fraternal equality with the lowborn, ignorant Bishop of Aix.

"The suggestions are all noble and good," he continued, "but they omit one detail. Time. There is little of it. We do not know why Euric and his army have decided to move no further until Clermont falls, but it is a mistake on his part. The town is no threat to his army. He could sweep past it to the sea at any moment he chooses, and there is a risk he will do so. How long will it take to raise an army in Italy, even if it can be done? Many months at least, as I am sure you realize. By which time there is every possibility that Clermont will have fallen and Aix and Arles and Marseille as well.

"If we are going to get help, we need it now. Within weeks. And, in my opinion, the only people who might assist are the Burgundians. Before anything else, I propose to go to them at Lyon and persuade King Gundobad to block Euric's advance to the East. He was brought up in Rome; his aunt was married to Ricimer and is a Catholic; he may be persuaded to help."

A feint; deceive the enemy that your main advance was merely a skirmish. Lull them into the feeling that the battle was not yet joined, so it might be over before they even realized. This, in essence, was Manlius's tactic at the meeting, which ended in unanimous agreement that he should first buy time, and then buy an army.

Thus it was that the end of Roman Gaul was decided by the enthusiastic nods of those who most wanted to keep it in existence.

HE GAVE a banquet that evening to end the meeting, and to impress on his fellows the extent of his power. There was no delicacy on this occasion; Manlius found the best musicians and cooks available, brought in his own servants and borrowed those of his family in the town. And toward the end he told them a story. It was nearly a parable, almost the first sermon he gave, for he was keen to educate them and prepare them for what he thought was inevitable.

"Let me tell you of my trip to Rome," he told them when they had eaten well and the last dishes were cleared, the musicians finished and dispatched. And when they had settled and he had their attention, he began.

"I was in the entourage of Lord Majorian, traveling there to cement his grip on the throne, going with a large portion of his army. My father provided a substantial number of troops for his cause from our estate, and I was taken to honor his contribution while he remained behind to keep control of the province. Remember this: I was with an army, and in the company of the only decent emperor to have held the throne for forty years. Did the Romans welcome us? No. Did they honor us? No again. Did the prospect of an emperor able to reassert the glory of Rome fill them with gratitude? No, for a third time. The first delegation which came out to meet us asked for money for games. The second presented a bill for quartering the troops. Even the senate, when he wished to address it, had to be bribed heavily before they would present themselves.

"That is by the by, perhaps. Rome has long been legendary for its rapacity, and I tell you nothing you do not know already. What I wish to recount is a conversation I had with Lord Ricimer, who had been master of the empire for years, though always in the background, and who eventually struck Majorian down. And, through his agents, my father also.

"He was barbarian by breeding, and barbarian by nature; utterly unlike those who see the glory of Rome and wish to emulate it. Not one piece of its civilization did he wish for himself. His manners, bearing, and deportment were almost painful to behold. The first time I caught sight of him—a short, bowed, scarcely shaven man, dressed in a rough tunic, with a truculent scowl—I took him to be a gamekeeper or some other servant. The person I was with laughed out loud when I asked how such a person could wander freely about the powerful senator's house in which we were at the time, and snapped his fingers at the man.

"'You, sir,' he called out. 'Yes, sir. You. Come here. This fine young man here'—he gestured to me—'wishes to know how a dirty gamekeeper like yourself comes to be wandering freely in this fine house.'

"He thought for a second, then replied, with a voice which sounded remarkably cultivated coming from such a source. The thing which struck me then, and continued to strike me thereafter, was its softness; he spoke so quietly you could barely hear him. Others have remarked on this as well. 'It may be because of one of two reasons,' he said. 'The first being that I own both the house and the senator. The second being that not so long ago another great man of this town did deny me entrance. But that is an old story; and he is long since dead.'

"And then he smiled, a smile of such dazzling beauty that I almost gasped for breath. We are told that we see the soul in such little details and if so, then this man's reputation must be wrong, for he had the smile of an angel, with beautiful white, even-spaced teeth lighting up eyes which were of a most remarkable blue—a legacy of his Visigothic mother, no doubt.

"'Your name, sir?' he asked of me. I told him immediately, with something of a stammer. I was scarcely twenty at this time and, although my training was complete, it had not yet encompassed situations such as this.

"'You are one of Majorian's Gallic entourage, then. What did he bring you for? Are you a cleric? A soldier? A diplomatist?'

"'None of these. If anything, I can lay some claim to being a poet,' I said.

"Ricimer laughed out loud. 'A poet? How useful! I am glad to see the savior of the Western empire has his priorities straight. So, sir poet, make me a poem.'

"I thought, in all my foolishness, that my chance had come. A vision of myself standing before the senate delivering a panegyric danced before my eyes.

"'Oh, willingly, sir. With the greatest of pleasure. The honor you do me . . .'

"But this was not what he meant at all. He wished to ridicule me, not honor me. My speech of gratitude was cut short.

"'Yes, yes. Come along then. Begin.'

"'But I need to prepare.'

"'A poet is full of song, I am told. Preparation is not necessary. Generals do not fight battles when they are ready; a good commander can turn any situation to advantage. The same with a politician and a statesman. Are poets different? Make me a song.'

"The tone of his words was playful, yet there was an edge to them. He was prepared to impose his will even in this little matter. The more I protested, the more would he push, until I gave way. I did not want an unseemly fight which I would inevitably lose, but I did not wish to make a fool of myself either. A difficult situation, as you can imagine. So, red-faced and covered with embarrassment, I began. Fortunately, I had that very morning been perusing Horace, which I had brought with me for the pleasure of rereading it on the very sites where the master has composed his immortal lines. I hope I offend no one if I say I am convinced his shade hovered over me at that moment, and gave me inspiration that I should not disgrace the name of poet.

"A two-line epigram only did I give him, two of the worst I have ever composed in technique, borrowing from but not imitating Horace as truly as he deserved. But they served their turn.

> 'Yet as I stand within the senate's halls,
> I hear wan stucco crumbling, dusty on the marbled walls.'

"The lines had a crude charm, I suppose, but could scarcely delight the heart of a connoisseur. Lord Ricimer, however was struck by them and, if I had made myself absurd by inventing the doggerel, he made himself the more so by commenting, in all seriousness, upon it.

"'Perhaps the poet does have his uses after all,' he said. 'For you seem to see more clearly than others superior to you in experience. They think Rome is still all-powerful; you in your poem state the truth, that it is crumbling, a mere illusion of what it once was.'

"He nodded thoughtfully, rapt with admiration, so I hoped, then heaved a heavy sigh. 'You surprise me, poet. Truly you do. We will talk some more. Come to my palace this evening. After dinner, if you please. I do not entertain, and you would not be flattered by any food I might offer you.'

"He turned on his heel and left the room, and also left me in a daze. My companion—whose attempt to show me up had collapsed so badly— at least had the grace to congratulate me on my good fortune. 'He has no companions, few advisors. No one knows his mind. If you can extract even a hint of what he intends, you will be able to trade it for whatever you want. But be careful. It is said that being Ricimer's friend is far more dangerous than being his enemy.'"

Manlius paused and looked around. No one had said a word, scarcely a cup had been touched since he had begun talking. He was telling them of prince and cities, of legendary figures in distant lands. Sophisticated theologians, men of God though they were, he had them enthralled. "I see from your faces that you are less interested in the progress of a young Gaul like myself, and more in the traveler's tale I have to offer," he said with a smile. "Perhaps you are right, for I have seen Rome. Once every Gaul of senatorial rank would have been there; now I know of only half a dozen people who have even traveled out of their own province. But I am one of them. I have seen Rome, I tell you. We hear differing reports, do we not, of this great city. The most beautiful, glorious city in the entire world, glistening with gold and marble. Or is it now a shattered ruin, ransacked and raped time and again after all its troubles, denuded of its wealth, stripped of its population?

"The answer is both; Rome has fallen from its glory, yet in its decrepitude is still more magnificent than the mind of man can easily imagine. I might even say that the barbarian armies might ransack it again and again and come back a third time, and what remained would even then outstrip all other cities on this earth. Stand on the Capitoline Hill, that sacred spot, turn right around and the city stretches before you, so vast you cannot see its end. The great Colosseum itself is bigger than most cities in Gaul, the shops still burst with the perfumes and spices and cloths of all the world. The libraries groan with precious works; at every street corner there is a statue or a monument to some hero of the past. It still boasts men of exquisite learning and women of extraordinary beauty. And ruling it all and all it owned, though always in the background, was Count Ricimer.

"I had expected Eastern pomp, as barbarians can rarely resist the sweets of luxury when they are ready to hand, and the palace he inhabited was grand enough—certainly the biggest such place I have ever been in. And yet he nested in it like a squirrel in an oak tree; most of the halls, all the dining rooms, baths, were disused even though beautifully maintained. Not a sound, not a person did I see in the entire place, even though I knew that guards must be all around. The entire building was in total darkness except for the light thrown by the torch of the two soldiers who escorted me to him. Outside, I was searched—efficiently but not brusquely—and then asked to remove my shoes. Then one soldier knocked on the door, opened it, and gestured me inside.

"Ricimer lay on a couch reading, but made no pretense of business. He got up—there was no one else in the room—and put the papers down on a little desk the moment I walked in, then turned to greet me.

"I was nonplussed by it all, so different was it to my expectations. I was not so naïve as to imagine that I had been invited because of my poetry— even had it been better, Ricimer was not one to have noticed the fact. Careful questioning had indicated that his lusts—if he had any—did not extend to young men such as myself. I did not consider it likely that I had been asked to give wise words on the state of the empire, although I allowed myself a few moments of fantastic imagination in that direction. In fact, I did not know what I was doing there. It never occurred to me then that the most powerful man in Rome had no one to talk to.

"He bade me sit on the couch—in this he was traditional—and asked me to pour him some wine, which I did, though I noticed that, although he put the cup to his lips, he never actually tasted it. He kept company with me, but did not join me. Then he asked me about my journey to Rome, and how our delegation was being treated. I answered frankly and honestly, for I considered that to do otherwise would be considered more insulting than to dissimulate. He did not wish to hear empty praise of a city for which he was known to feel little but disdain.

"'We are treated as you might expect, Excellency,' I said. 'As provincials scarcely worth talking to. Although since news of your invitation this evening circulated somehow, I find myself suddenly popular.'

"He smiled. 'They still fear me, I think. And will do so until they kill me. They hate me, but cannot do without me. How is my fame in Gaul? Am I thought of as the barbarian, destroying Rome simply to keep hold of power for himself?'

"'As you say yourself, sir; it is thought shameful that Rome should be under the sway of a man like yourself who is no Roman.'

"'But what does it say of Rome that it submits to me so easily? I am powerful despite being hated. Yet no one lifts a finger to curb my authority. Do you know why?'

"'A man with a powerful army is hard to curb.'

"'Oh, no. A knife thrust will do the trick. As many people have discovered in the past. No; it is because Romans no longer care to resist. They want an easy, trouble-free life, living on their past, going through their ancient ceremonies, reading and rereading books written half a thousand years ago. The present is of little interest to them. They leave it to me; and as long as their lives are not troubled, will continue to do so. You think of me as scarcely lettered, no doubt. So I am, but I have read some of the histories. I know of the republic and of the old virtues. Such people as the Romans were then would never have tolerated a man like myself except as a servant. Never as a master.'

"'But if you give them what they want, then you are their servant.'

"He considered this, then shook his head. 'Perhaps. But not a true servant. I am the servant who encourages his master to be drunk every evening so he cannot see to the honest running of the household, does not realize I am sleeping with his daughter. I am that sort of servant. I did not choose this role. I wished to do otherwise, to serve Rome, but it is no longer worth serving well.'

"'But with your power, your authority, and your skill, you could insist on this. I do not flatter you, I hope; your expertise in generalship is well known and often proven. But did not Julius Caesar, then Augustus, then Domitian, then Constantine all take a somnolent empire and force it awake, make it defend itself, renew its institutions?'

"Again a shake of the head. 'Do not tempt me. Those days are gone, and will never come back. All the people you mention merely had to take control of Rome. They did not have to fight against Rome itself. It took Domitian all the resources of the entire empire to fight back the challenges he faced. Do you think a man such as myself could do the same with less than half of one, when the more powerful part is hostile?'

"'I do not understand you. Why do you say that?'

"He looked at me with an ironic smile on his face. 'You are indeed provincial, young man. You see nothing except your own concerns, only what is right in front of your face. You complain about the encroachments of Visigoths and Burgundians. You come here asking for troops, and are confused and upset when no one provides them, worried that the empire is so paralyzed it cannot even defend itself anymore. Let me tell you a secret. It does not wish to defend itself.'

"'I know there are many demands on the armies. . . .'

"'No,' he interrupted me. 'You misunderstand what I am saying. Let me put it differently. The emperor in Constantinople will do whatever he can to ensure that peace does not come to the Western provinces, that the barbarians do win more and more territory, and that all of Gaul falls to barbarian tribes as Britain and Spain have already fallen. This has been their policy for half a century.'

"'That is ridiculous.'

"'Sixty years ago, Rome was sacked. Thirty years ago the Burgundians attacked in Gaul. On both occasions, the barbarians were hurled back and yet on both occasions they were offered huge tracts of land within the empire. It is these lands and peoples which now threaten the rest of Gaul and Italy. They were utterly defeated and could have been expelled, as had happened before. Yet they were settled instead, given land and revenue. Why?'

"'A mistaken policy, hoping they would prove controllable.'

"'You have a lower opinion of Imperial wisdom than I have. No. The empire does not make mistakes. Not consistently over half a century, and on a matter like this. It was no mistake. It was deliberate, and successful. The policy was to weaken the Western empire fatally, in order to strengthen the Eastern part dramatically. It has worked well.'

"'You make no sense.'

"'Let me explain again. How many usurpers of the throne, rebellions, pretenders, uprisings, and mutinies have there been in the last century?'

"'I don't know. More than I can count.'

"'Yes. Some have succeeded, some not, all have been expensive, some hugely so, resulting in years of civil war. Nearly all have come from the West—Constantine himself from Britain, most of the others from the army of the Rhine, Spain, or Gaul. Until the barbarians were settled, and the Western provinces so weakened they could no longer field pretenders. The armies were too weak, the barbarians were more interested in squabbling amongst themselves. How many Visigoths or Burgundians have set their eyes on Constantinople? None at all. And the East has been calm, and prosperous and rich; the imperial crown has passed from one man to the next with no bloodshed—or no more than is usual.

"'And the cost has been merely the dismemberment of troublesome provinces which, in any case, never provided much revenue; it was always gobbled up in Rome long before it got to the Golden Horn. Gaul has cost huge sums of money, and provided little in return except trouble. Much better to fragment it into pieces so small it can harm no one but itself.'

"'You are saying we are abandoned. Rome itself is abandoned?'

"'Look at it from the point of view of, say, a citizen of Antioch, or Alexandria. Older and more glorious than Rome in some cases, richer by far. Why would anyone shed a tear if those upstart Romans, so arrogant, so condescending, suffered a little?'

"He paused and looked at me seriously. 'All the world will be shocked should Rome ever fall. But preventing the perpetual civil wars was the main priority of all rulers for more than a century. You cannot say this has not been achieved. And what has been lost? What will be lost?

" 'We would be no longer Roman.'

" 'Why not?'

" 'We could not take office in the state. My father was consul, my uncle magister milites. What would remain for me?'

" 'Empty titles, for the most part. Which cost the possessor a fortune in entertainments and charity.'

" 'And yet we have an emperor in the West now determined to challenge the threat in Gaul.'

" 'Ah, yes. Majorian. And how long do you think he will last?' "

Manlius paused and looked around him. All his dinner guests had sat quietly, listening to this tale. When Manlius had left Ricimer's presence he had gone home, thinking quietly of what he had heard. He had thought of Majorian, the emperor he had accompanied to Rome. And what a difference there was! Majorian was a good man, one striving to do his best, but an ordinary man nonetheless. Ricimer was different, altogether exceptional, the sort you encounter, perhaps, once in a lifetime. Maybe not even then.

"For all that," he continued, "you know the result. Majorian was killed, his successor was murdered, and his successor was also killed, all probably on Ricimer's order. Every emperor who wished to raise an army or move against the Goths went to an early grave. Was it because he was bribed by Constantinople, or because he believed any such move was doomed to fail and would dissipate resources on a fruitless task? I do not know.

"He is dead, anyway. But I remember his last words as I left. 'The empire is not disintegrating because of the barbarians, but because of itself. One part will not fight, the other half cannot. The next time you have a barbarian army on your frontier, remember that well.'

"You want me to go to the emperor, if you can find one, and persuade him to send an army, so we might save Clermont and restore the writ of Rome. Let this story give you some hint of how much success I expect, and why I counsel approaching the Burgundians first. For any success with the emperor will not come swiftly if at all. And, I say again, we have little time."

He almost stretched out his cup of wine to spill the dregs in libation, but held back at the last moment; it would cause offense, and spoil the effect.

BECAUSE OF MARCEL'S fervent appeal, and because his need, and the need of his country, was so apparent, Julien Barneuve accepted the invitation to become a lecturer, a writer of articles, and an examiner of the works of others. A censor and a propagandist, to those few who disapproved; his own ambivalence was such that he used these terms himself. He was given leave from the university where he worked, and his colleagues happily allowed him to go, pleased at the prospect of someone so eminently sensible taking on such a position. Curiously, he enjoyed the work, and found the sensation of doing something worthwhile a pleasing one. For France needed reassurance, needed to know that chaos was controllable and that government was still firmly in the hands of the French. He needed such reassurance as well. Every time he managed to find an allocation of paper for a journal that might have been forced to close down, he felt a small tinge of pleasure, just as he felt a sense of achievement every time he gave a talk on the radio or at a public lecture in Orange, or Avignon or, once, in Vaison itself. Every time he persuaded an editor to hone a critical point so that it was less offensive, he felt he had been useful. Marcel was under siege from within, but at no stage did those seeking to undermine him have an opportunity to use Julien's department to level accusations of incompetence or laxity at his administration. Julien became skilled at making little things seem grand, at constructive delay, at semi-mendacious reports that gave the impression of great activity. But he also did his job, telling himself it was necessary to do so. And, as he traveled through the south of France, in the zone unoccupied by Germans, and gave talks to a variety of meetings, he could feel the stirrings of pride in the audience, and knew that, in his small way, he was helping his country heal something of its wounds, keeping the fragile tissue together.

He never talked about politics, for which he had a disgust that remained and, if anything, grew. Rather, he talked about what he knew; about history, and the way France had grown. He talked about the vicissitudes of the past and how they had been overcome; reminded them of the dark days of other invaders and how, in the end, they had been thrown out. He talked about how the country had grown until it filled its natural frontiers, breeding to produce the French out of the Bretons, Normans, Provençals, Basques, and all the other races who had occupied or passed through in the past. He talked about liberty, and the Revolution and the Rights of Man. None of these did he ever subject to the sort of scrutiny he might have deployed with a scholarly audience; rather, he portrayed their mutual history with an eloquent fervor, discovering reservoirs of patriotic pride he never knew he possessed and which swept over his listeners like a calming, inspiring flood.

He once even talked elliptically about Jews, by delivering a talk on the Avignon papacy in which he mentioned Pope Clement and his act of mercy during the plague, protecting the Jews against those who thought them responsible for the infection. Would he have done such a thing had he not been French? For reason and mercy was bred in the soil of France, breathed in the air. It was part of the national spirit.

Julien gave this talk in Orange, because the topic was very much on his mind. His daily work was not onerous and, indeed, proved a lighter burden than the teaching to which he was accustomed. In the gaps, he had time to go back to his notes and papers and found that the past provided a welcome refuge from the gloom of the everyday. There was much he had accumulated over the years, and much he had never looked at. It was because of the war that he turned his attention to Olivier de Noyen properly; this young man who had such a role in the regeneration of learning in a dark age carried a special appeal for him at that time.

The matter of the Jews also came to his mind for the same reason; even so strict a historian, so determined to exclude the present, could not help but be struck by the contrast between the sudden shaft of magnanimity lighting the dark days of the Black Death and the vindictiveness of the present. For in the most perilous hour of Europe's history, at a moment when more than a third of the entire population was dying in the most hideous agony for reasons no one then understood, the pope extended his protection over the people popularly assumed to be responsible. It accomplished only a little; across the continent, ghettos were destroyed, synagogues razed, and people killed. But on French soil—or soil that became French—a man born and brought up in France stood up and offered an alternative. "They shall not be compelled, because obedience without faith is worthless; they shall not be punished, because punishment without understanding is pointless." Thus the great bull that he issued; the Jews were not wiped out; indeed many came into Provence, into what became Southern France, and their descendants remained, to cause many of Marcel's present headaches.

"Please don't go mentioning Jews again," Marcel said wearily when they met a week or so after his talk. "I'm sure you were making some general historical point of no great relevance, but it doesn't sit well at the moment. Not the way you did it, anyway. I have had six letters of protest, and the policeman sitting in on the meeting was highly critical. I don't need it at the moment."

HIS ROLE GAVE him some small influence and knowledge, and he used it to try to find out what had happened to Julia and her father. He had not been particularly worried about her, as it never occurred to him that her father's will in this, of all things, would be denied. He assumed, rather, that Claude Bronsen had gone to Marseille, found his daughter, and got on the first boat to North Africa. The fact that he had heard nothing from her—no letter, no message—was itself reassuring. She always turned to him; that was his role, and it was one from which he had never shrunk, and she knew it. Had she been in any serious trouble he would have heard.

It was only when he received news from a list distributed around the Préfecture—an unremarkable, routine document, mainly intended to alert bureaucrats of housing in the region no longer occupied and now available for requisitioning—that Bronsen had been interned and had died in the camp that he began to panic.

"What is Les Milles?" he demanded of Marcel one morning. He met him as the préfet was walking across the Place de l'Horloge on his way to the office. A sunny morning, with the first breath of spring in it. Julien had taken to eating his breakfast in a café nearby, though the experience— once full of so many different little pleasures—gave him little joy now. Even though the tide of refugees was ebbing, and the air of desperation was fading, the city that he knew so well seemed changed by the experience. There was a bleakness, even a hardness about it he had not noticed before. The buildings themselves seemed more grim, more evocative of a harsh and cruel past, as though the recent miseries had reminded the stones of what they had seen take place before them in the course of so many centuries.

He almost didn't notice Marcel as he marched across the square. Still determined in his gait, his slight figure just fending off a hint of the ridiculous, the pompous in his stride. Only someone who knew him well, like Julien, could see how he stooped a little more each month. Only at the last minute did Julien finish his coffee—although its bitter, unpleasant taste reminded him of no coffee he had ever drunk before the war—throw down a few coins, and hurry to catch up with him. Marcel stopped and looked at Julien as he approached, and put the question without any ceremony. "Good morning Julien," he replied. "Have you been lying in wait for me?"

"No. I just saw you. What is Les Milles?"

"It's a processing camp. For illegal aliens. Nothing to worry about," he replied. "A routine sort of thing for foreigners wanting exit visas. Got to put them somewhere so they don't vanish. Why do you ask?"

"I have just heard that Julia Bronsen's father has died in it."

Marcel grunted. "The Jewish financier? What do you expect me to say?"

"He was French, and he died there."

"Evidently he wasn't French, or he wouldn't have been there."

"He was a citizen. He had a passport."

"Not the same thing anymore. And as for dying, that's a shame. But people die. There's a lot of it about at the moment. He must have been— what? Sixty? Seventy? It happens."

"So why lock up old men?"

"Don't be ridiculous, Julien. Those people in these camps are lucky. They get housed and fed free of charge, all their wants and desires looked after. And they're hardly under arrest. It's for their own safety, you know. Feelings are running pretty high about people like that. As far as I'm concerned, the sooner people like him leave the country the better."

"He won't be leaving now, will he?"

"Evidently not. And as I say, I'm sorry. But it is not in my area, and I didn't know he'd been taken in. So don't get angry with me. He was your friend, I know. And if I can do anything practical to help, just ask. But don't ask me to mourn someone I didn't know and probably wouldn't have liked even if I had."

"In that case can you find out what happened to Julia? She was meant to be meeting him in Marseille. They were going to leave together."

Marcel's eyes narrowed as he thought. Favors were currency, to be hoarded and used with care. Julien, for the first time, felt like a petitioner.

Eventually he nodded. "I'll make inquiries. All right? Can I go to work now?"

BUT AT LEAST when he made a promise, he delivered. A week later news came through. Julia was living in a pension near the docks in Marseille, trying to get all the exit visas she needed to leave the country. She had been there for four months and was likely to remain there, for it was daily getting more difficult to get out.

Julien could not work out whether he was more hurt or angry that she had not contacted him; in any case both emotions were overwhelmed by worry for her. It was getting difficult to travel, but the trains still ran sporadically; as soon as he could he went to Marseille himself to get her.

The reality was much less bad than his imaginings of squalid hotels, prostitutes, and the poverty of hunger; she was living in a tiny little hotel hard up by the docks, along with a dozen others in a similar situation. The owner was irrepressibly cheerful, remarkably so as it seemed that the chances of anyone paying her the full amount they owed was small.

"That is war," she said philosophically as she took Julien up to her room. "But what can I do? If I throw them out then I get others who cannot pay either."

Julien knocked and walked in. She was lying on the bed, smoking a cigarette, disheveled and with dark shadows under her eyes. She leaned forward onto herself when she saw who it was. She looked dreadful; tired and very frightened. He went to comfort her, but she waved him away. "Get out, Julien," she said.

"What?"

"Five minutes. Come back in five minutes."

He shook his head in surprise, but did as he was told. Stood outside on the narrow landing underneath a hissing gas light, until she opened the door once more and let him in. She'd put on a clean dress, combed her hair, tidied the room. The effort distressed him far more than the first sight of her; for the first time in her life she had been reduced to the conventional. His fury at her bubbled over because of it.

"Why didn't you write to me? What are you doing here? Have you taken leave of your senses? What were you thinking about?"

She opened the window to let in some fresh air, even though it was cold outside. "I like the noise of sea gulls," she said. "I think I'd like to live by the sea. I always enjoyed my stays in the Camargue."

"Julia . . ."

"Sorry. But if you ask rhetorical questions you can hardly expect an answer. If you must know, I didn't write because I couldn't manage it, because I didn't know where you were, and because I haven't exactly been thinking straight since my father died. Did you know about that?"

"I heard. I'm sorry."

"Yes, of course. So am I."

She shut the window and sat down once more on the bed.

"But I am not as destroyed by it as I thought I would be. Strange, don't you think? I think it is, anyway; I have a sense of liberation. I am penniless, bereaved, hiding in this horrid little room. The man who looked after me selflessly all his life, who comforted me, protected me, helped me, loved me without reserve is dead, killed in a dank little prison for no reason. The world, the worthwhile part of it at least, seems to be coming to an end. And my main reaction is to feel more free than ever in my life. And at the same time I sit here transfixed like a frightened rabbit, and sooner or later someone will come and take me away as well.

"I'm a Jew, you know," she added seriously, looking at him with an almost childlike intensity.

"I thought you might be," he said with a faint smile.

"Well, I didn't," she replied. "Not really. My father always pretended we weren't; I know nothing about it at all, but now the government says I am one, so I suppose I must be."

"I don't see why you're so worried. You're French; they're only arresting foreigners."

"Only foreigners," she echoed. "That's all right, then. Except I'm a foreigner as well. Another piece of news. I always thought I was French. I was convinced of it, in fact, but no: My mother was German, and I was born in Germany. My parents were traveling there at the time; my mother was ill, it seems, and they went to take the waters. I was born in Baden-Baden. Do you understand what that means?"

Julien nodded. "It means the sooner you get out the better."

"It does. But I can't get an exit permit without showing my identity card, and the moment I show that, I have my citizenship taken away and the police come round. So, I sit here thinking about my new liberty as an orphan. And, I must say, I have been drinking somewhat too much. Do you know, I've been drawing, after a fashion? I got some children's crayons. Do you know what I've been drawing? Flowers. Vases of flowers. The world is falling to bits, people are locked in camps, I'm stuck in this place, and I have been drawing flowers."

It was not her situation that shook Julien but her response to it, the overly dramatic way she spoke, the ill-considered gestures, the way in which she had forgotten so completely the way she was that she seemed almost a different person.

"You must get out, and you must let me help you," he said. "I've come with money and the names of people who might help. Will you let me?"

She looked at him blankly, and nodded.

JULIEN WAS NOT certain how many laws he broke over the next five days; certainly there were quite a few. He derived no pleasure from it, but had no fear either. No alternative ever crossed his mind. Her safety was the only thing of concern. It was a strange transformation in him as well; up to that point he had scarcely even walked on the grass in a park before; throughout that period most people who were arrested and sent to camps were caught because they could not bring themselves to break laws that they knew to be cruel, even though they knew obeying would lead to disaster. The habit of order was not easily broken; once it was, it was not easily repaired either.

By this stage he was no longer wealthy, as one effect of the war had been to destroy much of the value of investments and savings. Even the money he nominally possessed was hard to obtain; when he heard of Julia's whereabouts, he had reverted to old habits last employed in Rome. He went to a dealer in Avignon and sold him his precious Cézanne. Not for very much, but he knew enough to realize that he was given as much as the dealer was likely to get for it himself. Again a favor, he knew the man well, had taught his son. Such things kept civilization going.

The money he received was just enough for the bribes, the tickets, the payments required to get all the bits of paper Julia needed in the time available. There were those who could help, those who would do so if prodded with a little gift, and those who could be persuaded to turn a blind eye by overstressing his connections to people of importance. He took risks, got everything she required except for the precious exit visa. This she provided for herself.

She was brought back to life by his activity on her behalf, and disappeared one morning at dawn, coming back only as dusk fell once more. Julien spent a day in terror, convinced she had been arrested; he made inquiries but no one had seen her. So he sat waiting; there was nothing else he could do, his fear growing at every moment. When he heard the handle turn and saw the door swing open, he felt sure it was the police, come to search the room.

It was Julia, who walked in calmly and greeted him as if nothing had happened. She threw an envelope on the bed. "Look," she said. "What do you think?"

She was exultant, smiling, herself again. Her hair was loose and the way she moved had returned to its normal ease; for the past few days she had seemed like a creature in a cage, constantly fearful of brushing against the bars and being reminded of its imprisonment. Now she walked like one newly made free. He looked in the envelope. It was the exit visa. "How on earth did you get that?"

She laughed, a delicate, musical peal of laughter. "I didn't. I made it. I didn't spend six months at the École studying etching for nothing, you know. I went to a specialist printer—don't look like that, he's quite safe. He's a Jew as well, and we Jews stick together, it seems—and he lent me his press and a couple of plates. I borrowed our next door neighbor's visa for an hour last night and copied it, then etched it and ran off a copy. The stamps I did by hand. What do you think? They're the best bits of work I've done in a year. Julien?"

Her insouciance, combined with the worry of the day, was too much. He rocked backward and forward on the bed, crying like he had never cried since his mother died so many years before. She knelt down in front of him, stroked him gently, and comforted him, then took him in her arms.

They were both entirely defenseless, and made love for the first time; in many ways for the first time in their lives, and they had both waited a long time.

EVEN BEFORE THE plague bacillus had reached Avignon, Ceccani's great adversary Cardinal de Deaux had floated the idea that the countess of Provence might consider selling the city and some surrounding territory to the church for a large and much-needed sum, for it was undignified for the heir of Peter to live, in effect, in rented accommodation, and firm possession would make permanent residency more likely. For years now he had been encouraging the pope in every possible building project, and when the idea was suggested that Clement should leave the city to escape the plague, he argued forcibly against the notion.

"A shepherd does not abandon his flock," he said when his opinion was asked, although what he meant was that, once he had left, he might never come back. "Your people need you," he added, meaning that if he earned the gratitude of the population, the contrast with turbulent, disobedient Rome would be ever greater.

A strange man, this de Deaux, someone who never would have gotten on well with Ceccani even if the practicalities of great power had not forced them into mutual opposition. For he was a born politician, who acted on his instincts rather than from any easily grasped principle. He had no interest in the sort of thing that so fascinated Ceccani; Olivier would have found no patron in him; abstract knowledge was important only if it served to advance the church. Even in appearance they were different, the Italian short and stout, exuding a chilly affability, the Frenchman tall and gaunt, with a permanent cold even in the full warmth of a Provençal summer.

The Frenchman won the argument about the plague, for Clement was disinclined to leave the city in any case, as he felt safer behind the thick stone walls of his palace. There he did little, but merely remaining became an act of leadership and courage. De Deaux also won on the matter of the purchase, and was sent to open negotiations with the countess of Provence—who guarded her independence from France jealously, and needed money to make sure it continued. Ceccani noted the move and knew it was de Deaux's attempt to end forever the possibility that the pope would return to Rome, where he should be.

Clearly, de Deaux had put in a great deal of advance work before suggesting the idea; permission must have been won from the king of France, who must have concluded that a richer, more secure Provence was a small price to pay for the possibility of permanent French domination of the papacy. It made his own plans the more urgent; he needed to ensure that the negotiations failed, that France would reject the very idea of giving the countess money, that the countess would cancel any sale. He needed to set them at each other's throats. Time was short. He needed to move swiftly; and he needed to cast a shadow over de Deaux, and weaken him.

While Ceccani watched and Clement retired to the top of a great tower in the palace to escape the plague, de Deaux put himself in charge of daily activities, acting in the pope's name. Thus, through him Clement consecrated the Rhône itself as a burial ground, so that corpses could be thrown in to be washed downriver to the sea, rather than rotting in the houses and the streets. He emptied the prisons and put the dregs they contained to work dragging the bodies to the water's edge. And he was doing his best to discover the source of the illness—if there was one—so that something might be done. Or, failing that, so that something might be seen to be done, however ineffective it was.

He also brought his Jew to Avignon to see if he could discover the source of the infection. Ceccani noted all the maneuverings, saw the purpose hidden beneath them. For Cardinal de Deaux was steering the papacy into earning the love of the population, cementing its presence there in their hearts as it had already done in their wallets, fixing it ever more permanently into the very ground of Provence. He was staking his claim to the succession at the same time that he was creating the atmosphere in which the negotiations to buy the city outright were getting under way. Time was very short. Ceccani knew that if he did not move soon, he would never move at all.

Gersonides was brought to Avignon not quite in chains, but as good as. Certainly he would have been shackled and tied to the back of a horse had he persisted in his initial reluctance to come. The two armed soldiers outside his door would brook no refusal. The rabbi had, with the greatest irritation, packed bag and books and accompanied them.

"I do not know when I will see you again," he said to Rebecca at the door. "The plague is not here yet, and I will not come back until it has extinguished itself in Avignon. I do not know if it travels with people, but it seems very possible. I do not wish to bring it to my own home because of a selfish desire to see your face."

To this woman he was as gentle as he was gruff and offensive to men like Ceccani, even though she was every bit as stubborn and self-willed as he was. What was admirable in a man was unseemly in a woman, however, and she had not found a husband, nor was likely to do so. Who, after all, would seek out a penniless servant, with no family, no history? He doubted if even the young Christian, befuddled by her though he was, would be so rash. Gersonides had accepted that the young man was truly besotted, had seen the war rage in him with interest, noted the appalled disgust on his face as the emotion swept over him each time he came. To fall in love with a Jew; so strong was the reaction, so real the complications, he even felt a little sorry for him. And then he saw that same face—a handsome face, he noted, well formed, ringed by curly fair hair that was rarely combed but generally clean—ease as the soul within accepted its fate. And Gersonides also relaxed, for he saw that the young man would not trifle with her, although he knew that there was, for the first time, a possibility that she would now leave him. But what would she do? How would she react? How would it end? He was fearful, for his desire not to leave her mingled with his wish for her happiness and his consciousness of the dangers she faced.

For Gersonides, she was, quite simply, the center point of his life since the death of his wife and six children, all of whom, one by one, had died—three at birth, two when they, in turn, had come to give birth, and one of sickness. For them he grieved, fully and without reservation, although with the stoicism that was his natural character. Rebecca, however, was different, for had she died, he would have died as well. She had come to him by chance, lost and bedraggled, and he had taken her in, fed her, and warmed her. She worked for him selflessly and with absolute honesty, listened to him when he wished to talk, kept quiet when he did not. In the two and a half years since she had come to his door she had replaced wife, daughters, sons, and family. To lose her was the one thing he feared, which was why, on one of the few occasions some hint of a suitor had been mentioned, he had always found reasons to reject the approach. He knew it was selfish, that he should give her up and encourage her to leave. But he could not do so, and he reassured himself with the thought that she evidently had no wish to venture into the world either. Until now, perhaps.

When he left that day, surrounded by papal soldiers, he was alarmed and Rebecca was terrified lest some charge—of necromancy, conjuring, or whatever—had been dreamed up against him. Only a few days previously, news had reached Vaison that near Geneva six Jews had been burned alive in their synagogue. Others in their own town had been spat on and kicked. It required little insight to realize that the atmosphere was becoming dangerous. So far no serious violence had been offered in Provence, but the stories circulated freely and if—or rather when—the plague itself took hold in the towns east of the Rhône, more than blows would be hurled at the handful of Jews who lived there.

A small group had come to Gersonides's house the previous evening for guidance, as he was known to be the wisest man in the region. He was not, alas, the most practical, nor even the most comforting. As there were no moneylenders in the town, he pointed out, they could hardly do anything of significance, like cancel debts until the plague was gone. If the Christians considered that a philosopher, a tailor, a doctor, and a cloth merchant constituted a serious conspiracy against Christendom, there was little they could do to disabuse them of the notion. All they could do was go about their business in their usual fashion, wear the stars that identified them, offer no remark or action that might be misconstrued.

"And one other thing," he said to conclude. "Should the plague arrive, it would be well if some of you died, preferably in great pain and in public."

He gave a watery smile but met no response; the Jews of the town respected the rabbi, listened carefully to his words even when they did not understand them, but never once came close to grasping his sense of humor.

And the following day, the troops came and took him away. There were not that many of them, they were not brutal, even though they had not been told the reason for the deed, but no one would have even thought of offering resistance in any case. Everyone knew full well that, if you resist two soldiers, ten are sent; if you resist ten, a hundred arrive. Best always to do as you are told and offer no provocation. Others might suffer if you do otherwise.

So Rabbi Levi ben Gerson took a few moments to pack what he needed—little enough, to be sure—and presented himself to the soldiers outside his door a few moments later. He got on a horse—a good sign that, for horses are an expensive means of transport, unheard of for prisoners—and went off with the soldiers. They said nothing at all on the journey, although one looked curiously at him and, he felt, would have talked if he had the opportunity; neither looked hostile.

Gersonides did not speak either; idle chatter was not something for which he had ever developed a taste or a skill. Had one of his companions tried to draw him into conversation he would have replied, and would have listened with interest to what was said, but he did not feel inclined to initiate any such discourse. He had quite enough to think about in any case, for he had trained his mind over the years not to waste time on journeys. He was compiling a text on the soul with which he was so far greatly pleased. But it was unfinished and parts were, he thought, ill considered. It was a problem that had sprung into his mind after one of the first meetings—lessons rather—with the young Christian who came to plague him so often.

"You see, Rabbi," the young man said, "it does not make sense to me. The man who wrote this was a bishop, after all. And yet he says quite plainly that the soul is eternal. That is, it is godlike and is not created by God. In addition he talks about our lives, how we must ascend back to God, but stay on earth as mortal beings if we do not purify ourselves here. I don't, of course, want instruction in Christianity from you, yet I was hoping you might be able to explain it to me."

That had been the opening remark—Gersonides's mind was wandering a little as his horse clopped along the muddy road—a request put politely but an order nonetheless. Explain this to me. Give me an answer. The young man was nervous, perhaps, or simply had the rudeness of all his type. But it had not stayed like that. Gersonides had replied with a question himself:

"Perhaps the two are irreconcilable. Would you then be able to consider the alternative account with an open mind, or would it merely confirm its worthlessness in your eyes?"

Then another question:

"You must explain something of your theology. Why is it so important that the soul is created by God rather than deriving from him?"

And a third:

"And the resurrection of the body. Is that what it is called? Yes; why the insistence of that, when the superiority of the soul is so clearly acknowledged? Why do Christians need their bodies so much?"

And so on; he knew the answers perfectly well, for the most part, for he had spent long years reading Christian texts—and Moslem ones and classical ones as well as the Torah and the Talmud, seeking out those flashes of light, those God-sent insights that, he had concluded, illuminate the minds of all men who are capable of recognizing them for what they are.

Considering he was neither priest nor scholar, the young man gave sensible, thoughtful replies—the more so, perhaps, for being untrained, for he had not learned what he should believe or should not believe. Present a statement to him in flagrant contradiction to all Christian doctrine and he could be persuaded to agree on its good sense, unless he remembered it was the sort of thing of which pyres are made for the incautious.

"And now you must go," he had said after two hours had passed and the sun was setting. "I have my prayers to attend to."

"But you haven't told me anything again," Olivier had protested. "All you've done is ask me questions."

"Just so. And if you want to answer more of my questions, then you are welcome to come again. Preferably a little earlier in the day, and, for courtesy, not unannounced next time."

"I came to you for answers. Very specific answers."

"So you keep telling me. And I will repeat the only answer I know. I have none. Not that I haven't spent the last forty years looking, but I find answers are as rare as golden eggs or unicorns. All I can do is help you look for yourself. Think of what Manlius says and apply it to yourself: 'A good act without understanding is not virtue; nor is an ill act; because understanding and virtue are the same.' That is what you are seeking. Understanding, not answers. They are different things."

He peered at Olivier, his face obviously hovering undecided between irritation and perplexity, then went to a box and took out a booklet.

"In your search, you might care to examine this. It is a manuscript I copied out myself, so be careful with it. It came to me via some friends in Seville, who had it from a great Arab scholar. I cannot vouch for its accuracy, for it is a Latin translation of an Arabic translation of a Greek original."

His heart sank a little when Olivier took the book in his hands, for that eagerness, that glint in the eye, that way he all but tore it from his hands was quite unmistakable. He would not be able to deny him entry the next time he came, would not be able to send him away or dissuade him. For while most of his other pupils—and he had been sent many over the years—had been prepared, willing, ready to learn, had been diligent, with Olivier it was different. He needed to learn; it was why he existed, and he would wither unless he could satisfy that need.

Could a man such as himself ever turn away a fellow soul, he who had also ached with that consuming need? Even if there was a long delay between leaving his room and the door onto the street shutting? Even if he heard the sound of voices below, the animated tones of Olivier, the soft replies of Rebecca that always drifted up to his room after he left, and seemed to get longer on each occasion?

 SUCH WERE HIS thoughts on the journey, not about the abstract complexities of the soul; for once his self-discipline abandoned him. He was not especially perturbed, however. The likes of him would hardly be singled out for any real reason. He had no money, no power, and no influence; moreover, all his work—such as it was—had been written in Hebrew. So, the pope had taken lessons in Hebrew, it was said, although when it turned out that these lessons consisted of little more than having the alphabet copied out, the learned Jew, proficient in six languages, none of which had been acquired easily, was less impressed. But, whatever the reason for his being taken to Avignon now, it was unlikely to be because of his philosophy.

In this the old man thought correctly, although even his equanimity was disturbed when he noticed that the little entourage was heading straight for the papal palace, still being extended and rebuilt despite the times. For Avignon in the grip of the plague was truly frightening; scarcely a soul to be seen, in the marketplace only a few traders, miserably trying to sell their wares to no customers. An air of foreboding and of panic all around, the blank expressions on the faces of those few people in the streets saying all that was needed about their terror. Was this in store for his own town? If it was, then dangerous days were ahead of them all. One little spark and their world would be ablaze. Somebody would pay heavily for this catastrophe. Even he could not help considering the possibility that his own journey deep into the palace might be the first installment.

He had been there before, when making one of his reluctant visits to see de Deaux, but the contrast between then and now could hardly have been greater. Whereas before the great courtyard where they all dismounted was full of people—clerics, petitioners, merchants, even a few pilgrims—now it was deserted. The air of authority had dissipated in the face of a far greater power. Even the mighty church was now no more than a feeble collection of mortal, frightened men.

At least, he thought as he was led up a grand staircase, then through a series of rooms, then up a narrower staircase, climbing high into one of the towers; at least the dungeons are underground. We are ascending to the skies, not descending to the depths. Every step upward is one of hope. Unless, of course, they plan to throw me from the battlements.

They came to a small door near the top of the tower; a soldier knocked, opened the door, and stood back to let him past. He stepped in and was almost overcome by the heat, which came blasting over him like a wave from a furnace. He took a step backward, and had to take a deep breath; instantly, little prickles of sweat broke out all over his body, and his thick winter cloak began to feel uncomfortable.

"Take it off, if you find it too warm," came a voice from the corner, near the huge fire. "Do you wish to speak in Provençal, French, or Latin? They are all I can manage, I'm afraid."

"Any will do," the rabbi replied in Provençal.

"Splendid. Latin it is," said Pope Clement. "Do you wish to kiss my ring?"

He held out his hand, on which was a vast ruby ring, shining brilliantly in the firelight. Gersonides stood absolutely still, not assenting, not refusing. The pope smiled cherubically and withdrew his hand.

"What do you think of these rumors that malefactors have been poisoning wells?" he began. "Please, by the way, do not stand too close to me. I have not been up here sweating myself into an early grave for the last ten days just to succumb to some miasma attached to your body."

Not only, Gersonides noted, was the pope sitting as close to the fire as was possible without his clothes catching alight, he was also swaddled like a monstrous newborn in clothes, thick piles of cloaks and blankets and scarves, making him look appallingly bloated. His feet were laced up tight in fur slippers and on his head was a fur hat, expensive, possibly brought all the way from Russia. His face, what could be seen of it, was beetroot red, covered in sweat that rolled freely down his forehead and heavy jowls into his clothes. All around, making it even more oppressive, were candles and incense burners, thickening the air with smoke and contrasting, conflicting aromas.

Gersonides had a headache already, and was beginning to feel faint. His replies were not as subtle and considered as they might have been.

"They are nonsense, Excellence. As any sensible man knows, they are nonsense."

"Cardinal Ceccani today made a strong case that you Jews are behind it all. We have people in the streets saying so as well. Holy men, good men, he tells me. He also says that we must make an example of you. Are you saying, then, that I surround myself with fools, and bestow my patronage on idiots?"

"If you are indeed surrounded by people saying such things, then it is a proposition that deserves consideration, Excellence."

The pope's face turned blank with shock at the impudence, and he peered through the smoke at Gersonides's face. Then he leaned back in his tall oak chair and let out a peal of laughter, his thick, pink jowls shaking from the noise. Gersonides stood as impassively as before.

"By heavens, I am glad we are alone here. You are rude, sir. Very rude, and considering the situation, very unwise. Are you always so?"

"I consider it the best way I know to honor my Creator. He wishes us to strive after the truth, does he not?"

"He wishes us to believe in Him."

"The one does not exclude the other."

"It does in the case of Jews, who refuse to believe the truth of their own Messiah. So much so that they murdered Him rather than honoring Him."

"You know, Excellence, that is a false step in your argument. You can only make such a statement to advance your proposition if the substance of it is accepted by the other side. Only then may you argue for the consequence of that proposition."

The pope wagged his fat, ringed finger. "So you believe in tempering truth with at least a little cunning. I am not dealing with the Jewish equivalent of a holy fool at least. I am glad of it. You are said to be skilled in medicine, astronomy, philosophy, logic, languages, conversant with all forms of ancient knowledge, your own and that of others, familiar with mathematics and optics as well as theology. Is all this true? Or is it just a story put around by a man as vain as he is foolish?"

"I must confess to being both vain and foolish," said Gersonides. "But also to having a little knowledge of all the matters you mention."

"Good. I wish to consult you on a matter of the most vital importance. Will you serve me honestly and truthfully?"

"If I accept the commission, I will perform it to the best of my ability."

"Another cautious response. Do you know what is happening in the world?"

"I know there is a plague."

"But do you know how terrible it is?"

"I have heard some reports. And seen that this city is in a state of terror."

Clement looked dismissive. "This city," he said scornfully. "They don't have the slightest inkling of it. So far there have been a few thousand deaths. That is all. And they are already panicking. I have priests, cardinals, and bishops running for their fat little lives when they are most needed. And it has scarcely started yet. Do you know what will happen here, and throughout the rest of the world?"

Gersonides made no answer. The pope picked up a sheet of paper and began reeling off numbers.

"Syracuse: ninety thousand dead out of a population of a hundred thousand. Genoa: sixty thousand out of seventy-five thousand. Florence, less than ten thousand souls left. Aleppo, wiped out entirely. Not a single man, woman, or child still alive. Alexandria a ghost town. And it goes on and on. The whole world is being consumed, and in a matter of months. Do you see what I mean?"

The rabbi was shocked. That the head of the church had better, more precise information than he possessed he did not doubt for a second. That it should be so terrible he had not suspected for a moment. For a few seconds he could think of nothing to say.

"I read also," the pope continued, "several reports that Jews die as frequently as Christians—and, I might say, as Moslems. God is being very evenhanded, and it seems possible—so many think already—that He intends to wipe out His creation in its entirety. We are in the middle of another flood, except this time He is sparing the animals. Only men and women and children fall to this sickness."

"If that is His intention, then there is nothing we can do about it, except pray for a reprieve."

"And if it is not, then we should see what we can do. You as well. Or do you prefer to sit in contemplation while all of creation is destroyed?"

"What do you want of me?"

"You know about astronomy. See if you can find the source of this in the heavens, and try to discover from whence it comes. You know something of medicine, as do many Jews. Consult with others and see if some way of preventing this monstrous sickness can be found. There was, if I am right, a great plague in Athens during the Great War."

Gersonides nodded. "It is described in Xenophon, of which I have one of the few copies."

"And another in Constantinople in the time of Justinian."

Gersonides nodded again.

"Study them. See how they brought it to an end then. They knew more than us; we might learn from them."

"In that case I must return home."

"No. I do not permit it."

"I have to consult my books and my charts. I can do nothing here."

"They will be brought. My entire library and the resources of the curia will be placed at your disposal. You may have anything you want."

"I want to return to my home."

"Except for that," Clement said with a wintry smile. "Do not force the issue. I have been kind, and will reward you well. Do not make me angry and never challenge an order you receive from me."

It was a revealing moment. The affable pontiff, willing to speak politely with a man such as Gersonides, showing real signs of learning and concern, yet a Christian prince nonetheless. Their positions were clear; the nature of the courtesy clear also. Gersonides bowed his head.

"I will make a list," he said. "But I insist that a message be sent to my servant immediately, lest she be afraid for my health."

"The messenger who collects your papers will tell her."

A nod. "Please make sure he reassures her."

And the rabbi was dismissed. The shock of what had happened, and the impact of the fresh, cold night air when he left that room was so intense that he fainted on the staircase and had to be carried to his lodgings by soldiers, ordered to do so by their captain, for they thought he, too, had succumbed to the plague, and their first instinct was to throw him into the moat.

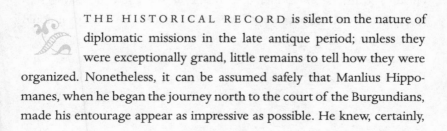 THE HISTORICAL RECORD is silent on the nature of diplomatic missions in the late antique period; unless they were exceptionally grand, little remains to tell how they were organized. Nonetheless, it can be assumed safely that Manlius Hippomanes, when he began the journey north to the court of the Burgundians, made his entourage appear as impressive as possible. He knew, certainly,

that King Gundobad was known for being cunning, and violent, but knew also that he had been in contact with the Roman world for long enough to appreciate the fruits of civilization. Gold and silver and jewels and fine cloth he did not take; these the king had in abundance, more than Manlius could assemble. To have taken such presents would merely have underscored his weakness, shown how little he had to offer. Changed days indeed from the time of his forebears, the sheer magnitude of whose embassies could in themselves awe a barbarian princeling into submission by the easy demonstration of excess. Worship me and all this shall be yours. Rome had survived and prospered for centuries by using the devil's words.

But no longer; now greater subtlety was required. Manlius could not project force, or wealth; there was little left of either. So he decided to strike at the king's weakest spot, his lack of cultivation. Instead of jewels he took books; instead of soldiers he took musicians; instead of a discourse to strike fear and generate submission, he prepared one of gross flattery, drawing parallels between the king and Augustus, noting the emperor's love of learning, and how his fame grew through the praise of men of letters. Let us agree, and I will do the same for you; that was the message, and hardly a subtle one. It was the balance that was important; Manlius needed a style that would awe through its complexity and sophistication but that could still be understood.

It would be an abuse of learning, a disgusting display, a shameful exercise. To praise an emperor and receive a reward, as he had done years ago during Majorian's brief and hopeful reign, that was one thing. Wheedling a barbarian chieftain was very different. Manlius took few of his lettered friends with him; he also took few priests, for the king was an Arian, and the last thing he wanted was some self-righteous cleric, burning with zeal to do God's work, trying to convert him, then denouncing him when he failed. The man's wife adhered to Rome; if she could not bring him around, a clerical harangue was unlikely to succeed either. But it could make him angry.

All this he did on Sophia's advice; he had talked the matter over with her. "To throw away the world to preserve the purity of literary style seems foolish," she had said severely. "You say this man has ruled with justice and firmness. That he was educated at Rome. That he is a man of moderate desires and tastes. To be cunning is no great failing in a ruler, I think. So why should he not be praised? You and your predecessors often delivered panegyrics to emperors who were distinguished only by their lusts, their violence, and their greed."

"Those were delivered to praise the office, and encourage the man to live up to it," Manlius said. "There is surely little comparison."

"There is every comparison. To praise an unjust man and refrain from lauding a just one is foolish. When, also, you desire something from the just man it is doubly so. Give him his due."

Manlius saw the wisdom of her advice, she who had always been so wise, and took his leave.

"I wish you the best of fortune, my dear," she said with a smile. "Do not forget that in everything you do, you must stand above faction and petty interest, and tread the road of virtue."

"Diplomacy and virtue do not make easy companions," he commented.

"No. But that is why you were chosen. Remember all you have learned. You know what is the right, and what is not."

He took his leave of her, and as he left, she picked up a book and began to read it. He caught one last glimpse of her through the window, sitting quietly in the courtyard, bathed in soft morning sun, her head nodding, already absorbed by the work she was studying.

ONE MORNING in early 1942, Julien insisted on a meeting with Marcel, whom in fact he saw only rarely at work, although they still met on occasion for a meal. He was a menial functionary, Marcel was in charge of the whole département. This time he insisted; went to the Préfecture first thing in the morning and waited, pacing up and down until he appeared, stumping along the corridor, battered briefcase in his hand.

"I need to talk to you," he said as Marcel nodded to him in surprise. "It's very important."

"It must be," the préfet commented as he showed him into his office. A grand room, though badly needing a new coat of paint. That would have to wait until after the war. "What is it that gets you so agitated?"

"Have you seen this?" Julien said, waving a folder in front of him.

"I don't know. What is it?"

"A list of books. To be taken out of libraries and destroyed. 'Degenerate literature,' it says. Marcel, they cannot be serious about this."

Marcel took the paper, fished his round, horn-rimmed spectacles from the top pocket of his jacket, and peered at the first page. "Hmm," he said without much interest.

"Did you know of this?"

"Of course I did. I also remember that a similar order came through some six months ago and you did nothing about it whatsoever. Nor, it seems, did anyone else anywhere in France. So now they've lost patience. That's what happens if you're obstructive. If you'd cooperated then and put all those books in store, they would have forgotten about it. Now they want more books, and they want them pulped."

"But look at the list!"

"Marx, Engels, Lenin, Bakunin. . . . A predictable choice, surely?"

"Keep going."

Marcel shrugged, so Julien read for him.

"Zola. Gide. Walter Scott. Walter Scott? What in God's name is degenerate about Walter Scott? Boring, I agree. But hardly a danger to national morale."

"That's committees for you," Marcel said wearily. "If you must know, I find it completely stupid as well, though don't quote me. But they will keep on going until it's done, and the list will get longer and longer. So go and do it. Now, if you'll excuse me."

Julien was dismissed and went marching down the corridor in a rage. He could not, would not do this. This was an outrage. He remembered how he had felt, the scorn and disgust when he heard of book burnings in Germany. Such a thing could never happen in France, he consoled himself. And now that was exactly what was happening. By direct orders of a French government.

Again, he thought of resigning, registering his protest, but then, once more, he thought of the cold, cruel man who was likely to take over his job; it was Marcel's subtle form of blackmail to keep him in place. For he had told him several times how only his protection stopped a rabid zealot, a crusader for moral and racial purity, from occupying his position. If that was what he wanted, then go ahead and resign. Look and see what would happen. . . .

Julien again sat on the memorandum, pretended it wasn't there, but no matter what he did he could find little comfort. A few weeks later he had to hold a meeting with the editor of a newspaper in Carpentras. It was a difficult meeting, and tried his patience. The editor was a venerable old man who had owned and run his paper for nearly forty years. Of the reporters who worked for him, two were known communists and one was a Jew. Of late, the paper had published a series of articles that were implicitly critical of the government, and that reported on the shortages of food and clothing. Julien, under strict instruction, had sent a letter warning of this, but he had paid no attention. Now he was under instruction to close the paper down.

"We cannot have this," Marcel had said to him. "Don't these people realize? Don't they see that whipping up resentment and criticism does nothing at all? If the marshal cannot talk to the Germans as the leader of a unified France, he can achieve nothing."

"Everything the paper said was true," Julien pointed out. It was a cold day; there was no heating in Marcel's office except for a small iron brazier that smoked badly. Julien felt asphyxiated by the fumes, and chilly in his ever more worn clothes. Even Marcel, he noted, was now badly shaved through lack of a good razor.

"It doesn't matter if it was true or not," Marcel snapped. "These people are making trouble unnecessarily. Sort it out."

And Julien had summoned the editor.

"You are going to close the paper?" the man said in astonishment. "Because we pointed out what everybody knows?"

Julien looked sad. "I'm sorry," he said. "You were warned."

"I do not accept it. There must be something we can do. I will give an undertaking—"

"You already have. Much good did it do."

The man thought. "The newspaper must stay in print," he said. "Fifty people work for it, and they won't find another job at the moment. There are the reporters, the printers, their families. . . ."

He looked down at the floor, staring at ruin and disaster. "Tell me," he said reluctantly, speaking slowly as if hating every word that came out of his mouth. "If I got rid of the reporter who wrote the article . . ."

"Who is he?"

"Malkowitz."

"I will inquire."

Julien went back to Marcel and made the proposition.

"This Malkowitz character. Is he the Jew?"

"I believe so."

"Excellent," he said. "A fine piece of work. The paper continues, we exert our authority, and we get rid of a Jew who should have lost his job six months ago if you had been doing yours. Come to think of it, take a look at all the papers. See how many Jews there are. Suggest to the editors that their supplies of paper would be more sure if they thought more carefully about the makeup of their reporting staff. Then maybe the Bureau of Jewish Affairs will leave me alone for a bit."

"Why? I really don't think—"

"Just do it, Julien."

"But, Marcel, apart from anything else it is quite unfair."

And Marcel exploded. The first time Julien had ever seen his friend display such a lack of control. "Julien, do not question me and do not waste my time with your quibbles. I have a département to keep running. I am faced with having to tell the good people of Avignon that two thousand young men are going to be rounded up and sent to work in German factories. I have acts of petty criminality and sabotage to deal with. I have Vichy and the Germans breathing down my neck all the time. I have Marshal Pétain coming to visit in three weeks' time. And if getting rid of a few Jews who probably shouldn't be in the country in the first place will get me a bit of peace and quiet, then the sooner they are dealt with the better. Now, see to it. Or I'll get someone else to do it. Understood?"

Julien retreated, taken aback by the outburst. He took the point. It was a question of priorities, and he could hardly criticize Marcel's reasoning. What, after all, were a few jobs in comparison to the utter collapse of an entire country? Nonetheless, he found the task distasteful and delayed doing anything about it for several days until Marcel prodded him again. And again. And eventually he talked to a few editors. Four Jews were fired. Three papers dismissed another five without even being asked. More would have done so had he insisted.

In return he went back to Marcel over the matter of the books. And won a compromise; Walter Scott would be put into storage, to be consulted only with special permission. Ten people had paid for his successful defense of learning. There was no connection; they were separate matters; it was a price worth paying. Eventually, it stopped going through his mind, trying to think of some other way he might have treated the problem.

AND THREE WEEKS LATER, in October 1942, Marshal Pétain came to Avignon and was greeted on the steps of the Préfecture by his loyal servant, Marcel Laplace. Throughout that short intervening period, Julien's disquiet grew as Marcel worked himself into a frenzy of worry. The police seemed to be in every café, every restaurant; soldiers were brought in to patrol the streets, suspected dissidents rounded up. Orders went out forbidding housewives to hang out their washing on the day of the great event. All flowerpots were to be taken off window ledges. Even so, leaflets mocking the marshal were distributed on the streets, and Marcel went wild with anxiety.

But, in Marcel's view at least, it was all worth it. The marshal arrived and expressed himself satisfied. A grand reception followed, and Julien was invited; he shook the marshal's hand, had those steady, deep eyes on him, and heard the speech that followed. He praised his préfet and hoped all would obey his orders; he criticized the legion, the bane of Marcel's existence, for having admitted undesirables, for being more concerned with power than ensuring good government. And gave a warning that their behavior would be watched in the future.

And when he left, Marcel was exultant. "Julien my friend, you see? Did you hear that? We've won. They've been beaten back. It's all been worth it. Now I can look after this place without being second-guessed and criticized all the time. Thank you, my dear friend. Thank you."

He drank glass after glass of a champagne carefully hoarded for a special moment; for Marcel had only one enemy in those days, the people who sought to weaken his authority. And his victory seemed complete; he had strengthened his position immeasurably, was finally master in his own house. He had won his war.

Exactly twenty-nine days later, on November 8, 1942, the German army swept south, out of the occupied zone, and extinguished what remained of Free France. They found the work Marcel had done in the course of the battle against his rivals—the lists of Jews and communists, foreigners and undesirables, the reorganized police force, the vast files on the subversive, the dangerous, and the discontented—immensely useful. And Marcel's life became complicated once more.

IN THIS PERIOD of darkness and uncertainty, Julien consoled himself by finally writing his article on Olivier de Noyen. It remained unfinished at his death, as he was never satisfied with it and did not really wish to end it, for it became a refuge he would have lost through its completion. The subject became in his hands a disquisition on loyalty, for he sketched out what he considered the truth of the poet's end, using for the first time the evidence about the Comte de Fréjus sent to him some years before. He wrote in the evenings and at weekends, after he had gone back to his apartment on the rue de la Petite Fusterie, and drowned himself in the past, staying in it until the next day came and he was forced back into a situation he found ever more difficult.

Beneath the scholarly proprieties, the article alternated between lyricism and bitterness, an exploration through history of the idea of loyalty to individuals and to political ideas, a reflection of his own situation and an attempt to come to terms with it. For he had established, he believed, the truth behind Olivier de Noyen's fate; the attack on him had nothing to do with Isabelle de Fréjus.

Rather it was because Olivier turned traitor and brought about the fall of Ceccani from the highest power. Olivier sold the secret of the cardinal's machinations to his greatest enemy, and if he had not done so, then Ceccani might well have been the next pope. Why did he do this? Surely not the desire for money; there was no evidence of that. Perhaps, though, for an ideal? Perhaps he felt that the papacy should stay in Avignon? But that was not convincing either.

Nonetheless, what he had done was there for all to see. The letter from de Fréjus to the seneschal of Aigues-Mortes, stating that he was to open the gates to the English troops when they arrived by ship, was in the Archives Nationales in Paris. The guarantee of money from Ceccani was in the ledgers of the banking house of the Frescobaldi in Florence. And the note in the daybook of the pope clearly indicated that details of the plot had been provided by the cardinal's "segretarius" who, at that time, was Olivier de Noyen. The plot failed; this was clearly known; Aigues-Mortes did not fall to the English; the papacy succeeded in buying Avignon and stayed there. It was easy and indeed inevitable to conclude that the failure of the scheme was because the pope intervened to make sure of it. Ceccani fell from papal favor, all his hopes of succeeding his master doomed. He was isolated and powerless, living out the remaining few years of his life visiting his dioceses. And as a final irony, on his death his great palace was bought by Cardinal de Deaux, his most bitter enemy.

Julien went back to the poems, those last lines written before Olivier was silenced, and in particular the one that contains the line "and I sink in heart-ache, like a ship in a storm." Not, says Julien, a reference to his love; this is not a love poem. For Olivier surely had cast off the safety of Ceccani's patronage, which had given him everything. And having thrown away the security of so great a master, there was nothing to protect him. The poem alludes to his betrayal and his consciousness of it. By implication it also suggests that Olivier was aware that retribution was close when he wrote, and that it was not unjustified. Loyalty has always been one of the highest human attributes. By the standards of his day and age,

Olivier's sin could not have been greater. He may have been a poet of considerable ability; in human terms he could not be judged lightly. The Comte de Fréjus was let loose on him in revenge. He was lucky to escape with his life; had Ceccani demanded more, who could have denied him?

And so Julien judged Olivier de Noyen harshly and without pity. He even referred back to Manlius and the example he set, using the text of *The Dream of Scipio* as the link; for Olivier knew Manlius's words, but had utterly failed to comprehend them, it seemed. "No one can possess wisdom if consumed by intemperance," says Manlius, quoting the Protagoras, yet Olivier's actions were surely intemperate. Another statement, this time derived from Cicero, also gave him comfort, for the wisest of all Romans stated that "you cannot act rightly by taking up arms against your father or your fatherland." Was that not what Olivier had done? For in that age without countries, Cardinal Ceccani was both father and fatherland to Olivier, and he had turned against both. Julien's own position was the more clear, surely?

It is significant, however, that Julien did not ponder the next passage from Manlius's manuscript until much later, for it might have brought with it further reflection. He had noted it years before in the Vatican library, correctly ascribed its origins to Theophrastus, then filed it away. "An amount of disgrace or infamy can be incurred," Manlius quoted, "if it is in the cause of virtue."

Had Julien been less influenced by his own predicament, then he might have looked harder and guessed the poet's motivations earlier than he did. He might also have considered the possibility that Manlius, in writing these words, was passing a verdict on his own acts, rather than providing a philosophical basis for them.

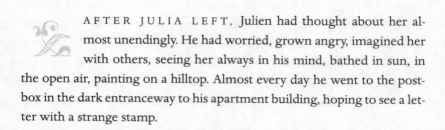 AFTER JULIA LEFT, Julien had thought about her almost unendingly. He had worried, grown angry, imagined her with others, seeing her always in his mind, bathed in sun, in the open air, painting on a hilltop. Almost every day he went to the postbox in the dark entranceway to his apartment building, hoping to see a letter with a strange stamp.

The concierge stopped saying anything to him after a while. Initially she had said, "Nothing today, Monsieur Barneuve," when he came down, but now she stopped and merely shook her head when he appeared every morning.

He had given up hoping for news by the time it arrived, quite unexpectedly, about two weeks after the German invasion of the south. He had finished his day's work, walked out into the ever quieter, dirtier streets, dark already with the streetlights unlit for fear of bombers—although the muttering of the cynical said this was a convenient excuse to cover the fact that there was not enough power to provide lighting anymore. The streets were deserted; the arrival of the German army had extinguished what little life there was left. Although people were getting used to it surprisingly quickly, few went out when darkness fell; only the occasional military truck was on the roads, and few people on foot except for patrols of either soldiers or policemen. There was an air of foreboding that hung over the entire city like a thick fog.

It was raining lightly and he hurried, crossing the road and putting his foot in a deep puddle that had opened up in the pavement the previous winter and had never been repaired. He stopped and looked down at his soaking foot and sodden shoe, his only decent pair of winter shoes, which he had taken out that morning and checked carefully to make sure their soles were still good. With luck they would last. This would not help them, and he cursed the war, the Germans, Marcel, the city, and the weather equally, for bringing their final disintegration that much closer. Then, more slowly and carefully, looking down at the ground, he walked the last couple of hundred meters to his home, standing in the entrance, shaking himself and brushing as much water as possible out of his hair and off his clothes.

He went up the stairs, into his chilly apartment, and even before he switched on the lights he fetched a towel. He stood by the window drying his hair, staring down at the steps of the church of Saint Agricole opposite. It was nearly eight; the doors were open and the last people at evening mass were coming out, each one pausing at the door, looking up at the rain as though they could see where it was all coming from, then hunching down and hurrying away.

Only one person there was not in a rush, standing close by the entrance, faintly illuminated by the light coming out of the open doorway. Julien stiffened. That turn of the head, set of the shoulders, that manner of standing. The patience of the way the woman let the rain run down her body rather than trying to find cover. He could see little, but he would have recognized her in any light or in any weather.

He ran down the stairs, forgetting his soaking shoe, not taking a coat or umbrella, and ran as quickly as he could across the street, bounding up the steps two at a time.

"Julia!" he called out.

She turned and smiled, and held out her arms to him. When he finally let her go he was soaked to the skin once more.

HE USED UP nearly a month's allowance of coal to get her dry, and rather than talking, spent the first few hours they were together fussing like an old hen over her. Taking off her clothes and arranging them around the fire to dry, making hot water for her bath, sorting out an old dressing gown for her to wear, then running out again to the shops to find something—anything—to buy for her to eat. They ended up having a feast around the fire of boiled rice, tomatoes, a little bread, and some grapes. Not grand, perhaps, but in the circumstances, a triumph.

And eventually, when she was warm and dry and clean, they began to talk. The room was in near darkness, and even though it was no longer cold they huddled close together, touching all the time. He could not bear not to be touching her, constantly reassuring himself that she was truly there.

"Why on earth are you here? Are you mad?"

In the intervening year her hair had become even more flecked with gray; she had lost weight and had acquired the gaunt, furtive look of the persecuted and the hunted. Her fingers fiddled constantly, and he realized that the calm and poise that had once been so much a part of her had gone. The clothes now hissing by the fire were a size or so too big, and threadbare; Julien realized for the first time how artful her previous simplicity had been. Only her eyes remained the same.

She was drinking as well; her third glass of homemade brandy—given to him by a farmer at Roaix, made in the man's own still—sat in front of her, already empty.

"I remembered how much you shouted at me for not coming to you last time I got into a mess," she said. "And I didn't want to risk that again. I hadn't anticipated that you'd be out so late." She had a faint, ironic smile on her face—which highlighted the lines growing around her mouth and in her cheeks. "On the other hand, if you mean what am I doing in France, it's a long story. But basically I discovered that going to America and being let into America are different things."

"So where have you been for the last year?"

"On a boat, and in various ports. I seem to have spent months in waiting rooms, waiting to plead my case. Which was listened to sympathetically until a decision had to be made. Then it was short and simple. No. I was in Havana, much of the time. Nice place. The boat docked there and the American authorities intervened. They were determined to stop us getting to the United States. Quite simple really: the politicians have promised that all refugees who ask for asylum in America will be given it, so they stop as many people as possible from getting close enough to pop the question."

She poured some more brandy. "Then back to Lisbon, and was thrown out of there, then into Spain, which was also too dangerous. So I thought that if I was going to be arrested, I would like it to happen at home. I missed you," she concluded simply.

"Being arrested will happen very soon," Julien said. "Nearly all Jews have been already."

She smiled, reached into her handbag, and tossed an identity card at him.

"Where did you get this?"

"Another one of my artistic creations. I forged my way out of the country, I forged my way back in again. I find I have quite a skill at these things. Identity cards are quite easy. I have a friend in Lisbon who is an artist, and he let me use his press. I'm quite proud of it."

"Madame Juliette de Valois?" he queried with a smile on his face. "Unnecessarily grand, isn't it?"

"Someone I knew when I was young. She died of tuberculosis when she was eight. Her father was a member of the Action Française and a great anti-Semite. It made me smile when I thought of becoming her. So, if necessary I can call on a birth certificate, you see. I also made myself a passport, showing I have been in Vietnam for the past eight years, hence no records of me in France. Residence permits for Hanoi, entry visa for Lisbon, and from then on everything is stamped and sealed quite legitimately. She had no siblings, her parents are dead. Very hard to prove I am not her. My only concern is that all these papers are too much in order."

"What about the death certificate?"

"She died in Saint Quentin, and the town hall was destroyed in the last war. I mean, she's perfect, don't you think? On the other hand, I am penniless, homeless, with only one change of clothes, nowhere to live, and have given away any possible source of income with my old identity. I can hardly sell paintings. Not that anyone would want to buy them, I imagine."

"And I am not the only person in Avignon who could recognize you."

"No. I wasn't sure it was the best idea. But—here I am, well fed, warm, and unmolested. Besides, when I look in the mirror I scarcely recognize myself. I'm surprised you did. It must be love. But I suppose I must go somewhere else."

"You will go to Roaix. You'll be safe there. And I will be able to keep an eye on you and make sure you don't get into any more trouble. As for the question of money . . ."

"Ah, yes."

"Do you have any at all?"

"No," she said in a curiously light way, as if acknowledging the irony of it all. "God only knows what I would have done if I hadn't found you. It's a strange feeling, being penniless. I suppose I should feel liberated from the material things of this world. In fact, it's very annoying. I do not like poverty. I do not see its appeal."

"I can let you have a little. But I don't earn much and my father's assets are largely useless and you can't sell anything anymore. So I am also without much in the way of resources."

"Come and live with me, then," she said lightly. "We can starve together and lead a life of Rousseauian simplicity. You can shoot rabbits, I will cook them for you. You can sit and read in the evening while I darn your socks."

"You can't darn socks, can you?"

There was just enough of a hint of suppressed desire for Julia to burst out laughing. Everybody in France, probably, had holes in their socks. It was one of the small humiliations of subjection.

"No," she said with a giggle. "I have never darned a sock in my life. But it can't be so difficult, can it?"

"And I know you can't cook."

"Julien, are you *refusing* me?"

And now he laughed. He felt the life surging back through him, like a house being occupied after a long absence.

"Officially, I suppose, you're not even married anymore."

"No. An odd situation to be in, I must say. But I can live with it."

"So marry me then. Now you have the chance."

The good humor and merriment were suspended the moment the words came out of his mouth. She put down her glass, then gazed at him carefully. "You're not even saying this because you feel sorry for me, are you?"

"You know perfectly well I'm not."

"That's good. I would have hated that."

"Well?"

"I will, kind sir. I will marry you," she said with a faint smile. "And do so with the greatest pleasure. But properly. Not under a pseudonym. When I can marry you as me, then I will do so."

Julien grinned in a way he had not managed, he thought, since the war broke out. "War is a strange thing," he said. "It makes people cut corners. Can we, perhaps, skip the marriage and get straight onto the honeymoon?" He went and got blankets and pillows from the bed, and they slept by the fire, Julien waking up periodically through the night to put on some more of the rapidly diminished bucket of coal. By the time morning had come there was none left. He would be living in the cold until the next supplies came through. And who knew when that might be?

The next morning Julien went to the railway station and collected her battered old case, brought it back, and strapped it to his bicycle. Then they began the long trek out to Roaix—pleasant enough in summer, much less so in winter, above all with the suitcase. Once, about two hours on the road to Carpentras, they got themselves all tangled up and both fell over, the bike crashing to the ground and the suitcase bursting open. Julien hurried to pick up all the bits, the bedraggled pieces of clothing, a hairbrush. "It's hardly worth it," he said, then looked up and saw her lip was trembling as she fought back the tears. It was all she had in the world.

"Oh, I'm so sorry," he said vehemently when he realized. "Don't cry. I was stupid. Don't cry." And he reassured her like he would a child, with all the tenderness he had, comforting, gentle, and loving.

"Leave it," she said. "You're right. It's not worth it."

"Absolutely not. It's coming."

They started arguing, a healthy, restorative dispute, were still fighting about it when there was a rumble behind them. It was a German truck, lumbering along the road. "I thought you said they didn't come over this side of the river?" Julia said. "Isn't this meant to be an Italian zone?"

"In theory," he replied shortly. "Not in practice."

The truck slowed, then halted beside them. A fair head poked out of the window and looked at them somberly. A young man, so far untouched by the war or any hardship. He smiled. "Where are you going?" Heavily accented but good French

"Vaison."

He thought, then shrugged. "I'll take you to Camaret, if you can tell me how to get there."

Julia was nervous, but Julien accepted and bundled the bicycle into the back, among all the ammunition the man was transporting. Then they got in. The young man talked all the way and fortunately didn't require much in reply. No, he shouldn't have picked them up, but don't tell anyone, eh? A couple arguing over a bike didn't seem much of a threat to him. It was their own fault for sending him off without a map. How was he expected to find his way . . .

A nice boy, eager to oblige, keen that the kindness be appreciated. When he dropped them off on the outskirts of Camaret, leaving them only twenty kilometers to walk, Julia said quietly, "Don't ever do that to me again." Julien looked at her. She was not joking.

THE NEXT DAY, after they had arrived in Roaix, he settled her in, showed her where all the wood was for the fire and the kitchen, the well, introduced her to the farmers living nearby as his fiancée, and asked them to look after her until he returned. This they promised to do, and they kept their word faithfully.

Then, when he left, Julia began to find her way around. About a week later, she went on a walk and discovered the shrine of Saint Sophia.

Even for the atheist and the rationalist, there are places in the world that are special, for no reason that can be easily explained. The footsteps slow, the voice lowers and speaks more softly, an air of peace works its way into the soul. Each individual has his own place, it is true; what is holy to one will not be so necessarily to another, although the reverberations of some are all but universal. And the chapel was Julia's place, every bit as much as Julien Barneuve's was the phoenix villa; she realized this long before she reached the top of the hill, walking up on his advice. "Pretty place," he told her. "Good view." She felt the air of anticipation well up in her, the peculiar mixture of calm excitement of one who knows their life is about to change forever. She sensed the chapel long before she rounded the last bend in the track and saw it surrounded by a clump of trees with weeds and wildflowers growing around its crumbling walls. She had never seen it before, but it felt comfortingly familiar. This sentiment she put down to the sense of safety she had been wallowing in ever since she had found Julien again and come to this place.

The door was not locked; there was nothing to protect. Inside it was clear that sheep and goats were perhaps the most frequent visitors. A small altar remained, placed there in the nineteenth century, an ugly reject from another church, bulbous and inappropriate, but better than nothing. And it was dark, as well; the windows were tiny and high up on the walls and were so dirty they let in little light, just enough to see the dozen or so bits of paper on the altar. Julia picked up a few, took them to the door, and looked at them.

"Dear Lady, should I leave my parents and live on my own?" read one. "Blessed Saint Sophia, should I go and work in Avignon?" was a second. "Thank you for your warning," a third. She was almost moved to smile, but there was something about the tidy peasant lettering, the way each missive had been folded carefully and neatly on good paper, the way each woman—for the writing suggested they were all women—must have toiled all the way up here, which made her refold each one carefully and put them all back in their place.

As she did so, she looked up and caught her breath as she saw what remained of Luca Pisano's work. The paintings were dreadfully damaged, blistering off in places through the effects of long neglect, scrawled on lower down by what she later realized must have been the hatreds of the Revolution, darkened by the soot of half a millennium's worth of candles, but still discernible; a saint reaching out to a man in a strange gesture, her hand over his eyes, something she had never seen before.

Instantly she was captivated; this was why she had come to this place, to see these pictures. This was the answer to her problem. She was ill equipped to study them closely; in her pocket she had only a box of matches, and even though she opened the door as wide as possible to let the thin winter sun stream in, she managed to see only part of the whole. But it was enough; the next day she returned, and set to work.

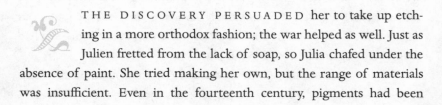 THE DISCOVERY PERSUADED her to take up etching in a more orthodox fashion; the war helped as well. Just as Julien fretted from the lack of soap, so Julia chafed under the absence of paint. She tried making her own, but the range of materials was insufficient. Even in the fourteenth century, pigments had been

brought from far afield. The war meant trade shrank to levels not seen since the days of Manlius Hippomanes.

She became obsessive about paper, learning its feel and different properties. She bought up old books for the blank pages at the beginning and end, and eventually tried her hand at grinding up old cloths to try to make the sort of rag paper preferred in the sixteenth century. Her fingers were permanently stained black with ink she also made herself from a recipe Julien found in a book in the library—the municipal library, now happily ensconced in Cardinal Ceccani's grand palace. She cut back her nails almost into the flesh, and soaked her hands in lemon juice for hours to clean them. The printing press she made herself—or rather she had the local blacksmith construct it for her out of an old mangle and a heavy iron frame that originally came from a bed.

She was proud of her creation; it produced results as good as any she had seen at the specialist printers in Paris, and the whole business delighted her artisanal inclinations. The unknown artist of the chapel, the master of Saint Sophia, as she called him, would have been proud of her, she thought. She had no money, but a good deal of time, and this she spent liberally, making meticulous drawings and drinking prodigious amounts of cheap red wine with the blacksmith, going over the design and the practicalities of construction. She began as supervisor to his work, and ended as his most menial assistant, filing off shards of metal, holding thick beams of iron as he beat and welded. And as he made the fine adjustments, she sat in his workshop with a plate of copper she had waxed herself and swiftly scratched out a study of Pierre Duveau at work, a serious man, slight for a blacksmith, with dark eyes and an intense stare.

He ended up with a respect for this overprivileged woman fallen on hard times, dressed in a man's shirt, her sleeves rolled up, her thick dark hair flecked with gray held back out of her face with a piece of string. A beautiful woman, he thought as he hammered, and a noble name, though she looked like a Jew to him. Not that he cared, as he mentioned to his wife. But what was she doing living in Julien Barneuve's house, turning up late one night and settling in to stay? His fiancée, didn't he say? Not, as his wife commented, that it was any business of his.

Pierre was not a man to give affection easily. Her willingness to assist and watch and learn did not entirely win him over, however, for he thought her interest unwomanly; her obvious intelligence and penetrating questions about the practicalities of slippage and downward pressure alarmed him, especially as she would not be put off by easy answers. Her perfectionism irritated, as she returned time and again with minor modifications and insisted that they be done precisely. And yet he was proud of the result, as others gathered around to stare in awe at the bizarre contraption. Julia bought the entire village a round of drinks to celebrate the final completion of the project, and made a joking speech of thanks for building the most useless mangle in France.

He was, however, touched and even a little flattered by the first work to be drawn from his device, though not nearly as pleased as Julia herself, as she inscribed, and presented it to him. "To Pierre, blacksmith extraordinaire, with thanks." It was the sketch she had done while she watched him work, which she etched in the acid that Julien had found in a chemist's shop in Avignon and brought to her one weekend, and then engraved with a dry-point to add fine detail to the face and arms. Not one of her most experimental works, almost traditional in honor of his calling. But still too abstracted and free for his wife, Elizabeth. "All that effort for such a thing," she said sourly as they looked at it on the kitchen table.

He laughed. "I like it," he replied. "I've even started to like her. A strange woman. Special, if you know what I mean. Educated. Intelligent. Accomplished. All the sort of things a woman would need if she was to keep Julien Barneuve. Permanently, that is."

This said with an edge to his voice, a hardness as he put the print down. He had it framed and hung on the wall to act as a constant reminder to his wife of the difference between an ordinary woman and a special one. She tried to take it down, or move it, but every time he put it back again, and would comment on how much he was growing to like it. He said it many times.

A sought-after work, now, for those who collect French prints. Only six were ever drawn off the plate before Julia erased it for more dangerous work later on. And few of those found buyers. She sold little; the dealer who had previously taken her paintings was in Paris, and inaccessible. And initially no one else would stock her work. She was now unknown, after all. Most were too considerate, or too dishonest, to say why they refused her. It was only when one looked closely at her, studied her face, then stared at the ceiling and said, "I just don't think I can sell *cosmopolitan* art at the moment, you see," that she understood. For some reason, she never thought it would touch her; not there, not in her painting. She almost said, "But I'm not Jewish," when she stopped, sensing that she had said those words too often already.

MANLIUS SET OUT the day after his discussion with Sophia and went north. He knew there was little time. Somewhere in Italy was Felix, spending money he did not have to raise an army that would never come; it would, in his imagination, march in an ordered fashion along the coast, then strike north, hurling itself against Euric's army, raising the siege of Clermont. Felix would establish his family's dominion over the whole of the province, the gentle balm of Roman life would return, and a peace of Augustan dimensions would fall over a contented land.

It was not to counter his friend and rival's ambition that Manlius left. It was because he knew, as his friend should have known, that Felix had gone to live in a lotus land of his imagination. Where what is desired is dreamed of as already happened, where obstacles dissolve under the weight of desire, and where reality has vanished entirely. For any army of barbarians marching under the Roman standard would accomplish nothing except looting, and the wrath of Euric would be the greater for the attempt to block him. In trying to save everything, everything would be lost.

So Manlius reasoned, and in order to accomplish his aims he made haste, as much as the roads and baggage would allow. He rode on a donkey—or rather, he took a donkey with him so that he could transfer to it when they neared the Burgundian encampment. A little detail, but an important one nonetheless. He was going as a bishop, not as a politician or a landowner, and needed to make this clear.

For the first time he gave a task to his adopted son when he left; it was time that his family assisted him, he considered. "Go into Vaison, Syagrius. Keep watch on the mood of the people there," he said. "Do nothing but listen; find out who is the most afraid, who is most on my side. I will need this information when I return."

Syagrius nodded eagerly; he had been waiting for such a commission, was desperate to show his worth. But Manlius took no leave of him as a father should of a son. Instead, he turned, mounted his horse, and began talking to the estate manager. Then he wheeled the beast around and rode off.

He talked little on the way; there was no one he wished to talk to. Of the thirty people traveling with him, not one had enough to say to tempt him out of his silence. Going through a valley toward the end of a day, after a hard drive that lasted ten hours, he saw the sunset, framed between the body of the hill and a decayed fruit orchard, long abandoned. The noise of wasps and bees gorging themselves on the fruit that had fallen unwanted to the ground was so loud they could hear it a full half hour before they passed by.

A bittersweet reference to Hesiod would have begun an exchange with more cultivated travelers, the theme developing into a discussion of the idea of descent, from the age of gold into the brute age of iron. Could the process be reversed? Could the age of iron be made to give way to a new age of peace and prosperity? What a pleasure to have such a discussion, to swim in the comfort of shared ideas and shared memories, to prepare for the encounter to come. Manlius instead had to have the conversation in his head, and later wrote it down (in edited form) as what became ff23–25 of Olivier's copy of *The Dream of Scipio*. He dwelt there on the divine and inevitability, a subtle (if inevitably sketchy) discussion of free will, pleased with himself for avoiding any reference whatsoever to the ponderous Christian contributions on the topic.

Are we fated or not? Can we individually alter what is to come? Are civilizations as a whole, mankind as a race, doomed to rise, then decline, from gold to silver to the brutality of iron? Was he—for this was the essence of the conversation he never had—fighting against the gods in trying to fend off disaster?

No, says Sophia. Polite but sure in her correctness, deriving the logic from Plato, but refined by near eight centuries of consideration into a form he would scarcely have recognized. You cannot change fate; even the gods (a reference here to Lucian, unspotted by Gersonides but picked up by Julien) are subject to the whim of Lachesis. She and her sister fates alone know what is to be, but they do not care.

The question is a false one, for the concern of man is not his future but his present, not the world but his soul. We must be just, we must strive, we must engage ourselves with the business of the world for our own sake, because through that, and through contemplation in equal measure, our soul is purified and brought closer to the divine. There is no reward for good behavior, as the Christians suppose, no judge to decide. The more nearly our soul resembles the divine, the closer it is able to approach the model from which it was formed and which it ceased resembling when it became tainted by the material on falling to earth. Thought and deed conjoined are crucial. Faith means nothing, for we are too corrupted to apprehend the truth.

Rephrase the question, then: Can Manlius Hippomanes, trudging northward with his small entourage, reverse the decline and restore tranquillity to the land? Possibly not, nor does it matter. The attempt must be made; the outcome is irrelevant. Right action is a pale material reflection of the divine, but reflection it is, nonetheless. Define your goal and exert reason to accomplish it by virtuous action; success or failure is secondary. The good man, the philosopher—the terms to Manlius were the same—would strive to act rightly and discount the opinion of the world. Only other philosophers could judge a philosopher, for only they can grasp what lies beyond the world.

DID MANLIUS DISPLAY a sense of humor in the *Dream,* of a sort utterly undetectable in any of his other writings? Certainly, there was a touch of the whimsical about it that added to the difficulty of its comprehension. For his *Scipio* was modeled in form but not in nature on the more famous work written nearly half a millennium previously by Cicero; the modifications look backward and forward simultaneously, bringing the past of Rome's golden age into association with a future that was dark and uncertain.

Cicero's great work—much commented on for nearly two millennia—was a part of his *Republica,* a final survey of the problem of civic virtue conducted through the mouth of Scipio Africanus, the most noble Roman of them all. In it the younger Scipio dreams he meets the older one and is shown the marvels of the universe, and has explained to him the way in which the actions of great men in society are part of the universal harmony, required by the divine.

Manlius re-angled the work and gave it a more melancholic, less optimistic twist. This time it is Manlius who is in reverie: The title refers to a dream about Scipio, not a dream by him, and it is occasioned by the prologue in which he discusses philosophy with Sophia. She mentions the famous remarks by Scipio when he sees Carthage ruined, and weeps lest the same fate befall Rome in its turn.

A pregnant moment; the sentence also inspired Saint Augustine to write *The City of God* after the sack of 410 brought Scipio's terrible vision to pass. Internal evidence suggests that Manlius must have read Augustine's great work; his treatise was the last pagan response to it, before the unstoppable momentum of Christianity extinguished all dissent. In his hands the sack of Rome by Alaric becomes the symbol of the end of civilization, the final extinction of anything of value. Manlius begins his journey of exploration in darkness, and is only slowly led by Sophia to a new light. Not the light of Christianity, that barbarian religion; civilization cannot be destroyed so easily.

Sophia takes him to the Capitoline and shows him Rome, burning and destroyed, and reassures him when he begins to weep: "Rome has fallen from its glory, yet in its decrepitude is still more magnificent than the mind of man can easily imagine. Stand on this sacred spot and turn around; see the city stretch before you, so vast you cannot see its end." And suddenly, from his vantage point, Manlius can see the whole world in the finest detail, can see men of goodwill rebuilding, stone by stone. He sees libraries reconstructed, and men discussing philosophy once more, and walking in fine gardens. "Philosophy cannot be extinguished, though men will try," she tells him. "The spirit seeks the light, that is its nature. It wishes to return to its origin, and must try forever to reach enlightenment."

"Most are unaware of the need," Manlius objects. "They prefer the foolish belief and the passions of the earth. They believe the absurd and shrink from the truth."

"No, they do not. They are afraid, that is all. And they must remain on earth until they come to the way of leaving it."

"And how do they leave? How is the ascent made? Must one learn virtue?"

Here she laughs. "You have read too much, and learned too little. Virtue is a road, not a destination. Man cannot be virtuous. Understanding is the goal. When that is achieved, the soul can take wing."

And so on; at every level, the Bishop of Vaison, Saint Manlius, launches attack after attack on Christianity, contradicting it at every turn. The soul is general, not individual; eternal, not specific in time. The body is a prison, not something meriting resurrection. Faith is corruption, Hope is deception, Charity illusion; all must be surpassed.

"But how must we live?" Manlius asks. "If man cannot be virtuous, can there be no good man?"

"Action is the activity of the rational soul, which abhors irrationality and must combat it or be corrupted by it. When it sees the irrationality of others, it must seek to correct it, and can do this either by teaching or engaging in public affairs itself, correcting through its practice. And the purpose of action is to enable philosophy to continue, for if men are reduced to the material alone, they become no more than beasts."

A remarkable sentence, which struck Julien when he read it, for Manlius completely overturns orthodoxy, whether Platonic or Christian. The point of civilization is to be civilized; the purpose of action is to perpetuate society, for only in society can philosophy truly take place. Only a man who realized civilization might not continue could have reformulated classical ideas in such a way; only a man contemplating drastic action could have penned such a self-justification. Only with such an aim could the pagan pretend to be a Christian, the friend abandon his friends.

As a piece of philosophy, it was not of the highest order; Manlius abandoned the syllogistic form and scarcely argues at all. Through the mouth of Sophia, he instructs merely. His style was as elliptical as usual, perhaps because it was hastily written. References and allusions peppered the pages but appeared to have been inserted unconsciously; Julien had to summon all his knowledge to track down the quotations from Aristotle, Plato, Plutarch, Alcinous, Proclus, references from lost works to which he could give only tentative attributions; then he had to analyze the mistakes and decide whether they were deliberate or accidental. And finally, he had to come to some conclusion—had Manlius made a genuine contribution to later Neoplatonism, or was it a semi-digested rehash of old ideas? Was the manuscript more use as philosophy or as a historical document?

It was so much easier for Gersonides, and easier still for Olivier, for the rabbi was largely, the Christian totally, innocent of the scholarly apparatus that revealed the complexity of the document.

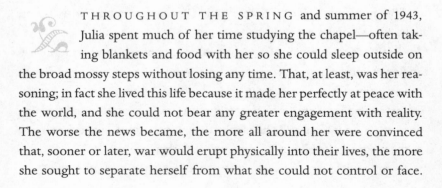

THROUGHOUT THE SPRING and summer of 1943, Julia spent much of her time studying the chapel—often taking blankets and food with her so she could sleep outside on the broad mossy steps without losing any time. That, at least, was her reasoning; in fact she lived this life because it made her perfectly at peace with the world, and she could not bear any greater engagement with reality. The worse the news became, the more all around her were convinced that, sooner or later, war would erupt physically into their lives, the more she sought to separate herself from what she could not control or face.

The idea, always in the back of her mind, that the tranquillity she enjoyed might soon come to an end made every breath of warm air, every scent of wildflowers, and every buzz of an insect many times more pleasurable and intense. Her senses were more alive than at any time she could remember, and she felt that she was, in her way, doing a service. For that sort of peacefulness was valuable; it was rare and endangered. She wished to store it up in her mind so that she might remember when the darkness fell.

Occasionally, when the solitude began to overwhelm even her, she would pack her bag and walk down the crumbly, slippery track to the village, to buy food or water, or sketch in the sun of the little square. She became, indeed, a figure of curiosity and some small suspicion; many were concerned at an outsider interfering with the shrine, and were fearful of her intentions. Within the first week of her discovery of it, she had numerous visitors—old women, young girls, shepherds—who just happened to find themselves nearby and came to investigate. Initially she was irritated by the waste of time, put off by the blank, dumb way they stood behind her as she worked, never asking questions, never showing any real interest that she could meet, never giving her a chance to explain herself.

But slowly the power of place settled over her; she no more resented them than she resented the goats whose bells clanged noisily outside as they fed, or the occasional sheep that wandered in out of idle curiosity. And eventually she discovered that they were proud of this saint, eager to answer questions about her. She began to jot down the stories they told her in a notebook before the setting sun made it too dark to read any-more, and as the weeks passed, she also jotted down variants in the sto-ries, grouping them into themes and categories, trying to distinguish the few kernels of truly old legend from recent accretions or borrowings. The saint's reputation for curing poor sight was one constant theme, as was her prowess at giving good advice, but she also, it seemed, had other pow-ers, particularly in curing all sorts of maladies. The affectionate way her limitations were recognized was also notable, and Julia first paid attention to this when the blacksmith's wife, Elizabeth Duveau, came up to the chapel one day.

She was working hard and didn't notice that anyone had come in behind her. Eventually a slight rustling sound made her stop her work and turn round. Elizabeth was standing a few feet away from her, staring stonily at her back.

"Oh, hello," Julia said. Elizabeth nodded and continued to look at her. Eventually, Julia realized she was looking at her left hand; she followed the gaze to try to work out what she found so interesting.

"No," she said when she thought she'd worked it out. "No ring."

"You won't be having children," she commented.

"I doubt it."

"You left it too late."

"Probably."

"Why was that?" came the question with that alarming directness she was slowly becoming used to.

She put down her paper with a sigh, her concentration gone. "I don't know. I've never met anyone I needed to live with until now."

Elizabeth wiped a bead of sweat from her nose. "Nor have I. But I've been married to Pierre for fifteen years. Her fault."

Julia looked perplexed. "Whose fault?"

She gestured in the general direction of the altar. "Pierre proposed to me in 1925. September, it was. I didn't love him, and I knew already he drank too much, but I was past twenty and laughed at as an old maid. I dreamed someone else might ask, but he didn't and no one else was likely to come along. So what could I do? I could go to the town and work as a servant or stay where I was and marry Pierre, who had good money as a blacksmith. A catch, he was. So I asked Sophia. She'd given good advice when I'd asked before.

"But not this time. She is not reliable in this area. Of course, she was never married herself, so perhaps that explains it. But she said I most certainly should marry him, and I took her advice."

At least it got the conversation off Julia's own life. "How did she tell you this?"

"The usual way. I dreamed that I was cold and hungry, living on the streets of Marseille, that no one would talk to me or give me work or food. So I took the warning, and stayed where I was, in the village, and married Pierre. And I have spent the last fifteen years wondering whether she was really trying hard enough."

"Why?"

She shrugged. "How long have you known Julien?"

"Oh. Years. Fifteen years. Something like that."

Julia felt the dark, inquisitive eyes studying her. "I've known him since he was eight." She said it in almost a proprietorial fashion, as though it gave her a superior claim of some sort.

"Does everyone know she is not very good at this sort of advice?"

She was thinking of something else, and Julia had to repeat the question before she came back. "Heavens, yes," she said eventually. "Even children know it. When they see a girl walking out with an unsuitable boy, they say she must have been talking to Sophia."

"How do you know she wasn't married?"

Elizabeth paused to consider a question she found strange. "Why would she have spent her life up here if she'd had a man and a hearth to tend?" The practicality of the response was unanswerable. "No; she was alone, and came up here to live in prayer. And was a good person, which is why people came to ask her advice even before they knew she was a saint. There were many miracles after she died, which is a sign. Of course, there are old stories."

"Which ones?"

She looked sheepish. "Old wives' tales," she said. "My mother used to tell me. But even she didn't believe them."

"Please tell me."

"Oh, it's about the blind man she cured. It is said that the first thing he saw when he began to see was Sophia's face, and he cried out in delight and said that he had seen her face in his dreams many a time, and that he had loved her all his life. And that he asked her to marry him, but she refused because she was virginal and pure. And he pined away with sorrow until she talked to him and brought him to God. But he always loved her, and swore that he would wait for all eternity until he could be united with her, and have her acknowledge his love. And she said she would wait until he understood what love was. It's something old women say to daughters to make them go to sleep. That's all."

She turned away to the altar, and Julia walked outside to leave her in peace. She sat on the steps in the sunshine, basking in the heat like one of the lizards that sat motionless all around her, looking down across the valley to the lavender fields beyond the woods. She fell asleep; must have done, for when she opened her eyes once more, the blacksmith's wife was already far in the distance, slowly picking her way through the stones and weeds.

Julia waved, but got no acknowledgment, then sat down for one of the best meals she had ever eaten, of bread and wine and salami. She felt entirely safe, and utterly happy.

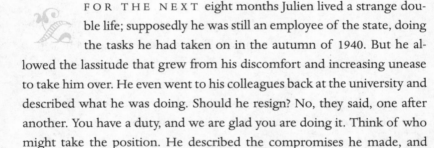 FOR THE NEXT eight months Julien lived a strange double life; supposedly he was still an employee of the state, doing the tasks he had taken on in the autumn of 1940. But he allowed the lassitude that grew from his discomfort and increasing unease to take him over. He even went to his colleagues back at the university and described what he was doing. Should he resign? No, they said, one after another. You have a duty, and we are glad you are doing it. Think of who might take the position. He described the compromises he made, and again they replied, Stay where you are. He even once went to Marcel and appealed to him, but met no help from that quarter either.

"Don't you see, Julien, that there is no room here for your delicacies?" Marcel replied with a sigh. "That your fastidiousness is out of place? Selfish? We have to keep government going. Have to keep it in the hands of men of moderation. Don't you see that?"

Julien continued to look uneasy, unconvinced. "And you are a man of moderation?" he felt like asking, but he knew the answer. Yes, Marcel was indeed, in comparison to those others snapping at his heels.

ONLY JULIA SUGGESTED a different course of action when he went back to what he now considered his real home to be with her. "You are doing things you dislike so that others won't be able to do worse. Are you sure that is not the case for everyone? Isn't that what your friend Marcel is doing? The policeman who arrests people in the night? The prime minister? Even Pétain himself? They are all doing things they would prefer not to in order to prevent worse. The evil committed by good men is the worst of all, because they know better and do it anyway. Isn't that what that manuscript of yours says?"

Her opinion contradicted those of so many others, but then she would not be affected by his resignation; all the librarians and journalists and newspaper owners and academics and teachers would be. He thought about it some more, anguishing in his indecision. And as he writhed, he came in late, if at all; memoranda and orders lay on his desk for weeks before anything was done with them, and then any work was bungled and performed incompetently. He read more, found himself obsessed with the minutiae of the life of Olivier de Noyen, to the exclusion of all else. His idleness was his refuge, and in this he was like many others in France in that period; laziness became political.

More and more, he left Avignon altogether and went east to Julia, traveling however he could. Sometimes there were buses, sometimes he managed to get a ride with a farmer on a horse and cart; most of the time he rode on his bicycle, the tires now long worn away and replaced with cloth, which he bound tightly to the rim of the wheels with wire. Once there, he would stay often for ten days at a time, finding excuse after excuse not to leave. When he did return to Avignon, he hoped to find he had been dismissed in his absence; no such good fortune ever awaited him.

When he came, he brought gifts for her, all sorts of things he would never have considered before the war. He spent time going around bookstalls finding old books with blank end pages that she could use for her printing, cutting them out in a way that previously would have appalled him. He knew every pharmacist in the city who would set aside the acid she needed for biting her plates. Ironmongers and scrap merchants received constant visits also, and would collect plates of copper for him, beating them flat into a usable shape once more. Once he discovered some oranges, and bore them to her in triumph; they ate them together on the flat grass outside the chapel door, getting themselves sticky as the juice ran down their faces and clothes. The wasps came, and Julia ran away screaming in fright; Julien ran after her, pounding at them with his hat to drive them away before they both scuttled into the chapel and shut the door, sitting in the darkness and laughing themselves silly.

Both of them were happy in a way neither had ever imagined. Often they scarcely even talked for days on end, but were merely in each other's company. She did her work, outside when possible, inside if not, and he did likewise. They would take such food as they could find with them up to the chapel and spend the day there, often sleeping there at night, waking up at dawn and eating a crust of bread together before washing each other down with the water Julien brought up from the river in an old metal bucket. Or she would go on her own and Julien would busy himself in the garden. He grew potatoes and tomatoes; there was an olive tree and a fig tree, and he carefully tended four tobacco plants, whose leaves he would pluck and press and dry and shred. They smoked the result with a couple of old clay pipes when cigarettes were unobtainable.

Julia returned to herself, and to her work, in his company and with the stimulus of the chapel. She slept, for the first time in two years, she said, and slept so hard Julien could scarcely wake her in the morning. Then she would bustle about making tisane, for there was no coffee, and went to see if the hen she'd acquired had laid any eggs. Generally it hadn't, but occasionally she would return from the henhouse she'd built, bearing the egg with the most immense pride in the bird's achievement. And she would boil Julien the egg, and serve it with all the ceremony of Escoffier himself, concocting one of his fragrant masterpieces in an age now long forgotten.

They were playacting, they knew, and the realization made it the more precious. They were living out the pages of a child's book, pursuing the life of bucolic simplicity to fend off the ever grimmer news that came through from the outside; the shortages, the arrests, the Allied landings, the bombings, and the murders that became daily events. There was nothing they could do about it except survive, and celebrate their survival and the love that grew stronger with every glance and every shared moment.

It was Julia who pointed out, when she read some of the late poetry of Olivier de Noyen, tossed onto the floor as Julien worked, that whomever he might have loved, this "woman of darkness, wisdom touching the light" (to quote one of his latest poems) surely could not have been Isabelle de Fréjus, at least not if her supposed portrait was truly her.

"Look," she said impatiently one evening, brushing her hair out of her eyes in the way Julien had first noticed on his Mediterranean cruise, and which he had loved ever since. A competent, businesslike gesture of someone whose profession was seeing, done with a slight toss of the head and which always left her face and neck and hair arranged in a perfect harmony. "Look at the damned woman."

Julien had finished his article for perhaps the fourth time, but was still not pleased with it. It had lain now for several months on his desk, and every time he had gone back to it, he had a feeling of impatience welling up inside him; he could not settle down and work on it again. It was true; everything he said about the poet was right. About the betrayal of Ceccani, the casting off of all accepted obligations. Yet he knew he did not have the whole picture, for although he could reinterpret some of the poems, others were stubbornly intransigent. They were love poems, and however much he might reconsider Olivier as a man, as a poet he could not persuade himself that his last words were anything but remarkable.

He mentioned this and she read both the poems—struggling through in the Provençal—and listened to his argument. Then she looked at the portrait of Isabelle reproduced in a guide to the *Musée des Beaux Arts* in Lyon. It came from a book of hours, and the attribution was venerable enough to be believable; Pisano had given it to her. Then she stated the obvious.

"I'm a mere painter," she said. "But were I a poet, I would never dream of describing someone with fair hair as a woman of darkness, whatever I might mean. It would be lazy, not to say incompetent. I think I would make myself work a little harder to make the metaphor match the physical appearance."

Julien grunted, then chewed his lip. "Well," he said reluctantly. "You're right, I suppose."

"Of course I'm right," she replied cheerfully. "Sorry."

Afterward, he let the remarks brew on their own in his mind. Of course she was right; of course this woman of darkness could not have had fair hair. Could not have been Isabelle de Fréjus. But the fact remained that Olivier had loved someone. Did it matter whom he had loved?

His mind turned the question upside down and presented him with a different solution many months later. From the notion of Wisdom he thought of Sophia, then of the chapel that Olivier had written about. This came to him in Avignon, and the next time he visited—in winter this time, when even Julia had stopped going up the hill because of the lack of light and warmth—he asked her about how the painter had portrayed Saint Sophia. She rummaged in the large folder she had made to protect her precious paper.

"I did some watercolors," she said, handing one over. "They're not so good. But she does have dark hair."

"And these?" he asked, picking up a pile of papers wrapped up in the same bundle.

"Ah, well," she said, settling down on her haunches, an air of anticipation, pleasure, about her.

So Julien looked, and instantly understood the self-satisfaction in her tone. He looked for a long time, picking up one, then the next, then the next. Eventually he looked up. "Congratulations."

It was deserved. She had finally overcome the barriers that he had so harshly pointed out to her some ten years before and attained a simplicity and originality that was breathtaking. Pisano had set her free; Julien never considered that he might have had a hand in it as well. She had taken his work and allowed herself to range over it; sketching parts of it time and again, renewing and revisiting, bending and breaking, stripping the image down and building it back up again. She gave the faces depth, then flattened them to abstraction, reduced them to a mere line, stressing first one feature then another, until she came to her goal, which was an almost perfectly harmonious blending of herself with his pictures. She now neither broke with the past nor imitated it; rather she grew out of it, extended it in unimagined directions.

She was leaning back against a chair by the fire and lit a cigarette; it was an important moment for her, she had three to get to the end of the month. "What do you think?" Still a little anxious, wanting compliments, but sure of getting them.

"These I would buy. Alas, now I don't have any money. You just don't have any luck, do you?"

She laughed. "I was going to give them to you anyway. They're my wedding present to you."

She picked up a pencil, and inscribed each one. "To Julien, with love from Lady Wisdom. January 1943." And she signed it with her own name. Next time he went back to Avignon, to his other life, he took them with him; he could not be without them.

THEY STARTED FROM opposite ends. Pisano is a master of form and is striving toward reality; Julia aches to throw off the tyranny of reality and reach the essential that lies somewhere underneath. In the quiet of the chapel they meet, briefly and only once. In the panel of Sophia curing the blind man, the toss of her head, the expression on the face, derived from Byzantium, coming through Rome and a hundred years of Siennese mastery but infused with the spirit of Olivier when the Italian caught him once looking at Rebecca, Pisano comes close to his goal.

And Julia begins with his painting, releasing what has been locked up in it for nearly six centuries. When she finished—the hour late and the light long since faded—she knew that she had found something she had been looking for for years.

Just as she had prodded Julien, so he had pushed her. He had made the connection between the Sophia of the *Dream* and the saint of the chapel, hinted they were one and the same, or at least derived from a common model. So she had used this; the blind man is not the recipient of a Christian miracle; rather he comes to knowledge; Sophia is not some evangelical saint but the vessel conveying that wisdom.

It was Marcel, of all people, who pointed out the obvious. Julien hung them in his apartment, removing some prints then on the wall to reuse the frames. Marcel saw them on one of his visits, rare now but all the more valuable to him for that, a reminder of the normality of friendship that Julien, despite everything, was still able to offer. Julien found his company ever more uncomfortable, but his need was so obvious he could not deny him.

On this occasion, Marcel looked at one of the pictures carefully, he who had no serious interest in painting beyond a conventional contempt for the modern.

"If you are going to have your portrait done, you really should get someone who can paint, you know," he said with a smirk. "*I* can tell it's you. But many people would miss it entirely. And don't think I don't recognize the woman, either. She left, didn't she? She did go?"

Julien nodded, cautiously.

"Good. If she'd stayed here she'd be in danger. If she was found, they'd take her. You do know that, don't you?"

He nodded again.

"Good," he said. "I'm hearing bad things. Very bad things."

Julien didn't ask him to elaborate. Marcel turned back to the pictures and grimaced. Then, abruptly, he picked up his hat and left.

Julien mentioned his comments about the pictures the next time he saw her. Julia turned deathly pale.

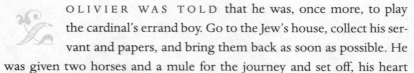 OLIVIER WAS TOLD that he was, once more, to play the cardinal's errand boy. Go to the Jew's house, collect his servant and papers, and bring them back as soon as possible. He was given two horses and a mule for the journey and set off, his heart beating hard at the prospect of seeing Rebecca again, and alone.

It was a day's ride, and he arrived in the evening and went straight to Gersonides's house. This was a kindness, for he knew that no one had yet told Rebecca that her master was safe and well, and he knew also that she would be frantic with worry lest he had come to some harm. So he knocked just as the rain, which had been falling in a light drizzle for the past hour, turned into a downpour, and stood there with water dripping from his hat and cloak and face as she opened the thick wooden door.

She thought he had come with bad news; the look on his face, made pale by the journey and the cold, suggested so, and she cried out with alarm to see the apparition on the doorstep.

"Oh, no," she cried, holding her hands to her face. "Oh, no."

Her grief was so real, and so wrong, that Olivier felt a similar hurt at having caused it, and stepped into the door and embraced her to give reassurance.

"No, no," he said softly, stroking her cheek, "you must not be afraid. I have not come to upset you. He is perfectly well. And is perfectly free."

These words, designed to calm her, seemed to have the opposite effect. Rebecca sank to her knees, sobbing loudly and with the tears rolling down her cheeks. Olivier let her go and suddenly became aware that the water dripping off his cloak was making her almost as wet as he was; also that a large puddle of water was forming on the floor and that the winds blowing through the door were about to blow out the candle. So he shut the door quickly then knelt down beside her.

"He has been commissioned by His Holiness to search for the cause of the plague," he said. "And I may say will be well rewarded for his assistance. He has agreed to help, and is staying in a fine apartment in the palace. He needs his papers, and he needs you. So I have come to get both. He sends his greetings. And that is quite all."

He put his hand under her chin and lifted it toward him, and when he saw her disheveled, tear-stained face, his heart melted in a way he had never dreamed possible. He had read the poetry and heard the songs since his youth. For more than two years he had willed his love into being, fixing on the abstraction he had glimpsed in the street and determining that he would feel the truth behind these songs. Then when it was in his grasp he had recoiled from it, wished it away and almost come to hate the reality that spoiled the simplicity of his vision. He had believed he was ill, gripped by a sickness as virulent as the plague, and he ardently desired a cure. And when he looked into her face that rainy night, he gave way, and wished to be sick forever.

When he touched her cheek he was at last rid of all artifice. He did not know whether she was beautiful or not, although some thought her so, a robust, rugged beauty that was a great distance from the soft, slightly pampered attractions of a woman like Isabelle de Fréjus. Her skin was too dark, her frame too strong, her hair too thick, her features too pronounced for her to excite any other poet than Olivier. But he knew at that moment that all the poems he had written had been for this woman, not for some ideal, and that he had loved her since before he was born, and would love her long after he had died.

Even though he had been brought up with the feelings of the troubadours, Olivier's reactions went far beyond any of the extreme but stylized emotions sanctioned in their songs, and the poem he wrote a few days later, just before the catastrophe struck him, was so excessive that even after the passage of centuries it has the ability to cause shock or, in the less sensitive, derision. But it was a real song, stripped of all mannerism and conceit, pouring out, however ineptly and inaccurately, something of what was within him.

As for Rebecca, she, too, felt winded by the intensity of his gaze and the surfeit of emotions that he caused deep within her. The way he dissipated her anxiety, the gentleness of his touch, and the reassurance of his presence stirred her in a fashion that was as irresistible as it was unwelcome. She had not spent much of her youth listening to songs of love and the forgiveness that awaits those who follow love's dictates. Rather, her sense of obligation and fear had deep roots and could not be torn out so easily.

She pulled back—gently, though, and with no anger, encouraging him even as she snapped the strong link that so briefly bound them together.

"You are welcome, for your kindness and your news," she said, and she could not disguise the tremor in her voice, nor its cause. "My thanks. Please sit by the fire and dry yourself."

"It is good of you to think of my comfort."

"You are dripping on my floor."

They looked at each other once more, and then both began to laugh without restraint. Every few moments one tried to stop, then looked at the other and erupted again. Olivier knew that he should take her in his arms then and there, and she knew he should do so, but the rules of life prevented him. The fact that he did not, that there was an absence where there should have been movement, made the stillness even more potent, lasting until both, finally, managed to wipe their eyes and stop.

Both knew full well what would happen sooner or later; the inevitable, fate, God's will—none of these can be denied or avoided or even postponed for long. But Rebecca tried her best, becoming the guardian of household purity in her master's honor even though he was absent. But the times were as extreme as their emotions, otherwise she would not have dreamed of allowing him to stay; would not have allowed him to eat with her, and would not have allowed him to help collect her master's papers—not that he was much help as he could not read the writing on most of them. Olivier noted that she, too, had trouble; indeed that she could barely read.

"I have heard it said that Jewish women are often well taught," he mentioned.

She hesitated for a moment and looked at him carefully. "Indeed," she said. "Some are. But all the education in the world would not help with handwriting like this."

She put down the papers. "I cannot do this now," she said, "not while I cannot see properly." They had a few good wax candles in the house, jealously saved for high days, and she had recklessly gotten two from the kitchen and lit them, only to find that the yellow sputtering light they gave off was little better than darkness. Gersonides's handwriting was as illegible in Greek and Latin as it was in Hebrew, so bad, indeed, that only he could even tell which alphabet his terrible scrawl was using. To make out in the darkness which manuscript was which was almost impossible.

"Come and sit by the fire," she said. "I will get some food while you warm yourself, and then you can tell me news."

"I thought you did not encourage Christians to eat in your houses? Or am I wrong?"

"We will not eat in yours, because your food is unclean. You may eat as much of ours as you wish. It is just that we do not like Christians in our houses. In fact, we do not like Christians, on the whole. But you may sit down. Unless you are uncomfortable being in a Jew's house."

"I am not at all uncomfortable," he said. "The fire is as warm as a Christian fire, the roof as strong, and the food will be welcome whether it is clean or unclean. I am merely confused, that is all. You are serving me with food, even though it is Friday and darkness has fallen."

"Rules can be broken under necessity."

"A Jewess who can barely read, who serves me with food and lights me candles and brings me wood for the fire on a Sabbath?" He smiled softly.

She sucked in her breath for a moment and looked at him in the firelight, but saw no anger in his eyes and heard no criticism in his voice.

"Why do you pretend to be a Jew?" he asked, eventually.

She hung her head. "Because I am even more unfortunate than one," she replied. "Because it is only among them that I have found safety."

He looked at her curiously. He could think of almost nothing more unfortunate than that.

She looked at him seriously. "My parents died when I was fifteen, and I went wandering; there was no one who would take me in, not to give me safety. I travelled around France but found no help, then crossed into Provence. I came to Avignon but that frightened me; I could find no one who wouldn't question me. Eventually I came here; the old man found me and said he needed a servant. He also wanted someone who was not Jewish to look after him on the Sabbath as well. But it is illegal for a Jew to employ a Christian. So for the outside world I pretended to be a Jew. He got his servant, I got my protection."

"And you like this life?"

"I love him. He has been as kind and as good to me as any father. He never criticizes, never hectors me, and would die rather than betray his trust to me. What more could I want?"

"You are one of those heretics, aren't you?"

She nodded. "If you wish."

"I didn't know there were any of you left."

"More than you think. A hundred years ago, the church murdered as many as they could find, but they did not find all. We learned discretion, and learned to hide ourselves. Now, if we are discovered we are almost safe, because we do not exist anymore, and the churchmen cannot admit they left the job undone. My parents were hanged for theft, which they did not commit, not for their beliefs, which they openly admitted."

"I heard a phrase recently. It begins 'The water of life . . .'" Olivier said, and looked at her expectantly.

"Yes?"

"What does it mean?"

"It means that we are all part of the divine, and that our desire is to return to the ocean from whence we came. We must purify ourselves on earth, and put aside our taste for material things, for the world is our prison, even though we don't realize it. We are in hell now; but we can escape it."

"And if we don't?"

"Then we are reborn, and must live again. This interests you?"

"I read it in an old manuscript. And heard it on the road when I was traveling."

The genealogy of ideas did not interest her, the similarities between Neoplatonic thought and her beliefs prompted her to no amazement or questioning. She nodded merely and fell silent.

"And us?" he asked after a while. "Is it evil what I feel for you? How can it be?"

"The flesh is the creation of evil. But the love is God's touch; it is our wish to become complete. It is our memory of God, and our sense of what we might become."

"Do you believe all this?" he asked suddenly.

"Do you believe that God took on material form and washed away the sins that his own wishes imposed on us in the first place? That our bones will come together out of the earth when a trumpet blows? That Heaven is to be locked into our bodies for all eternity?"

"I do," replied Olivier stoutly.

She shrugged. "Then we would say you are still in the darkness, that you understand nothing of yourself or creation. That when you do good, you cannot know it, and when you do evil you cannot stop it. You are ready for nothing, and will get what you wish, which is to stay in your prison."

"And you?"

"I know when I do evil. I think that makes me worse than you."

"What do you mean?"

She thought carefully. "When they came for my parents I was outside, picking berries. I heard what was going on, but did nothing. I hid, and watched them being taken away. Then I ran, and kept running. I never came to them in their prison, never brought them food. I abandoned them and left them to die knowing their daughter's faith was so feeble she would not admit who she was or what she was. And I am still hiding and pretending."

"Being burned alive is virtuous? What would it achieve?"

"You don't understand. I have condemned myself to spend the rest of my life in hatred, for those who did this to my mother and father. I cannot escape it. I wished to live quietly until I died, and could at least hope that death would come soon. But then you came along, and made me want to live. Do you see?"

Olivier shook his head in bewilderment. He didn't see at all. She stood up abruptly, took one of the candles, blew out the other, and walked away from the fire out into the small room with thick stone walls where food was kept cool. The house was small; one room downstairs and another upstairs, serving all the purposes they needed as bedroom, study, with a place to eat and sit and read and pray. There had once been a great crush, when Gersonides's wife was alive and all his children were there, but now it was almost empty. It was warm, though, and the food was wholesome and plain. Olivier ate it eagerly and in silence. Neither was able to talk.

When he had finished, she finally asked, "What news is there of the plague? People have begun to sicken here. Some have died already. How long will it last?"

"That is for your master to discover, I think," Olivier said. "But if the stories are true, then it is only just beginning. I heard someone say yesterday that in Marseille there is scarcely a man left alive. The same stories come from other places as well. Some people think it will be the end of the world. The second coming."

"Or perhaps the first. Is no one safe?"

"No. Everyone dies. Young and old, rich and poor." He stared briefly into the fire. "You and me. And at any time. In half an hour we might sicken. Or next week, or next month. There is nothing we can do."

"Except pray."

"We are abandoned. There is a tale that in Nice a priest went to his church to pray for deliverance for the town, and many people came out of their houses to go with him. No one had yet died there, but when the priest turned his back on the congregation and raised the host, he uttered a groan and fell down, and black pus began to run from his mouth. Half an hour later he was dead, and the congregation left him there, lying in front of the altar. Within five days they were all dead as well, every single one of them. There is no help in prayer; it merely seems to make God the more angry. That is why I am here. Your master needs his papers if he is to discover anything of use."

She smiled wanly. "In that case we must sleep. Your cloak will soon be dry, and you may sleep by the fire. If you wish you can get some more logs to keep it blazing all night."

She stood; he stood as well and came close once more to reaching out for her, but something in her eyes told him it would not be welcome yet. Then she took the candle and went up the rickety stairs to the bedchamber, where Olivier could see the faint light and shadow playing through the gaps in the floorboards. He heard also her say her prayers, a strange sound, almost music but not quite, so alien to his ears that he almost shivered. He crossed himself and prayed as well, then wrapped himself up in his cloak—still wet despite having spent so much time in front of the fire—and lay down to watch the flames in the grate. She came down to him half an hour later; when they were finished, she cried herself to sleep in his arms. Olivier did not know the cause, but as he comforted her he grew certain it was not because of him.

CARDINAL CECCANI DIED in Italy in 1352, some rumors suggested by poison, and was buried in Naples. A hasty, careless internment befitting a man who had—no one knew why—fallen utterly from favor. He was placed in a vacant grave in the cathedral of Naples, which was then covered with a slab of marble. His name was eventually carved on it. That was all; unlike other more fortunate cardinals, he had no grand tomb with a carved representation of his appearance in life. The only reminder of what he looked like came from the painting by Luca Pisano, high up on the wall by the entrance to the cathedral.

But thanks to the Italian's skill, his face remains, and is known. No such fortune attended either Manlius Hippomanes or Sophia, or Olivier or Rebecca. Their faces exist still, but only Julien ever half suspected who they were. Many times he had thought of what they might look like, and imagined Manlius to be like his prose: stiff, formal, somewhat severe yet with a hint of his wit about him—in the eyes, or the mouth, perhaps. He dressed him in his mind in traditional Roman clothes, even though by his day no one had worn the toga with any regularity for nearly three hundred years. He was influenced, perhaps, by the fanciful imaginings of André Thevet, cosmographer to the king of France, who published a set of idealized engravings of great Frenchmen and Gauls in 1584. Certainly, he tended to imagine a face that fitted in with his supposed character.

Ceccani's portrait was a perfect reminder of the foolishness of the mind, for what Pisano painted bore no relation whatever to what Julien knew of his character. There he stands, half obliterated by peeling paint, wearing a huge hat that makes his head seem childlike and innocent as he contemplates the Virgin and her child. The shoulders are rounded, almost with a stoop, the gorgeous robes he wears look as though they are suffocating; perhaps Pisano caught something of the way high office and great power bore down on him. Only in his eyes is there a sign of calculation, or of cunning. That, of course, might have been a trick of the light. But why should people appear like their character? Who in Julien's knowledge did?

And whose character was fixed in any case? Did Julia look as she was, for example? And if they did, then Marcel Laplace should have had an entirely different face, not the chubby, childlike, innocent one he in fact possessed.

It was Bernard who pointed this out to him. A strange thing to discuss at that moment, perhaps, but then it was a strange meeting, organized hurriedly and in shock after Julien met him one Friday morning in February 1943, two months after the Germans had invaded the south and extinguished the pretense that France still existed in anything but name and memory.

It was just outside the café where he often had lunch; he came out, nodded to the owner, crossed the rue de la République, and began to walk back to his office; and as he strolled along trying to remember the last time he had tasted meat that was truly worth eating, a man came up, slipped his arm through his, and said quietly, "Good afternoon, my friend. I trust you ate well? Keep walking. Don't slow down, and please don't look surprised."

So he did as instructed; it never occurred to him to do otherwise. "I want to talk to you," Bernard said as he guided him down a narrow, empty alleyway. "Tomorrow would be best. Where do you suggest?"

And Julien had suggested the cathedral. High above the esplanade, next to the papal palace, dominated by a gigantic gilt Virgin, it was out of the way, rarely visited these days for there were few casual voyagers anymore, and it was too isolated to attract any but the determined worshiper. It was always dark and ill lit, offering a refuge for those who wished to sit without being noticed. Bernard nodded and slipped away; Julien kept on walking. It took him under a minute longer than usual to get back to his office.

It never occurred to him either not to keep the appointment; he went there exactly on time, stood on the forecourt overlooking the huge and deserted *place* and across to the river, then went inside to walk around as he waited. He ended up by the entranceway, staring up in thought at Cardinal Ceccani's face, paying homage to the one power indisputably greater than his own.

Bernard was late. Bernard was always late, one of those who could never understand the irritation such a habit could produce in others. He wandered in fifteen minutes after the appointed time, walking with a strolling gait that suggested a man without a care in the world. He peered up at Cardinal Ceccani.

"Not a man to be trusted," he said. "Who is he?"

"The patron of Olivier de Noyen," Julien replied impatiently. "Bernard, what are you doing here? Did you change your mind?"

"Not exactly. You like de Noyen, don't you? Why is that?"

"Bernard . . ."

"Tell me. You made me read him once. I found him a dreadful bore. Hysterical, out of control."

"I am finding things out about him. He is more interesting than you think."

He grunted. "Good to see the war is making you concentrate on the important things in life, then. Anyway, to answer your question, I didn't change my mind. I went to England, and now I'm back, to be part of the Resistance. My name is not Bernard Marchand, you understand. Shall we walk? Will you hear my confession?"

So they walked down the cathedral until they found a side chapel neglected by the faithful with no candles burning, only a small baroque altar to Saint Agatha, and a few pews. Bernard led the way in, and half-closed the iron grill to discourage any sudden outburst of devotion, and they sat down in the gloom of the dim light filtering through the dirty stained glass.

"To resist in what way?" Julien asked.

Bernard said nothing; instead he stared up at the painting of the saint and cocked his head to one side.

"Five weeks ago, I hear, in Tours, a German soldier was shot by people calling themselves resisters," Julien commented to fill the silence. "Fifteen people were taken hostage. Six were executed. Two weeks ago, just outside Avignon, more resisters wanted to blow up a member of the Milice. They killed four other people in the blast. Is that the sort of resistance you have in mind, Bernard?"

"It's a war, Julien."

"Not for us, it isn't. We are not fighting. The Geneva Convention, remember? Noncombatants sit tight. Leave the fighting to soldiers. Do that and we are safe; we have the law on our side."

"And the Germans are great respecters of that, I know," Bernard said quietly.

"It has limited them a little. Break it, have civilians take up arms, and there will be no restraints on them at all. Our job is to watch history take its course, and survive it. Or people will die pointlessly. Does that not bother you?"

"It makes the Germans watch their backs. It makes them realize there are French people who will fight. It builds morale among the Resistance. It is not pointless."

"The Germans take only part of the blame, you know. Your heroic fighters are not winning so many hearts."

He snorted. "I don't care about people's hearts. They'll celebrate in the streets soon enough when the Germans are beaten. What is important is that we take a part in that defeat. Nothing more. Otherwise we will either have anarchy when the war is over, or a settlement dictated by the Allies. This is not a time when responsibility matters. Responsibility means not doing anything."

"Like me, you mean?"

"Dear me, no. You have chosen your side. All those articles, those speeches, your job. We know all about that. What do you think you're doing, Julien? I know you, or at least I thought I did. I knew you weren't a raving communist, of course, but what are you doing working for Vichy? For that moron Marcel, of all people. And now for the Germans?"

"I'm not working for the Germans," he answered stiffly. "I was asked by Marcel to write some things for the newspapers. Give talks, that is all. And then I was asked to be in charge of paper allocation. Which means I decide who gets published, which journals and magazines survive, and which close down because they have no paper to print on. Do you know how hard I have to work to keep some papers going? How often I turn a blind eye to things?"

"But how often do you not turn a blind eye? How often do you say no?"

"Sometimes. But not as often as those who would do my job with more zeal."

Bernard remained silent, his point made. He found it all so easy.

"Look, Bernard, while the Germans are here life must go on. Not as we would want, not as it was, but it must continue. Not everybody can scuttle off to London and take a high moral tone. And by living with them, cooperating, we can change them, humanize them. Civilize them."

"I see."

Bernard stood up, finding the sanctity of the chapel overpowering. He led the way out into the nave, then headed for the fresh air outside. There he stood, all disguise and caution thrown to the winds. It had always been his great weakness, that impatience, Julien thought. It will kill him one day.

"You are being unusually vain, if I may say so," Bernard said quietly. "You, on your own, are civilizing the Germans and the reptiles they have brought to power here. Are you sure it goes only one way? What if they corrupt you, rather than you civilizing them? Are you ready to risk that possibility? Two years ago, would you have denied anybody the right to publish their magazines, print their books? Even thought of it? And now you do it every day and say you are doing it to protect civilization. And they have lost; you know it as well as I do. They lost the moment they attacked Russia and declared war on the Americans. It is only a matter of time now."

"And when they are defeated," Julien replied, "it won't be because of your efforts. It will be because of the English and Russian and American armies. An act of sabotage here or there will make no difference. It will just make things worse for those who live here. And you will be caught and shot."

He nodded. "I know. Someone was sent here before me. We think he survived six weeks before he was captured. He accomplished nothing, as you say."

"So now you come. Why?"

He smiled. "Because I was ordered to. Because these people are in my country and they shouldn't be, and because the government has been stolen by mediocre gangsters. Someone has to fight them; you're not going to."

"Very noble, but I don't believe you. When did you ever do something because it was right? You do things because you get pleasure out of them."

"At some stage, probably within three months, I shall be captured, possibly tortured, certainly shot. You think the prospect gives me pleasure?"

"Yes."

Bernard paused, then laughed. "You're right, of course. Partly, anyway. It's the challenge of survival, of doing something. Do you know, I intend to beat the odds? I intend to be there to watch the Americans or whoever march in. And when that's done, there will be accounts to settle, you know."

"Is that a threat?"

"No. It's a fact. If I'm lucky, I'll be able to moderate the rage of those less forgiving than I am."

"Another threat?"

"A warning, this time."

"You'll be doing the same as I am now, then."

"In a sense. But I shall be on the winning side. And, I might add, on the right one."

They were walking down the steps and across the *place* and out toward the walls, then on again down to the river's edge.

"How is little Marcel?"

"Older. More lined. More short-tempered."

"As are we all. Are you still on good terms with him? Still friends?"

"Yes. I think so."

"Sooner or later," he said, "I will need to sound him out. He may be contemptible, but he is not stupid, and he is supposed to control what administration is left around here. An empty title, to be sure, but better than nothing. I would like you to be the conduit between us."

"Your messenger boy?"

Bernard considered this. "Basically, yes. I trust you, he trusts you. Neither of us trusts each other. He might listen to you even if he refuses to listen to me."

"Are you serious?"

"I thought it would appeal to you. You have always tried to keep the peace between us; now you can do it on a grand scale. If I can reach some sort of understanding with him, then there will be a greater chance of holding things together when the Germans withdraw."

"If."

"When. It may take three years, it may take ten, but sooner or later they will be destroyed. My task is to make sure we do not destroy ourselves in the process. So at long last Marcel and I will have a common purpose. I would prefer to have him shot; and he would no doubt be happy to do the same to me. But we will need each other, and eventually he will realize it. I want him to know what to do when he does come to that conclusion."

"Is that all?"

"Yes," he said. "Nothing else. Well . . ."

"What?"

"I'm working on my cover story, something which means I can travel often, and without attracting notice. I cannot have a job, as that would mean too many people being involved and having to conceal my journeys. I have to be my own employer, doing something which will account for my income at the same time. So, my dear, I'm going to be an art dealer."

He bowed solemnly. It was so unexpected, said with such panache, that Julien burst out laughing in surprise. "You?" he said incredulously. "An art dealer? Never say this war doesn't have its comic side, then."

Bernard grinned back. "I know. It's not something which will come naturally. But apart from my incapacity, it's a perfect occupation, although I have to do it properly to be convincing. I need artists to provide me with pictures, put on a little exhibition or two, invite people, make a show. I also need the names and addresses of painters scattered throughout Provence so I can always say I am visiting them when I am on my travels. They will be in no danger. To them I really will be Paul Masson, dealer in art, struggling to make a living in times of trouble. When I am arrested and they discover who I am they will be as surprised as anybody. Will you help? I'll need names of painters, that sort of thing. Anything will do. Good, bad, or indifferent. It makes no difference."

"I'll give you some names. And I'll ask Julia. She'll know some others."

"She's still here?"

Julien nodded. "She's safe."

"No, she's not. She's not safe at all. There are rumors coming through to London about what the Germans are doing."

"What rumors?"

"That they are killing as many Jews as they can. I don't know whether it's true, and I imagine it must be exaggerated, but certainly if she is caught she'll be sent to a camp in the east."

"I've tried. But it's not so easy, you know. You couldn't help, could you? Get her out?"

He shook his head. "I've my own people to look after."

Julien shrugged. "She probably wouldn't go anyway now. She's convinced herself she's safe. She's in the Italian zone, after all, and the papers she made herself are better than the real ones."

"Made her own papers? How?"

"She forged them. She is remarkably good at it."

Bernard thought about that for a moment. "So in theory she could produce dozens of them?"

"Why do you ask?"

He paused, and looked carefully at Julien. "A deal. If she will make false identity papers for, say, a couple of dozen people, then I will get her out of the country when they're delivered."

"That's friendship, is it?"

"It is these days."

"I'll ask." Julien turned on his heel and walked away.

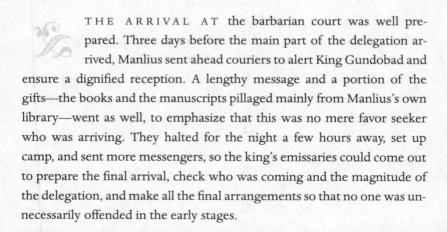

THE ARRIVAL AT the barbarian court was well prepared. Three days before the main part of the delegation arrived, Manlius sent ahead couriers to alert King Gundobad and ensure a dignified reception. A lengthy message and a portion of the gifts—the books and the manuscripts pillaged mainly from Manlius's own library—went as well, to emphasize that this was no mere favor seeker who was arriving. They halted for the night a few hours away, set up camp, and sent more messengers, so the king's emissaries could come out to prepare the final arrival, check who was coming and the magnitude of the delegation, and make all the final arrangements so that no one was unnecessarily offended in the early stages.

Manlius did not receive the king's messengers when they arrived at his camp, preferring to hold his own appearance in reserve to create a greater effect. He also kept himself out of the initial encounters by saying he was at prayer; all around his tent, guards ensured silence, and a reverent hush was maintained. The bishop was communing with God, a useful reminder of his position and a hint that the king would be negotiating with the supernatural as well as the earthly. He continued to use this technique in years to come, leaving negotiations that were locked in obduracy as if to pray, and finding when he returned—often many hours, and in one case two days, later—that the combination of his godliness and their being imprisoned in a room for so long had resolved the conflicts in his favor.

After all the preparations were made, he approached the king's court. Manlius changed into a simple white tunic and cloak, unadorned with any jewelry save for his ring, and mounted the donkey. The carefully considered artlessness, the lack of magnificence as he plodded in—being careful to be some way ahead of the rest of his party, to suggest he came alone, needing no help but God's, mindless of the things of this world—created a wonderful effect on the Burgundians, by now used to delegations from all over Gaul striving for grandeur and instead appearing pathetic.

The king responded in kind; this had been arranged in advance. He stood with half a dozen courtiers, and came forward to help Manlius off the donkey himself in a gesture of respect, then kissed the ring on Manlius's outstretched hand. A murmur of approval went up from Manlius's party, all of whom could be relied on to spread details of the scene around the province on their return.

The king was respectful of the church; he was humble before God, even more, he gave his support to the offices of Rome. All this from a schismatic Arian, all this in stark contrast to Euric of the Visigoths, who humiliated the ministers of the church, all this to indicate the degree to which he had absorbed civilization during his years as a hostage in Italy.

Half the work was done in this single gesture, indeed Gundobad's standing was the higher because he was a heretic and was still so respectful. The other half, perhaps, had already been done. It may be surmised that chance was an absent deity at the meeting; that the warm welcome, the deference, and even the conclusion of the meeting had been hammered out in the shade, through countless letters of varying precision, and innumerable meetings between the envoys of Manlius and the representatives of the king.

It was little more than theater that the multitude witnessed that bright morning—the encounter canceled from the previous day, supposedly because of a slight indisposition on Manlius's part but in fact because the weather was dull and overcast, a bad omen for the superstitious, an altogether too gloomy atmosphere for the more practical, not conducive to optimism. The clear skies, the warm sunshine that enveloped the actual encounter instead was a sign of the light and safety to come, a new morning, the dawn of tranquillity after the storms and threats of the all too recent past.

Then the king and Manlius went into the basilica, which had been roughly converted into the royal palace, its sound roof the main reason for its choice, and retired to a suite of rooms in the back, once part of the law courts, for the private discussion. Again a symbol; Manlius was received as an equal, not as a suppliant; the books and manuscripts, the small statues and the holy relics he presented were to mark a man of justice and cultivation, not a bribe to assuage the violence of the barbarian. Once more, the fine details were noted with approval. The diplomatic work was already completed; Manlius's battle for the hearts and minds of his flock was under way. Manlius even allowed himself a small burst of confidence; what he desired was within reach. He, not Felix, would conjure up the armies to march to Clermont and block Euric's designs.

 HE TOLD JULIA about his encounter with Bernard when he again made his pilgrimage to the little house in Roaix, and they talked about the offer.

"In fact, I'd be quite prepared to do a little light forging in any case," she said. "If he can get me out of the country, then all the better."

"You're prepared to go?"

"Probably. Although I'm not sure it might not draw more attention to myself, make it more likely that I get noticed. You look doubtful."

"It's an extra risk," he said simply. "That's all."

"And it would be doing something. With the added bonus of getting out of here to somewhere truly safe. Will he keep his word about it?"

Julien thought. "I've never known him not to. On the other hand, I do know I've never put myself in the position of having to rely on him for anything important. And this is important."

"I would like to do it, though. There are times when merely surviving is not enough."

"There are times when merely surviving is a major achievement," he said.

"Two different outlooks on life, there," she commented ironically. "But I will do it, in any case. Depending on what he wants, of course. How do we get hold of him?"

"Through a postman in Carpentras, apparently. He always had a sense of melodrama, I'm afraid. That is how I am meant to get a message to him about Marcel, if he ever decides he wants to discuss things."

"And this will be your contribution, will it? A go-between?"

He nodded. "When needed. Unless those two are brought together, they—or rather the people they represent—will fight each other. Marcel's police, Bernard's resisters. The Germans will go, and civil war will result. Bernard needs Marcel to counter the communists, and Marcel needs Bernard."

"Why?"

"Because otherwise someone will shoot him."

And then he got on his bike once more and pedaled to Carpentras, leaving a message that Julia would prepare the plates and do the work; Bernard should supply the names and photographs, and also lay plans for getting her across the border into Switzerland or Spain. Then he went to see the préfet and talked to him.

Marcel gave a dismissive wave. "The Resistance?" he said with a sneer. "What do I think of them? What are they? Communists? Gaullists? Monarchists even, so I understand. Their ranks swelling every day with opportunists willing to risk the lives of others so they can pose as heroes when other people have won the war for them. They care about France and are willing to sacrifice French people in its name. But I do not pursue them anymore, if that's what you're asking me. The Germans have occupied us, they can do it. I am happy to leave it to them. Why do you ask?"

"I was wondering if it might be a good idea to talk to them."

"Talk to them? To a bunch of criminals? You must be joking."

"One day it might be wise."

"One day it might be. I am not a politician, nor a turncoat, Julien."

"No. You are an administrator. And it is your job to see that good governance continues. That's what you told me in 1940. You have the same task now, surely."

"Why do you ask all this, Julien?"

Julien hesitated. "Because I have been given a message to pass on to you. That when you wish to talk, or make any sort of contact, then there will be people ready to listen."

Marcel gazed at him. "I could have you arrested merely for saying that, you know."

"I know. But it would not serve any purpose. I am not in the Resistance, Marcel. You know me well enough for that, I think. My opinion of these people is not so very different from your own. But I was given this message—which I did not seek out—and I promised to pass it on. Now I have done so. And if ever you want a message passed back, then let me know, and I will discharge that duty as well. For friendship's sake."

"For friendship's sake . . ." Marcel said thoughtfully. "I see. Now, whose friend are you, Julien?"

He shrugged. "That is all I will do. I did not volunteer, but you can trust me."

"I see."

Marcel changed the subject. They never spoke of it again. Not in those terms, at least.

IN MANY WAYS, Manlius's task was simple; settling the price was the only complex part. He wanted Gundobad to move into Provence; Gundobad was perfectly happy to do so, up to a point. The price was high; higher even than Manlius had dreamed: He had imagined that the king would ask to assume all the rights, titles, and revenues of a Roman governor. It would preserve the form, if not the reality of *romanitas,* and give Manlius enough space to persuade his fellow landowners to accept the offer. They would get, after all, a firm hand capable of ending the constant bleeding away of the population, able to put down—with whatever savagery was necessary—the incursions of the landless.

The annexation, of course, had to be dressed up and presented properly in the hearing of the court and for the sake of Manlius's entourage, and it is a pity that the formal speeches of both sides—given in the basilica, after the private negotiations had taken place—did not survive in identifiable form. Faint echoes only survived, fragments in the Burgundian code, in Fortunatus and in Gregory.

"Excellency, son of Rome, we are here to demand that you live up to your responsibilities as her trusted friend. You know how Rome's enemies press her from within and without; you know how her armies have been sent off to fight her enemies overseas, and you know how men of ill will seek to exploit certain circumstances for their own ends. Serfs run away, the grass grows in field and streets, bandits roam the roads, and all because they think that the province from which I come is weak and defenseless. All because, I should say, you do not see your duty, your obligations clearly. Why was it that Rome took you to her bosom for so many years, educated you, covered you in honors and dignities? Was it so you could live out your life amongst your own people alone, remembering the glories you have seen? Or did she have a purpose in her generosity? Did she, the all-seeing, know even then that when that little boy of six arrived that he would one day rise to great importance and power, take up his God-given role as a high official in the empire?

"It is time, Excellency, for you to accept the responsibilities for which you were so carefully trained. Time for you to take on the position of magistrate and commander of Gaul. The people in the streets, even, began to laugh and doubt at your idleness, wonder whether you do not care for Rome, think that perhaps foolish voices have dissuaded you from your clear duty. You must still those doubters, accept the offices which are clearly yours, and take on the burdens for which you will receive only gratitude."

There was much more besides, flowery phrases and ornate compliments carefully dressed up as threats and warnings. Meanings within meanings that only the long practiced could devise and understand. In speaking thus, Manlius addressed the king as a fellow citizen; the proposed annexation was to be dressed up in Roman clothes still. And the king replied in kind:

"Good Bishop, I stand here with tears of remorse in my eyes as I hear your justifiable reproaches. My idleness cannot be excused, except by a determination to give recompense through my devotion to duty henceforth. You have shamed me into seeing my negligence, and with God's help, I will take up the burdens of office you so rightly say must be mine alone. I had wished someone else would assume these onerous tasks, for which I am scarcely fitted, but I see now there can be no escape. I will assume the offices both civil and military which are currently empty. I will restore order within and without the land, return it to prosperity and a respect for the laws which have been in place for generations. I will defend the church, and guard its rights. You were right to come here, and I thank you for your cruelty. I criticize you only for your delay."

The king's court applauded; more important, Manlius's entourage noted all the points he made. Maintaining Roman law rather than imposing barbarian custom; reviving old offices; defending the province against the much harsher Euric; respecting the rights of the church; and, most important, protecting property and taking a firm line on runaway serfs. If he was as good as he promised, it was agreed, then Manlius had pulled off a master stroke.

The real discussions took place that evening, with the king and the bishop alone. And it was at this moment that Manlius was confronted with the choice that he had hoped to avoid, for he was too intelligent a man not to realize that it was a possibility. All his skills, all his wisdom were brought to bear, probing the king, finding out his strengths and weaknesses, seeing how far he could be controlled and where he must be left alone.

Gundobad did not want to rule in the name of Rome. Did not want to continue with the pretense of being a servant of something that was a mere phantom in the mind. His sense of pride, of his own importance, matched his full awareness of Manlius's need. He had made the calculations carefully: He would lose some standing amongst the landowners, but would gain mightily amongst his own people and his personal reputation would rise hugely. He would rule as king of the Burgundians, beholden to no one, acknowledging no one greater than himself.

Manlius then had the choice: He could have stability, safety, the freedom to live in peace without Rome. Or he could have a short while—perhaps only months—to be a Roman still.

He accepted Gundobad's demand, had decided to do so well in advance of the need to do so. To sacrifice a name was a small thing. The deal was as good as any man could achieve and better than most could dream of. Gundobad was no fool and was endowed with more of the human virtues than many an emperor. He was also aware that, for all the acting, Manlius had few other options. He admired the bishop for the consummate skill by which he made best use of his resources; realized he would make a fine and useful ally, was impressed by the open-eyed way in which he grasped at an outcome that would have been anathema to most of his contemporaries, but still had no intention of going beyond the bounds of common sense.

And he would not, he said almost as an afterthought, move much farther south than Vaison itself. The rest of the province would have to fend for itself. Nor would he march to relieve Clermont.

By this stage, all artifice had been laid aside; windy words and compliments were abandoned. Rather two men of power were sounding each other out, each grappling with the will of the other, wishing to avoid failure.

"Clermont is vital; it must be saved," Manlius said icily. "Relieve it, block Euric there, and the entire region will greet you as a savior."

The king nodded. "I realize this, My Lord Bishop. But I also know full well that Euric is not a man to challenge lightly. I could, as you say, relieve Clermont. At the moment this is no great problem. He has committed a fraction of his men to the siege. But what then? He commands incomparably greater resources than I do. In order to ensure success, I would have to send every man I have there. And that would leave much more open to him. Let me put it plainly: I can save Clermont for a while or I can save your territories permanently. Not both."

"I was sent here to find a guardian for the whole of Provence. Am I to go back and say that I have saved my own part of it, and am abandoning the rest to Euric?"

"I am afraid that is the choice you must make."

The meeting ended there; Manlius needed to think. For the first time he wished he could pray as well. Later, as he lay on the bed in the accommodation the king had provided, he was scornful of his hesitation. Prayer, indeed. Even he, it seemed, was being corrupted by the weakness of the Christians. This was not a matter for God; this was a matter for himself. This was why he existed, to take decisions, to make choices.

It is hard to describe his mood as he lay there for so many hours. If not prayer, it was a form of contemplation, although of a fiercely active variety. He did not glory in his power to affect the destiny of so many people, that he held their fate in his hands, that his decision would mean so much. Nor did he fret about what others would think of him, wonder whether he would be considered a traitor if he did this, or weak if he did that. He considered what would be the best decision, and as he understood all too well, the choice was simple. Either part of Provence would be saved, consigned to the hands of a man who, although barbarian, had been educated at Rome, was tolerant of its religion, would respect its laws and enforce them justly, or none of it would be.

So he formulated the problem, simplifying his options by not considering alternatives. He could have raced back, thrown his all behind Felix, and taken the risk. His friend's military skills were formidable; if he stripped all his estates and handed over every man to him, then perhaps he could win a victory that would reverberate through the world.

But that would mean exposing his own lands to depredation; it would mean there would be no one to prevent his labor abandoning their tasks and walking away. It would mean admitting the error of his own strategy, and undermining his own authority, which was desperately needed to maintain order. All for a possibility. Perhaps Felix could win a victory that had eluded emperors for half a century. But it was more likely he would fail, and achieve nothing but to bring the wrath of King Euric down on the whole region. He had said that, if all else failed, he would stand by his friend and they would die together. He had meant it. But all else had not yet failed. The choice was not so stark.

HE RETURNED to Gundobad the next morning and accepted the terms.

"Can you guarantee there will be no opposition to my troops? I will not weaken myself in civil disturbance or opposition."

"No. But if you move quickly there will not be much. You must arrive with sufficient troops within a month. Otherwise opposition may coalesce."

"And who might be the leader of it?"

Manlius thought for a moment, staring into the dead, empty grate. "A man called Felix," he said eventually. "He is wedded to the Roman solution, and is liable to oppose this arrangement. He is popular, and holds large properties. He could mobilize a small army if you give him enough time."

"We had better not do so, then," said the king with a smile. "And it would be as well to make sure that he presents no danger afterwards either."

"Handled properly he would be a valuable ally, and a good advisor. You have virtues enough to win his support, in time."

Gundobad grunted. "I will be the judge of that," he said. "And I will not take risks for your sake. Euric will take Clermont and will move east, as you say, and I must be impregnable by the time he does. I cannot afford to be distracted by internal opposition. The matter must be solved before I move, otherwise you will get no help from me."

Manlius said no more. He left the king's presence and went back to his quarters to reflect some more. He left for home the following morning.

IT WAS ONE of the little ironies that, for many months, the only real outcome of the encounter in the cathedral was that Julia once more began to sell her work. It was a bizarre arrangement, but Bernard needed pictures of all sorts to carry off the illusion of being a dealer, and she, stripped of her identity in all other respects, wished to have some existence in a world in which she was otherwise invisible. Besides, money was short, and the prospect of earning anything by selling her work was irresistible. Periodically, Julien would meet a go-between in Avignon, and would give him a bundle of paper—sketches, watercolors, and etchings, the chronicles of her life and her encounter with Saint Sophia. She even signed them in her own name, but carefully dated each one 1938, to give the impression they were coming from some long-stored stock of work. Inside the packages were some freshly made, newly aged identity cards of different varieties.

Julien was not at all happy about turning into a courier for the Resistance; all his arguments against their activities were unanswered. But if he had not delivered them, then either Julia would have done so or the opportunity to get her out of the country would have been lost. And every time he handed over his package, he also delivered a message: When will she leave the country? Are you nearly ready? Each time the same reply came back: Soon. With a list of more names to go on more false papers. Each time he suppressed the feeling that nothing would ever get done. Bernard was his friend.

The paintings and prints were Bernard's passport, which he carried with him to show to soldiers, militia, and police who might stop him, wondering why he was in a particular place at a particular time. Look, he would say, I am taking these to a potential client. Times are hard, but even so some people remain interested in art. What he did on these peregrinations no one truly knew; his biographer, who published a book on him in 1958, failed to discover much about his activities. The book alluded to events of importance without ever managing to pin down much, and thus perpetuated the air of mystery that had always been his style. His role was shadowy, using the aura of London's approval to impose himself on the disparate groups who would have as cheerfully killed each other as the Germans. Persuading them to work together, pursue a common policy, giving neither too much nor too little to all the factions that sprouted up. Ensuring that none became too big or powerful, a need that required him, on occasion, to sow dissent and mistrust. He was not liked but, despite the fact that he had nothing except his own personality and a fitful advance knowledge of gold and guns dropped by aircraft on dark nights, he was feared and respected, in his element.

He settled in Nîmes, where he was unknown, and rented a small shop, which he opened as an art gallery. He did the job properly, and even began to enjoy it. He assembled enough paintings to put on little exhibitions, and invited members of the German army to private views. He gave speeches of welcome at parties, talking about the ability of art to overcome differences in politics. Clichés about the contrast between arts of peace and war dropped from his lips. It was cheeky of him; the paintings were not of the sort to appeal to the military mind, but he found the reputation he acquired more than useful. In public he was considered at best an apolitical merchant, solely interested in making money. At worst he was detestable as a collaborator on the make, going out of his way to make the occupiers feel at home. In between these opinions lay the space he needed to get on with his work.

Sometimes, though, he even sold something. One afternoon, a captain from the intelligence bureau in Nîmes, a man from Hamburg, a linguist who had heard only ten days previously that his wife and two children, his father and mother, had been killed in a bombing raid, came into the gallery. He had not been able to do his work analyzing signals picked up from the constant chatter of radios to the south, uncoded, terse remarks that, sometimes, could be made to reveal a glint of gold. He no longer thought it mattered; he knew the war was lost and suspected, for the first time, that he didn't care much.

He'd been wandering the streets for more than an hour by the time he passed by the rue de la Republique, and came into Bernard's little gallery because he wanted a distraction from his own mind, constantly churning over the same memories and thoughts.

He spent nearly an hour staring at the etchings, thoroughly worrying Bernard, who had never been detained by any image for more than a minute. He thought initially the Gestapo was about to swoop down on him and knew there was nothing he could do about it: He was not so foolish that he kept a gun anywhere near him. Then he noticed the tears coming down the officer's cheek, and took reassurance from the spark of light reflecting in the liquid as it ran through the stubble on his pallid face.

"Who are these by?" the officer asked eventually. "Who is he?"

"She," he corrected. "An artist called Julia Bronsen."

"They are magnificent."

Bernard looked at them. Truth to tell, he had never really looked at them before, and saw nothing special now. But he knew his job. "Ah, yes. They are special, indeed."

"I will buy them all. How much are they?"

Bernard gave an outrageous figure. The man looked disappointed, so Bernard lowered it, a little. He bought all eight.

"I would like to meet this woman," he said as Bernard wrapped them up—in newspaper, it was all he had.

"Not possible," Bernard said. "She lives a long way from here. Besides—"

"She would not want to meet me?"

"She is Jewish."

The captain nodded. "Then at the least please convey to her my profound admiration for what she has achieved here."

He bowed, with a little inclination of his head, and walked out of the shop. Julia was absurdly pleased when she heard the story.

THE ACCUSATIONS against Gersonides and his servant came just before the first soldier guarding the pope fell sick and died. Until then, all in the papal palace, its new but unfinished walls rapidly reinforced and barred to the world, had dared to believe that what could keep out men could keep out death itself. They had, after all, nothing else to put their faith in, and they could do little except hope and patrol the walls. The hope was misplaced, although the newness of the building—much of it not even complete or decorated—seems to have offered some protection; by the time the soldier fell, many thousands had already died in Avignon itself.

The charge was not leveled by Ceccani himself, of course; that would have been far too obvious. He merely indicated at the correct moment that he had believed the report the moment he had heard of it, and gained praise for his efficiency and vigilance. Rather, one of his palace creatures, a priest from a good family who hoped for advancement, leveled the charge, going to the palace seneschal. Again, the paper lay in the cardinal's archive, and was read by Julien in Rome.

"I saw the Jewess pouring liquid from a phial into the well last night," he said. "It is the well which provides water for His Holiness."

It says much for the seneschal that, although a shiver of terror ran down his spine at the words, he still kept calm and tried to ensure that the correct procedure was followed. Even in such times, even for a Jew. He was not so much a good man, but he was a good soldier, and believed in order, correctly followed. This was fortunate, and for Cardinal de Deaux it was vital. Had the seneschal barked out orders then and there, the soldiers would have run to Gersonides's chamber and killed him and Rebecca within minutes.

THE ARRESTS WERE the opportunity Ceccani had been praying for; almost daily he heard more of the way that morality and order were crumbling as men recoiled from what they saw all around them. License and lust spread their tentacles throughout the world, men turned from priests and the church and cursed God; unless they could be given some hope, then all authority would crumble.

He sought an audience with Clement, to try once more to make him realize the size of the disaster sweeping the world. Not the numbers dead, but the effect it was having on the living.

"Daily, I get more and more reports; I hear of men and women, complete strangers, coupling in the streets, in full view of passersby. Husbands and wives abandoned, even sold to others. I hear of children thrown into the streets to starve, of men killed for no reason, of priests insulted and spat upon, of churches spurned. All authority and all law is crumbling, Holiness, and rather than bring men back to God, making them see their sins and repent, the church is thrusting them further away. It is a matter of urgency that order be restored and that a lead be given. All they are crying out for is direction. And you must give it; you must stamp your authority on this situation now."

The pope wiped his brow of the sweat that prickled down it; he must, Ceccani thought, have lost a third of his weight by sweating in the past few weeks, sitting up in his tower and roasting himself like that. He looked warily at his cardinal; he did not like him, suspected him of constant intrigue, but knew also of his intelligence and diligence. Cardinal Ceccani wanted power, and perhaps even wanted to succeed him, of that there was no doubt. But it was also true that few others so deserved the office, or had such an elevated concern for its defense.

"And what am I to do, Ceccani? Offer a cure? Bring back the dead? Hold up my hand and bid this plague be gone? Prayers are fruitless, intercession has achieved nothing."

"You must give hope, and understanding. And above all you must move swiftly to counter those who are using this situation to undermine the church. The friars, the mendicants, these people calling themselves the flagellants. They offer scourging and penance and the people flock to them, abandoning the church as they go. And they offer an explanation, the only one: that God has sent this plague as a punishment for the evils of mankind and of his church, which has led men astray."

"Do they, by God! We will see about that."

"No, Holiness. You cannot defeat these people. If you move against them, then the people will hate you the more; they care for the sick and offer them hope; the church at the moment is doing neither. You must not attack them, you must place yourself at their head."

Clement looked at him impassively. "Go on. Tell me what you have in mind."

And Ceccani sketched out the way the church could let them loose against the Jews and destroy them in the same way that it had devoured the heretical Cathars, and thrown back the Muslims from Jerusalem. Give the people a purpose, an opportunity to destroy their enemies, those who wished them ill. He saw the temptation of glory dancing in Clement's eyes, reflected in the firelight, and knew he was halfway to his goal.

PART THREE

EVEN THOUGH an entire continent was engulfed by war and the south occupied, Julien paid little attention to the German presence until shortly after Bernard had come to see him and announced, somewhat prematurely, how he planned to take control of the region once the occupiers had gone. He always thought on a grand scale, his friend. Until then, the war had been an abstraction, whose reality was sensed only through the shortages of food, the new laws and decrees, the air of despondency that could be sensed in the wind and in the expressions of men as they passed by. The emptiness of the streets, the fact that even a single vehicle attracted attention when before streams of them went unnoticed.

And, of course, through the absence of those people who vanished, taken away to be offered as sacrifices to placate the powers in the north. The foreigners, some Jews, men drafted in to feed the factories of Germany with manpower, others who fled to the hills to avoid being taken or to join the Resistance. The war was a collection of absences but had no real physical presence for him until the day a single truck rumbled into the main street of Vaison, stopped, and the driver got out. What the Germans called Operation Anton, the occupation of Southern France, had been under way since the previous November, but demarcation disputes with Italy over who was to control the area east of the Rhône meant troops generally passed through on their way to the coast. The hilly land east of the Rhône was of no great military importance; it was not the way any invading troops landing in the south would come, if they had any sense.

It was a Saturday morning and the driver was lost. Throughout history, a good general has been he who knows where his army is; a great one he who can say with some assurance where it will be tomorrow. In the case of this soldier, this one-man occupying force, he had been told to join a convoy going to Marseille. But no one had told him where the assembly point was. He had waited for three days, then set out from Lyon on his own to try to catch up.

He was fresh from school; had been in the army only twelve weeks and had not one iota of military fervor in his body. He had hoped desperately for a posting far away from the slightest hint of any fighting, and had used what small influence he possessed—he came from a military family that, collectively, was ashamed of him—to join a unit defending a small island off the Brittany coast, spending his days fishing while hoping that the might of the Allied powers would decide it had better things to do than assault an island with a population of 278 people.

But much of the German army moved south into the previously unoccupied zone, and the young man could only reassure himself that things might have been worse: He could have been dispatched to the eastern front instead. He was swept up in the vast redeployment and got lost as he drove through the night, hoping to find someone—anyone at all—who could tell him where he was, where he should be. He came to Vaison, far from the road he should have been on, and got out to ask directions. He looked around him with an air of perplexity on his face. He was too innocent to wonder whether he should have been afraid, all alone in this town, with no one knowing where he was, driving a truck full of food that the inhabitants would have eaten with the greatest pleasure.

Julien saw him as he stood there, blinking in the bright early sunlight. The youth looked at him, wondering whether he was a person to ask for directions, then walked into a shop. Julien watched him waving his arms as people do when they cannot speak well. He pointed, first in one direction, then in another; the shopkeeper pointed as well. He pointed to some bread and was given it, tried to give some money in exchange, but the shopkeeper waved him away, would not take it. An ambiguous gesture, not friendliness, not disdain, a cautious mixture of both that acknowledged the occupier while also taking account of the news that the fortunes of war were swinging, that the air of invincibility was fading. He mentioned the incident to Julia later: hardly the embodiment of military prowess, he said. Difficult to imagine that the defeat of France had been encompassed by such a figure.

The soldier walked back to his truck, looked around, then drove off. Julien watched that as well; he had not moved once. Julien said so, and described every movement to the investigators who came a few days later, trying to find out who stopped the truck six miles down the road, made the youth get out, then butchered him and left him to die while they stole the supplies he was transporting.

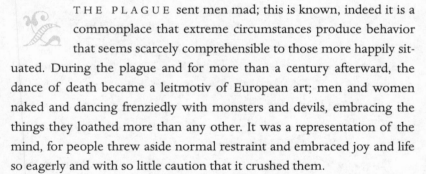

THE PLAGUE sent men mad; this is known, indeed it is a commonplace that extreme circumstances produce behavior that seems scarcely comprehensible to those more happily situated. During the plague and for more than a century afterward, the dance of death became a leitmotiv of European art; men and women naked and dancing frenziedly with monsters and devils, embracing the things they loathed more than any other. It was a representation of the mind, for people threw aside normal restraint and embraced joy and life so eagerly and with so little caution that it crushed them.

One such was Isabelle de Fréjus, whose absurd passion for Pisano provided all the proof necessary that love is a sickness, a dangerous disease that corrupts and destroys all around it. Since he had sketched her and addressed her by the walls of the town, he had grown in her mind until he towered over all other thoughts. She dreamed night and day of him, imagined being held by him and submitting to him in a way which revolted her when she thought of her own husband. Initially she tried to pray that the thoughts would leave her alone, but soon she stopped; the madness took hold and she no longer wanted them to leave. Where the lurid visions came from she did not know; how they arose unsummoned was also mysterious, but soon she stopped fighting them and began to summon them like an incubus to come and comfort her.

Then she passed from mere daydreaming. The longing was so great there was nothing—no action, no distraction—that could shake it from her mind. She had no respite from the moment she woke until the moment she submitted to her dreams at the end of the day. And when it was annnounced by her husband's chamberlain that they were now to leave Avignon and head west into central France in the hope of outrunning the sickness, she became sick herself. What if her painter should die? What if she never saw him again? Could she live, how would she die if the thing she desired most of all had slipped through her hands? The morality she had learned from the priests had no power against such thoughts. The sanctity of her vows before God meant nothing to her. She would willingly trade her life and her soul, joyfully submit to an eternity of torment to lie in his arms for one single night, to have that release he alone could provide, which she had imagined so often.

This fever of the mind, this plague of the soul, gripped her and twisted her until all she dreamed of, all she desired was to sin. And the night before she was due to leave, she could abide it no longer. As the servants and members of the family bustled about —those left, for the plague had already struck the house, killing six servants and her own grandmother and sister—packing cases as quickly as possible to make their escape, Isabelle put on her cloak and slipped through the door.

"I'm going to say goodbye to my friends. Who knows, we may never meet again," she said. It was another sign of the times that she was allowed to go unchaperoned.

Pisano lived in a mean area that had the great virtue of being inexpensive, for Avignon had learned to love greed, and the influx of the papal court forty-three years before had created such a need for space that despite the injunctions about fair price, even cardinals sometimes had to live in houses scarcely fit for priests. Only the areas so low in reputation even the most desperate shunned them could still be afforded, and here, cheek by jowl with the city's Jews, settled first one Italian painter, then nearly all the rest who came to try their luck.

The area was not entirely unknown to Isabelle; the city was not so big, nor women so protected. She had been to the Jews' quarter on many occasions, but never alone, and never at night. Huddled in her best cloak, with no one to light her, she walked swiftly through the streets, her sense of unease mounting as they became smaller, more crooked, darker and meaner. Finding the Italian's lodgings was not easy; she had to ask several times. Getting into the house was more difficult still as it was already boarded and barred to the outside world; she had to knock loudly on the thick oak many times before she heard the noise of feet coming down the stairs.

It was not what she had imagined; in her mind she had thought of a discreet arrival, wafting into the Italian's room, his arms and his bed with no one else even aware of her presence. Then home again before dawn, through deserted streets, with only her flushed cheeks and look of content hinting at what had taken place. Instead half a dozen people—the housekeeper, servants, people in the streets and the houses opposite—had seen her and must have noted her, for she did not dress, walk, or behave like someone from the quarter.

A less courageous, less mad woman would have taken warning and gone home before irrevocable damage was done. But she had only one idea in her mind, and she never even considered turning back. She knocked on the door until she was let in and the landlady, cursing wildly, came and hammered on the door of the room. Olivier emerged, yawning from tiredness, then came down. He had spent the evening with his friend, and had been up talking too late; he was locked out of the cardinal's palace, which now shut its doors the moment dusk fell. Those outside would now have to take their chances. So Olivier had begged a space on Pisano's pallet and was the first to hear the knocking. He woke up swiftly when he saw the woman at the foot of the stairs; he knew from her eyes he would be having to find somewhere else to sleep that night.

They whispered together, so the landlady, notoriously inquisitive, should not hear. Then he took her upstairs.

"You must be crazy coming here," he said as he led the way. She didn't reply. All she had said was that she had to see her Italian.

"You should go home. I will accompany you. It's not safe."

"No thank you."

Olivier showed her in, thought of going in as well to remonstrate with Pisano, but then decided to leave well alone. He dressed himself at the top of the stairs, wrapped himself up in his cloak, for the night air was cold, and walked up and down the street. While he marched he cursed friendship and women and Italians with all the venom only the truly poetic can manage.

ISABELLE STAYED nearly two hours, then Pisano let her out again, and she began to walk home, a sane person once more in a mad world. The madness had protected her, given her immunity from harm. Now she was herself again, she knew she was vulnerable. She accepted it almost as her punishment, and was not surprised when she turned down a blind alley, totally lost, then heard footsteps behind her.

The comte was also in the grip of the devil; he had seen the look on her face as she slipped out the door, and was aware she had never looked that way for him. He followed her, all the way to the moment that she knocked on the door of Pisano's lodging. While Olivier was pacing up and down the street, he stood silently in a doorway, waiting, his fury and torment rising to such a pitch that he thought he would burst. And when Isabelle came out of the house, he followed her again until he was sure no one was nearby.

She scarcely had time to realize what was happening, and was so weak and puny, with her well-bred arms that had never lifted a weight and soft legs that had never been forced to run. Nor did she have time to scream, for his strong fingers tightened around her windpipe the moment he came close enough.

She had half-turned when she heard the footsteps, but did she see who dragged her into the dark doorway of an abandoned house to squeeze the life out of her in his blind fury? Did her eyes beg for mercy as she sank to the ground, before they glazed over? Certainly she was unconscious before the knife stabbed time and time again into her body, and felt nothing as it slashed, one final time, across her throat in the last, extinguishing burst of rage.

The count threw the knife onto the ground beside her and stood for a few moments, heaving from the exertion. Then he walked off, pulling his cloak up above his head as he rounded the turn into the main street. But not fast enough to avoid the eyes of Olivier as he walked up and back in the cold one last time.

TWENTY-SIX WERE arrested because of the murdered soldier; the strange mind of German military authority had decided on the number—precise, and not to be violated—for reasons not even they understood.

A town that previously had seen little of the war suddenly felt it in its full barbarity; its feeling of vague security because of its presence comfortably in the Italian zone was abruptly destroyed. There was a list, drawn up in advance, as there always was in these circumstances, but no attention was given to such precision anymore. Once, such things were carefully, meticulously done; notables—doctors, lawyers. Two masons. Three shopkeepers. Four artisans. One person who might have been a communist. Two good Catholics. People from the town and from the outlying villages. No women, no children, no one whose death could lead to accusations of being unfeeling or brutal. Such was the original pattern before civilization really crumbled. But this sort of care was in the past; there was no time for precision anymore. The revenge alone was the point. The trucks swept into the town and rounded up the first twenty-six people they saw; herded them together and marched them off to the school, which had pupils and teachers evacuated at five minutes' notice.

Hector Morville was not a man for such a crisis. He was deputy mayor of Vaison for no reason at all except for the fact that people liked him, and he so obviously enjoyed the little drip of honor that it brought. His wife had died, it was the town's way of sympathizing. Doing something to bring him out of himself. The mayor often feigned illness before meetings—he was a lazy, if healthy man—so that Hector could wear the full insignia of office and swell up with pride as he sat at the head of the table. No one made fun of him, though it would have been easy to do so. His pleasure was too simple, too pure, to be spoiled by cynical laughter.

Now he was terrified by the sudden burdens of office, petrified by the danger overhanging his friends, people he had known for years. The crisis aged him within hours from being plump and shiny—like many, his family had a small farm that had turned to producing remarkable amounts of food under the stimulus of shortage—to being gray and stooped. An old man suddenly, with all the doubts and hesitations of the elderly.

And so he consulted Julien, his childhood friend, when he bicycled into town that evening to find out what was going on. Elizabeth Duveau was one of those arrested, bundled into the truck merely because she was walking across the main square of Vaison after buying some cloth in a shop. It had received a supply of cotton; every woman for miles around had heard of the event and had come to Vaison to see what might be had. When she did not return, the village of Roaix had collectively turned to Julien to do something about it. Julien came to the deputy mayor to discover the details, such as he knew them.

"They have not been harmed?"

"I don't know."

"What do they want?" he asked. "Tell me, what do they want?"

"I imagine they want the people who killed that soldier."

"Do we know?" asked Julien, who knew very well.

Everyone knew. The moment the town heard of the murder, they knew who had been involved. The two men had been seen near the town that evening, then had disappeared altogether when the body was found and had not been seen since.

No one could guess where they had gone; they had long practice in making themselves scarce. They were not the most admirable citizens of the town, one in particular was a known drunkard, but they had their own robust courage. When the order came for them to submit themselves and go to work as laborers in a German factory, they talked together and decided to refuse. They had never been disciplined, never been good at school or good workers. They had never learned to obey orders. Wartime turned these traits into virtues. One night they disappeared into the hills and woods that they knew so well, and the police and soldiers knew not at all.

After a while more people joined them and they became resisters, sometimes without even being aware of the transformation. Some were heroes, some were trying to escape the German factories. Some were idealists, some patriots, some joined because they loved violence too much, some because they abhorred it completely. Some had clear political objectives, some merely wanted to defeat the Germans, or to bring down the current government of France. Some fought for country, some for God, some for their families, and some for themselves. All were prepared to fight, although how they were to do so, and who they considered their enemy was not always clear. It was groups like these that Bernard was supposed to weld into an effective force capable of doing real damage to the Germans, and groups like these that so terrified Marcel.

"We cannot have these people in this town murdered because of them," said Hector.

"What do you suggest we do?"

"We hand them over."

Hector had never been a practical man. He still lived in a world where you told the police, the police did something. It was his own form of resistance to pretend such a universe still existed. He was at the end of his imagination, all his ideas used up. He had briefly put up a moment's defiance, but all for naught. He sank back into his habitual impotence and shook his head sadly, as he always had when faced with something so imponderably wrong.

"That is not so easy," Julien pointed out gently. "And perhaps not wise, either."

"You have contacts, Julien. You are important. You know the préfet. Go and see him. Talk to him. He'll be able to do something."

Julien gazed sadly at him. His faith was touching.

"What do you think?" he asked Julia when he pedaled back to the house. She was still with him; Bernard had not yet made any arrangements to get her out and it looked now as though he never would. Months had passed by; Bernard didn't even trouble to make excuses anymore. Yet the demands for more identity cards and documents kept coming. Julien hoped that when Bernard had made the agreement he had intended to keep it, but he was no longer sure. Julia had done everything he wanted and more. Anyway, it would be quicker now, so Julien dryly remarked, to wait for the Allies to come to them. Not that he minded so much; there had been no hint of any danger, and the days passed in such perfect happiness—peace, almost—their own tranquillity the greater because of the daily news of the fighting that sooner or later would engulf them all.

She was covered in ink; before he'd lived with her Julien had never realized quite how messy, quite how physical was the life of a painter. It gave added impetus to his constant search for soap. He looked at her fondly as she tried to scratch her nose with some part of an arm that wasn't covered in her particularly sticky brew of homemade ink, then took mercy on her and scratched it himself.

"Now I know why the Renaissance painters had assistants," she said in relief. She looked in the mirror. "Dear God, just look at me!"

An old shirt without a collar, a pair of his old trousers rolled up at the bottom so she wouldn't trip over them, no shoes, hair tied back with a piece of string, she looked utterly beautiful and more happy than he had ever seen her.

"Go," she said, after studying herself carefully. "Of course you must go. What is there to lose? You must do something for these poor people, if you can."

Julien left an hour later. He would, he reckoned, be back the following afternoon, and he promised to see if there was any soap or paper to be had. They were, he acknowledged with a smile as he left, the two most valuable things in the world.

IN 1972, shortly before he died, a journalist-turned-author came across the name of Marcel Laplace and wrote a book about Provence in wartime. His work was part of the reevaluation of the war that at that stage was just beginning to get under way, but was still more concerned with exonerating than accusing. Old accounts were settled, long-hidden deals and accommodations brought to light. In Marcel's case the cost was not high; he was already ill by then and his mind had trouble concentrating; he was beyond recrimination and had no need to defend himself. His record and reputation spoke for itself.

Marcel, by then, was a man so loaded with honor that he was one of the great men of the state. He had been of major importance in different branches of the French civil service for nearly a quarter of a century after the war and had played a part in the economic miracle that had restored French pride in the 1960s. A technocrat, the epitome of technocracy, who had perfected his art in Avignon during the war, while putting into effect the policies for national renewal dreamed up in Vichy.

The journalist delved into his past and found much that had been forgotten. The book that resulted avoided the bureaucratic detail, the memoranda, the orders, the meetings, the appointments that were the daily bread of collaboration. He could have made much more of the administrative orders Marcel had issued, which showed him time and again going beyond the requirements of both régime and occupiers in his desire to please, gaining himself space to maneuver at the expense of others. A careful examination of the way he applied the *statut des juifs* would have shown that many people lost their jobs who might have survived had a more indolent préfet been in charge. That edicts on reforming schools, closing nightclubs, banning meetings might have been softened in more cautious hands.

All this was mentioned, but it was not what he was after; rather, the author chose to concentrate on the single event that summed up the drama and confusion of war. And he chose as his one telling anecdote the moment on August 14, 1943, when Marcel, according to his own recollection, first tried to make contact with the Resistance, a courageous decision that finally bore fruit in the weeks before the liberation the following year. For when the German army was beaten back, civil war did not break out, chaos did not ensue. Civilian government resumed and reprisals were kept to a minimum. Once more, Marcel served his country and his département well. The author picked up that he and Bernard had been to school together; under his penmanship they became friends, closer than friends, blood brothers reaching out a hand to each other across the divide of ideology and the noise of conflict. Trust, simple and human, triumphed over fear and hatred, and ensured the swift reintegration of military and administration, the reestablishment of civilian government, at the first possible moment after the Allied armies had pushed the Germans back north.

. Thus the journalist imagined a conversation in which Marcel was told of Bernard's presence in France, and has him sitting at his desk, considering how to proceed. Does he inform the Germans? Pass the information on to his own police? Or does he step out of legality and enter the dark world of the clandestine? Someone like Olivier de Noyen would have constructed a semi-theological scenario, with a very literal devil tempting the bureaucrat into evil, an angel arguing for the opposite. Manlius Hippomanes with his classical and pagan background would have mimicked the judgment of Hercules, with a long and highly intellectualized discourse in which the moral issues are debated—with personifications of Vice and Virtue to help out—before Marcel makes his reasoned choice.

Given the way the drama was constructed, all three must make Marcel the hero, as did the author of the book, or at least the centerpiece of the affair. Everything focuses on his decision, and this is where the journalistic distortion creeps in. For Marcel never made a choice. He never considered alternatives. He never doubted for a moment that the actions he in fact took were correct. And, of course, the journalist did not suspect the existence or the importance of Julien Barneuve in the matter.

THE PROBLEM was simple: Manlius regarded the Burgundians as the best hope for the security of Provence. He could make a distinction between one group of barbarians and another, while his friend Felix saw all as a threat to the ideal of Rome. By the time Manlius left the king's palace and began his trek back home, the starkness of the opposition was clear to him. Events had made them enemies. One or the other must give way. And time was short; the Burgundian king was willing to move his army to a line south of Vaison, but would not invade. He wanted no opposition, and if there was any either he would not come at all or he would feel free to pillage at will. Then everything Manlius had tried to achieve would be lost. Their savior would become their destroyer.

As he voyaged, the journey taking ten days when a generation ago it could have been done in two, Manlius was confident that he could carry the day in the town and the region; his position as bishop gave him an unrivaled, indeed a unique voice to the townspeople, and there was, of course, no doubt that his estates would obey. Nonetheless, he was aware that there would be opposition, and that with Felix at its head, it could be formidable.

He was reassured by the belief that Felix had headed south, to try once again to raise troops to send to Clermont; it was because of this confidence that the news Vaison had rebelled against him under the leadership of Caius Valerius came as such a shock. It was one development he had not foreseen, for like Felix himself, he had never taken seriously the devout but simplistic fool whose bishopric he had taken.

In fact, Caius had been preparing since the moment Manlius was elected some four months previously, and knew that the absence of both the bishop and Felix from the region gave him the one chance he was likely to get. Within hours of the delegation leaving for the court of the Burgundians, he began to move with those he had persuaded, bribed, and frightened into supporting him. The church was captured, and its treasury—newly filled with Manlius's gold—opened. Work details were set onto the walls, building and strengthening. All of Manlius's men in the town were disarmed and given the choice: abandon their master or have their hands chopped off so they could not fight for him. Most chose the former option. No move was made to deprive Manlius of his position, however; that would be done later; charges of peculation were prepared to lay against him when he returned. For Caius did not underestimate his bishop or his cousin, and knew that he had little time. Manlius was immensely powerful, and could raise a substantial number of troops from his estates. Moreover, the townspeople were uneasy; Manlius had been elected by acclamation. He had the support of Faustus; he was God's representative.

Nor could the town be easily prepared for a siege, or defended. The walls were feeble and weak. The inhabitants had almost no idea how to fight. Caius sent urgent messages south, along with all of Manlius's gold, to hire mercenaries, but nothing had happened. Until they arrived, or his cousin Felix returned with troops to face a fait accompli, a full and open declaration of war against the bishop was unthinkably stupid.

So Caius Valerius worked to prepare the walls, and to stiffen the resolve of the townsmen. Here something dramatic was needed; something to ram home just how unsuitable Manlius was. Who better than Sophia to make this point?

The rumors about her had already started in any case. It took little effort to fan them into a flame of outrage. Sophia was strange, haughty, and aloof. She spoke in a way—the purest Latin, in fact—that the Gallic ear could scarcely even understand anymore. She practiced medicine, so easily confused with necromancy. She was, undoubtedly, the bishop's consort, he who was supposedly dedicated to celibacy and chastity now his wife had gone to a woman's house. Above all, she was a pagan, who preferred the company of Jews to good Christians, who openly sneered at the truth and had corrupted the mind of youths throughout the land with her teaching. Sophia, when she heard this last, laughed out loud. She couldn't corrupt them even if she wanted to.

She was in the habit of coming into the town every few weeks, not so much because she needed to—her slave was more than capable of seeing to her small needs—but because she needed to breathe the air of civilization, however diminished and provincial it might be. She stayed in the great house Manlius had given her, generally only for a day or so, and went walking through the streets, listening to the noise of human activity, constantly surprised by how much it reassured and soothed her. For she had absorbed little of pastoralism in her education; she lived in isolation on her hill to escape the omnipresent signs of decay, rather than to bask in the revitalizing aura of nature. Nature, indeed, she had little time for; she had always been a city dweller, and was more appalled by cruelty of the wild than she was awed by its beauty.

Besides, she had begun to give instruction to Syagrius. The young man had come to her one day and asked to speak. Then, in a rush, he had asked her for lessons, his eyes beseeching her not to turn him away or ridicule him in the way that his adoptive father did as a matter of course. Sophia would never have done that; but she did not, initially, want to instruct him either. She knew perfectly well that he did not ask out of any craving for philosophy; rather he wished through her teaching to come closer to Manlius and demonstrate his worth.

Ordinarily, she would have refused, but now she had no other pupils, and as he stood there, proud but so young and lost, his wish to win Manlius's respect and affection so clear, she could not turn him away. Instead, with a sigh of misgiving she had smiled, and agreed. "Of course. It would be a pleasure." His smile of relief and gratitude—a charming smile, with real beauty in it—reassured her.

"And the first thing you can do in my company is to stop standing to attention like that. I will not be your teacher but your guide. I will help you, not instruct you. This means you must speak freely, and I forbid you to believe anything I tell you. Do you understand?"

A look of puzzlement and distress crossed his face. Sophia's heart sank. "Come in, young man. But if you call me 'my lady' once again I will throw you into the street. You will, I hope, think of me with respect. But I have not earned it from you yet. When I have, you may address me thus."

And so she began with poor, simple discourses. His ignorance was total, the lad was scarcely capable of understanding the basics. Sooner or later, he would say:

"How can you say this? The Bible says . . ."

"What do you mean that life is a quest? What are we looking for? Surely faith should be enough."

And she would try to explain in a way he could understand, but knew that she lost him, almost every time. "Now, how can we define the difference between understanding and believing?" she would say, continuing because he wanted her to continue, and she was determined not to stop as long as there was any hope that, one day, she might spot some flash of recognition in his eyes.

But she never saw it; his mind was long closed, barricaded by priests and Bibles. She was not strong enough, not a good enough teacher, perhaps, to burst through and let in the light of reason. She should have given up, but she saw also that, although Syagrius's understanding was feeble, his soul was good. There was no malice or cruelty in him, nor did he ever give up, even though at times he came close to tears in his desperate wish to understand. "Let us take our premise that the individual soul likens himself to God through the refinement of understanding reached through contemplation, and that virtue is a reflection of this understanding . . ."

A cliché of philosophy, repeated endlessly for near eight hundred years; Sophia hardly even thought it controversial. Even in Marseille, she had never had the proposition queried. However, it came to the ears of Caius and he saw it as the pyre on which Manlius might be consumed.

The bishop's woman taught that men could become God. She challenged the Almighty, taught youth that no savior was necessary, that faith was absurd, that she was the equal of Christ. She contradicted Revelation, poured scorn on believers, and all the while was supported and defended by Manlius himself. What sort of bishop encourages men not to believe?

She was sufficiently unworldly, or perhaps arrogant might be the better term, not to notice that more people looked at her askance as she walked through the streets; that there was more muttering as she emerged from her house. She paid no attention; the opinions of such people had never been of the slightest importance to her; their talking no more registered with her than the noise of buzzing flies occupied her mind.

Southern Gaul was not like the East; monasticism had not taken so strong a hold that hundreds or even thousands of monks were gathered in almost every town. Yet there were many who had gathered informally in such associations, often moving in and taking over abandoned villas or town buildings, asserting—sometimes violently—their ownership and priding themselves on the purity of their faith. More than anyone, perhaps, they feared invasion, for an Arian, heretic king would have little sympathy for them and be open to the complaints of aggrieved property owners.

It took little to persuade them that True Religion must be defended, and that the corruption Sophia represented should be stopped. On the morning before Manlius held his first meeting with the Burgundian king, they gathered outside her house and waited for her.

There were only about a dozen; no more were needed, although the crowd grew larger as time went on. Several were drunk; such things were common, for most were young and were scarcely under any control. For all that, they had no idea what to do but were waiting for someone to give a lead.

When Sophia came out of the house, she paused as she saw them. It crossed her mind to go back inside, for even she sensed the menace in the atmosphere. Had she done so, history would have been subtly changed in innumerable ways. But she remained true to the philosophy she had practiced all her life; she was not afraid, and after a brief moment when the lower, more treacherous part of her mind sent a surge of alarm through her body, she conquered the fear and restored herself to tranquillity.

Then she began walking down the street, toward what had once been the forum but now scarcely merited the name of a market square. Ahead of her was Syagrius, waiting for her. She relaxed, felt the relief flowing through her, and was angry with herself. He would not hurt her, she knew.

"You are in danger," he said. "You must come to a place of safety now. Come with me."

And she went with him. He took her to the church, and barricaded her in.

WHEN ISABELLE'S BODY was found, news of the event raced around the town as fast as the plague. Her husband himself came for the body, and even though his sense of outrage was still uppermost in his mind, he also felt regret for the loss of this pretty, feckless, disobedient girl of whom he had been fond. At the same time he was aware, of course, that he had acted justly, and that moreover he was now free to marry again and produce the legitimate heir that she had denied him.

Nor did he want to delay quitting the town more than necessary. He was a thoroughly frightened man; the plague was one reason, but he also wanted to get to the safety of Aquitaine, safe on English territory when the French realized who had been responsible for opening the gates of Aigues-Mortes, due to take place in only a week's time. But his wife's foolishness the night before had thrown all these plans into disarray, and he would now have to stay for a few extra days. So he gave instructions that the packing should continue, and concerned himself with laying a complaint to the authorities about the murder. With luck he would still be able to set off before it was too late, and if he went alone, abandoning his household and telling them to follow in their own time, he might yet be able to outrun any pursuers.

It took only a few hours for the magistrate to discover that Isabelle de Fréjus had gone the previous night to the house near the Jewish quarter where Luca Pisano lived. This was clearly stated in two of the depositions contained in an individual folder under Reg. Av. 48 in the Vatican archives, whose existence Julien noted first in 1924 but which he did not pursue until much later. Despite the difficulties of the war, he wrote to Rome in early 1943 and requested that someone copy out this folder for him; it was done because he was known to the archivist, and because he was a man who, at that time, commanded respect as a supporter of Vichy.

He should have had his interest piqued much earlier, and he had a residual annoyance with Julia's father when it finally arrived. For he remembered well that he had a choice that day, either keep on working in the insufferable heat, or abandon it, walk out the doors, and go for a long lunch with Claude Bronsen. He had also managed to get permission to see the Golden House of Nero, and wished the older man to see it as well. The temptation was too great. The file remained unread for another eighteen years.

When it did arrive, he understood what he had missed, and why he should have paid more attention. The murder should have been dealt with under common legal procedures, yet it had been quickly plucked out of the hands of the magistrates and dealt with by a papal appointee. The report clearly stated that Isabelle de Fréjus had gone to see the painter Luca Pisano. Combined with the fact that his poetry of love had been written for someone else, then the whole tale of Olivier's end, of how he murdered his mistress and was mutilated in revenge, was demonstrably and totally wrong. Nonetheless, he had been attacked by one of Cardinal Ceccani's own people. What had happened?

The count himself had a dilemma; Isabelle could not be tainted with the sin of adultery; he had his pride, and yet even a cursory investigation would uncover why she had been in that part of the city. And as he stood in the little alleyway staring at the body he had so grievously assaulted, waiting for his men to come and take her back to his house, he suddenly realized how to extricate himself from the potentially dangerous and embarrassing situation. A crowd had gathered behind him, restless and uneasy, staring at the figure on the ground and the pool of blood, still wet and shining in the morning light, as it ran off in a great stream of scarlet. There was an air of terror that he could feel among these people, who had grown so inured to death over the past few weeks that one more should not have even been noticed. But this was different, of course. As the plague was taking so many, for someone to die of violence seemed ten times worse than usual, an almost unbearable act of evil.

"It was the Jews." The first time it was muttered, the count did not hear it. Only after it became almost a chant did he pay attention to what was developing all around him. He turned and saw a tall man with a thin beard, his face disfigured by the scabs of poor living, repeating the phrase, looking around him slyly to make sure the refrain was being picked up by others. He began beating time with his fist, so the sound rose and fell; soon it was accompanied by stamping, getting louder and louder.

More and more people joined in; the crowd overflowed into the street, and down the street, young and old men, men and women, women and children, all chanting and stamping their feet, moving restlessly. Then there was a pause and the collective noise petered out. A sudden silence of waiting. "Kill them," the bearded man shouted. "Revenge."

"Yes," shouted the count. "I demand justice."

The crowd responded with a roar of pleasure.

JULIEN TRAVELED back to Avignon the moment he decided that, even though it was likely to be useless, he had to intervene with Marcel, try to get him to do something to save the hostages. This time there was no help on the road; no military trucks stopped anymore, farmers and their carts had vanished, holed up now on their farms, keeping out of the way. Everyone knew the fighting was getter closer.

It took him eight hours on his bike, but it was now a trip he did almost without noticing, only the heat of midafternoon slowed him down; then he had to stop for an hour or so to seek shelter. He didn't even feel tired when he arrived to see Marcel.

There was an air of abandonment about the Préfecture; he'd not noticed it before, or perhaps it had grown in his absence; the corridors that once resonated with purpose, with a mission, now seemed desolate and irrelevant. He was recognized at the door, walked in, and went straight to Marcel's office. It would not have mattered if he had been a total stranger, the lassitude had spread even here. Even the bureaucrats seemed like those who sit idly at night, feeling the thunder approaching, doing nothing except waiting for the first flash of lightning.

Only Marcel, it seemed, was still fighting, hoping that simple activity could fend off what even he now accepted as inevitable. His desk was piled high with papers, files were strewn across the floor; he sat there, head bowed, scribbling furiously in the purple ink he had affected when young and never given up. Julien often wondered what the appeal was. Bernard once remarked he thought he could smell a little touch of incense in his writing.

"Marcel, they've taken hostages in Vaison."

"I know," he said, not even looking up, still scribbling. "They told me. Good of them, don't you think?"

Finally he abandoned his bits of paper. "The water gave out in Carpentras a week ago. Did you know that? I've been trying to find somebody to repair it. Simple enough, you'd think. I can't even find anyone to go and look." He shook his head, then threw his pen down and rubbed his eyes, covering his whole face with his hands before finally looking at Julien.

"If you've come to ask for help, there's nothing I can do. It is entirely out of my hands and I've already done everything I can think of. Made representations, of course. Protested. Sent telegrams. Tried to get what is left of the government involved. Even been to see the German High Command. But . . ."

"Nothing?"

"No. Not long ago, pointing out how this would damage relations might have had some effect. You remember when the Resistance blew up those trains? Six railway workers were shot for it. I bargained them down; they wanted to shoot twenty. Now they are desperate. They don't care who they kill anymore. Do you know any of these people?"

"Several," Julien replied shortly. "I even took communion lessons with one of them. Marcel, there must be something . . ."

"No," he snapped. "There isn't. Nothing I can give them. Believe me, I've thought, and asked. And all I've got is that if the people responsible are caught, then the hostages will be freed. It's what they always say, of course." He shrugged helplessly. "I'm at the end of my tether, Julien. I can't do this much more. I have responsibility without power. I spend my time trying to restrain people to stop things getting worse, and I am helping people whose war is lost. Everybody knows it now. The Allies will soon land here, in the north, and they are advancing from Russia. The Germans are beaten. Hooray. And here I am, trying to make sure there is something still standing when they go. And that means keeping things as calm as possible. There must be an adminstration of sorts still working when they leave, just as there had to be one when they arrived. But I don't expect I will get many thanks for it. And, while the world is falling down, do you know what I get? Demands for Jews. Can you believe it? We are not filling our quotas, it seems. Can I order the police to round up some more. Unbelievable." He looked at Julien curiously, as though an idea had come into his mind.

"Give him to me, Julien," he said quietly.

"Who?"

"Bernard. I know he's nearby. It's obvious from what you said. Who else would choose you to be his errand boy? Why else would you talk of friendship like that? He's back here. I know it. He would satisfy them. He'd save the hostages. Give me Bernard, and I can trade him for those people."

Julien stared at him, then shook his head. "I can't. I couldn't."

Marcel considered the reply, then looked at the floor for a few seconds. "My apologies. You must excuse me for a few moments. There is something I must do. But please don't go; I need to talk to you some more."

He walked out, and Julien sat, puzzled but patient, for nearly an hour before he returned. His manner had changed; it reminded Julien of something he'd seen before, he couldn't quite remember what it was.

"Julien," he said, sitting on the edge of the desk, bending over close, creating a sort of intimacy. "Give me Bernard. Tell me where he is, how I can find him. All I need is a promise, and I can get these executions at least postponed. Please, tell me now, to stop worse happening."

"I can't," he replied sadly. "You mustn't ask me that. You know you shouldn't."

"I must have him," Marcel continued. "It's a matter of life and death, don't you see? I cannot allow twenty-six innocent people to die if there is anything I can do to stop it. Don't think I'm doing this lightly. I know full well that if you give him to me, I'll be signing my own death warrant. I know what will happen to me the moment the Germans go and the Resistance move in. "

Julien shook his head. "No. Arrest me if you must. But the answer is no."

And Marcel, still undecided, broke the moment of friendship, got up and walked to the window, stared out over the *place* so he would not have to meet Julien's eye.

"I have telephoned the police in Vaison," he said softly. "I have told them to go to Roaix and arrest Julia Bronsen and take her into custody. You can have her back if you give me Bernard."

And Julien stood up and screamed, for the first time since the woods near Verdun, when he thrust his bayonet time and again into a German soldier. "No!" he shouted, and rushed forward and started hitting Marcel with his hands and his fists. Marcel was no match for him; he had not spent much of the past couple of years walking and cutting wood. All he had was what remained of his authority. He held up his arms to fend off the blows, bent down to avoid hurt, and waited until Julien's despair brought him to a halt.

Marcel seemed to draw strength from the reaction; it removed his last vestiges of doubt. He sat down at his desk once more, the bureaucrat again, commanding through his calm. "What did you think, Julien? That you could take her to live with you in a small village without anyone noticing? That no one would figure out who she was or what she was? She was denounced weeks ago, my friend. The wife of a blacksmith, I recall, reported her. I knew who it was the moment I saw those new pictures on your wall. Why do you think she hasn't been questioned, taken in as a Jew living under a false identity? Hmm? Because I have protected her. Me, Julien, because I knew who she was, and I am your friend. But I cannot afford friendship anymore, if it is not reciprocated. Twenty-six innocent people will lose their lives."

"She is innocent as well. She's done nothing."

Marcel brushed it away. "I'm not arguing, Julien. It's too late for that," he said wearily. "Give me Bernard. Tell me where I can find him. If you don't, I won't protect her anymore. I have to supply Jews. She will be one of them."

Julien bowed his head, crushed by the words, all the arguments he might have summoned, all the reasoning like so much dust before the enormity of what Marcel had done.

He didn't even think. He simply agreed.

MANLIUS HAD anticipated that some form of trouble would erupt during his absence. He was aware that he had not won the love and obedience of his flock, and that many people of influence actively resented him. He had not, however, forseen anything quite so severe. When he heard the news he returned as quickly as he could, accompanied by a hundred of Gundobad's best troops, pressed on him to demonstrate the new friendship between bishop and king. He accepted the offer, knowing they might become more than a useful symbol of amity. Then, at the head of these—an aristocrat again, no longer a bishop—he marched back to Vaison, leaving his small force a few kilometers out of the town while he approached with a few dozen of his own men.

Like all of his class, Manlius had received a military training in his youth. Unlike Felix, he had never fought, but the basics of war were ingrained into him so deeply that he could assess any situation instinctively. He pulled up his horse outside the main gate and sat looking, the beast whinnying and tossing its head as he stared. A dreadful silence covered his followers like a blanket, and on the walls a single townsman stared back. Manlius looked at him. He was old, unfit to fight, afraid already.

What did they think they were doing? he wondered. Did they really think that people like that could withstand Gundobad or Euric? Did they not see that they were committing suicide?

Slowly Manlius wheeled his horse to the left and walked it around the outside of the town. He went alone, making himself a target, knowing that they would not dare attack him when he was so exposed. He was their bishop. They would not go that far. Something else must be in store for him. He could imagine it all too easily. The horse walked along, Manlius thought and considered, but as he did so he carefully examined the walls and his contempt grew. Why was he even bothering trying to save these people? They were like children, even worse, like people in their dotage, capable of unreasoning anger but incapable of rational thought or action. The walls, built a hundred years before and then allowed to fall into semi-ruin, had been patched and repaired, but could be overcome by half the soldiers he had with him. In places they were scarcely eight feet high, with wickerwork stuffed in the gaps to make them seem stronger than they were. Elsewhere it had fallen down already, the work was so badly done.

Did they think he would not use force against people who had excluded him from his own city? For Manlius now considered himself the ruler, the owner of the town. It was his, to do with as he liked just as he exercised total authority over his villas and their inhabitants. They were not excluding a bishop they disliked. They were in active rebellion. And he knew he was not going to make the same mistake his father had made. He had hoped to avoid having to choose, but he had no option.

He could call in the Burgundian soldiers and they would take this place within an hour. But that would make him dependent on Gundobad, a pensioner to his power. This, he knew, he would have to solve himself. So he thought, and while he pondered, the gate opened enough to let out one person before shutting again.

It was Syagrius. To Manlius, the shock was almost palpable; of all the people who might desert him, he never thought that Syagrius, who had so much to lose, would throw in his lot with his enemies. He had always considered him too stupid, too malleable, to cross him in any way. That must have been his error.

Why had he been chosen now? To show how little support Manlius had? To make him realize that even those closest to him would abandon him? All of Manlius's training came into play, to ensure that not one jot of emotion passed over his face as the young man approached.

"My Lord," Syagrius said. "I have come to tell you that it would be unwise to try to enter this town as bishop. If you do, I fear the Lady Sophia may come to harm. They want you to submit yourself to arrest and prepare to answer charges of gross peculation and abuse of the office and trust placed in you by the diocese. This is the message I have been told to give you. I dare say no more, though I would gladly do so. When this is concluded, I will explain what has been happening."

No dramatic words met this pronouncement. Manlius did not turn black with anger, or rail against the ingratitude of the messenger, or the temerity of the message. He could easily have made Syagrius tremble with fear, for their relative positions were such that his anger would have been formidable.

But he controlled himself, as the Roman of old, and sat impassively and detached on his horse. On the other hand, now was not the time for subterfuge, or for bargaining. He could not show hesitation, or any hint that he was prepared to compromise on his rights.

"Report back this reply: that I was elected by acclamation and that I have the power of God and of the law on my side. That I will brook no opposition. That I will enter this town as bishop within the hour."

He dismissed all but six of his own soldiers, sent the rest back to the cemetery outside the town where he had left his Burgundians, refusing to acknowledge the hurt he felt, or the scale of the betrayal. Syagrius wished to consign him to oblivion, and whatever happened, he had succeeded. He no longer had even an adoptive son to carry on his name. Only his own efforts were left now. Manlius turned his horse, then paused and dismounted.

"No," he said. "Syagrius, come back here. I wish you to bear a stronger message; these people will not understand anything less."

Syagrius turned and stood waiting as he approached. Manlius walked up to him and as he drew near, he nodded at a soldier.

"Kill him," he said. Then he turned his horse around and returned to his baggage train containing the gifts that King Gundobad had given him as a token of esteem and selected a large, gold-encrusted box. He did not look around and never saw the look of strangled disappointment and panic on Syagrius's face, the way he sank to the ground and died, still kneeling, clutching the place where the blood flowed from his body into the dusty ground. Nor did he see the way the faces of those on the walls turned from eager interest to terrified horror at the event. He knew already the effect the demonstration had had on them.

Then he collected some men, two dozen of his own guard, and led them to the weakest spot in the walls. A small crowd followed him around on the battlements, watching, uncertain about his intentions. Manlius, changed now into his most gorgeous episcopal robes with the bishop's ring glinting on his finger, scanned them carefully. No man of real authority was there, neither Felix nor any member of his family.

A ripple ran through the little crowd, and Manlius looked up again and saw Sophia, looking at him impassively. Two guards stood on either side of her, and she was chained by the wrists. What Caius lacked in skill he was prepared to make up for in the threat of violence. But he had not learned when threats work, and when they merely incite.

He looked at Sophia once more, silent and immobile. She looked back at him. For the first time, their glances communicated little. What was she thinking? What was going through her mind? Was she frightened or calm? Was she watching and assessing him? Approving or disapproving? Would he follow his public duty, or his private desires? How would he interpet these? Would he accept defeat, or refuse to be intimidated? Years of discussion between them had been passed in analyzing the abstract. Now it was time to apply that teaching, for Sophia to see how much her best and last pupil had truly learned. This at least he understood; he saw nothing of the walls, the people, did not notice the faint smell of jasmine in the air, or the sudden silence that fell over the crowd on the walls. All he noticed was her curious look as she stood there.

He ordered the box to be brought, and held it up high above his head, then knelt in the dust.

"Blessed Mary Magdalene, true servant of the living God," he began. "You who lived among us, bringing your teaching of God's word to those incapable of understanding, forgive us for our sins, and help these poor people see their folly. I beseech you, through this most holy relic, bring men back to their senses, end this strife, and open up this town. I pray you, My Lady, help these poor, weak men about to approach these walls and give them divine strength to tear away these defenses. Strong though they may be, they are as nothing in comparison to your power. Let the walls crumble under their touch, fall when they push, give way according to your wishes. And enter, My Lady, into the hearts of those wicked sinners who so abused you, and let them sin no more. Let them truly repent, and your mercy and intercession will save them. But if they persist in their wickedness, let their town be razed, their families scattered, and their punishment be complete."

Not a long speech, but declaimed with all the force of someone brought up to oratory, his voice pulsating and projecting his will with enormous force. Even as he finished, and bowed his head then stood up, he saw that the effect had been made. The apprehension on the faces of the defenders had turned to despair already; they had turned pale, they fingered their weapons nervously. They would not, could not, oppose him.

He gave the order, and his half dozen men moved forward and began hacking at the pathetic wickerwork palisade. Within minutes holes appeared and then, with an enormous tearing and cracking, it gave way. The soldiers pulled it aside and threw the pieces into the shallow moat, then gave out a great cry, "Thanks to the blessed Magdalen! Long live the Lord Bishop." One by one the defenders threw aside their weapons and went down on their knees, the foreheads in the dust, as Manlius stepped gingerly, careful not to trip or stumble and spoil the spectacle, over the rocks and boulders onto the wall and then into the town itself.

"Let us go to the basilica to celebrate this deliverance," he cried. "And afterwards I call a meeting of the town."

With one soldier bearing aloft the empty box, he walked all the way to the basilica. As he went he could sense the atmosphere. He had won this round, but not yet their hearts. They were in awe of him, but that would not last.

OLIVIER HEARD the noise from his bed; it woke him up as he lay there beside Pisano. The Italian snored with the peace of contentment; Olivier had slept only fitfully, still too ill-humored to rest. The noise of people shouting, reduced to an incoherent rumble over the distance, woke him properly, and he lay there for a while, trying to figure out what it might be. Eventually, he levered himself up and stumbled down the stairs to fetch some water from the well, and also to see if there was any bread or soup left over from the previous evening.

The old woman was excited; she had just come back from seeing for herself. "Have you heard? The Jews have murdered a woman; butchered her in the street." She was exhilarated by the violence she had just witnessed. It took some time to get the story out of her, but when he did so, Olivier turned and ran back up the stairs, his heart pounding. He shook Pisano violently. "Wake up, wake up."

His friend came around slowly, then groaned and turned over again. Olivier pounded him with his fists to get his attention.

"What is the matter with you? Leave me alone."

The Italian was in a good mood, despite being hit in such a fashion. He had slept well and soundly, surrounded by the sweetest dreams; the aroma of Isabelle still clung to his body, the memory of her lingered in his mind.

"Pisano, she's dead."

The painter lay there for a moment as the words filtered into his mind and made sense to him. Then he sat up abruptly. "What?"

Olivier repeated what he had heard, and as he provided the details, his friend sank back onto the bed and groaned. In truth, his feelings for Isabelle had been as weak as hers had been strong for him; he had been flattered by the attention, more than pleased to pick up the delicate fruit that fell so easily from the tree, excited by the heady mixture of danger and sin. But Isabelle had been an adventure, a pleasure, and his response to her death was only in small part distress for her dreadful end. More in his mind was the immediate awareness that he was in deep trouble.

"What happened last night?" Olivier asked.

"What do you mean? What do you think happened?"

"Luca, don't be stupid."

"I don't know what happened," he replied testily. "You tell me. I was in here."

"When she left here, someone must have grabbed her, dragged her down an alley, and slit her throat. They are killing the Jews for it."

"Maybe they did it, then."

"Luca, when I came walking along the road I saw her husband coming out of the alleyway."

"Oh, dear God."

"You have to get up; we have to go to a magistrate and stop it."

The full impact of the danger he was in suddenly swept over the Italian. If de Fréjus could calmly kill his own wife, what would he do to the man who cuckolded him?

"Oh, my God," he repeated, sinking back onto his pillow. "Oh, my God."

"Come on, then. Get up. Luca . . . ?"

"Do you think I'm mad?" he said, recovering himself enough to answer, then getting out of bed and fumbling for his clothes in the shuttered darkness.

He began walking around the room, collecting clothes and equipment and stuffing them into a large canvas bag as fast as he could, panic obvious in his every movement.

"What are you doing?"

"What do you think I'm doing? I'm getting out of here."

"You can't do that. You have to go to the magistrate, say what happened."

"Are you mad now? Stand up and say, 'Please, sir, that countess, that woman married to the Comte de Fréjus, wasn't killed by the Jews. She was murdered by her husband because she was committing adultery with me just before?' I wouldn't even have time to sign a statement, he'd kill me so fast."

"But unless you say what happened . . ."

Pisano shrugged. "What? De Fréjus goes free? He will anyway. All the Jews are killed? They will be anyway, the way things are going."

"You can't just run away."

"Watch me."

He was being coarse, brutal, unfeeling. Deliberately so, wanting to push aside all memory of what had occurred the previous night. In his mind he was halfway there. She had never come to the house; he had never given Olivier a beseeching look to go and spend a couple of hours walking the streets. She had never walked over, kissed him, given him no choice about what happened next. He had not fallen asleep, thinking that in all the time she'd been there, they had not exchanged more than six words. She had come, and gone, and now the whole encounter was merely a fantasy, a dream that had never taken place. As long as he was not confronted with the gossip and the details, that was how he could keep her. If he could leave immediately.

His bag was packed. All he had to do was walk out of the house, hire a donkey, and go.

"You're really running away?"

He grunted, then turned around. "Olivier, my friend, believe me. I may have been wrong not to make sure she got home safely, I may have been wrong to let her stay here in the first place, but I'm not going to get killed for it. Promise me you will say nothing. Nothing will be gained by it."

Olivier hesitated, then promised.

Pisano turned and ran down the stairs, the door crashing as it slammed shut. His world was collapsing all around him, and like many another, he felt the need to go home, to see the hills and fields and people who had given him life. He never reached them. The nausea began four days later, even before he reached the coast road that led down into Genoese territory; the sweating began an hour afterward and the black, stinking pustules erupted in his armpits and then all over his face that night. He was traveling alone, wanting no company out of fear, and would have been able to find none even had he so wished. The roads were empty, and those who were on the move were going in the opposite direction, away from the sickness and carrying it, all unknowingly, farther and farther into the heartland of Europe.

He died alone, without comfort or sacrament, with only his mule for company, it as indifferent to his suffering as he had been to its distress at the weight of baggage he had loaded onto its back. After he died his whole body erupted into a mass of black pus, creating such a stench that the mule slowly wandered off, into cleaner, fresher air. Even the rats refused to chew on his carcass. He did not win his place as one of the great founders of Italian painting, as he believed he deserved. The pages of Vasari do not mention him even as a pupil of anyone; he won no great commissions from church or town or noble patron; nor did he ever have the chance at fixing his immortality onto the walls of his beloved Siena.

THEY HAD lived in a dream of their own imagining, believing that they had barricaded themselves from reality, shut out the world, created a place of perfect safety by their own efforts and the strength of their emotions. It was the shock of realizing how much of an illusion that had been that so numbed him that he spoke automatically to Marcel's questioning and probing.

But, crushed though he was, capable really of thinking only of her, he still responded with a flicker of calculation, enough to win himself time; and with time came hope, for the two are really aspects of the same thing.

No, he said, he did not know where Bernard was. He had been given a means of contacting him, that was all. A message to be relayed through who knew how many intermediaries. And only two messages to send; that was his entire purpose. He could say he had some of Julia's pictures ready, or that Marcel wished to discuss matters with him. That was all; anything else would be ignored. He had to deliver the message on his own, with no supervision, otherwise Bernard would not come. He needed a car as well, for the message had to be delivered in a town some way from Avignon, and time was short.

He would, he said, tell Bernard that Marcel would meet him, at his house in Roaix. Tomorrow. At four o'clock. Marcel could make whatever arrangements he thought necessary.

"One condition, though. I deliver this message, Julia goes free. Once I've done it, I will go straight to the prison and collect her. I will telephone when I get there, and you will give the orders that she is to be released. I will take her away, and you will promise she will not be troubled in any way again. If you do not agree, I will not leave this office."

Marcel agreed. He was glad to do so, genuinely glad. "Believe me, I wish her no harm, Julien," he said. "Even you will scarcely be as happy as I when she walks through those gates."

Julien did not answer. He walked out of the office, with the keys to Marcel's car in his pocket.

WHEN THE POLICE came for Julia, driving out of Vaison in their car, they were angry at the assignment, not least because they had been told to take her into Avignon and they barely had enough fuel to get there. They had been husbanding their limited supplies for weeks now, and considered that to use it all up on such an errand was an absurd waste.

She answered the door on their knock, and looked more surprised than worried to see them there. "What's up, gentlemen? Lost your way?"

She was still dressed in the dirty ink-stained shirt, the arms rolled up, her hair pinned back loosely, falling around her neck. Her hands were dirty; she had been working.

The policemen were uncomfortable; none truly believed they should do jobs like this; the government had set up a special department for rounding up Jews, and they disliked having to do the dirty work for others. One of them, indeed, was ready to tell her that they would come back, that she had half an hour to disappear into the hills. All would have been quite happy had she not been there. These were not cruel men; in a few months' time one would abandon his uniform and join the Resistance himself; another would risk trouble for giving a young man and his family precisely the opportunity he was not quite ready to give to Julia. Only the third disliked troublemakers and communists more than he did the Germans, yet even he acted with no zeal when it came to rounding up people for deportations. He did his duty, as did the others, hoping that a higher authority—the préfet perhaps—would intervene and prevent this matter getting out of hand.

"Is your name Julia Bronsen?"

Her lips tightened as she realized that the moment she had feared then managed to put in the back of her mind had materialized so suddenly in the middle of a hot, quiet summer afternoon. The words changed everything; the heat became humid, the light sound of the wind through the trees around the little house faded into silence, and she knew she was very afraid. She said nothing; she could have said no, the lady of the house has just gone into Vaison, but did not know the police would have tried to believe her.

"And are you a Jew?"

Again, she could have denied it, produced all her identity cards, all the official bric-a-brac she had made for herself, but did not; she'd been busy that morning working on some new cards for Bernard and was more terrified of their coming in and seeing these than she was of being arrested. There was little she could do; they evidently knew she was not Juliette de Valois anyway. And if the police came in, dozens of Bernard's associates would be vulnerable, and Julien would also be arrested.

Besides, she realized she did not wish to deny it anymore.

So she looked at them firmly and said, "Yes, I am."

She begged a few minutes to prepare herself; checked there was nothing incriminating; packed a bag, asked to stop at the village, where she quickly asked the priest to get a message to Julien. The police did not come in the house; they should have done so, but they were hoping she would take the opportunity to run out the back door. She would have been pursued, of course, but they would not have done a very good job of it. It was too hot for running; only those in fear of their lives could run on a day like that.

But she didn't. Instead she walked to the car and sat peaceably in the back as it drove over the bumpy tracks to the road, then turned onto the main road to Avignon. She felt very calm, if annoyed at her ill fortune. Julien, she knew, would intervene and get her released. Why had he worked for Marcel for all this time if not in anticipation of a moment like this?

OLIVIER WAS IN a state of shock as he walked through the streets, unnaturally quiet now that the fury had abated, with only the smell of burning wood from the Jewish quarter to give a hint of what had happened only an hour or so before. Dozens of people had died, many buildings razed, their possessions—few enough—not even looted. This was holy rage, not to be deameaned by theft. The storm had blown, then suddenly died away; men who were screaming, throwing stones, beating bodies with sticks, suddenly found their fury exhausted, and they stood there seeming not to know what they had been doing or why they had been doing it.

Calm, and the appearance of normality, returned, but as he crossed the town and made his way to the cardinal's palace, Olivier could feel the chaos lapping at his heels. The feeling that all sense was turned upside down became stronger still when he arrived, made his way to his master's private chamber, and begged for an audience.

"Not now, Olivier," Ceccani said. He was staring out the window to where he could just see the papal palace, still covered in the impedimenta of building, though all work had now stopped.

"Forgive me, sir, but this is truly important," Olivier began.

Ceccani said nothing, and Olivier used the brief moment to catch his attention.

"The wife of the Comte de Fréjus has been murdered, sir."

Ceccani turned and arched an eyebrow. "So?"

It was gossip, pure and simple. Nothing to attract his attention as yet.

"She was murdered by her husband, I am sure. But the people are blaming the Jews, and there was a riot this morning. Many have been killed, and more will be soon unless something is done."

Ceccani had not risen so far without being able to unravel implications, and the implications of implications, in an instant. His good fortune was so great that he knew that divine favor was responsible for it.

"Why did the count kill his wife?"

It never occurred to Olivier for a moment not to say; Ceccani was master of them both, nothing could be concealed from him, and in truth, Pisano never intended that it should be when he extracted his promise.

"Because the lady was with Luca Pisano shortly before her death."

Ceccani said nothing.

"She came to him, sir," Olivier went on. "He did not seduce her."

"Spare me the details, Olivier," Ceccani said with a wave of his hand. He sat down in his chair by the broad oak table covered with papers and parchments, and thought.

"So," he said after a while. "The Jews are under suspicion of causing the plague by poisoning wells; we have solid evidence of it with Cardinal de Deaux's creatures caught trying to murder His Holiness, and now they have murdered the innocent young wife of a nobleman. It is God-given, Olivier my boy. Just as the church could put itself at the head of Christendom by calling for a crusade, then again by wiping out the heretical Cathars, so it can do so again, now, by wiping out these people, once and for all."

His eyes shone as he saw the possibilities. At last, people would have hope once more, convinced they were attacking the source of their troubles. The authority of the church would be restored as it placed itself at the head of the despair, and channeled it into purposeful action. And once Aigues-Mortes had fallen, and the papacy was forced out of Provence, then it would return to Rome as well, immeasurably strengthened and ready, once more, to impose itself on all of Christendom.

This was the first Olivier had heard of the arrest of Gersonides; he had not been to the palace for several days, and the arrests had not yet been broadcast abroad. Would not be, until the battle for power within the palace was decided. He turned pale at the words and gripped the back of the chair to balance himself.

"What? What did you say? Who did you say tried to murder His Holiness?"

He sounded so grieved, so incredulous, that Ceccani omitted to reprimand him for his interest in things that were none of his business. "Just as I say. Gersonides and his servant are both in the dungeons. One of them was caught emptying a phial of poison into the well."

"But that's ridiculous. They are innocent, sir. They must be."

"Maybe they are," said the cardinal. "Maybe the Jews did not kill Comte de Fréjus's wife either. But in the current state of panic no one would believe it. We must use what God gives us."

"They must be freed, sir. Both of them."

Ceccani looked at him curiously. "Why?"

"But . . . sir—"

"Olivier, you are meddling. We are dealing with great matters here.

The whole course of Christendom is at stake and will be determined by this. That is my concern. These two Jews, guilty or not, give me an advantage. They will confess to this crime. If I have to torture them myself, they will confess to it. Now, if you please, leave me in peace."

But Olivier stood his ground, terrified of his own defiance but unable to retreat. "No, sir," he said eventually. "You cannot do this. They must go free."

Ceccani turned toward him. "And you insist on this?" he said coldly.

"I do, sir."

The cardinal waved his hand. "You are angering me, Olivier. I have always indulged you. You are wayward and foolish, but I have always been kind to you. But you do not—ever—interfere or state your opinions on matters which do not concern you. Do I make myself clear?"

Olivier took a deep breath, his heart pounding with his temerity. "But—"

"Get out of my sight, Olivier. Now. Or we will both regret it."

Olivier, shaking with terror at his daring, bowed and retreated.

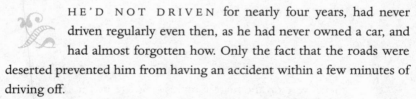 HE'D NOT DRIVEN for nearly four years, had never driven regularly even then, as he had never owned a car, and had almost forgotten how. Only the fact that the roads were deserted prevented him from having an accident within a few minutes of driving off.

The liberty he felt was extraordinary; sitting behind the wheel of the black Citroën, wheezing along at forty kilometers an hour in a machine that had scarcely seen any new parts since the war began, and that had been patched and mended with true ingenuity by mechanics to keep it on the road. Under any other circumstances he would have found it exhilarating, almost godlike to travel thus, alone in the world to be so privileged.

He had no such sensation, though; in his mind there was only one thought and the rest of him was cold and numb. He did not think of the consequences of what he was about to do, or debate the nature of the

choice. Had Marcel been responsible alone, had it been German investigators who had uncovered Julia's secret, he could have understood. It
was something he was even half prepared for. But it was not. The only
thought that had gone through his mind was that Julia had been denounced by Elizabeth Duveau, someone he had known for thirty years,
someone whom he had befriended as a child and who, he thought, had befriended Julia in her turn. And that she had been arrested because he had
come into Avignon on Julia's urging to try to save the woman who had denounced her. And that all of this had happened because one day Elizabeth
had come to him, and he had reached out to her.

He arrived in Carpentras at three o'clock and went to the post office,
where he asked to see the postmaster.

"I need to send a telegram to a Monsieur Blanchard in Amiens," he
said. "It's very urgent, about his sister who is ill. Is that possible these days?"

"I'm afraid not," the man replied, cautiously and steadily. "Perhaps you
might step into my office, and I will see what can be done for you?"

He led the way into a back room, and there Julien delivered the message, specifically designed to lead his friend to his death. Marcel, it said,
wished to talk, tomorrow at his mother's old house. He would meet
him there.

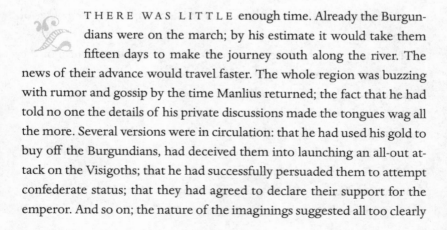

THERE WAS LITTLE enough time. Already the Burgundians were on the march; by his estimate it would take them
fifteen days to make the journey south along the river. The
news of their advance would travel faster. The whole region was buzzing
with rumor and gossip by the time Manlius returned; the fact that he had
told no one the details of his private discussions made the tongues wag all
the more. Several versions were in circulation: that he had used his gold to
buy off the Burgundians, had deceived them into launching an all-out attack on the Visigoths; that he had successfully persuaded them to attempt
confederate status; that they had agreed to declare their support for the
emperor. And so on; the nature of the imaginings suggested all too clearly

that the populace was not yet ready for the truth, which was the only possibility not generally canvassed.

Manlius had only a few days to prepare the region for what was to come next. He also knew that he could not permit his opponents to intervene again, for once Felix returned they would be that much more formidable. The imbecilic Caius Valerius was no serious foe; Felix with his reputation and ability was very much more daunting an opponent. Manlius had to win over the people to his side, and had to ensure Felix did not get the chance to offer any alternative. He must present the result of his maneuverings and compromises as though they were God-willed. Shouting and dispute—however admirable in principle, however much in the tradition of the Rome they admired—was unacceptable.

He also had to persuade the great landowners to follow him, and they required different sorts of arguments to the ones that would sway the townspeople. However devout they might be in their souls, in all other respects they were hard-nosed. What sort of deal had Manlius achieved? Would Gundobad rule with a heavy hand? Would he enforce the laws on tax that were beginning now to slip? Would he defend their rights and return errant serfs? If Gundobad would serve them, enrich them, strengthen their position, and rule in a way Rome no longer could, then they would accept him. And those who would soon lie outside Burgundian protection would simply have to fend for themselves. He had saved what he could. It was better than nothing.

Successful governance with no true authority in law depends on convincing others to do your bidding, which in turn means acting in ways that they consider appropriate. From this need came the event that won Manlius his later sanctity, the conversion of the Jews of Vaison because of his miraculous powers. It was this occurrence—transmitted in garbled form through an interpolation in Gregory of Tours' *Historia Francorum,* although this is merely a summation of his work on lives of the Gallican saints, lost now but available to Gersonides when he was teaching Olivier de Noyen in his study in Carpentras— that won Manlius the authority to proceed as he wished, winning over his diocese and convincing his brother bishops that he was indeed now a true Christian. It says much of Manlius's skills as a politician that the moment the events took place he saw their potential and moved to exploit them.

Was it a considered policy, though, this dramatic event that seems to have led to the conversion of some 150 Jews, the razing of the one synagogue in the town, and the expulsion or death of those recalcitrants who refused to comply with his will? Certainly Manlius was not greatly exercised by the presence of so many Jews in Vaison, for although they remained a self-enclosed enclave, they paid their taxes and kept themselves quiet. Their existence did not offend him. And yet he must have known full well that moving against them would strengthen his hand immeasurably. As he himself had bowed his knee at the altar without in any way feeling as though he had betrayed his beliefs, so it is unlikely that he considered for a moment that the reluctance of the Jews to embrace Christ in their heart was a proper reason for them not to do so in public. And he was a ruthless man, short of time, born to authority but never yet having had the opportunity of exercising it. Gentle, eloquent, cultured, and refined he might be, but these qualities were bestowed on those who deserved them, and that was a narrow circle. To others he was, all admitted, just and fair, but he would brook no interference with the proper exercise of his authority.

The great events were begun three days after he had reentered Vaison by a Jew called Daniel, an utterly dissipated young man all but shunned by his community because of his criminality, violence, and cheating. He had always been so, cruel to his family, idle and insulting, so much so that he was, in effect, expelled from their midst. He was a woodworker, but of no great skill or application, and it was generally accepted that he spent much of his time in theft. When a priest went to his family's house one day and demanded either compensation for someone he had defrauded or that Daniel leave the town, he responded by going to the church, throwing himself in front of the first priest he saw, and demanding to be baptized. He had heard that converts such as himself were greatly welcomed, showered with money and opportunity and, as he now had nothing to lose except a family that hated him and a community that wished only his absence, the prospect of such favor became irresistible.

He was conducted to Manlius, who interviewed him and was repelled by his evidently low character; but, as the deacon pointed out, we were all sinners in the eyes of God, and Daniel's character might change once accepted into the church. Manlius was more skeptical, but could find no reason to deny the request and, in any case, was well aware of the value of such an event, especially once stories went into circulation that his own interview had been the cause of the young Jew's dramatic request. So Daniel was given rapid and cursory instruction in doctrine, and the following Sunday, a ceremony of some noise and grandeur was prepared for the baptism. This was the occasion of Manlius's first sermon, in which he inflected orthodox doctrine with the teachings he had absorbed since his youth. It is not the case that he stated baldly that the life of man is but part of a journey, that the soul cannot ascend to God until it is purified and clean. The implication was there, however, and it was a conception that derived from Pythagorus, and was restated by Plato before finding its place in Christianity through the idea of Purgatory.

His argument was far too complex for most of the congregation; rather it was a clarion call, a warning to his fellows that, although he might be a neophyte, he did not intend to abandon his beliefs through gratitude. From then on, and for the rest of his life, he delivered his sermons, arcane, erudite, and complex, knowing that his audience would not understand them but knowing also that the repeated presentation of such sophisticated ideas would indeed have an effect, if only a small one, deepening and refining the bundle of coarse superstitions that Christians called their religion.

Even had he ventured into complete and coherent heresy, however, the congregation would have forgiven him. For Manlius spent a considerable sum of money to provide a spectacle the likes of which they had not seen for years. He had already begun rebuilding and extending the church, now he rerobed the priests and offered food in plenty and at no cost after the event. For this, they were all to parade through the streets to the now generally disused forum, led by Manlius and with the new convert, robed in white, just behind him.

However, the route from the basilica ran alongside the street where most of the town's Jews lived, and they were enraged by the way the church's triumph was being so noisily proclaimed. Even so, there was little anyone could do, but Daniel's brother, deeply shamed by his elder sibling, climbed to the top of a building and, when Daniel passed by underneath, tipped a large jar of oil over him.

Fortunately, none hit the bishop, else the consequences would have been very much worse; had his cloak been touched, even the slightest drop staining the pure white wool, then the anger of the crowd would have been uncontrollable. But the aim was true; only the newly baptized Daniel was touched, and he shrank down with a scream, thinking that worse was about to follow.

His fear ran through the crowd, and when one pointed up at the roof to the departing brother, they all cried out and began to give chase. It was a hopeless task; Vaison was hardly a big town anymore, but it was more than large enough to conceal one person who did not wish to be discovered. Their anger could find no outlet, and so they went to the one place where they knew Jews could be found. The synagogue was not grand, and did not in any way resemble the buildings that either Olivier or Julien would recognize. Rather, it was an ordinary house, with one larger than average room at the back, big enough to accommodate fifty or so people at one time; when there were more, on holy days, the extra would congregate in the small courtyard outside. It had been there a long time, more than a century, since the number of Jews in the town had increased enough to support it, and everyone knew where it was.

There was no plan to what happened next; the building was set on fire because, once the crowd arrived outside its doors, no one knew what to do next. Had someone with authority managed to keep up, worked his way to the head of the crowd and taken control, there would have been no violence. But, in the absence of such a figure, leadership descended to the most brutal, and it was one of these who first picked up a stone and threw it into the building, then kicked in the door. Half a dozen charged in and only one of these took some embers from the fire glowing in the grate and used them to light the hangings.

It was a small fire, which did little damage in itself; its main effect was to enflame the crowd, who sensed that the thin curl of smoke and little flicker gave the permission to continue. From then the destruction increased and engulfed the whole building. When the real fire, the one that reduced it to ashes, took hold, there was not a piece of furniture, hanging, or book left intact. The noise of the crowd increased to a pitch, then gave way and sank back to silence as the flames blazed, the energy of their anger transferring to the conflagration, and reducing them to mere spectators. Then they simply stood and watched what they had done, scarcely even remembering that it was they who had begun this. And after a while they began to disperse, their anger spent, their vengeance taken, and their lust satisfied.

In terms of violence, it was not a serious business. Compare it with the orgy that convulsed Constantinople a few decades later and left fifteen thousand dead after a week of riots. Compare it to some of the coups and civil wars that had engulfed the empire in the past century. Compare it to the traditional and accepted behavior of troops taking control of a city after a siege. The violence of Vaison killed no one; even Daniel's brother escaped unscathed, and while Jews felt obliged to stay indoors for a day or so, even they did not consider themselves under great threat. Indeed, their anger was directed not so much against the Christians who had destroyed their synagogue—even though they deeply resented the assault—as against the family that had brought this calamity upon them: the useless Daniel and his equally violent, headstrong brother. Neither of them was worth any loss.

The importance of the incident was not the violence; many communities of all sorts had suffered very much worse. Rather, this lay in the fact that it became woven into the fabric of Christian, Gallic history, embedded in a framework of theological justification, given purpose and meaning, a past and a future, through the words and deeds—misreported and twisted though they were—of Manlius Hippomanes.

For Manlius saw the opportunity finally to make himself the undisputed leader of the town, to put himself in a position where he commanded such love and respect that he was invulnerable. And he took it, grasped it with both hands.

The following day he delivered his second sermon. Less considered and far more effective than his first. Little of what he said was completely new; the desirability that the Jews should throw off their blindness and recognize their own Messiah was something of a commonplace and had been for well over a century. Revulsion at the way they had murdered their own God was not new either. Disdain for—or more properly incomprehension of—Jews was also common, although it was little different in form to the bewilderment that had once greeted the unsocial, uncivil, and coarse behavior of Christians themselves. None of this was innovative; nor did passion give the words their power, for Manlius regarded Jews with no more disdain than he regarded Goths, Huns, slaves, serfs, and townsmen—anyone not of his family or rank.

It was his logic that impressed, that finely honed skill taught to him by Sophia and which he applied to all that he said or did, reaching out to conclusions and stating them because of their rationality. The Jews were disobedient; they had disobeyed their savior, and now they disobeyed those who took their authority from the savior. Consequently, the path was clear. They were to be given three choices. They could convert, they could leave, or they could die. It was necessary for all Jews to be eliminated for the divine plan to be fulfilled, and the church, through Manlius, put its full authority behind this noble plan.

Manlius wished to be remembered as a man of letters, the voice of reason, a philosopher. This he intended to be his immortality. But all of this was buried for nine hundred years until Olivier briefly unearthed his work, and it was then lost again until Julien discovered it in the Vatican archive. Instead, such influence as he had came through a trifle, an instinctive reponse to a political problem that he had largely forgotten about only a few months later. For in one sermon he managed to bind all the diverse elements of disapproval into a coherent polemic. He asserted not merely the right of the church to insist on conversion, but also its duty to eradicate false belief by whatever means necessary. His learning, skill, and eloquence were bent to the task of asserting the church's right—his right—to absolute control, and he brought all his scholarship, everything he had learned, to the task of weaving the proofs necessary to back up his desires.

Faced with such a call, the reaction was swift. Manlius achieved everything he desired, doubts about him faded away, his advocacy of the treaty with King Gundobad was accepted almost without question. Over the next week, fifty converted, a hundred and four left, and five died. The incident was recorded, passed from mouth to mouth, written about in letters, and eventually, many years later, found its way to Gregory, the saintly and able Bishop of Tours. He recorded it twice—once more or less accurately in a manuscript lost in the fifteenth century, and once less so, transferring the events and the words to Saint Avitus a century or so later, repeating the same story because the simple repetition excited in him not suspicion that his source was doubtful, but joy that the same events occurring twice confirmed the will of God. Through him, and others who borrowed his arguments and turns of phrase, the words of Manlius echoed down the centuries, becoming fainter and stronger by turns, whispering into the ears of Clement, of Olivier, of Gersonides and his servant Rebecca, and on to Julien, Bernard, Marcel, and many, many others. This was his immortality.

 JULIEN DROVE BACK to Avignon afterward, ran out of fuel outside the railway station, and abandoned the car by the side of the road. He left it unlocked and walked straight off, looked up at the goods train, immobilized on the tracks above him, puffing pathetically. He sometimes thought all the trains in France had spent the last four years sitting idly at stations, waiting for some order to be given. Nothing moved anymore, except in slow motion.

He headed for the lycée that had been converted into a makeshift prison. His lycée, indeed, where he had enjoyed the triumphs of youth before he volunteered for the army in 1917. Where Bernard and he and Marcel had first met. And he understood the passion that Marcel felt at this moment, how he wanted so much to triumph at last.

He remembered the schoolroom, probably still decorated with the same tables of the alphabet; he remembered the smell of the place, the way the paint peeled in the corridors. The maps, though, would have been changed, taken down so that Alsace and Lorraine would not be shown as French; the bust of Marianne, symbol of republican France, which used to decorate the hallway, had no doubt also vanished, removed and put into storage on Marcel's order some three years previously. But unchanged would be the teacher's podium, where Bernard had once taken his penknife to the teacher's desk.

Everyone had watched him do it; a crowd had gathered around, laughing and sniggering. Only Marcel had stayed at his desk, conscientiously working, doing his best as usual to keep up, making best use of his time. Had Julien been one of the crowd? He could not remember. He remembered it only as a filmgoer; the scene in black and white, the giggling children, the sudden hush and scramble as Monsieur Julot the teacher came back into the room; the suspicious look, and then the questioning.

"What has been going on here?"

And how had he accomplished it? How had Bernard managed to get the blame poured onto the top of Marcel's innocent head? "Julot is a Jew," Bernard had scratched, and the beating Marcel received was severe, not because of the vandalism, although that was serious enough, but because of the magnitude of the insult. Bernard put his arm around him afterward, said he was his best friend, made him feel better.

"No one here of that name." He had managed to get into the building, demanded to see the officer in charge, and explained why he was there. He had come for Julia.

"Don't be absurd. The préfet said she was here. I am to telephone him, and he will sign the order to have her released."

He shook his head again. "All the Jews were moved out this afternoon; orders of the General Commissariat for Jewish Affairs."

Julien stared. "What?"

The man sighed; a bored sigh of one who has to deal with complaints far too often. "There was a convoy to pick up Jews. It was short of numbers from Marseille. So . . ."

"Who said that?"

The man did not reply. What did it matter? It was not his concern.

"Where has she gone? What are they doing with her?"

Another weary shrug. "You're asking the wrong person. I am merely in charge of guarding this place."

"You must know something."

The panic in Julien's voice struck a chord. Some sort of human connection was made. "Look, I don't know. All Jews are to be taken to an assembly point, then they will be transported to work camps. That's all. Now, go away."

"Where is she? Please tell me."

He sighed. "They were all taken to the railway station," he said impatiently. Anything to get him to go away. "And that's where they will still be, I imagine."

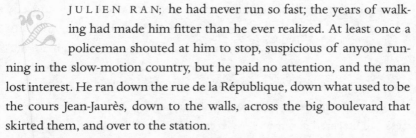

JULIEN RAN; he had never run so fast; the years of walking had made him fitter than he ever realized. At least once a policeman shouted at him to stop, suspicious of anyone running in the slow-motion country, but he paid no attention, and the man lost interest. He ran down the rue de la République, down what used to be the cours Jean-Jaurès, down to the walls, across the big boulevard that skirted them, and over to the station.

It was quiet; he tried to block out what that meant. As he ran in he started shouting uncontrollably. "Where is the train? Where is the train?"

The few people there paid him no attention, beyond curious looks. He ran to the platform, found a guard, and grabbed him. "Where is the train?"

The guard pushed him off roughly, and Julien lunged forward again, then tripped and fell heavily on the concrete. "Please," he said, panting so hard he could scarcely speak, "I beg you, tell me."

"What train?"

"The one that was here. With the people on it. The convoy."

"The Jews, you mean?"

He nodded.

The guard paused, and looked down the line. Nothing here, his gesture seemed to say. "It was in the goods yard. It went ten minutes ago."

He looked at Julien for a moment, considered offering him some help.

Then he looked at the clock; his shift was over, he was late. It had been a long day. He flicked his cigarette onto the tracks and walked away.

OLIVIER TRIED to think, for a while, that something might be salvaged from the catastrophe, but knew he was fooling himself. He knew and understood nothing. Ceccani could feel the great sweep of history whirling around him, and thought in centuries; he had taken on the guardianship of the soul of Christianity. He was prepared to sacrifice, himself and others, to discharge his duties toward Christendom, and to obey the will of God. Daily, he grappled with mighty matters of an import Olivier could only guess at; the poet was a mere human, Ceccani something more than that.

Although he understood this much, it meant little to him. His universe was smaller, more petty and more circumscribed. Having buried Althieux, seen Pisano run away frightened for his life, been close when a man murdered his wife, smelled the charring of a riot, knowing that the plague threatened them all, he found he cared little for the future of Christendom, was indifferent to the power of the papacy. This was not his business. All he cared about was Rebecca and Gersonides, locked away, liable to be tortured and killed. His mind was insufficiently grand to see further than that. And indeed, he realized he was not even preoccupied with Gersonides; he felt—for now he felt only and could not think—that everything in creation, his soul and hers, the soul of all men, depended on her continuing to live.

He walked the streets all afternoon and into the night, the only person in the entire city mindless of the plague, knowing full well that it had no power over him whatsover; that although it might one day claim him for its own, it could not do so until he had reached the decision that he knew he must make sooner or later. He could bow to the wishes of his master, obey the laws of men as they were unwritten but understood. For Ceccani had given him everything—money, encouragement, a place in the world, even something approaching friendship. In return he expected loyalty; it was a fair bargain, freely entered into and universally recognized. No one would accept that throwing that over was justified. It was not self-interest, although the consequences of breaking the ties that bound him to Ceccani would be terrible enough. Rather it was a matter of honor, the simple fact that nothing could possibly justify what would be a breathtaking treason. Olivier was considering playing the part of Judas; a squalid little Judas betraying his master for no reason except for what the world would consider a base infatuation.

Nor was there anyone to talk to. Pisano would have talked him out of it with a laugh, made him see the absurdity of his conundrum, ridiculed him back to sense. Althieux would have been more considered, taking the argument through countless authorities, classical and biblical, before coming to the same conclusion. But one was on the road to Italy, the other was dead.

Olivier had only his own mind, filled with the metaphors of poetry and half-understood readings from philosophy. And the phrases of Sophia, relayed through Manlius, came back to him, hammering inside his skull. "Any amount of disgrace or infamy can be incurred if great advantage may be gained for a friend." And again: "The action of virtue is rarely understood by those who do not understand philosophy." Again: "Laws formulated without the understanding of philosophy must be constantly questioned, for the exercise of true virtue is often incomprehensible to the blind."

He slept on the steps of Saint Agricole, along with half a dozen other beggars, and considered how he had first glimpsed Rebecca some two years before. He again saw her walking past in her heavy dark cloak and remembered the feeling that had torn through him as he looked. And he decided that the emotion that welled up in him that day was itself a sign from God, that he had to obey it.

Dawn came eventually; his companions of the night rolled over and groaned one by one, and as the light rose, Olivier stood up with a sudden surge of determination and walked off, pausing only when he got to the great walls of the palace. He considered going again to Ceccani, considered going to de Deaux, but dismissed both ideas. He thought of begging for Rebecca alone, saying she was not a Jew, but knew this was hopeless. Ceccani was reaching for the whole world; Olivier knew he could never deflect him with anything so simple.

He walked in through the huge gates of the palace, nodding familiarly to the guard, whom he had known for years, but wary lest some alert had been put out for him, in case Ceccani had managed to read the mind he had had such difficulty understanding himself. But all was well; nothing happened, there was no shout or running of feet. In the great courtyard he stood uncertainly, lost and bewildered once more until his confusion was broken into by the clear, pure sound of a bell ringing through the morning air.

He almost fell to the ground in thanks as he heard it. It was the sound for the musicians and the singers to leave their studies and gather in the chapel, dutifully waiting their master. For them to sing their hearts out before God's earthly representative. Clement, frightened and blockaded in his tower though he was, could not live without music. It was his life and his greatest pleasure. Even the plague could not deflect him from it. Even as the bodies were carried through the streets, he had ordered that any musician who left the palace without his permission would be arrested. If they had to die for his tranquillity, then so be it. There were some things this strange man could not do without.

And as the bell tolled, he would be putting on his robes, descending the stairs, and processing through the great corridors and chambers of the palace to the chapel. He would be alone and isolated, for he had ordered that no man must come near him in case he communicate the plague. Then he would sit until the music had finished and he could scurry, refreshed, back to his protective chamber high in the sky.

Olivier hurried, taking all the shortcuts he knew by instinct after so many years. There was a side door to the chapel where the acolytes entered and left as the services demanded. Olivier got there before anyone else and ducked through it. Then he concealed himself behind one of the huge Flemish tapestries Clement had commissioned to make the place more pleasing to his eye. And waited.

At any more normal time, he would have had no chance of approaching Clement; the moment he stepped forward, the guards who always hovered nearby would have fallen on him and dragged him away. Clement had an affable persona in public, but took the prospect of neither injury nor insult lightly. True, he was at his least exposed in the chapel, the heart of his own palace where only his immediate circle was allowed. Still, the guards remained, for he knew well that men of God were not necessarily men of peace.

The plague had changed the great ceremonies; Clement wanted as few people as possible around him. Moreover, he had a fine sense of occasion, and refused absolutely to look absurd. Rather than entering in with one priest behind him, no assistants and no one to watch, he strolled in alone with a goblet of some drink in his hand, sat heavily on his throne, leaned back, and called out to the officiating priest:

"Come on, then. Get on with it. I haven't got all morning."

The priest bowed and made a blessing. The choir, looking solemn or bored or resentful according to their characters, filed in and the singing began. The new music, rising and falling, twisting in and out of itself, doubling back, created in the air for as long as it lasted a perfect resemblance of the wonders of creation, and the love of God. Too complex, it seemed, for man to grasp as a whole, but so beautiful that Olivier again thought of Rebecca and Sophia and their belief in the evil of the world. So it might be, he thought. The world of spirit might be far finer, more pure, and closer to the divine. But nothing that can produce such beauty can be irredeemable; if men can produce such harmonies, hear them with their ears, sing them with their voices and their instruments, there must be goodness in the material.

Then the contrast, between the calm beauty of the music and the dire state of his own predicament, came back to him once more. He stiffened and prepared himself as the music came to an end, and an echoing silence descended on the chapel, broken only by the pope beating on the arm of his throne with his hand and calling out in a loud voice, "Very fine, very fine, boys. My thanks to you all. Makes me feel better already. Now, get out of here, and tomorrow I'd like that piece you did last week again. By that Italian fellow, you remember?"

The choirmaster nodded and bowed, and with a loud cackle of pleasure, Clement bounded out of his throne, bowed solemnly to the altar, then rubbed his hands.

"Nothing like a bit of music for stirring up an appetite, I think. I'm starving."

He turned, took a step toward the door, then stopped as he saw Olivier, standing in front of him. There was a moment of screaming silence as Olivier realized how alarming he must look—unshaven, swaddled in a dirty cloak, the look of the hunted about him already. He kneeled down swiftly when he saw from the look on the pope's face that he was frightened out of his wits.

"My deepest apologies, Holiness. My name is Olivier de Noyen, one of Cardinal Ceccani's people. I wish to beg for an audience."

Clement peered at him more closely. "De Noyen? Good God, man, what's with you? You look like a gypsy. How dare you come before me in such a state?"

"I apologize again. I would not have done so if it had not been urgent."

"You'll have to wait. I want my breakfast."

"This is more important than breakfast, Holiness."

Clement frowned. "Young man, nothing is more important than breakfast." He looked exasperated, but saw in the dogged look on the young man's face that there was something he should hear. This was not frivolous, a demand for a favor, or yet another madman who believed he knew how to cure the plague or bring the Muslims to Christ.

"I will not readily forgive this."

"As you choose, Holiness. What you do with me is of little importance as long as you hear me."

Clement signaled to one of the guards at the door, who stepped forward. "Search him," he ordered. "See he has no weapons. Then bring him to my chamber."

And with a mighty scowl and a ruined morning, God's vicegerent on earth stamped out of the chapel.

"WELL THEN? Get on with it. What is so important that you ruin my music, my breakfast, and my morning?"

"Holiness, do you wish to take the papacy to Rome?"

"A strange way to start. Why do you ask such a thing?"

"Because you may have to. There is a plan to make sure you have no alternative but to leave this city. Aigues-Mortes is to be delivered to the English. When it is, the king of France will blame the Countess of Provence and want you to condemn her. You will have a hard time refusing him, I think. And if you condemn her, your chances of buying this city from her, or even remaining in it, will be small."

Clement's mind, subtle in matters of theology, was direct when it came to statesmanship, but now it hardly needed either. He scarcely needed to think at all to grasp that such an unfolding of events would be catastrophic. He would be reduced in an instant from serene overlord of Christendom to wandering priest, or at best a local magnate, battling against the petty warlords of Rome. Who would allow him to be peacemaker between French and English, to dictate the policies of the empire, to call up and direct a crusade, when he could not even keep his own house in order?

"You know this? Or is it something you have imagined to win my attention?"

"I am a mere servant, and a poet, Holiness. I have no taste for intrigue. I could not have invented this. I have read a letter, setting out just such a plan."

"From? To?"

"It was written by the Bishop of Winchester. To Cardinal Ceccani."

Clement sat down and thought. Then he wagged his finger at Olivier. "I know you, young man. You are Ceccani's favorite. And yet you come here to tell me this? Why would you do such a thing?"

"Because I want a reward." He could have given a long justification to exculpate himself, to demonstrate that he acted with honor, appealed to higher motives. He did not do so; he was selling his master; he knew it and did not wish to disguise it.

"And that is?"

"I want my teacher and his servant released from this place. The two Jews. They have done no wrong, the accusation was made simply to weaken Cardinal de Deaux. And I want you to stop this campaign against the Jews before any more people die. If all Jews are threatened, then so are they, as long as they live."

Clement waved his hands in irritation as if to dismiss the very idea. "The world is crumbling into ruin. Armies are marching. Men and women are dying everywhere, in huge numbers. Fields are abandoned and towns deserted. The wrath of the Lord is upon us and He may be intending to destroy the whole of creation. People are without leaders and direction. They want to be given a reason for this, so they can be reassured, so they will return to their prayers and their obediences. All this is going on, and you are concerned about the safety of two Jews?"

Olivier stayed silent. He was not meant to reply.

"I wish to do something which will make my name light up history," Clement said. "I will be remembered as the man who rid the world, once and for all, of the scourge of these people. Who eradicated a daily offense against God. For more than a thousand years they have had their chance, and for all that, they have spat on the truth as they once spat on our Lord. This is the moment to strike against them. Do you doubt it is a noble thing? A necessary, justified act, delayed for too long already? The Jews must convert, or be killed. Ceccani is right; it will bring men back together with a common purpose; reunite them with the church. I have merely to say the word, and it will be done."

Olivier lifted his head and looked at him. "Then do not say it, sir. A conversion by force cannot be pleasing to God, only to men. The Lord built his church on love and faith, not on lies and threats. Obedience is nothing without faith. When Saint Peter took up a sword against the soldier, He took that sword from him and healed the man's ear. And you are his heir on earth; take the sword from Ceccani's hand as well; do not do what he suggests. Rather, do the opposite; extend your protection and love to these people, just as Christ loved sinners as much as he loved those who had faith. Live up to the name you chose when you ascended to Peter's chair. Be clement by nature, as well as by name. Let that be your memorial. So that in the future men will think of you and say, 'He had such love for humanity he gave the cloak of his protection even to the Jews. And by doing so, let all men see that as God is love, so is His church, even for the worst sinners, and for those most deserving punishment.'"

Olivier took a deep breath, then continued: "Otherwise, you will spend the rest of your life wandering the world, homeless and friendless. Men will laugh at you, no one will listen to you. Because I will not tell you how the gates of Aigues-Mortes will be opened, or when, and you will not be able to discover enough in time to stop it."

Clement was sitting, listening to his words carefully, not throwing him from the room as he deserved. Olivier had touched something in him, he knew. But he was not there yet. "You have not yet convinced me this is anything other than some sort of elaborate trick," he said. "You say you have seen a letter, but you do not produce it. Is there such a thing? If there is, perhaps it was written by one of his enemies? You say you have a letter proving Cardinal Ceccani is guilty of the most terrible betrayal of me, and yet here you are, wandering around this town in broad daylight, quite un-molested. If I were Ceccani, I would have cut your throat before you came near me."

"He does not know I am here. But there is a letter."

"Give it to me, then."

"I cannot. There is no time. Either for you or for me. The torture of the two Jews will start soon, if it has not already. There will be more riots in the streets when night falls. And you must move quickly if you are to save Aigues-Mortes for the French."

"You are suggesting I take severe measures against a cardinal who is my closest advisor, on your word alone? No, young man. How do I know you have not been suborned by de Deaux? Or maybe you have a dispute of your own with Ceccani and wish to ruin him in revenge? You are un-convincing. I will do nothing on the basis of what you say."

He was half-convinced, Olivier knew, and very worried. Clement knew quite well that it was a scheme Ceccani was capable of devising. But he

was not sure enough to act. Not ruthless enough, perhaps. Ceccani would have done so already, on half the evidence. But the pontiff was a gentler, more pacific man, less able to think ill of people, and who found disturbance almost painful. Olivier found his prize slipping from his fingers, and so tried his final throw.

"Holiness, you say you are surprised I have not been silenced. So am I. I do not think my safety will last long."

He paused. "Send someone to find me this evening. If I am still unmolested, then I have not proved my case, for why would anyone wish to do me harm?"

Olivier stopped, and looked carefully at the pontiff. "If someone has attacked me, then arrest him as the person who will deliver Aigues-Mortes to the English for the cardinal. Interrogate him, and discover the truth. You will also remember that the man who conceived this plan is the one who is also urging you to begin a crusade against the Jews. And you will think about that carefully before you follow his advice to soak your name in blood for his purposes."

Clement considered. "Very well. I accept your offer. By this evening we will know whether you are a liar or a fool."

"As for my friends, I am not trying to force you to save these two people; I leave them to your mercy and ask for no more."

The pope rose; he liked nothing more than to demonstrate his generosity and his mercy. "The pope must know how to behave like a prince" was his belief. He liked no man to leave his presence unsatisfied.

"You may take them," he said with a wave of his hand. "I give them to you. One condition though. And that is that you tell me why any Christian should place himself at risk to save Jews, either a brace of them or the entire people."

Olivier thought, and then accepted his failure. He had spent much of his time in the last few months trying to wrestle with the thorny questions Manlius Hippomanes had thrown at him, and he now understood for the first time the difference between clever patterns of words and the answers of the soul. "I do not know, sir," he said. "I can discover no reason or justification for it, and do not wish to. I am neither a theologian nor a philosopher, a lawyer nor a politician. I cannot find reasons; my skill is to sing about the impulsions of the heart, and that is enough."

Clement grunted. "Very well. If you want to play the fool, then so be it. Go away. Give me a convincing demonstration of your case by this evening, and I will reconsider. But if you don't . . ."

He paused and thought.

"But if I don't . . . ?" Olivier prompted.

The pope did not smile. "Then I will kill every Jew in Christendom, including your teacher and his servant."

JULIEN STOOD ON the platform of the railway station for nearly half an hour, not knowing what to do. His mind had closed down. Only one train came through as he stood there, full of German soliders heading south, rattling and squealing, filling the atmosphere with thick coal smoke. The days of triumph had gone; they were traveling to be defeated; everyone knew it.

Eventually he shook himself, walked away, and found himself going back to the Préfecture. There was nothing else he could do. Only Marcel now could help in any way; so he went to beg.

He was, as usual, sitting neatly at his desk, going through papers, oblivious of the heat and the little trickle of sweat running down his temple into the frayed collar of his shirt. He looked up at Julien, with the defiant glance of a guilty man.

"What have you done?" Julien said quietly.

He shook his head. "It wasn't me, Julien. Believe me, I didn't do this. She was taken to the detention center, then the people from Jewish Affairs came. They didn't know she was not to be moved. They wanted all the Jews. She had admitted she was one, so they took her. I only heard about it five minutes ago."

"A mistake?" he said incredulously.

Marcel nodded. "I'm sorry," he said.

"Get her back, Marcel. Phone ahead, say there's been an error. Say she's wanted for interrogation. Say something. Say anything. You can do it. You're the préfet, for God's sake."

"It can't be done, Julien. These convoys are run by the Gestapo. They don't stop them because of requests from French officials. If she hadn't signed a statement saying she was a Jew, I could have done something, perhaps. Why did she do that?"

Julien shook his head, dismissing the question. "What happens to her now?"

Marcel paused. "Do you want the official, reassuring answer? Or the one we both know?"

He didn't reply, so Marcel continued. "Officially she will go to a labor camp. Conditions will be harsh but fair. She will be kept there until the war is over and then, no doubt, released."

He hesitated, got up, and stood facing Julien, his hands in his pockets, his face looking down at the floor for a few moments.

"But you know as well as I do that is a lie, and that she will die there," he said. "They are killing them, Julien. They said that's what they were going to do, and they're doing it. I'm sorry. I truly am. This is not what I intended. I wanted only to save the lives of twenty-six innocent hostages."

Julien stood there, quite immobile, until Marcel came and touched him on the arm. "Come with me," he said. "Let's get out of here for a while."

He allowed himself to be led, along the corridor with the worn linoleum, down the stone stairs, and out into the oppressive heat of the afternoon. They walked, quietly and companionably and for a long while silently; good friends, almost. The sort of walk that Marcel had always valued, and which Bernard so disdained. Together they crisscrossed the city, seeking out the dark and shadowy streets where the sun could not penetrate; past the steps where Olivier had first seen Rebecca, past the place where he had been attacked and where Isabelle had been murdered.

And Marcel stayed with him, saying nothing, hoping only to give some comfort with his presence, the assurance of his friendship. Eventually, Julien began to talk.

"When I was at Verdun," he said quietly, "I saw things which were more appalling than you can imagine. I saw civilization coming apart at the seams. As it weakened, people felt free to act as they pleased, and did so, which weakened it still more. And I decided then it was the most important thing, that it had to survive and be protected. Without that tissue of beliefs and habits we are worse than beasts. Animals are constrained by their limitations and their lack of imagination. We are not.

"So that is what I have tried to do, all my life in a small and insignificant way. Anything would be better than another collapse like that, because I was certain that another would be final. No coming back. And I told myself that no matter what politicians or generals did, they were merely the barbarians, and everyone else had to defend what was truly important from them; keep the flickering flame going. People like Bernard and you were what I detested most of all. Neither of you was even honest enough to admit you wanted power.

"I was wrong, and I only realized it when you told me Julia had been denounced by the wife of our local blacksmith. Odd, don't you think? I have seen war, and invasions and riots. I have heard of massacres and brutalities beyond imagining, and I have kept my faith in the power of civilization to bring men back from the brink. And yet one woman writes a letter, and my whole world falls to pieces.

"You see, she is an ordinary woman. A good one, even. That's the point. You are not a good man. Bernard is not a good man. Nothing either of you do can surprise or shock me, or worry me. But she denounced Julia and sent her to her death because she resented her, and because Julia is a Jew.

"I thought in this simple contrast between the civilized and the barbaric, but I was wrong. It is the civilized who are the truly barbaric, and the Germans are merely the supreme expression of it. They are our greatest achievement. They are building a monument which will never be dismantled, even when they are swept away. They are teaching us a lesson which will echo for hundreds of years. Manlius Hippomanes buried his ideas in the church, and those ideas survived the end of his world. The Nazis are doing the same. They are holding up a mirror and saying, 'Look at what we have all achieved.' And they are the same ideas, Marcel. That was my mistake."

"The Germans are trying to win a war, Julien," Marcel said. "And they're losing. They're desperate, and that makes them even more brutal than they are usually."

"You know that's not true. They knew the moment the Americans entered the war they'd lost. Before then, even. They may be mad, but they're not fools. What they're doing goes far beyond the war. Something unparalleled in human history. The ultimate achievement of civilization. Just think about it. How do you annihilate so many people? You need contributions from so many quarters. Scientists to prove Jews are inferior; theologians to provide the moral tone. Industrialists to build the trains and the camps. Technicians to design the guns. Administrators to solve the vast problems of identifying and moving so many people. Writers and artists to make sure nobody notices or cares. Hundreds of years spent honing skills and developing techniques have been necessary before such a thing can even be imagined, let alone put into effect. And now is the moment. Now is the time for all the skills of civilization to be put to use.

"Can you imagine a greater, a more enduring achievement? This will last forever, and cannot be undone. Whatever benefits we bring to mankind in the future, we killed the Jews. No matter how great the advances of medicine, we killed them. However high our achievements may soar, however perfect we become, this is what is at our heart. We killed them all; not by accident, or in a fit of passion. We did it deliberately, and after centuries of preparation.

"When all this is over, people will try to blame the Germans alone, and the Germans will try to blame the Nazis alone, and the Nazis will try to blame Hitler alone. They will make him bear the sins of the world. But it's not true. You suspected what was happening, and so did I. It was already too late over a year ago. I caused a reporter to lose his job because you told me to. He was deported. The day I did that I made my little contribution to civilization, the only one that matters."

"If you think that, why didn't you throw your lot in with Bernard, then?"

"Because he's no better. He promised to get Julia out of France and then did nothing about it, because he needed her to forge papers for him. If that placed her at risk, then so be it. If she got caught, it didn't matter.

He spends his time thinking about the future, and in the present his people kill soldiers and bomb barracks. They don't sabotage many convoys taking away the Jews. It's not a priority. There are more important things to do.

"'The evil done by men of goodwill is the worst of all.' That's what my Neoplatonic bishop said, and he was right. He knew. He had firsthand experience of it. We have done terrible things, for the best of reasons, and that makes it worse."

Marcel was trying to lead him back to his apartment; they got to the entrance to the museum, closed now. "I think you should go and sleep. You haven't had any rest for a long time."

"What about Bernard, Marcel?"

"It's out of my hands. All the information has been given to the Germans."

"'Has been given'? You mean you gave it to them already?"

"Yes. I gave it to them. I had to, otherwise those people would have been shot this evening. If they manage to arrest Bernard, they will be let go."

"And then what? He is tortured to death?"

Marcel sighed. "What can I do, Julien? What would you do?"

He shook his head. "I don't know."

"Go home and sleep. It is out of your hands. And out of mine. We are powerless. We always have been."

And Julien did go home, but before he did so, he watched Marcel slowly and heavily go into the church across the road. He was going to pray; he found it a comfort. Not for the first time, Julien envied him the solace.

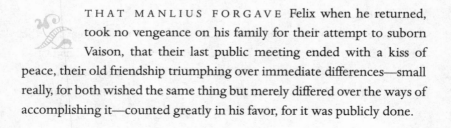

THAT MANLIUS FORGAVE Felix when he returned, took no vengeance on his family for their attempt to suborn Vaison, that their last public meeting ended with a kiss of peace, their old friendship triumphing over immediate differences—small really, for both wished the same thing but merely differed over the ways of accomplishing it—counted greatly in his favor, for it was publicly done.

Afterward, he begged Felix to come to his villa for more substantive talks. The invitation was accompanied by all sorts of reassurances that the friendship of the soul must always triumph over minor material estrangements. That Manlius was, and always would be, his true friend. In these dangerous times any sort of disunity amongst those who truly were of importance would allow civil strife to come to the surface. In the name of the rationality they had always espoused, Manlius begged Felix to come and talk to him, that their differences might be settled.

Felix responded—not enthusiastically, but readily enough; it was the last flickering of their old friendship. Besides, Manlius now had the upper hand in the delicate balance of the town's affections; he had come to some accommodation with the Burgundians; and Felix needed to know urgently what exactly he had agreed to do.

So he came, and the spirit of peace returned. They retired to his villa, and arm in arm they walked once more, and for a while the comfort of civility extended itself over them both.

"I wish this had not happened," Felix said. "Much will be lost if we are separated."

"We needn't be," Manlius replied. "We will always walk through these gardens, smelling the flowers in bloom and watching the sun on the water's surface."

Neither wanted to break the moment, to talk about why they were meeting. To do so would have acknowledged that their last afternoon together was a chimera, existing now only in their desires, not in any reality. The hearts of both men ached for what was passing from their grasp. The days spent in conversation, the letters received and read, the responses made to them. Their shared pleasure in a well-cropped fruit tree, an admirable vista recalling some work of literature, a subtle blend of spices at an agreeable dinner party.

"Do you remember," Felix said eventually, "that time we heard of the Greek musician in Marseille? How we both went down there as fast as we could, and bid to hire him for a month? How the price went up and up, until the poor man was bewildered and thought we were making fun of him?"

Manlius laughed. "And eventually he had to intervene, and promise to come to both of us, one after the other. But you got him first."

"And you discovered that he knew the whole of the *Iliad*, and could recite it in the old mode. So beautiful it was."

"And all the more enjoyable for watching the faces of our guests when they realized they were expected to stay and listen to it for eleven days."

They walked some more, basking in the warmth, until Felix finally broke the spell. "I think that Gundobad does not read Greek," he said quietly.

Manlius almost cried out in protest. Not yet. Let us enjoy this a little while longer before it is taken away forever. But he knew that sooner or later it would come. It could not be delayed.

"He is a good ruler, educated in Rome. Willing to take advice from people he trusts. His wife is a Catholic and he will not interfere there. And he can block Euric."

"He is a barbarian, come what may."

"So was Ricimer, and Rome itself bowed before him happily enough."

"But Ricimer bowed in turn to Constaninople. Gundobad will not do so. Will he?"

"No. He wishes to be king, owing allegiance to no man."

"And the Burgundians are not numerous. Do you seriously think that they can relieve Clermont and defend the whole of Provence from Euric?"

And here was the moment. The end of it all, for civilization was merely another name for friendship, and friendship was coming to an end. Manlius wished not to speak, wished he could say something else, suddenly come up with a great plan that would convince his friend so they could meet the coming challenges together. But he could not.

"He does not intend to."

Felix took some time to absorb the implications of this. He was not a slow man; far from it. He simply had trouble believing what he heard.

"Go on," he said, almost in a whisper.

Manlius took a deep breath. "I did my best to persuade the Burgundians to march to Clermont and block Euric there. They would not do so. Instead, they will move south to a line a little beyond Vaison, on the left bank, so that they command the river. That is all I could get them to do. And I believe they have begun their march already. Clermont is lost. So is all the land down to the coast. Those who live there had best make what peace they can with Euric, or he will impose his own terms later."

He glanced at his friend and saw that there were tears in his eyes. "Manlius, Manlius, what have you done?" he said eventually. "You have betrayed us all. Sold yourself and abandoned everyone else. Did he reward you well, this new master of yours? Did you go down and kiss his feet? Are you learning his language, so you can lie to him the better?"

"My friend . . ." Manlius said, resting his hand on Felix's arm.

"You are no friend of mine. A man of honor would have preferred to fight to the last, side by side with his friends. Not sell them into slavery to save himself and his estates."

"The way is open for you to bring troops from Italy. Did you find any?"

"There is no time now. The moment Euric hears the Burgundians have moved, he will move as well. He must. You know that, don't you?"

Manlius nodded.

"Not that it will concern you. You will be safe, all your lands protected by Gundobad."

"And if I hadn't? What then? Do you seriously think that even if you had a year, or two years, you would have found any troops worth having?"

"Yes."

"You know there are none. Any you found would have put up a paltry show of fighting then joined the winning side. And the Goths would have destroyed everything in vengeance. As it is now, they will be blocked. The sea on one side, the mountains on the other, and the Burgundians on the third. They have to keep moving. Eventually they will wither and die."

"And will anything be left when they leave?"

Manlius shrugged. "There is a chance."

"Yes. There is one chance."

"What do you mean?"

"A show of strength, to demonstrate that we are not to be walked over.

If we can throw back the Burgundians, then Euric will think twice about trying as well. He is besieging Clermont still. He cannot commit his forces to little wars all over Gaul. It will give him pause. And in that time we can raise troops from somewhere, even if we have to melt down every statue in the land to pay for it. That is our chance. Give me your aid, your money, and your men. We could leave in a few days, you and I, and others would join us."

"I have already given my word."

"The Bishop of Vaison gave his word. After tomorrow, you may not be the bishop. You have called a meeting. Very well, then. We will see who is the more persuasive."

Manlius nodded, distracted by the noise of two slaves standing nearby, hewing at a log with a long-handled axe.

"We must not argue now," he said sadly. "Too much is at stake for heated words. Let us pause and think, and talk again later."

OLIVIER COLLECTED the authorization from Clement's secretary, dictated brusquely and signed with a blotchy blob of wax, then ran off to the section of the palace that was being used as a prison. He stood there, haranguing the guards as they shuffled about, unlocked the door, and let the prisoners out, their release as abrupt and as unexplained as their initial incarceration.

When she came out, dirty and disheveled, she looked confused, uncertain, and frightened, not knowing whether she was being released or taken off to be tortured or killed. Then she turned, ever so slightly, and saw Olivier. She couldn't even smile, she just ran to him and gripped hold of him so tightly it seemed that they must become one person, inseparable and indistinguishable. He bent his head down and smelled her hair, felt it against his cheek, rocked to and fro delighting in her touch. Neither said anything; even the guards stood back and let them be.

With the greatest reluctance, they had to pull apart; such moments do not last in this world, they merely offer a hint, then are whisked away.

"You are free. I've come to take you away." It was all he said; he had used up all his poetry and needed to say nothing else. "Come quickly."

The old rabbi, standing by and seeing all, needed little encouragement. He had no idea what had happened to him; it was what Christians did. He sought no further explanation. Philosopher he was, but no fool; he now wanted to get out of the palace and the town as swiftly as his old legs could carry him. He had no money, and no donkey or horse. Weighed down with books and manuscripts—for these he refused to abandon—the three of them walked up to the ground and out into a courtyard. It was still morning, a fine and beautiful day, the most beautiful there had ever been.

They walked slowly through the streets of the town until Olivier made them sit down and wait while he ran to find a donkey. As he left them, he was overcome with a fit of shivering despite the heat of the morning sun. The realization of what he had done came over him like a sickness, and he felt the chill of loneliness. He was alone, and without any protection. He had no one to go to for help. As he walked he felt hunted already, knowing that retribution would be swift and hideous. He dared not go back to Ceccani's palace, his home for the last ten years, but could not behave as Pisano had done and run away. He wanted to, though, wanted to race across the countryside as fast as he could and catch up with his friend Pisano. Then they would journey to Italy together, and Olivier would—what? He did not know; all he knew was that the greater the distance between himself and Avignon, the safer he would be.

But what of his other friends? What about this woman he had fallen in love with, and her master, grumpy and ill-humored though he was? If he left, they would die sooner or later, and it says much again for the limitations of Olivier's vision that this was the way he saw it. If all the Jews died, so would they. He was making no grand gesture, did not want to guarantee his own eternal fame. He did not even want to save the Jews; they were not his business. All he wanted to do was make sure that these two people were not harmed when they deserved to be left in peace. A foolish, wasteful, and futile gesture; even he knew that.

He came back with a donkey, after giving all the money he had in exchange. He walked it back to them in bare feet, and helped load Gersonides's books—he was coming to hate books, he thought as he struggled to tie them in place—then the old man himself. And he handed the halter over to Rebecca.

"Leave the city immediately. Do not go home, or anywhere where there are Jews until you are sure you can do so safely." He said it brusquely, without detail. He knew that if he started talking to her properly, he would never be able to stop.

"But you are coming with us?"

"I have things to do here."

"What things?"

He shrugged. "Important things. Things which don't concern you. I would like to go but I can't. And you must. It is too dangerous to stay here."

"No," she said. "You have to come, too."

He turned to Gersonides, sitting as patiently on the donkey as it was bearing his weight. "Sir?" he appealed. "Tell her to go with you."

"I think it would be best, my dear," he said gently. "Olivier will no doubt race to catch up once his business is done." He looked at Olivier and saw there was little chance of it, whatever he had planned.

"Of course," Olivier said stoutly. Then he moved over to talk to him quietly.

"You will make sure she stays with you and doesn't come back here?"

"Of course. A counterfeit Jew can die as readily as a real one, I think."

"I cannot say goodbye to her properly."

The old man nodded. "Probably not."

Olivier smiled. "Goodbye, sir. I think you sense how much I have valued knowing you."

"No. But I will comfort myself with guessing until you return."

Olivier took a deep breath, then turned and bowed in farewell. Gersonides nodded in return, then thought of something.

"That manuscript you brought me, by that bishop. It argues that understanding is more important than movement. That action is virtuous only if it reflects pure comprehension, and that virtue comes from the comprehension, not the action."

Olivier frowned. "So?"

"Dear boy, I must tell you a secret."

"What?"

"I do believe it is wrong."

JULIEN COULDN'T SLEEP, of course; there was never any chance of it. Instead, he walked around the apartment, so beautiful and usually so reassuring, but found no rest or respite. Not that he was thinking; a dullness had settled over him the moment he was told that Julia had been arrested, and had never lifted. He had not thought or felt anything since then. He found himself looking at the four pictures she had given him so proudly, so full of promise; she had solved her problem, but he had not managed to find any answer to his own, and she had now paid the price for it. His understanding, such as it was, only came when she was taken. Marcel had been right, of course; just as Pisano had turned the blind man and the saint—Manlius and Sophia, as he now thought—into Olivier and the woman he loved, so Julia had found her solution by continuing what he had done, transforming them once again into herself and into him. A triple portrait, around the same theme: making the blind see.

He looked out the window, hoping for distraction in the ordinary bustle and movement of the city, but there was virtually none. No people walking up and down going about their business, most of the shops shut. Only one car, its driver leaning against the bonnet smoking a cigarette. Where did he get that from? Julien thought. And he looked again, more carefully, and realized.

Friendship had its limits. Marcel had sent the police to watch him, make sure he didn't try to leave and warn Bernard. He was to be, once more, an accessory to a murder. The realization snapped him awake; he could feel the surge of thought through his mind as he grasped what was going on. He had not gotten to the station on time, managed to achieve nothing to save Julia. But he could at least refuse to accept this as well.

He made his preparations quickly; changed his clothes, put on his stoutest shoes, ate what little food there was in his kitchen—some olives, a piece of hard, dry bread, a tomato, a small piece of cheese; they had all been there for a week or more and were scarcely edible. Drank a glass of wine that was close to being rancid, and wondered if he had ever had a meal that tasted quite so unpleasant.

Then he left the apartment, walked down the stairs and into the courtyard. There was a high stone wall that separated the house from the one behind; too high for him to climb. He went to the concierge and asked to borrow a chair.

"I am going to climb over the wall and go into the next street. There is a policeman outside. I want you to do something for me. If he asks, say that I went upstairs to go to sleep. Say I have not come down again and you have not seen me since. Will you do that?"

The concierge nodded, a little twinkle in her eye. Her husband, he knew, had spent years in jail for robbery before he had died; she herself had been in enough trouble with the police over the years for her nearly to have lost her position when one of the building's occupants discovered it. Julien had argued for her to be left in peace. Had she ever done anything wrong? Then let her be. She knew of it, and was grateful.

"You'll never make a good burglar, Monsieur Julien, if that's what you're thinking of doing. Best give it up before you get into trouble. Some people are just not made for it. My Robert, now, he was hopeless, so I know."

He grinned at her. "I'll bear it in mind And I'd better go."

"I've not seen you. Don't worry. I wouldn't talk to a policeman even if my life depended on it. Never have. Don't hold with them."

He nodded, and climbed the wall, making such a bad job of it that the last thing he heard as he fell heavily to the ground on the other side was a sarcastic cackle.

Then he started walking, passing through the gates of Avignon as the sun was beginning to set, doggedly pounding along the road as it grew dark. He reached Carpentras at about one in the morning and thought of stopping for a rest, lying down somewhere for a few hours' sleep, but kept going; he had had enough sleep in his life and needed no more. Instead he headed north, and as dawn broke he passed close by the hill with the shrine of Saint Sophia at the top.

He was far too early to go to his house; Bernard was not due there until the afternoon. So he climbed the hill and took refuge in the place where Julia had been so happy. As he reached the top and saw the chapel nestling in its little copse of trees, he saw also the bits and pieces she had left behind the last time she had been there—a bundle of papers, an old tin can she used for washing her brushes, a scarf she wrapped around her head to keep the sun off. Julien picked it up and felt it, then put it to his face and smelled her for the last time. And her smell finally made him break down as he had not managed to do before at the train station, or with Marcel, or in his apartment. There he had still been in command of himself. Now he was no longer; he sank down onto the grass, his whole body shaking and his whole mind overflowing with grief.

It was only the heat as the sun rose higher in the sky, and the realization that time was passing, that eventually forced him to banish all such thoughts; but when he finally stood up he had accepted that she would not come back and he would never see her again.

He went into the chapel and looked at the pictures she had studied, and saw them through her eyes. He looked at the picture of the blind man and Sophia, her gesture so tender, his so responsive, and saw again how she had made it her own. She had lost herself in this old work, her personality dissolving into it, so that she had been set free. The immortality of the soul lies in its dissolution; this was the cryptic comment that so frustrated Olivier and which Julien had only ever grasped as evidence for the history of a particular school of thought. He had known all about its history, but Julia knew what it meant. He found the realization strangely reassuring; she, it seemed, had come to understand everything that Sophia had tried and failed to teach Manlius, and which he had never understood himself.

Did that make it any better? Did it lessen the horror of what she was enduring? Or of how he had contributed to it? Of course it did not; nothing ever could. She was on a train, in the hands of monsters, and while she journeyed to her death he sat here, looking at pictures. Julien had sunk into complete impotence, where he had nothing left he could do. Everything he had ever thought or learned, all his tastes and cultivation had gone, stripped away by this one fact: She was gone, and he could not prevent or change anything that was to happen.

Olivier had made a protest against great ideas for the sake of a small humanity, and had illuminated it with his own suffering. Julien could not even do that; his life was already over and with it any opportunity to accomplish something of worth. All he could do was signal that he understood, at least, how much in error he had been, and hope that someone might, in turn, understand him.

He closed the door of the chapel carefully, breathed in the warm air, so fresh after the slight dankness inside, and began walking down the hill.

FELIX LEFT THAT EVENING, his retinue bumping along the unrepaired roads, the few soldiers with him on the lookout for brigands, who were becoming ever more adventurous in their depredations. They were in something of a hurry, for Felix had much to do before the confrontation with Manlius. Supporters to prepare, soldiers to ready, for he did not doubt that fighting was likely, and much though he regretted it, he felt there was now no choice. One of them would have to give way; only one person could emerge triumphant, for the stakes were too high for compromise.

They went some ten miles before they paused, and stopped by a stream to water the horses. It was then that the attackers struck. There were perhaps six of them, although as no one survived, the number remained conjecture. Felix himself was the last to die, his head severed from his body in such a way that it went rolling down the slight incline and came to rest in a patch of primroses growing on the riverbank.

But at least he died knowing who had killed him. The last thing he saw before his life was extinguished was the blade of the long-handled axe as it swung through the air, glinting brightly in the spring sunshine, and he recognized the man who had been hewing wood on Manlius's estate the day before.

WHEN THE BURGUNDIANS arrived, they behaved with exemplary correctness, eliciting admiration from the population for the way in which they were kept in order, without looting or pillaging. A contrast to soldiers in the pay of Rome, it was pointed out by more than one person. Only in one area did they act with less restraint; the estates of the family of Felix were attacked immediately and by the end almost the entire clan was eliminated, the villas burned, the land transferred to the king for distribution to his own people.

This was as it should be; no one mourned them, for by then they knew his true duplicity, and were the more won over by their bishop, their savior. For Manlius told them, with trembling voice, eyes filled with tears, how he had discovered the truth about his friend, how he had been in secret negotiation with Euric, planning to hand over the land to him in exchange for favors. This had been the true reason, he announced in a dull, resigned voice, why he had moved so fast to invite King Gundobad to move south, why he had abandoned the idea of going to the emperor for troops. There was no time if Felix's treachery was to be countered.

The news came as a shock, but the impact was salutary. Gundobad was hailed as a savior and entered into his new patrimony without a sword being drawn in protest. And Manlius, his chief advisor, began teaching him about ruling, about the law, and about justice. About how to be a king, not merely a chieftain.

He was at his greatest in those years; he felt it was what he had been born to accomplish. The constant, intricate details of administration, of justice, of reevaluating and reassigning tax revenues, the delicate discussions and persuasions needed to steer both rulers and ruled toward an understanding and even appreciation of each other. It was due to him that war never came between the Burgundians and Visigoths, that the destruction all had feared never happened. And the culmination of his achievement was the code of law, the *Lex Gundobada* as it was known to Julien, which encapsulated the triumph of Roman civilization over its tribal successors. The Roman people submitted to barbarian rule, but the barbarian rulers submitted to Roman law.

It took years of unremitting work before his labors were complete, and when he was satisfied, he went back to the great villa that had been almost desolate for so many years and opened up the doors and lived in peace once more. It was much changed; the huddling masses of laborers had been cleared away, but there had been no time and no money to restore the garden. Cracks had appeared in the fabric, holes in the pavements and mosaics, for despite his efforts the labor force had continued to evaporate, the towns to shrink. Cut off from much of its old places of trade, with travel ever more dififcult, society continued to wither, albeit at a slower, more gentle pace.

He was satisfied, nonetheless; he had achieved all he had aimed at, and more. And now he could rest. So he hoped, but no peace came to him. The hole in his soul grew bigger by the day, for he had lost Sophia, the woman who had guided him and taught him for all his adult life. He had wanted her praise, her thanks, or at least her understanding, and had gotten none of these, even when he finally finished his last work, the *Dream*, and sent it to her.

HE HAD SEEN little of her since the arrival of the Burgundians, for he had much to do and she had withdrawn to her little house on the hill. When he had secured her release from captivity she had not even thanked him. He thought he understood why; for Sophia yearned for the release of death, and would have no gratitude for the man who had postponed what she so ardently desired. She had left with scarcely a word, and he had been too busy to follow, although he made sure that she was properly protected and looked after. His occasional letters went unanswered, and eventually, after he had sent her his manuscript, with a dedication to the great god Apollo and his consort

Wisdom, he went to see her. He was puzzled, offended even, by her silence. And he wanted her praise.

"That you will not have," she said when she divined this part of the reason for his visit. She was sitting under a tree beneath which a servant had fixed up an awning of white cloth; there she sat on the ground, knees crossed and hands together.

"I never thought that I had managed to teach you so little," she continued, with a sadness and a distance in her voice that he had never known before. Often in the past, she had been angry with him, furious at his obstinacy or his inability to understand. But that had been part of her love; this time she talked like an acquaintance, someone who cared nothing for him. The realization sent a chill through him.

"I admit it," he said with a forced smile. "But what there is is all due to you."

"Then let me be cursed for it," she said quietly, "for if I am responsible for what you have done then I bear a heavy guilt. I taught you as much as I could and you used it to massacre your son, your friend, and the Jews. And you have become a saint. You are a saint, Manlius; the people say so already. When you are dead you will have your shrine and your prayers."

"They are nothing to me if I do not have your good opinion, my lady."

"And you do not have it. The moment you ordered the death of Syagrius you lost it forever. He did not betray you; he stayed in Vaison to ensure I came to no danger. He kept watch on me night and day, offered himself as a hostage until you came back. Your response was to kill him, without inquiry, so you could make a grand gesture before all the town. And to yourself, and to the shade of your father. You would not show weakness, would you, Lord Bishop? You would not expose yourself as your father did, and hesitate, and be merciful. He did, and died for it. His cause was lost. That was not a mistake you would make. You learned from him as you learned from me."

"What he did—or what he failed to do—is the cause of our current distress," Manlius said stiffly.

"Nonsense," she replied harshly. "Do you think one man can make a difference? If he had lived another twenty years, would it have conjured up armies? Given the people of this region the will to fight? Made Rome able to defend itself? No. Your father's quest was doomed from the start. He knew it, and he died as a man of honor, choosing not to do wrong, so that at least he would leave behind something noble. Would that you had his qualities. You have chosen instead to pile injustice on injustice, corpse on corpse. Felix knew nothing of what his cousin was doing, but your response was to kill him, and to kill his entire line, because you wanted to deliver a peaceful province to Gundobad. And because you needed to win the minds of the people, you slaughtered the Jews, who had done neither you nor anyone else any ill. On such things do you build your civilization, and you use me to justify it all."

"I have brought peace to this land, and security," he began.

"And what of your soul, when you use the cleverness of argument to cloak such acts? Do you think that the peace of a thousand cancels out the unjust death of one single person? It may be desirable, it may win you praise from those who have happily survived you and prospered from your deeds, but you have committed ignoble acts, and have been too proud to own them. I have waited patiently here, hoping that you would come to me, for if you understood, then some of your acts would be mitigated. But instead you send me this manuscript, proud, magisterial, and demonstrating only that you have understood nothing at all."

"I returned to public life on your advice, madam," he said stiffly.

"Yes; I advised it. I said if learning must die it should do so with a friend by its bedside. Not an assassin."

She looked up at him, with tears in her eyes. "You were my last pupil, Manlius. And you have made what you have done into my legacy, as well as your own. You have taken what I had and corrupted it. Used what I taught you to kill and justify your killing. For that I will never forgive you. Please leave me alone now."

She turned back to face the valley and closed her eyes in contemplation. Manlius waited for a moment, hoping she would begin talking to him once more, then turned and walked away. He never spoke to her again.

JULIEN HAD ONLY glimpses of what Olivier did in the last few hours before he was attacked. Olivier himself scarcely understood what he was doing; he did not proceed rationally, but rather went by instinct, almost in a dream. In many ways, he was behaving purely selfishly, in contrast to the idealism that motivated both Ceccani and Cardinal de Deaux in their different ways.

He left the palace and walked through the streets of Avignon until he saw a servant of the Comte de Fréjus, someone he had seen before. He walked up to him. "Say, my friend," he said. "Would you do me a favor?"

The man turned and nodded in vague recognition.

"Would you run straight to your master and say you saw me? Say I am going to the house of the Italian painter Pisano. Tell him the news: that I said I know who murdered his wife, saw the culprit with my own eyes, and that I will inform the magistrates this afternoon. Make sure he understands. I know who murdered his wife."

The man frowned in puzzlement.

"Do not ask me questions," Olivier said urgently. "Just discharge this service, and I will be in your debt forever."

And he turned and walked away. He went back to Pisano's lodgings. He waited for four hours, during which time he wrote his last poems, the final four that came down to Julien, including the most puzzling of them all, the one that begins "Our lonely souls swim to the light . . ." a verse that only Julien ever properly understood, its strange imagery, and tone oscillating between the regretful and the joyous being too eccentric to be readily appreciated.

And then they came, as he knew they would. Olivier folded his papers and pushed them under the door of Pisano's neighbor, with a note that he should take them to the pope. Then he knelt down to pray as he heard the footsteps coming softly up the stairs. He looked up and saw the Comte de Fréjus himself with three other men standing in the doorway.

"I have been expecting you," he said quietly as they came in.

THE REST OF the story took place in public, although what it meant was swiftly obscured. Only Clement, perhaps, held all the strands. When de Fréjus fled, leaving Olivier bleeding on the floor all but dead, his hands smashed beyond use, his tongue cut off so that he could never tell his secret to anyone, the news traveled fast. The count was seen entering the building, seen leaving it two hours later covered in blood; the screams as Olivier was tortured were heard for hundreds of yards around. No one dared intervene. It was then that the story began to circulate that the assault was revenge for Olivier's murder of Isabelle de Fréjus; the tale protected the count's reputation, for no one wanted the truth made public, but it did not fool Clement. A horseman left the papal palace within the hour, heading for the Countess of Provence's court; the comte's seneschal was removed from Aigues-Mortes and the command taken over by her own cousin; extra soldiers were sent in. The English force materialized off the coast, waited three days, then sailed back to Bordeaux.

As a power, Ceccani was finished, his desire for the papacy to return to Rome dead. He even returned to his bishoprics, visiting each in turn and winning a reputation as a good shepherd of his flock, in contrast to the absentees of Avignon, who took their dues but gave precious little in exchange.

And three days after the attack, Olivier had his reward as he lay in a quiet room in the papal palace, attended by the pope's own physician. For Clement was a thorough man; he not only blocked Ceccani's plan for Aigues-Mortes, he moved to demolish the power base his cardinal had built himself as well. The great bull *Cum Natura Humana*, a thunderous declamation that echoed across the whole world, was issued. The Jews were innocent of any charges laid against them in the matter of the plague. They were the fathers of nations, as was now the pope himself. To injure them was to injure the pope, and all Christians as well. Clement took them under his personal protection. Anyone who harmed them in any way would be excommunicated and would have to answer to the pope himself. They were not to be attacked, nor to be forcibly converted, for obedience without faith was pointless. They were to be left alone.

And those people who attacked them, the men like Peter the flagellant and all his followers, were excommunicated, to be hunted down. And all those who helped them were to be excommunicated as well. They were to be chased from the society of men, spurned and shunned, thrown out of any town they approached or arrested, and kept imprisoned until they repented. Rather than using them to persecute the Jews, he turned the full force of papal power and authority on the persecutors. The results were not swift, but they were effective; the assaults on Jews spluttered out, bit by bit, the flagellants and those who came to the surface under the cloak of their piety were crushed.

It was—and is—an extraordinary document, with a few antecedents but no parallels. The sound it made, true, was drowned out by other more raucous voices; the tumult first stirred in Provence by Manlius proved more attractive and more tempting. And yet the little flicker it represented stayed alight for long enough, embodying something of the soul of Olivier de Noyen, and communicating itself down through the centuries until it whispered into the ear of Julien Barneuve as he trudged the last few kilometers to his house.

OLIVIER LIVED OUT the remaining part of his life in the monastery of Saint Jean outside Vaison, whose abbot was appointed under the guidance of Cardinal de Deaux. He arrived one night, in a litter escorted by the pope's own troops, and no one in that place ever knew his story. All they knew was that he was under the protection of their cardinal, and of the pope himself. He had rendered great service to the church, it was whispered, although what this was was unclear.

He did little in that period; could not talk and could not write. Nor did he attend services unless he had to. Rather, he sat in the sun most of the time, read a great deal—his friends sent him manuscripts to read as they were discovered—and walked. His favorite place was the chapel on the hill about a day's march away, where his friend had begun painting the life of Saint Sophia. He slept there often, and spent much time in prayer to the saint; it gave him great comfort.

And Rebecca came to him there. Gersonides and she returned to their house when peace came back, and they felt safe. The ordeal had weakened the old man, though; she knew it would not be long before he died.

Olivier tried, and eventually managed, to communicate to her that she should marry, if possible. Or she would be utterly defenseless in the world. But it was not what she wanted.

One day as they were sitting together, looking out over the hills, she stood up suddenly and turned to him. "You were wrong in what you did, you know," she said. "To protect me, I mean. I did not deserve it. You suffered for nothing."

He reached out and tried to touch her, to get her to be quiet, but she pulled away from him and continued, the words coming out in a rush now she had summoned the courage to speak at all. "I was born in a small village near Nîmes, and someone betrayed us. There was a monastery nearby and the case was taken to the abbot. And at the end of it, he gave orders that everyone accused of heresy should be executed. They told me it was merciful, that otherwise the monks would come and do as they had before and kill everyone in the region. That this was a kindness on his part to save many others. But still my parents were killed by this act of kindness.

"I ran to the fields and wandered for six years before I came across my master. He found me and took me in and looked after me until I was ready to look after him."

Olivier looked anguished, made the childish gurgles and chortlings that were the nearest he could now get to speech to interrupt her, but she went on doggedly nonetheless. "That abbot was a great man, and became greater still. A few years later he began to be known as Pope Clement the Sixth.

"When you came for me that night, to take me to the palace, I knew the temptation. I took a potion my master had, which he had always told me never to touch as it was a powerful medicine, dangerous if not taken with care. I put it in my bag, and when I got the chance, I poured it into the well. The moment I'd done it, there was a great shout, and someone grabbed me."

She paused and smiled. "I tried to explain, you know. I said it was all my doing and tried to tell them why. But they weren't interested. They thought I would never have done such a thing without my master's instruction. The stupid thing is that it wouldn't have worked anyway. Gersonides has told me it was quite harmless when diluted to such an extent. I wanted to confess, but my master said there was no point. No one would believe me, because they wanted to believe Jews were poisoning wells."

She went down on her knees and kissed his cheek. "You are a good man, Olivier, far better than I am. I hated, and risked the life of my master, and subjected you to this for my hatred. And you now must hate me, too, and I know you will never want to see me again."

He leaned forward and took her in his arms; he wished more than anything to speak to her and reassure her; his heart was full of wonderful poems; all sorts of words and phrases sparkled in his head, none of which anyone but he would ever hear. But he held her nonetheless, rocking her gently backward and forward, doing his best to stroke her hair with his arm, kissing it with his lips.

"Do you want me to go?" she asked eventually. "Please don't tell me you do."

He shook his head fervently, and then she returned his embrace, and they stayed there together for a long time.

He lived for another six months before the burden of his wounds finally pulled him down. Rebecca was with him at the end; the abbot of the monastery understood enough to know she would be his best comfort. And so it proved; Olivier died in almost perfect happiness. The only blemish on his contentment was not knowing when he would see her again. But he believed in eternity, and knew it would not be long.

AS JULIEN WALKED to his house, he began to reach a state of calm that had long eluded him. He arrived at the house about fifteen minutes early; it gave him just enough time to send out a warning that Bernard would be able to see from miles away, something that would make him turn around and go back. He dug up the etched plates from the place where Julia had hidden them and took them into the little kitchen of the house, then got a bottle of the acid she used for biting the lines into the metal, and poured it all over them. Bit by bit the lettering would be erased; that part of his job was done. He lifted the floorboards and took out the little pile of papers inside and put them on the floor. He was not thinking anymore; he merely did the job he set himself, his mind completely empty.

Then he prepared himself, and made a pile in the middle of the living room of all his old notes and papers, his manuscript on Manlius, useless because so wrong. The notes from the Vatican. His draft on Olivier, also erroneous in nearly all respects except for the analysis of the poetry, which still had some merit. None would be missed. They were a record of wasted time and misunderstanding only.

These he stacked carefully, then surrounded them in turn with wooden furniture, the old curtains. Beside them he put his last two-liter jar of kerosene for the little heater, and the bottle of eau-de-vie that Elizabeth Duveau had once given to Julia. A welcoming present, a gesture of friendship.

His last cigarette he took from the packet and put in his mouth, the box of matches on the table, then picked up the kerosene and eau-de-vie and splashed it liberally on the papers and over the furniture. He needed only a few moments for the fuel to soak in; when he judged the moment was right, he took a long puff on his cigarette and exhaled. Then another; his last pleasure. He blew on the end until it glowed brightly and flecks of ash flew off and floated through the beams of light coming through the open window, then dropped it, quite carefully as with all he did, in the middle of the pile of notes.

THE FIRE TOOK hold quickly, sending a billowing column of smoke into the hot summer air, easily seen for miles around by the approaching platoon of Germans, and also by Bernard. The soldiers rushed to the scene but could do little; Bernard, in contrast, took the warning; he turned around and vanished swiftly into the woods he knew so well.

He survived another six weeks before he was captured and killed. Two days after Julien's death, twenty-six civilians were shot in the quiet courtyard of a farm a kilometer or so outside Vaison.

Mid fourth century AD Roman Empire divided into an Eastern Empire, based on Constantinople, and a Western Empire, based on Rome.

380 Christianity becomes the official religion of the Roman Empire.

406–9 Barbarian invasions of Gaul.

410 Sack of Rome by Goths under Alaric.

416 Visigoths arrive in Gaul.

455 Rise of Ricimer to take control of Italy.

457 Majorian becomes emperor in the West.

461 Majorian killed on the orders of Ricimer.

472 Death of Ricimer.

475 Fall of Clermont Ferrand in central France to Visigoths under King Euric; Burgundians annex cities in Rhône valley; Visigoths annex the rest of Provence.

476 Deposition of Romulus Augustulus, the last emperor in the West, effective end of the Western Empire.

1310 Clement V settles in Avignon to escape civil unrest in Rome.

1328 Philip VI ascends throne of France.

1334 Start of building work on papal palace in Avignon.

1337 Outbreak of Hundred Years' War between France and England.

1342 Pierre Roger elected pope; takes the name Clement VI.

1346 Battle of Crécy; English army under Edward III defeats French forces; large numbers of hostages taken.

1348 Arrival of the Black Death; Clement successfully negotiates to buy Avignon from Joanna, Countess of Provence. Plot to deliver Aigues-Mortes to English forces fails.

1350 Death of King Philip of France.

1352 Death of Clement VI; death of Cardinal Ceccani.

1378 Church splits, with one pope in Rome, another in Avignon.

1410 Schism healed, papacy reunited and once more permanently resident in Rome.

1928 Right-wing riots in Paris nearly topple the Third Republic.

1929 Start of Great Depression.

1936 Left-wing Popular Front government in France; outbreak of Spanish Civil War.

1939 Outbreak of World War II.

1940 Fall of France when German army invades through the Ardennes forest; collapse of Third Republic, with France divided into the northern part, occupied by Germany, and the southern part, controlled by a government in Vichy led by Philippe Pétain. Launching of a "national revolution" that includes a *statut des juifs* to limit the number of Jews in certain occupations.

1941 Germany invades Russia; United States enters war.

1942 Deportations of Jews from France commences in the summer.

1942 October 10: Pétain visits Avignon.

1942 November: Operation Anton. German army marches to take control of French southern coastline.

1944 August: Allied forces invade southern France, liberation of Provence.

ACKNOWLEDGMENTS

With thanks to Felicity Bryan, Mih-Ho Cha, Eric
Christiansen, Catherine Crawford, Dan Franklin,
Robert Gildea, Julie Grau, Lyndal Roper, Georges-
Michel Sarotte, Lucinda Stevens, Nick Stargardt
and once again, Ruth Harris.

ABOUT THE AUTHOR

IAIN PEARS was born in 1955. Educated at Wadham College, Oxford, he has worked as a journalist, an art historian, and a television consultant in England, France, Italy, and the United States. He is the author of seven highly praised detective novels, a book of art history, and countless articles on artistic, financial, and historical subjects, as well as the international best-seller *An Instance of the Finger-post*. He lives in Oxford, England.